Di Morrissey AM is one of the most successful and prolific authors Australia has ever produced, publishing twenty-nine bestselling novels.

She trained as a journalist, working in newspapers, magazines, television, film, theatre and advertising around the world. Her fascination with different countries, their cultural, political and environmental issues, has been the catalyst for her novels, which are all inspired by a particular landscape.

Di is a tireless and passionate advocate and activist for many causes. She is an avid supporter of Greenpeace, speaking out on issues of national and international importance. She established The Golden Land Education Foundation in Myanmar (Burma), and is an Ambassador for Australia's Royal Institute for Deaf and Blind Children (NextSense). Di also publishes and edits a free community newspaper, *The Manning Community News*, www.manningcommunitynews.com.

In 2017, in recognition of her achievements, Di was inducted into the Australian Book Industry Awards Hall of Fame with the prestigious Lloyd O'Neil Award. In 2019, she was made a Member of the Order of Australia.

To find out more, visit www.dimorrissey.com and www.facebook.com/DiMorrissey. You can follow Di at @di_morrissey on Twitter and @dimorrisseyauthor on Instagram.

Also by Di Morrissey
In order of publication

Di
MORRISSEY
The NIGHT TIDE

PAN
Pan Macmillan Australia

Pan Macmillan acknowledges the Traditional Custodians of country throughout Australia and their connections to lands, waters and communities. We pay our respect to Elders past and present and extend that respect to all Aboriginal and Torres Strait Islander peoples today. We honour more than sixty thousand years of storytelling, art and culture.

First published 2022 in Macmillan by Pan Macmillan Australia Pty Ltd
This Pan edition published 2023 by Pan Macmillan Australia Pty Ltd
1 Market Street, Sydney, New South Wales, Australia, 2000

A catalogue record for this book is available from the National Library of Australia

Typeset in 12.5/16 pt Sabon by Post Pre-press Group
Printed by IVE

Chapter image credits: Prologue, Aleks Khan/Shutterstock; Chapter 1, Taras Vyshnya/Shutterstock; Chapter 2, Kevin Wells Photography/Shutterstock; Chapter 3, Sergii Sobolevskyi/Shutterstock; Chapter 4, K. Luzzi Paul/ Shutterstock; Chapter 5, Scapigliata/Shutterstock; Chapter 6, Lukas Gojda/ Shutterstock; Chapter 7, DroneGo Sky Scouts/Shutterstock; Chapter 8, Patrick Jennings/Shutterstock; Chapter 9, Sandra Lass/Shutterstock; Chapter 10, Grindstone Media Group/Shutterstock; Chapter 11, Serge Vero/Shutterstock; Chapter 12, Valeri Vatel/Shutterstock; Chapter 13, Sven Hansche/Shutterstock; Chapter 14, A Kisel/Shutterstock.

The author and the publisher have made every effort to contact copyright holders for material used in this book. Any person or organisation that may have been overlooked should contact the publisher.

Di Morrissey and Bill Roberts, the father she loved, at Pittwater.

In memory of Bill Roberts and little Michael Roberts.

And for all my special memories of
Pittwater, New South Wales.

Di Morrissey, 2022

Author's Note

Di Morrissey as a child at Lovett Bay, Pittwater.

I LIVED AT PITTWATER, New South Wales – which inspired WestWater in this novel – when I was a little girl . . . what a magical place it was then.

The poet's house mentioned in this novel is inspired by my childhood memories of visiting an elderly lady at the end of our bay, who had a roomful of books. I told her I didn't have many books so I made up my own stories in my head.

She told me very seriously that when I grew up, I must put my stories in a book one day so others can enjoy them, too.

Thank you, dear Dorothea Mackellar.

Di Morrissey with Spike, the family dog, back in Pittwater.

Acknowledgements

Many, many thanks to . . .

Dearest, Boris Janjic, for the years we've shared and those to come. Thank you too for the love and support during the last two years of lockdown!

My children, Dr Gabrielle Morrissey Hansen and Dr Nicolas Morrissey, who share love, advice, laughs as well as my grandchildren – Sonoma, Everton, Bodhi and Ulani. I'm so proud of you all.

My editor, Liz Adams, such a great friend and editor from the Byron days who shares daily news, gossip and advice (wanted or not!) and tough love over editing. We both share that special bond of the love of books and words, as well as friendship.

To my new excellent and charming publisher, Alex Lloyd. You are a special joy! Especially as you are so organised and efficient smoothing my journey from prose to publication with calmness and humour! I owe you a bubble or three.

As I do all my loyal family at Pan Mac: Ross Gibb, Tracey Cheetham, Katie Crawford and the sales team, Adrik Kemp and the marketing crew, Bri Collins for her meticulous copy editing, and especially my charming and whip smart publicity gal, Clare Keighery. And of course the unsung heroes at IVE printers.

Not forgetting legal eagle, Ian Robertson. Also super agent and dear friend, Jane Novak. Thank you both!

While this book is fiction, I reflected on important influences from my Pittwater days as a kid – my darling mother, Kay Roberts, Uncle Jim Revitt and his 'bestie' Jim Bird, Mary Stackhouse and sons John and Tony, Chips and Quentin Rafferty, George and Marcia English, Pat and George Farwell, my childhood mate Shane Egan, and the weekender girlfriends Ailex Williams and Diana Bridgewater.

I also share some stories from the late judge Jim Macken, who so loved Coasters Retreat.

Thank you Rick Jamieson, Gilgai Farm and Helen Thomas of Picayune Farm for the horse-breeding information.

I have an abiding interest in architecture and remain a fan of the late dear Sergei Malnic and Jutta Malnic. I am an admirer, too, of Pittwater's Professor Richard Leplastrier AO.

When the theme of this book came to me, I spoke to several people who continue to suffer the pain of not knowing what happened to, or the whereabouts of, a loved one, and so they suffer enduring loss and wondering. Thank you for sharing.

And, as for the past thirteen years, the small white shadow always at my feet or heels – loyal Mina.

In addition to the dedication to my father, Bill Roberts, I must also dedicate this book to the late Rosemary Revitt, my wonderful aunt, friend and confidant. So many happy years shared with my adored late Uncle Jim and the boys, David and Damien, who carry on the legacy of decency, integrity and kindness.

Prologue

THEY WAITED TILL FIRST light. In a dreary mizzling rain and cold mist, the two helicopters rat-a-tat-tatted into the dawn on a sad search.

One swept around the foreshores and bays of the quiet reaches of WestWater on the northern fringe of the city, circling over the hunched deserted Crouching Island that guarded the entrance to the ocean.

Like a small insect, the other helicopter flew over the rugged state national park, which rose above WestWater like a vast wooded ocean of hills and gullies.

Finding a missing person in such terrain seemed an impossible task.

Guided by the spotters seated beside them with high-powered binoculars, the pilots zeroed in to investigate any unusual shape, flash of colour or disturbance.

'Be a bit easier if we knew what he was doing out here . . . How many days has it been?' commented the spotter.

'Two or three. It's a mystery. We only know he lived in the area.'

'Too far away from the city lights for me.' The spotter focused on a bulky object that was wedged between rocks where a creek emptied into a bay. 'Hey, what's that?' He directed the pilot's attention to the spot.

The message crackled into the cockpit of the second chopper, whose pilot acknowledged and responded, angling to change direction.

Two police officers in their launch looked up as the helicopters suddenly began to converge on a site towards the water's edge.

'Must've seen something. We'd better head over.' One called in to alert the base of their movements.

Shortly afterwards, ambulance and police sirens woke the families who were not yet aware of the unfolding drama in the quiet Sydney backwater.

*

Sam Sutherland held his mug of tea as he stood on the deck of his house, peering through the trees that filtered his view of the curving bay.

His wife joined him, tightening the belt of her dressing-gown in the misty dawn light.

'Do you think it might be him? At last.'

'Could be, thank God. Bring this nightmare to an end.'

'Poor Maggie. I don't know how she's coped all this time. It's been a very long few days.' She shook her head sadly. 'If it is him, at last we'll know what's happened.'

Sam nodded and they stood quietly for another moment before Sam drank the last of his tea and turned.

'C'mon, Gloria. Shake a leg, there'll be a lot to do. We're the nearest; we've got to be ready in case we're needed.'

As they moved to go indoors, they saw through the trees the flashing blue lights of a police car as it wound down the hill to their neighbours' home.

*

Maggie leaned forward anxiously from the back seat as the police car pulled away. Outside the house, Gloria held the hand of Maggie's youngest child, while Sam kept the others inside to finish their toast before getting ready for school, trying to keep things normal for them for as long as possible.

Maggie felt a heavy darkness pressing in on her. This had been their home which they'd built and loved, in a stunning place they'd never expected or imagined to be able to live and raise a family. A home where there'd been so much love and laughter.

'You all right, Mrs Gordon?' asked the policewoman.

'No, I'm not. I've been dreading this.' Her hands twisted in her lap.

'It's better than not knowing,' said the policewoman, trying to be kind.

*

The room seemed cold. Bare and clinical.

The policewoman and a man in a white coat stood beside Maggie, speaking gently.

Maggie felt she was looking down from a great height, and the man's movements seemed to her to be in slow motion as he lifted the white sheet from the gurney in front of them.

The face was white, covered with grazes and wounds that must once have been red with blood where now the skin was like stone.

Her hand flew to her mouth.

'I know this is difficult, Mrs Gordon. We just need . . .'

He trailed off as the distraught woman stepped back awkwardly, unable to take her eyes from the face of the man lying before her.

Wildly she gripped the policewoman's arm and cried in an anguished voice, 'It's not him! It's not my husband.'

And burst into tears.

I

THE DIM WINE BAR, not far from the Sydney Opera House, was crowded, a warm haven of comforting bursts of laughter, loud voices, the aroma of food, and somewhere in the background, a muffled music track.

The normally spectacular harbour view was obscured in the darkness, the harbour and city lights dimmed by spattering rain.

No one noticed.

The bar was a short walk from Sydney's Parliament House in Macquarie Street and a popular haunt for government staffers.

Heads close together, they leaned towards each other to be heard over the noise as they dissected the results of their election loss.

'Julie was good. Strong, honest. It's a real shame.'

'Maybe too honest. Blunt sometimes, telling it like it is. She ruffled a lot of feathers.'

'Do you reckon she'll run again? She has young kids.'

'I thought she had good numbers. Clearly not good enough. Live and learn.'

'Win some, lose some. Even if she does run again, in the meantime, she lost, and we're all out of a job.'

'Let's not get into the whys and wherefores right now.' Dominic Cochrane looked around at his five colleagues, all staff of the now former state member. 'The bottom line is we have to start looking for work.' He paused as Kristy, who'd worked for him directly, threw back the last of her drink. He knew she was a single mother. 'You going to be okay, Kristy?'

She nodded and shrugged. 'I put feelers out, just in case.'

There was some friendly outrage that she had taken precautions in case they lost, when the rest of them had believed they would, and had to, win.

'So where're you moving to then?' asked Dominic.

'Press Services Incorporated. They're diversifying into radio and regional press as well as mainstream media. I'll be writing releases to start with. I can do a lot from home which fits in with the kids' school and stuff. What about you?'

Dominic shrugged. 'I hadn't thought about it seriously till tonight.'

'Our gal was good. Smart. Genuine. Really believed she could make a difference. We got overrun with too much shit and trivia,' said Andy, one of Julie's other staffers.

'Then she'll get in next time. Did you keep notes? Could be a book in it,' Kristy said to Dominic.

Dominic paused, and Andy laughed. 'You do want to write a book! You and every other policy adviser I know,' he added.

'Yeah. And I want to win the lottery,' put in Hamish, Julie's press officer.

'Look, you're not wrong . . . but I need to find a way to survive in the meantime.' Dominic sighed.

'Rent your place out. Find somewhere cheaper and pay off your mortgage. Then get the book-writing out of your system. Maybe by then Julie will have been re-elected, and you'll be rehired.' Kristy made it sound like a no-brainer.

'Maybe easier said than done.' *Time to change the subject*, Dominic thought. 'Anyway, whose shout is it?'

Andy jumped to his feet. 'Mine.'

As senior policy advisor, Dominic had worked with the group for two years and felt they'd become a good team. He hadn't seriously addressed the future beyond tonight, but he was beginning to see that he should have. Kristy's words struck him with the cold reality of his situation. He'd need to look for a new job come tomorrow. How to find cheap but reasonable accommodation while renting out his apartment to pay his mortgage, just in case a job didn't immediately appear?

*

Two weeks after the election, the dust had settled. Dominic's usual interest in the direction the opposition party might be heading had waned. Everyone had moved on, trying to find jobs in allied fields.

He'd had a couple of job offers, but Dominic couldn't work up any enthusiasm to move into the business world. A corporate advisor's job paid a small fortune, but Dominic couldn't bring himself to represent, sell and pitch to big companies with dubious associations. He was a people person, articulate and a good organiser. But for the moment he couldn't decide what to do with his talents.

His mother finally pinned him down.

'You can't still be busy. Are you job hunting? I'm really sorry that Julie lost. We would have voted for her if she'd been representing our electorate.'

'Thanks, Mum.'

'Now, you have to come and visit on Saturday. Cynthia and Jeff and the kids are coming over for an early barbecue dinner. You've been so busy with that election, we all need to catch up.'

'Great, sounds good.' Anticipating her next question he added, 'And, by the way, I don't have any plans for my future just yet.'

She chuckled. 'Well, I'm sure you'll have a lot of options. And you have so many friends in such different fields, who knows, eh?'

'Yep. I've been making a few enquiries. So what time on Saturday?'

'Any time. The earlier the better. Cyn and the crew will be here by four, so come early and we'll have a quiet drink together before the kid chaos descends.'

*

Dominic drove along the quiet street where his parents lived in what the real-estate writers called 'Sydney's leafy north shore'. Over the years his parents had renovated and landscaped as the area's bushy backyards became tennis courts and swimming pools.

Dominic realised he hadn't seen his family for weeks in the election madness. They could be exasperating, in the way most families were – he knew, for instance, that his mother would waste no time in grilling him about his future plans – but he loved them and also liked their company. He was close to his sister, although their lives had gone in separate directions these past few years. Her kids were happy and well adjusted and his brother-in-law, Jeff, a lawyer, was nice enough.

Sue Cochrane met her son at the door and hugged him tight. Dominic knew she was pleased she and his father could spend time with him alone before Cynthia and her family arrived in a flurry of kisses, kids and food. And, it turned out, there would be other guests, too. Dominic was not entirely surprised. Ever the social butterfly, Sue had also invited a handful of friends and acquaintances.

Inevitably, over dinner, one of the guests, a wealthy schoolfriend of Cynthia's, launched into a diatribe about politicians and the fallout from the recent election, and turned to Dominic, wanting to hear some salacious 'pollie gossip'.

Dominic wasn't keen to debate or engage. 'I'm out of politics,' he said simply.

Noticing his unease, Cynthia tried to steer the conversation away. 'So what's the plan?' she asked him.

'Aha, now you can expose the inner workings of political life!' said the schoolfriend.

'Yes, you've been saying for years you've got a book in you,' said his father.

'I know. But I couldn't write while I was working. There was never enough time,' Dominic deflected.

'Did you keep notes?' asked Nigel, a stockbroker friend of the family.

Dominic nodded. 'Material's not the problem. Having the time is one thing, but I haven't had the headspace before now, either.'

'A book will take months! How will you pay your mortgage?' asked Sue.

His sister frowned at her mother. 'Give him a break, Mum. Let's not discuss his finances! This is a social occasion.'

Dominic put down his knife and fork. 'Actually, one of my colleagues suggested I rent out my apartment and find somewhere cheaper to live to pay the mortgage. So I'm thinking I'll start looking for a place. Then I might be able to afford to write fulltime – for the short-term, anyway.'

Nigel leaned forward. 'Look, I might be able to help with that, and do us both a favour. I'm going overseas for six months. You can stay in my place if you like. It's small, private. Quiet. Good place to write. On the water. It's a converted boatshed at Flounder Bay in WestWater, just sits there empty a lot of the time. I'd be happy if you housesit. Feed the birds some fish occasionally.'

'Are you serious?' asked Dominic.

'Are *you*?' Cynthia asked Dominic in some surprise.

'Come over tomorrow and have a look,' suggested Nigel. 'I'll give you the run-down.'

*

Dominic drove along the winding beach road, thinking that this was a place for holidays and not somewhere you'd want to commute to the city from each morning, let alone home again in the evening. He'd been to a few parties out here on the northern beaches side of the city over the years, and had been sailing with friends, but it had been a very long time since he'd had a proper look around.

The area had once been a quiet backwater, but it was

now triple gold real estate: privacy, water views, a boat mooring. Luxury getaways abounded, holiday escapes for the rich fleeing their harbourside mansions and the city, Dominic supposed. So he was more than pleasantly surprised to find that Nigel's 'boatshed' was indeed 'just a boatshed', a sprawling building on a decent jetty. However, it had been modernised, transformed from dark and musty boat storage to a small but comfortable home. Behind it, a barrier of trees rose up the hill, screening a large house almost hidden from view.

Nigel was already there and came out to greet him.

'My parents owned all of this but you can see the problem,' Nigel explained, waving an arm towards the hill. 'Bloody hike down here from the house. The old steps are gone now. They had a flying fox to take supplies up from the boat when the old ferry used to deliver to our jetty. That era is long gone since they put a road in up the top of the hill. Mum and Dad liked to sit on the patio looking at the view over the treetops. It all became a bit too much for them in the end, so they sold up. But the family is sentimental about this place, so the land was divided in two and I bought the boatshed from my parents.'

Dominic pointed at a name plate on the wall next to the boatshed's front door, which read: *The Pavilion*. 'Was that a more ambitious plan back then?' He visualised a great airy pavilion on this waterfront, thinking how fabulous it could be.

'That was the name of the big house. Although they're now owned separately, we kept the name,' said Nigel. 'There are neighbours, you can just make out their place through the trees.' He pointed away to the right, up the hill. 'They're a couple who've been here since Mum and Dad moved here in the seventies. Can't say I know many people around here any more, though. The road splits behind the houses and that's called the upper circle. We're known as the link road as it runs along the foreshore then joins the upper road. People along the top road rarely come down here to the waterfront. Not many of the old boatsheds are being used any more. Seems a bit of a missed opportunity to me. If your book doesn't sell, you could become a developer, flipping sheds to seafront sales,' joked Nigel, hurriedly adding, 'though that's the last thing we want!'

Nigel ushered Dominic inside and walked through to the double bi-fold doors onto the little front deck, which he opened. Dominic stood in the middle of the main living–dining room, looking around him and then out to the deck, and beyond that the jetty and the view. The space was compact and comfortable but it felt spacious with the doors folded tightly to one side, opening to the sweep of WestWater. The deck was sunny and inviting, a good place to grow a few plants in pots, Dominic thought. It was another thing he wanted to try his hand at while he had the chance.

'Well, this place has had a stunning makeover,' he said appreciatively.

A small kitchen and bar as well as a bedroom and ensuite ran along one side. Along the sea wall was a small stone patio lined with flowering shrubs. A shaded swing seat, a wooden table and benches beside a barbecue made a welcoming entertaining area.

'My ex-wife did it. There's a small runabout – a tinnie – if you need to go visit someone on one of the yachts or cruisers out there.' Nigel nodded to the flotilla of expensive boats moored in the distance. 'It's very quiet here most of the time. There are parties occasionally. People come down and go out to their boat with a bunch of booze and food, then they party like there's no tomorrow and never leave the mooring. There is a small community in the area, the locals. You'll only ever spot them at the general store and post office a kilometre or so down that way at The Point.' He grinned. 'All in all, this is a pretty good place to write a book, I reckon.'

'I'd say so. What would you like me to pay for this?' Dominic asked.

'I don't need any payment if you want to stay. It'll be good to know someone's here. Don't want hoons crashing here or vandals smashing the joint. Not that this area sees them much. Pretty good security when there's money living nearby.'

'Internet any good?'

'No problems. So, when do you want to move in? Does next week work for you?'

'Hell, yes.'

They shook on it.

'Good luck with the book, Dominic. Of course, if you just want to laze around on the deck and take in the view, that's fine by me.'

*

'So you're really going to live in Nigel's boatshed? What about your flat?' His sister was stunned.

'Rented it in two days, Cyn. The mortgage plus utilities is covered. I'm a free man without a job – for six months, anyway.'

'Well, good for you. You'd better make the most of it and churn out a book, then.'

Dominic smiled. 'Churn is not the word, sis. It's a

creative endeavour, requiring much thought and intense dedication burning the candle at both ends.'

She laughed. 'Yeah. With a bit of fishing thrown in.'

*

A week later, Dominic moved in and decided to take a few days to get settled.

He hadn't brought many possessions: a few clothes and books, personal stuff, and a heap of folders and note-books along with his laptop and phone charger. He knew he could probably buy or borrow anything he needed or had forgotten. He'd cleaned out his flat when he rented it save for the basic furniture, so his belongings, a few rugs and furnishings, paintings and books were stored at his parents'.

As he was unpacking in the boathouse, he found a portable vacuum in a small cupboard and, behind it, an old guitar. He pulled it out and found it to be in reason-able condition. He'd had a few guitar lessons at uni and had planned to take it up more seriously, but once he graduated he'd never had the time. But he had time now, he thought.

He strummed the instrument and sat down to tune it, and found it had a warm, mellow sound. Smiling, Dominic spent the next half an hour picking out some tunes his fingers remembered even if his brain didn't. He made a mental note to look up some guitar music and give it a proper go.

After a few days, Dominic still had little desire to do anything very much at all. He fished, fed the stray cat that hung around, cooked for himself, read some of the books in Nigel's bookcase, and took the little boat around the stretch of sheltered coves and bays where, from out on the water, he had a better perspective of the hills of the national park rising above the hidden upper roadway. Through the screen of trees he could see glimpses of a number of homes backing onto the dark hills, themselves a green smudge between the water and the sky. Along the waterfront, when the tide ran out, mudflats were exposed.

It felt like another country.

Sitting on an unravelling cane chair on the deck of an evening with a beer in hand, Dominic realised that, a bit like the old chair, he too was unwinding. The tightness and tension he hadn't realised he was holding in his body had eased.

Now he didn't grab the phone instantly when it rang. If he was dealing with a fish, he let it ring out till he was ready. This would have been unthinkable ten days ago. But, he realised, very little was truly urgent enough to warrant an immediate response.

He told himself and his family that he was taking some time to mull over ideas and themes for a book. His family left him in peace, apart from Cynthia who texted with 'just touching base. All okay?' queries until he stopped bothering to answer. He reassured her and the others that he was just fine. Loving it, even.

Dominic supposed this time of reflection, or dead stop in his life, was the sort of thing women talked about when they went to retreats, spas, took up meditation, or were recovering from a divorce or some traumatic event. He didn't know any male friends who'd dropped out; not in their thirties or forties, anyway. Who could afford to just stop working? Cynthia had probed him about his savings and plans but he'd shrugged off her queries, reassuring her that he was secure enough for the time being.

Dominic had been paid fairly well in Julie's office and

had made a lot of contacts, both in the media and in other industries. But it occurred to him now to wonder, what would he be doing in ten, twenty years' time? He had never worried about the future, had never had a Big Plan for his life. He'd accepted positions as they were offered and, thus far, they'd always come around when he needed them. He knew he was smart, quick thinking and affable enough to make friends easily, and he was well liked among his colleagues.

He couldn't ignore the fact that his work had impacted his personal life, though. Two serious relationships had faltered at the long-term stage, when discussions over 'our future' had fallen at the final hurdle. Meeting women had never been a problem. They were attracted to his ready smile and easy, friendly manner, and he'd inherited his father's handsome features. His brown hair had a habit of flopping attractively on his forehead, and he dressed well. Cynthia had once declared her brother a catch. But he knew he had always spent too much time at his desk or attending work functions. Girlfriends tended to give up on him due to his lack of time and the pressures of his job. He was always too busy.

Dominic looked out across the calm water towards Welsh Island, dotted with beautiful houses and jetties. Beyond Welsh Island, the tranquil bay of WestWater continued past the wild shores of the deserted Crouching Island, acting as a sentry to the Pacific Ocean. His gaze lost in the vista of the sprawling backwater, Dominic felt momentarily lonely, but the feeling was fleeting. Although he enjoyed socialising, he was quite comfortable in his own company. He had taken to listening to the radio news instead of buying the papers, and was less addicted to checking the online news sites. He knew he was lucky to have this time of contemplation and solitude, and he intended to make the most of it.

*

'Damn! Missed him. Took the lot,' Dominic muttered to himself as he scratched around in the tackle box for a lead trace and new hook.

The evening tide was on the turn. The wind had dropped and the surface of the water looked newly ironed. Casting out once again, and hoping for a fresh fish for dinner, he thought, *I could get used to this*.

There was a distant splash and he turned to the spread of mudflats being swallowed by the tide. He could see a rippling school of small fish, baby mullet maybe, darting in formation in the shallows. He briefly wondered how he could possibly net some of the little fish for bait or to feed the stray cat which appeared intermittently.

He glanced further up the hill to the neighbour's home through the trees, where the previous evening he'd heard laughter and voices out on the deck. It was nice to know he wasn't entirely alone; sometimes he felt he was the only human in the sweeping curve of the bay.

As he was about to turn back to his line, his attention was caught by a dash of colour and movement. Deftly moving from rock to rock along the shoreline below the hill was a figure in blue.

A slim girl, childlike in her movements, danced across the rocks, her feet barely touching each one before rising to skip to the next. Sure-footed and dainty, he was reminded of a nimble gazelle. She was watching where she leaped but moved without hesitation. It was clearly a path she knew well, but she kept her eyes to the ground nonetheless.

He was loath to call out in case she misstepped. But as she approached his jetty she turned onto the flats, squelching into the soft mud, so he called to her.

'Hi there!'

She reacted in surprise, looking around before she saw him at the end of the jetty as he rose from the up-ended bucket and cushion he'd been sitting on.

He waved. 'Where'd you spring from?' he called.

She pointed up the hill.

He gestured to the boatshed. 'I just moved in. So we're neighbours.'

She nodded. 'Any bites?' she asked as she walked towards the jetty.

'Some good ones. Lost my hook a few times.'

'Bream. Or a flattie, probably.'

She was possibly fourteen or fifteen, he thought. Tomboyish and slight.

'Want to join me? I have a spare line.'

'Sure.'

There was no shiver in the loose boards in the jetty as she walked lightly along it. She gave him a slight smile as she reached him. 'Hi, I'm CeeCee.'

'I'm Dom. Actually Dominic.'

'I'm actually Cecily. Cecily Hope. So how long are you staying here?' She sat on the edge of the old jetty, swinging her legs, reaching for a prawn as he gave her a hand reel.

'Is a handline okay? There's a rod back on the deck if you prefer.'

'This is fine, thanks. I won't stay long. My grand-mother will start to worry.'

'Who's your grandmother? I haven't met any of the neighbours yet.'

'Oh, my grandparents are Gloria and Sam Sutherland. We're to the right along the track up that way, past where Nigel's parents used to live.' She turned and pointed up the hill.

'So you know Nigel and his family?'

'Yeah. Everyone sort of knows the locals who've been here a long time.' CeeCee threaded the prawn onto her hook.

'Makes sense.' Dominic nodded to the water. 'I was hoping for a fish for dinner.'

'You can't go far wrong with throwing a fish on the barbie,' CeeCee said sagely.

He glanced at her as she swung the line like a lasso and it spun out to plop into the water twenty metres away. 'Nice one. Do you fish a lot?'

'Not regularly. Only when I come here and visit Nan and Grandad. Mainly school holidays.' CeeCee studied him through her tortoiseshell-framed glasses. 'What do you do? Are you on holidays?'

'Not really. I wanted a change. I'm staying here while I do some writing.'

CeeCee jagged her line then wound it in and inspected her empty hook. 'Baited. Well, I guess I'd better get back.'

'You've been out walking?'

'I went around to see old Snowy Burns. Nan likes me to check up on him when I come over here as he lives out in the bush and it's a bit of a hike for Nan now. Too hard for her to get there. He's pretty old, and stubborn, Nan says.'

'Who is he? Why does he live in the bush?' asked Dominic.

'I don't know why, really. Snowy's just always been here. He has a rough sort of shack, but he seems to like it there.' She neatly secured the hook and dropped the reel in the bucket.

'Well, it was nice to meet you. If I get a decent couple of fish, I'll let you know and you can share them,' said Dominic.

'I mightn't be here. I just visit when I can.'

'Did you grow up here? Wonderful spot to live, no wonder your grandparents haven't moved.'

'My mum grew up here.' CeeCee jumped to her feet. 'Might see you next visit. I'll tell Nan about your fish offer. Just in case.'

CeeCee hurried back along the jetty where she spied the cat lying in the late-afternoon sun on the deck outside Dominic's door. 'Are you feeding Woolly? The cat?' she called back to him.

'Yes. Shouldn't I? Is that what the poor thing is called?'

'He's a con artist. Begs from everybody. He'll move on. Don't feel sorry for him!'

Dominic waved. 'Story of my life! See ya.'

*

The following afternoon, standing at the refrigerator and wondering what to make for dinner, Dominic heard CeeCee calling him.

'Hey, Dominic, Nan sent me down to see you.'

'Come on in,' he said, closing the fridge and turning to see CeeCee in the doorway. 'Just deciding what to throw on the barbecue. Had no luck yesterday. Fish went away with the tide, I guess.'

'Oh, shame. Anyway, Nan said would you like to come up for dinner with us? Very casual.'

'That sounds nice. I'd love to. What time?'

She shrugged. 'About six-ish, Nan said, or whenever you're ready.'

'Thanks. I'll clean up and see you then.'

'Sorry you didn't catch anything.'

He smiled. 'That's fishing for you. It was just nice sitting there watching the sun start to go down.'

'We'll get one next time.' CeeCee grinned and darted away.

*

The sun still felt warm on his back as Dominic picked his way up the hill to the big weatherboard home that was probably considered 'Swedish modern' back in the late seventies. The spacious wooden deck, flagstone terrace and flowering trees and plants blended inconspicuously with the native vegetation.

CeeCee greeted him, calling down to him from the deck, 'Go round the side, there.'

Around the house at the main entrance he saw the garage and a precipitous driveway leading to the road above. The garage and house were accessed by a flight of steps made of old railway sleepers. Flourishing fruit trees flanked the entrance and shoes were lined up by the front door.

The door was opened by a wiry, muscular woman who radiated fitness and energy even though she must have been in her seventies, Dominic thought. She beamed at him.

'Hello, you must be Dominic. I'm Gloria. Oh, please, you don't have to take off your shoes if you don't want to. Come in.'

They shook hands then she turned and led him into the sitting room where doors and glass windows without any curtains had a panoramic view of the spread of bays and hills. The deck wrapped around the exterior like a protective hug.

'So you're looking after Nigel's place for a bit? Are you comfortable down there?' Gloria asked.

'Totally. Too much so. I'm not doing any work.' Dominic handed Gloria a bottle of wine.

'There was no need, but thanks. We don't mind an occasional drink on the deck. Like now. Shall we? This is my husband, Sam.'

Sam loomed large, balding and affable with a strong handshake and cheery smile.

'Good timing,' said Sam. 'How're you managing in the boatshed?' He led the way out onto the deck, where comfortable chairs including classic settler's chairs were lined up facing the view, a little like a cinema.

'It's terrific. Well laid out, everything I need. I feel very lucky that it fell into my lap when I needed it.'

'Smell the roses while you can, lad. Well, the mud, salt and fresh air, anyway.' Sam smiled as he sank into a settler's chair, stretching his legs in front rather than dangling them over the straight wooden arms as was the design for weary stockmen's booted legs.

'Did you work in the outback, Sam?' asked Dominic.

Sam chuckled. 'Yeah. You can tell I'm a bushie, eh? Mind you, that was in my young and fit wild days. Once Gloria came on my radar, that was the end of that.'

Gloria appeared, handing Dominic a glass of wine and Sam a beer and smiling indulgently. 'You should have heard him whinge when my father wanted him to move to the city. But he did.'

Sam gave a small smile. 'I wasn't one for an office job. I'd worked with my dad, had a small holding, ran a few cattle. The drought in the mid-sixties did us in. So I went from the land to the sea. Not that I was ever much of a swimmer. But I did my Masters certificate to qualify as a skipper, and after we got married I got a job as a ferry master at Castle Beach, running all around WestWater. I know every creek and bay in this area. And in the old days, every family.'

'That's quite a change of lifestyle,' said Dominic, noticing the warm smile the couple exchanged.

'Never thought I'd end up living in a place like this,' said Gloria. 'Change from the southern suburbs where I grew up. We love it and won't move till they have to carry us out. 'Course, it's got a bit more gentrified than when we first came here.'

'Yep. It was rustic fibro cottages and whatever people could afford to bang up. Weekenders mostly,' added Sam.

'It all changed when they upgraded the road,' said Gloria. 'Almost put Sam out of work.'

'I went from ferry captain to charter boat. Then started fishing trips. Reckon I was a bit ahead of my time. No cocktails and nibbles when we went out to sea past Crouching Island back then.' Sam grinned. 'I'm back on the ferry now. A shorter run, but still the best way to get round the bays and over to Welsh Island.'

'So what was the social life here like?' asked Dominic. 'It still seems a little, well, isolated. Individualistic. A lot of space between you, lots of trees screening you. I mean, it's private and pretty, but . . . it seems everyone keeps to themselves.'

'I'd shoot myself if I had neighbours you could hear and see and almost touch,' Sam said with a grimace.

'I think we have the best of both worlds. Privacy, peace and prettiness. And only a short stroll or cooee to a neighbour if we need them or want to visit,' said Gloria.

'It might seem quiet, but we have a strong little community. And we've had some great parties here over the years.'

'And a few accidents,' said Sam. 'It's all very well walking home along a bush track, drunk as a skunk. Or getting in and out of a boat, three sheets to the wind, but you have to know what you're doing or stay on the orange juice all night so you get home in one piece.'

'It used to be the city people who came here and got into strife,' added Gloria. 'But now with the road people have to be careful not to be over the limit when driving.'

They sipped their drinks in the twilight. Sam was reflective as he said quietly, 'Seems now it's just us old-timers living around here fulltime. Lot of empty houses.'

'That's 'cause young families can't afford the big modern houses up on the top road. It's all holiday rentals now. Unless they have rich parents, I s'pose.' Gloria sighed.

'Debt. Kids are sunk in debt. Live for today . . .' Sam shook his head, and then seemed to decide that was enough morose talk for one evening. 'What are you doing with yourself, Dominic? Our CeeCee said something about writing?'

'That's the idea,' said Dominic. 'I was working for a member of state parliament. She lost in the last election, so before looking for another similar job I thought I might take time out and explore new horizons; you know, rethink what I really want from life. Well, from a career. I'm toying with the idea of trying to write a book. But so far I haven't actually seen past the view from the jetty.'

Sam chuckled. 'Well, seems like a good place to contemplate the future to me.'

'It's peaceful and beautiful for sure. But it's not dull, either. We've had our times over here, haven't we?' said Gloria quietly.

Sam nodded. 'A bushfire in the mid-seventies was a close call. The fire came straight down the hill to our back gardens and in the gullies to the water's edge. Wallabies were leaping into the bays everywhere. We lost quite a few homes, boatsheds, even a couple of boats.'

'Poor old Baldy died too.' Gloria looked at Dominic, explaining, 'He was a funny old draught horse that somehow found his way over here. Must have been lost in the bush for months before he was adopted by the Stackhouse family. Lived with them for years. He got frightened by the fire and headed to the water, then fell in and drowned.'

'So sad really,' added Sam. 'They towed him over to the front of Happy Gove's place and sent him to the bottom. Fed the fish for bloody yonks. Happy reckons he fished up the odd fetlock and hoof over the years.'

'Happy was a bit of a yarn spinner,' said Gloria. 'You know who he was? The movie star?' When Dominic looked a bit blank she added, 'One of our first Aussies to make it in Hollywood. They made him a sort of lanky cowboy type. His name was Howard Gove but he was such an easygoing larrikin they nicknamed him Happy.'

'Yes. I think I've heard of him,' said Dominic.

'We heard all about it as he was the one who set up a fund to help the Wynn family after their tragedy.' Gloria shook her head sadly. 'It was before our time. Apparently John Wynn was a lovely fellow who started a little water taxi service over to The Point from the bays before the road came along. He had his eighteen-month-old son with him one day while the mother was shopping. Little fellow fell overboard. Just the two of them on the boat. John jumped in to try to get to him. Both drowned.'

'Oh, how tragic,' said Dominic. 'No life jackets?'

'It wasn't the done thing in those days. Besides, the waters here are usually so calm.'

Dominic nodded. 'Tragedy can come so quickly and quietly sometimes. When least expected.' It felt like a trivial cliché but then, it always did with such things. He wondered how to change the subject and continued, 'CeeCee mentioned she'd been to visit an old chap who lives in the bush here?'

'Old Snowy,' said Sam. 'He's an odd one. A Vietnam vet so he's carrying a lot of baggage. Been here for years. Just opted out and lives quietly. He can't cope well with the modern world. We all watch out for him.'

'That's nice. So this is actually a close-knit community,' said Dominic.

Gloria nodded. 'That's for sure. We can all go weeks or more without any contact, though. Then we get together and pick up where we left off.'

Sam added quietly, 'But if there's a problem or anything happens, we're all there straight away.'

Gloria glanced at him. 'Sadly we can't always make things right. A drowning. A fire. An accident or whatever. The worst thing, though, is when there's a tragedy and you never find out exactly what happened or why.'

Sam nodded. 'Some mysteries are never solved.' He looked at Dominic. 'That's the worst – the not knowing. Happened to a local family here years ago. A good family man just disappeared off the face of the earth. No rhyme or reason.' He shook his head, looking perplexed.

Dominic read between the lines. 'Well, suicide is a dreadful and tragic thing –'

'They don't know even that! Hard to hide your body if you've suicided, and his was never found,' said Gloria briskly, then stood up. 'Right, tea's nearly ready; I'll just go dish up. Come in when you've finished.' She looked at Sam nursing the last few inches of his beer.

'Good-oh.' He paused. 'This is a good place, Dominic. Good people. Trouble is, you never know what's going on in a family. You can live side by side with people for twenty years and then, wham! The last thing you expected happens.' Sam drained his beer and eased out of his chair.

Dominic got to his feet too, unsure what to say. 'I guess it can happen anywhere, Sam. You think you know people . . .' He trailed off, then followed Sam's sturdy figure as they went inside and headed to the dining table.

Sam pulled out a chair. 'Hey, something smells good. Take a seat, son.'

Gloria marched in carrying a hotpot, CeeCee in her wake.

'Hi, Dom!'

'Hi, CeeCee, good to see you.' Dominic smiled.

'Thought a stew might be a change from fish for you,' put in Gloria. 'And CeeCee made a baked custard with poached pears for dessert.'

'Preserved pears from Nan's tree.' CeeCee smiled proudly.

'It smells wonderful. Thank you both so much,' said Dominic.

Dinner was a light-hearted affair as the proud grandparents prodded CeeCee to talk of her ambitions as well as probing Dominic about his plans and life in the backrooms of the political movers and shakers. In turn they filled him in on their views on local politics and the shortcomings of their council.

'I think they pretend they don't know we exist. In some ways it's good to be in a backwater. But as you may have noticed, the area around us is becoming posh and pricey. A lot of exclusive clubs and gated homes and swish boats that cost as much as a house,' said Sam, shaking his head.

'It's creeping ever closer, too. We've been far enough away from the city for people not to be too interested in our properties; our patch down here off the link road has always been considered a bit inconvenient. The upper road has the big new homes with the sweeping views, and till now they haven't seemed to notice there's a little community along the waterfront here. Which is fine by us. Another glass of red wine?' asked Gloria.

*

As he made his way down the hill after dinner, Dominic glanced back through the trees and saw a dark silhouette on the front deck watching his progress. He raised a hand in farewell.

It had been a pleasant evening. Dominic had found Sam and Gloria salt-of-the-earth people. CeeCee, although she didn't say a lot, had been polite and attentive before excusing herself. A nice family.

As Dominic reached the boatshed the motion light shone a sudden yellow beam on the back door as a patchy dark shadow darted past him.

'Bloody cat! It's too late for food. Go catch something.'

But he relented, considering the destruction from roaming cats at night, and put down a saucer with a small handful of raw mincemeat on it. 'Here you go, Woolly.'

Later, Dominic stretched out in bed, familiar now with the night sounds of lapping water, an occasional splash of something diving or jumping, and waves sploshing against the rock wall as the wash from some passing boat finally reached shore.

Tentatively the cat crept onto the bed and started pawing the sheets into a nest by his feet.

He'd really enjoyed meeting Gloria and Sam, Dominic reflected. He wondered what the rest of the neighbours were like. Living most of his adult life in the city where he'd barely seen or spoken to his neighbours, Dominic had rather forgotten the pleasure and reassurance of knowing you had good people close by.

It seemed this was a community who watched out for each other without intruding. And, in stark contrast to his last few years, these were people who were not seeking favours or acting in expectation of a quid pro quo . . . you scratch my back and I'll scratch yours. Like his parents, this was a generation of people who were simply good friends and neighbours, who expected only the same in return.

The machinations, vested allegiances and manipulations of those who held a sliver or more of power were not part of this world, and it was refreshing. People like Sam and Gloria were decent straight shooters, whose word was their bond. A handshake meant a deal. And they would be there in any emergency.

It gave Dominic a sense of comfort, security and, sadly, a wish that the Sams and Glorias of this world had a lot more say in running the joint.

He slept well.

2

THE SWEAT RUNNING DOWN Dominic's face started to dry as the sun came out and filtered through thick stands of gum trees. The rich tangy smell of eucalyptus oil was clearing his head.

A sunny morning walk to explore some of the national park had somehow become a confusing and tiring hike. He really wasn't sure where he was. He'd followed the dirt track that wound up the hill behind the boatshed, and as he headed higher and deeper into the bush he'd found the old fire trail which supposedly led to a headland with magnificent views over WestWater.

The fire trail started above the small township at The Point, which Dominic hadn't yet visited, and wound along a ridge, so he'd impulsively taken what he thought looked like a short cut but now realised was probably only an animal track. Exactly where he was and how to find his way back to Flounder Bay or a road, let alone the boatshed, he had no idea.

He paused, glancing at his phone to find there was no reception and the battery was almost flat. He'd been walking for three hours. He had little water left in his flask. He turned his baseball cap around to shade the back of his neck.

Just retracing his steps would be almost impossible as he'd forced his way through the scrubby bush assuming he'd get to the main track or the ridge with an outlook so he could get some idea where he was. At one point he'd come to hip-high grass so he'd pushed through it into a small clearing only to startle a dozing wallaby which had pounded away in alarm.

Dominic stood still now, turning slowly and hoping he'd get some indication of which direction to take. He looked at the angle of the sun, which was almost directly overhead. His glance at the phone had confirmed it was nearly midday. Surely he couldn't be totally lost? He concentrated and found he could hear the occasional faint hum of a distant car.

He decided on a direction and set off, wishing he'd worn long pants as his legs were getting scratched by the undergrowth, sharp twigs, thorns and a variety of razor grasses.

Suddenly he was in full sun as the stand of gums thinned out and large boulders poked through the undergrowth. Clumps of bushes were studded with small flowers and the hillside grew steeper, but he was glad to be out of the canopy of trees, despite the burning sunlight. He hoped he'd come to a peak or ridge which would give him his bearings.

He watched where he put his feet, aware of possible snakes in the long grass, and heaved himself upwards. And then, reaching a cluster of sandstone rocks, he pulled himself onto the largest to find he was suddenly gazing across a great expanse of scrubby bushland, and dipping into the vista in the far righthand distance was a strip of blue water.

He realised he was thoroughly lost.

Dominic sat down to rest and decide what to do. The phrase, 'like a shag on a rock' came to mind. He shook his head. How the hell had he managed to strand himself in the middle of nowhere? It had been foolish to set out without more water or a clear idea where he was going.

Bracing himself against the rock, he arched his back to stretch tired muscles, and his fingertips touched some sort of indentation. He glanced down, then shifted to one side. He stared at the surface of the ancient rock. He was sitting on a carving of a large fish.

Clambering down, he walked around the rock, studying the engraving, then reached into his pocket and pulled out his phone to take a photo only to find it was completely dead. He was about to shove it back into his pocket when there was a bellow from behind him.

'Hey! You! No bloody photos!'

Dominic spun around in surprise.

A short, stocky older man was glaring at him, his expression fierce. He was dressed in khaki shorts and a matching shirt, wore heavy boots and long socks and looked unkempt. Greasy white hair hung beneath a battered army hat, its side pinned up in traditional Anzac style. He was carrying a sturdy stick which he leaned on now.

'Who're you?' he snapped at Dominic. 'You bloody lost or what?'

Dominic gave a hesitant smile and lifted his arms. 'Yep. Lost, all right. My name's Dominic.'

'Why you poking around up here then?'

'I just came for a walk, to get a feel for the place. I heard there's a great lookout somewhere up here. I'm living in a friend's boatshed at Flounder Bay,' he added quickly.

'Oh yeah? Who'd that be?'

'Nigel Fullilove. He's gone overseas for a bit.'

'Yeah. I know it.'

'I just can't figure out how to get back down there.' Dominic took a step, but the old man was instantly alert.

'So why you taking pictures?'

Dominic gestured at the carvings on the sandstone. 'I just thought these were amazing. But anyway, I couldn't take any photos, my phone is flat.' He shrugged.

'We don't like people taking pictures. Putting them out there so people know about this place. You planning to come back up here?' the old fellow asked suspiciously.

'I doubt I'd find my way back up here again,' said Dominic pleasantly. 'I'd just like to find out how to get back down to the water.'

'Lot of water around here. Bays and coves and backwater spots you wouldn't know was there. Mostly you can only get in by boat,' said the man. Squinting at Dominic, he seemed to decide any threat had passed. Dominic watched him pull a tin from the top pocket of his shirt, take a plug of tobacco from it, then take a flimsy cigarette paper and stick it to his lip as he deftly rolled the tobacco in the palm of his hand.

'So you never been up before?' asked the man, as if double-checking Dominic's story.

'Never. You a local then?'

'Sorta. Why're you staying down there in the shed?'

'Nigel loaned it to me as he's away and I was after a quiet place to do some writing.'

'You another one, eh? Been a few writers, a poetry woman too, who used t'live around here.' He paused as he rolled the tobacco in the paper and licked its length, smoothing it into a sleek cylinder. He stuck it between his lips as he reached for matches. 'Just so long as yer not one of them nosey archaeologist types.' He swiped the match along the box, put it to the cigarette and took a deep drag as the end flared. 'Or pretending to be.'

Dominic was puzzled for a moment then saw how the older man was glancing at the carved fish on the rock face. He smiled. 'I gather this is an Aboriginal carving. Old, is it?'

'I reckon. Hundreds, maybe thousands of years old. They did a lot of them through here. The sandstone is pretty soft.' He paused, taking another drag on his cigarette, then seemed to make up his mind. 'You gotta know where they are, though; some don't show up well. Gotta toss water on them 'cause they're so faded. Carvings haven't been touched up for many years, probly.'

'Would you show me some?' asked Dominic.

The man glanced at him, some of his suspicion resurfacing. 'Guess so,' he said slowly. 'Gotta be careful who knows they're here, though. Vandals and such. Mostly stupid, smart-arse kids.'

'And what about archaeologists?' asked Dominic carefully. 'There must be a lot to study up here.'

'Don't want 'em round here,' said the man bluntly. 'Next thing they'll be bringing in tourists and picnic tables and rubbish and the place'll be shot. There's a few know about all this but they keep it quiet. Some of the old men have passed on stories,' he added enigmatically. Then he started walking and said over his shoulder, 'Come on. I'll show you the way back down.'

Relieved, Dominic followed the grumpy odd fellow as they clambered around the big flat sandstone rocks, finally asking, 'So what's your name? You live around here, right?'

'Yep. Been here a good time now. I'm Sergeant Johnathon Burns. But everyone calls me Snowy.' He pulled off his hat to show the thin covering of blinding white hair. He gave a hint of a smile.

'Ah. I know who you are. I've met the Sutherland family and they mentioned you. Nice people.'

Snowy nodded. 'That CeeCee is a good kid.'

CeeCee's reference to checking up on a spiky old man who lived in a shack was fairly spot on, thought Dominic, as the tough older fellow sat beside him. 'Are there snakes around here?'

'Never know what you might run into up here,' Snowy replied vaguely. He peered into the distance and Dominic got the impression he was looking more into the past than being alert to the present.

'So, you heading back to your place?' Dominic tried again to draw Snowy into conversation. 'Can you point me in the direction I should go?' he added.

'I'll take you down to the track,' Snowy answered gruffly. 'And I'll show you something interesting. But you're not to share it. Okay?'

'I understand,' said Dominic, beginning to wonder if the old fellow might have a tenuous grip on reality.

Snowy led the way without further comment, and Dominic noted that he didn't hesitate or take his bearings or even look around, but seemed familiar with the route through the bushland. However, he walked with a bit of a limp. Dominic kept his eyes down, following in the old man's footsteps until they reached a hillock overlooking a gully beneath them. Snowy paused, leaned over and rubbed the stub of his cigarette on a rock, spat on it and put it in his pocket.

They were standing in knee-deep bracken surrounded by large boulders. A tree was growing from beneath one of them, its roots gripping the rock, which seemed to join other boulders that had erupted from the earth like huge ancient pustules the colour of dried blood.

Snowy parted the bracken with his stick, stomping his booted feet.

'Lie down.'

'Sorry?' Dominic stiffened. And as Snowy jabbed his stick and pointed, Dominic saw that there was a shadow beneath a boulder which he realised was an opening, as if a slice had been taken from underneath.

'Push yourself along in there a bit. There's a crevice and then you'll see an opening at the back of the tree.'

Dominic felt a bit silly lying on his belly and wriggling forward as Snowy directed, then he saw how the ground suddenly sloped and widened like a yawn.

'Pull yourself forward and stick your head down in there,' instructed Snowy.

Dominic wedged his shoulders against one side and leaned forward then gasped as he realised he was facedown, his head protruding into a large rock alcove beneath him.

He was lying on top of the roof of a small cave overhang. Light was coming in from whichever direction it faced.

'Wow, where is that? Can you get down in there?'

'Look to the sides and up on the right-hand side.'

Dominic craned his head and then caught his breath. That hidden underground cave was home to a wondrous secret.

'Wow,' he breathed. 'There're handprints! And a kangaroo. Beautiful! How old are these? Who did them? What is this place?'

'Wallaby. Could be thousands of years ago. It's not underground, the shelter is below us . . . The light comes from the entrance down there. Tough climb to get in, though.'

Dominic struggled upright, brushing grass and leaves from his hair. 'That's incredible. Very moving. Must be extraordinary to be inside it. Thank you for showing me. I'll keep it to myself.'

'Good.' Snowy nodded. 'Bit more of a walk along here and then I'll show where to head down to Flounder Bay.'

They set off again and were silent for a few minutes before Dominic asked, 'So what do you do with yourself, Snowy? You've been here a while, I believe.'

The old man didn't answer immediately and seemed to be deciding what to say, or not.

'Sam said you were in the army? Vietnam?' prompted Dominic gently.

'Yeah.' Snowy hesitated, then added, 'No thanks for it, but. Treated like scum when I got back. No one cared for any of us. Left to ourselves. Shoulda got organised sooner. Talked to the other blokes. Even our families didn't know, understand.'

'Yes. That must have been hard,' said Dominic quietly.

'We got on with it. Life. What else you gonna do?'

'That's true. Been any bad bushfires around here?' asked Dominic, remembering Sam's mention of fires.

'The fire in seventy-nine was real bad. Few homes lost. Cleared out the holidaymakers though, so that was good.' He glanced sideways at Dominic. 'You gotta be a certain kinda person to live here.'

'Living round Flounder Bay? Or the WestWater area generally?' asked Dominic, thinking the look Snowy gave him was some kind of test.

'It can look peaceful enough, but there've been tragedies, accidents, and things you don't want to know.'

'Yes, Sam and Gloria mentioned a drowning, a bushfire, some fellow who went missing . . .'

'Yeah. Odd one, that,' interjected Snowy. He stepped over a small log. 'You never really know people, do ya, eh? Must be hard to live like that . . . always wondering, like. What happened, and why.'

'What did happen, do you think?' asked Dominic, falling in behind Snowy as the undergrowth became too thick to walk side by side.

'Dunno. The bloke just never came home one day.'

'Didn't want the reason made public, I suppose?' hedged Dominic to Snowy's back.

Snowy's shoulders lifted. 'Who knows? They stayed, anyways.'

'The wife? The family? Really?'

'Kids all grown up now. She's still here. Patient woman, I'd say.' Snowy stopped and pointed. 'Right. Push your way down there a few hundred yards and you'll come to the track along near those gum trees. Follow it east and it'll take you towards the water and the bottom road. You'll know your way from there.'

'Can't thank you enough, Snowy. You certainly know your way around. I owe you one. Stop in for a cuppa or a beer next time you're in Flounder Bay.'

'Dunno about that. I don't socialise. I only get out when I'm feeling good, like today. Just t'check up on things,' Snowy muttered.

'Well, it was my lucky day. Thank you.' Dominic reached out and shook the old man's hand, surprised at how soft it was compared to the weather-beaten face and slight but stocky body.

Snowy gave a gruff sort of farewell and turned and headed off without a backward glance.

*

Compared to the morning, Dominic's trek back was easier, though he was weary when he hit the old bitumen road along the waterfront.

As he trudged along he heard a car behind and stepped to one side to let it pass. The car slowed then pulled over in front of him. It was a smart royal-blue luxury four-wheel drive, and the top was up. As he approached, a woman climbed out of the car.

His first impression was that she was tall, blonde, smiling and had great legs. She wore shorts, sneakers and a tight T-shirt. She lifted her hand.

'Hi there! You lost? Or need a lift? You look a bit done in. Been hiking?'

'Sort of. I got lost. Was rescued by an old bloke.' He caught up to her. 'Thanks anyway.'

'Do you want some water? I have some.' Without waiting for an answer she pulled the door open and leaned across the front seat, her shorts tightening across her shapely rear.

She handed him a flask of water.

'Thanks, I won't say no.' He took several long gulps. 'Ahh. Nice and cold.'

'Where're you headed? There's not much out here. Happy to drop you anywhere.'

'That's kind of you, but I haven't got much further to go now. I'm in Flounder Bay,' said Dominic.

'You on a boat?'

He shook his head. 'Nope. Are you?'

'Oh, I live nearby.' She gave him a big smile. Despite her attractive, slightly sexy look, her haircut and its colour, skilled make-up, professional manicure, expensive gold necklace and watch gave her the aura of coming from money.

He handed her back the flask. 'Thanks so much.'

A car passed them.

'Hop in, you look bushed. Where in Flounder Bay are you? The upper road?'

He walked around the car, easing himself into the low-slung passenger seat. 'No, the link road. On the waterfront, I'll show you.'

'No worries. I'm Alicia, by the way.' She got in and pulled her door shut. The interior smelled of genuine leather and something sweet. Whether it was a car freshener or some fancy French perfume, he couldn't tell.

'I'm Dominic.'

As Alicia drove confidently along the winding road he couldn't help feeling bemused by all that had happened in one day. She chatted easily, confidently.

'So you live here or have a holiday place down here? Great spot, isn't it?' she said.

'Yes. I like the peace and isolation. Only been away from the big smoke for two weeks.'

'Ah, a bit of a chill-out. Nice. You should come out to the boat for a drink.'

'Is this a boat you live on, or fish from, or what?'

'It belongs to my boss. There's a few of us here for his birthday. No fishing allowed.'

'That sort of boat.' He grinned.

'It's not a wild party boat if that's what you're thinking. The old man is in his eighties but likes company. We're moored in the lee of Welsh Island. Where's your place?'

'Not much further.' He pointed. 'Just before the turn-off to the upper road. I'm in a refurbished boatshed along there. You can leave me here, thanks a lot.'

'Pleasure. Here's my card, give me a call if you want to come out to the boat.' She leaned over to the handbag resting by Dominic's feet, her hair swinging against his arm, and again he caught the sweet smell of her perfume.

She gave him a smile as he took the card. 'Sorry I didn't come across you earlier and save you a walk.'

'The idea was a nice walk to see the views. Getting lost wasn't in the plan. Many thanks.' He held out his hand and she shook it firmly, lingering briefly before her fingers slid from his palm. Or did he just imagine it?

He turned, and as he walked away from the road he had the feeling she was watching him in her rear-view mirror.

'I'm sounding a bit desperate,' he chided himself with a chuckle.

*

Showered and feeling better, he leaned back in his deck-chair and drained the last of a cold beer.

'I'm stuffed, Woolly. What a day,' he said to the cat, who was lying in the late-afternoon sun in the doorway.

Next thing he knew, his phone was ringing inside on the charger. He blinked into the twilight, realising he'd dozed off. He debated whether or not to answer, but the sun had gone down and it had grown cool. He wanted a warmer top and another beer. He went inside and picked up the phone.

'I was just about to hang up. Were you fishing?' said a friendly voice.

Rob Talbot, who Dominic had met at university, was probably the closest thing he had to a best friend. Over the years they had borrowed money from each other, taken trips together, fallen in and out of love with various women – once, memorably, with the same girl, who'd then spurned them both – and shared family tragedies and triumphs. The last few years they hadn't been in such close contact, but when they met up it was always like old times, and each knew the other would be there in a crisis. Rob was divorced after an impetuous marriage in Bali, and Dominic had given up following the vicissitudes of his romances.

'Rob, mate. No, I was asleep. I did a massive hike today.'

'Wow, that's impressive. Where'd you get to?'

'No idea, actually! Got a bit lost, in fact. The bush-land is really rugged around here.'

'Hope you weren't chased by local wildlife!'

'Could've been. It's all national park, unfenced, wild, native bush. Very unspoiled. Ran into a wild species or two, though. Big day.' He yawned.

'You sound buggered. How's the writing coming?'

'Next question.'

'That good, eh? Did you see the great article in the new issue of *The Monthly*? Great reporting. Too bad, as your minister is going to be sorely missed.'

'That's politics for you. We did our best,' said Dominic,

picking up his half-empty warm beer. 'I'm a bit over it all, to tell you the truth.'

'I can believe it.' Rob sighed. 'Anyway, sounds like you're keeping fit, at least. What else you up to? Met any of the on-trend movers and shakers that hang out round there?'

'Actually, I got a ride in a four-wheel drive with a nice-looking chick the last kilometre or so after my hike. She's staying on some party boat with her old rich boss by the sound of it.' Dominic chuckled.

'That'd be right. I saw a group in the social pages "celebrating" at WestWater last weekend.'

'You read the social pages now, Rob?'

'Every so often, just to keep tabs on who's who in the zoo. Never know, I might want to pitch something to them.'

Dominic smiled. 'Ever the entrepreneur. What are you flogging now?' Last Dominic could remember, his old university friend had been in advertising and media and dabbled in promotions, produced music clips, had set up an online radio network, and was now in IT working with a team developing dating apps for singles.

'I've been working on some broadcast programs, mostly online. You coming into town at all? Thought it was time we caught up,' said Rob.

'Not really. Don't have a reason to and I'm rather dug in here.' Dominic paused. 'If you're heading this way chasing influencers or anything, come over for a drink. Stay the night, whatever.'

'Sure I won't be interrupting?'

'I'd enjoy the company.'

'Can I bring any rations, supplies, sustenance from the big smoke? Refreshments are already on the list, of course,' said Rob.

'I've got most things covered, mate, but maybe some meat? We're a bit over fish, it seems.'

'We? Am I intruding?'

'I share my bed with a stray cat,' said Dominic with a grin.

'Jeez, Dom, you need some company. How's Saturday sound?'

Dominic laughed. 'Great. Take the bottom road along the waterfront. It's very private but you'll find the boathouse.'

'Looking forward to it.'

Dominic hung up. *Be good to have some company for a short visit*, he thought.

At a loose end for the evening, he was tempted to wander up to see Sam and Gloria and tell them about Snowy 'rescuing' him. The more Dominic thought about the feisty old man the more intrigued he became. He just felt there was something more to him, another layer to the crusty, disillusioned veteran. But he was tired. Darkness closed in and the now familiar night noises began, the lapping of the tide around the piers, birds settling for the night and a stiffened breeze in the trees. He fed Woolly, made his dinner, poured himself a glass of red and settled comfortably in front of the TV.

*

Early the next morning Dominic pulled up outside the local quaint old general store at The Point. He glanced at his watch. Door to door, a twelve-minute drive. He should walk it next time, he decided.

When he'd moved in, he'd brought supplies from a big supermarket in The Vale, the nearest centre on the way from the city to WestWater, and he went there whenever he needed to do a big shop, but he'd rather go local when he only wanted to grab little things like milk and bread. Although now he was here, he was beginning to wonder what sort of shop this was. The store looked like it had perhaps had a different life as a shed, warehouse or depot of some kind. In old-fashioned script under the somewhat faded general store sign were the words: *D and D Props*.

A bell jingled as Dominic walked into the crowded space filled with boxes, crates and a table labelled *Local Produce* which had fruit and vegetables piled in baskets, and lettuce, spinach and herbs in jugs of water. Shelves lined the walls and divided the main room while at the rear there was a large freezer cabinet. Fresh flowers in buckets of water gave off a sweet scent. *It just needs the smell of baking bread to complete the folksy image*, he thought.

'Good morning,' came a cheerful welcome.

Dominic turned to see a slim woman in her sixties or seventies with cropped grey hair smiling at him. She was wearing jeans and a loose shirt with the sleeves rolled up, and her hands showed weathered skin and blunt nails. Incongruously, earrings of dancing elephants in tutus dangled from her ears.

She held out her hand. 'I'm Deidre. You must be the new fellow staying in Nigel's place.'

'How did you guess? Yes, I'm Dominic.'

'I thought you'd be in before long. CeeCee described you. So, you settled in? What do you need?'

'I have a mate coming to stay for the weekend. Need some basics. May I browse?'

'Of course. Meat and deli things over there,' Deidre waved a hand, 'dairy and local cheeses, dips and such in there. Fruit and veggies at the front – lots of local produce – and tinned and packet stuff on the far shelves. I can slice you some ham, corned beef or salami. The baker will be dropping in his excellent baked goods any minute. Do you want me to keep a newspaper for you each day? Oh, and there's wine and liquor and beer in the back fridge. Cleaning stuff back there. Look around, you never know what you'll find. Daph – my partner – orders things behind my back.'

'You've got an amazing range,' said Dominic. 'Looks like I'll want for little.'

'You go ahead and browse. Here's a box to put your goods in. Most customers bring it back next visit and reuse it or we have a pile of string bags you can use.'

'My grandmother always used one of those,' said Dominic.

'Daph makes them. Hell on your fingers crocheting that twine, but they work well and are strong.' She handed him the box and excused herself as another customer came in.

Dominic started collecting things as he wandered around the shop, putting them in the box as he went.

'Finding everything?' Dominic turned to see another woman smiling at him. 'You met Deidre? I'm Daphne. We wondered when you'd pop in. How's your book writing going?'

Dominic threw back his head and laughed. 'No secrets around here.'

'When you've been here as long as we have, you get to hear everything,' Daphne said with a chuckle. 'I said to Deidre we should have been a newsagency first and foremost. We're generally first with all the news.'

'So how long have you been here?' Dominic asked.

'Let's see, we came here in the seventies. Got fed up

with the city. We quit our jobs at the uni and it just so happened this place came up. It was a run-down though busy petrol station then, but once the big road went in The Point became a backwater.'

'And that's just how we like it,' said Deidre, coming over to join them.

'What university? Were you lecturing?' asked Dom curiously. The two women spoke well and had a confident, self-possessed air about them. Daphne seemed more refined compared to Deidre's outdoorsy look, but both had a presence and voices that spoke of a good education.

'I lectured in art history, Daphne worked in the library. Huge job. Of course she wanted to organise this store in some sort of Dewey filing system,' said Deidre with a smile.

'Thank heavens we left before I had to be retrained and it went digital!' said Daphne in mock horror. 'I'd better go and serve Mr James; he wants his milk and papers. Nice to meet you, Dominic. Anything we can do for you, just let us know.'

'You been here ever since the seventies? You've seen a few changes then?' Dominic asked Deidre.

'Not a lot, actually. Which is how we like it. Some residents come and go. We don't count holiday people or weekenders, really. But the core of the community are still here, or their families. We're so glad Nigel kept the boathouse. We miss his parents.' The door jingled again and Deidre glanced over. 'Well, happy shopping, and enjoy your weekend with your friend.' She smiled and went towards the counter which sported, Dominic noticed, a modern computer.

As he got back into his car, he again spotted the shop's sign and realised what the *D and D* stood for. The two women must have a lot of local knowledge between them, he thought. Plus they had a surprisingly good selection of stock. He decided he would definitely be a regular at the general store.

*

Rob arrived mid-morning on Saturday carrying some good wine and a couple of steaks.

'Thanks, mate. I'm not exactly slumming it here after all, I've found an excellent general store, but this is all very welcome.'

'I was expecting a bit of a desert island! But look at that view. I would find it hard to drag myself out to bother finding a supermarket, too. Man, this is some kind of oasis. Are the creative juices flowing?' asked Rob.

'Not particularly.' And seeing Rob's surprised expression, Dominic went on, 'What I thought I wanted to write about seems . . . I don't know, passé? Trivial?'

'Dirty politics isn't what I'd call trivial, mate.'

'But it's a case of shit happens. It's not exactly ground-breaking news. The reality, sadly, is pretty mundane,' commented Dominic.

'Anyway, Julie is probably pretty pleased she's not in government with the mess they're in now. And you're well out of it too,' said Rob with a laugh.

An hour later, unpacked and stretched out on the deck-chairs at the front, Rob was relaxing. He wore a T-shirt that had a somewhat phallic image of an old-style microphone on the front with a smirking green frog draped on top of it with the words, *Keep up! Hop onto the Pond Podcast* circling the image.

Rob stretched. 'I see why you're chilling out here. What a spot. This is why the rich party animals like it. But then, when you have a mansion out here and a floating gin palace at your disposal, what's not to like?'

'The company?' Dominic raised his eyebrows. 'This isn't a palace, but I enjoy my own company . . . and of course, the company of select friends such as yourself,' he grinned.

'I agree. However, there are houses tucked up in them thar hills.' Dominic chuckled at Rob's terrible accent. 'Have you met any of the neighbours, other than the old bloke who rescued you?'

'Only one family. But at some stage I might check out the others. Seems like there could be a story or two about the old days here. I don't know who has Nigel's parents' old place up the hill behind us. Hey, do you want to take a spin around the bays and have a bit of a look? Nigel's got a tinnie here, tethered to a tree by the little workshed past the barbecue. I assume there's fuel there.'

'That sounds like a plan.' Rob gazed across the water. 'Isn't the Rangers Tavern over there, next to the yacht club? We could putt-putt to the pub. Nicer than driving. Have a hamburger and a beer after the tour of the bays?'

'Good idea. I've heard the Tavern has excellent chilli prawns. Be back in time for the incoming tide, throw a line in. Oh, and wear your swimmers, in case we pull into a bay or something.'

'Can't we swim in the nude?'

'Perhaps not, it's a sunny weekend, lots of visitors about. During the week is okay. Up to you.'

Dominic checked the small metal open boat. It would be crowded with four people but was generous for two, and it had a decent outboard motor, a good rope and anchor. Three life vests were crammed under the rear seat by the tiller. There was also a long gaff – a pole with a metal hook secured to one side – beneath the seats with the oars.

'Looks pretty shipshape to me.'

'We got a full tank?' asked Rob as he stepped into the boat and sat in the middle seat. He had a light sweater knotted over his shoulders, wore sunglasses and a cap with the same frog logo as his T-shirt.

The engine started second pull, and with Dominic at the tiller they headed out of Flounder Bay into the expanse of WestWater.

'Welsh Island to port,' Dominic called over the sound of the motor. 'Nigel said they used to get good oysters off the rocks there.'

'No more?' asked Rob. 'Pollution?'

'Don't know. I don't think you're allowed to take wild oysters any more.'

From out on the water they could see homes scattered among the trees on the hillsides.

'More people living here than I thought,' said Dominic.

A short while later they steered slowly among moored yachts and cruisers to find a spot at the long jetty of the WestWater Yacht Club, where small boats and dinghies were lashed to the wooden wharf.

'We could just pull the boat up on the sand,' suggested Rob.

'Nope. Tide's coming in, it's safer here. Okay, let's head to the beer garden.'

*

Two hours later they returned to the tinnie with some wine and prawns for dinner in a mini-esky and headed back out of the crowded marina.

'What's that bay over there? Look at those boats,' said Rob, whistling in appreciation.

'I think it's Torpedo Bay. According to the map and brochures at Nigel's, that's the bay opposite Welsh Island. Evidently it's a good picnic spot, sheltered with shallow water. I believe a lot of the luxury cruisers moor overnight or for the weekend in there.'

'Party central. Let's go in as we go past and have a stickybeak at how the other half play,' said Rob.

Dominic guided the tinnie away from the jetty and increased their speed across the open water. The moment they rounded the headland into the large curve of the bay with its sheltered strip of beach at the base of steep hillsides there was little wind so they could speak in normal voices and didn't need to shout over the engine and the breeze.

'Some serious money in here,' said Rob, gazing at the yachts and cruisers.

'Yeah. The mooring fee to stop here is astronomical, I believe. Do you want to go ashore?'

'What's there?'

'The brochures say a camping ground at the back beach where there's a lagoon. Public toilets and cold showers. We might as well have a look, we don't want to seem like perving interlopers or celebrity seekers.'

'Who'd be here? Celebs? Politicians?' asked Rob as they puttered between the moorings, sliding past a large yacht where lunch was in progress on the deck – laughter, chatter and the clink of glasses drifting to them.

'Rich people,' said Dominic as they headed slowly towards the sand. 'Like them.' He tilted his head towards a large sleek white cruiser with half-a-dozen people on the foredeck and others in the lounge area as well as the upper deck by the wheelhouse. 'Probably has eight large staterooms plus smaller cabins and eating and entertaining areas. And look at the toys.' Dominic pointed to the jet skis, rubber duckie and water skis neatly stacked at the stern where gold letters announced the boat was named *Tamsin*.

Dominic cut the engine and the runabout glided onto the beach. Rob hopped out and dragged the boat through the shallows till it was firmly on the wet sand.

Further along there was a canoe, and a sleek speed-boat was anchored in the shallows of the sandy foreshore, but no one was in sight.

'Nice spot to picnic. Why wouldn't more people come ashore here?' wondered Rob, looking at the shady grass under silky oak trees back from the beach.

'No ice? No staff to wait on you?' suggested Dominic dryly.

'Well, that could be arranged.' Rob laughed. 'Let's have a swim. Where's the lagoon?'

'Around the corner of the little sand spit, I think.'

As they headed around the bend they heard shrieks of laughter and voices. The broad lagoon came into view, and Dominic saw it was fed by a creek which curved away around some thick bushland at the base of the hills. Several couples were standing at the edge of the water while others floated in the shallows.

Dominic nudged Rob, indicating the picnic rug and baskets, cushions, a couple of fold-up chairs and a beach umbrella. 'They've got the right idea.'

Rob shaded his eyes. 'Do we join them? They sound like they're having a good time.'

'Let's just go in here. Room for everyone,' Dominic suggested.

Rob pulled off his T-shirt as Dominic kicked off his shoes and shorts.

One of the girls in the party spotted them and waved.

Dominic was pulling his T-shirt over his head when Rob muttered, 'Who's that waving? Look at the legs!'

Dom dropped his shirt on the sand and turned to see the girl walking from the water towards them. There was no mistaking the long brown legs and blonde hair.

'Hey! Alicia,' he called.

'You know her?' whispered Rob.

'Sort of.' Dominic strolled towards Alicia. 'We have to stop meeting like this,' he called.

She laughed, shaking water from her hair. 'Small world out here, I guess.' She turned to Rob and held out her hand. 'Hi, I'm Alicia.'

'Rob.' He shook her hand. 'You've nabbed the best spot.'

'Happy to share it. We locals know the best spots, isn't that right, Dominic?'

'I haven't been a local very long. How's the water?'

'Refreshing. The shallows are warm, but it's chilly deeper in. Come and meet the others.' Alicia turned back towards the lagoon.

They waded in and introductions were made as Alicia explained how she and Dominic had met.

'Are you all local?' asked Rob. 'I think I should move from the city, this is too good.'

'Just here for the day,' admitted one of the girls.

'Gaye and I work together,' Alicia said with a smile.

'Are you guys on *Tamsin*? The big . . .' Rob caught himself and said, '. . . cruiser out there? Beautiful boat. Do you live on it, Alicia?' he added.

Alicia shook her head. 'No. It's our boss's boat. Though I've done some nice trips on her.'

Rob turned to the other two girls, but Dominic knew he had an ear open to what Alicia was saying. There was no doubt she was the knock-out in the looks department, and Rob hadn't missed it.

Two of the men with them announced they were hungry, and they all waded from the lagoon.

'Come and join us,' said Alicia. 'We've got plenty of food.'

'We have some fresh prawns we just picked up and some wine,' said Rob eagerly. 'Right, Dom?'

'Sure. I'll go get them.'

'No worries,' said Alicia. 'We have a big esky of ice here.'

Rob gave Dominic a smile and a thumbs-up as he headed back to their tinnie to fetch the prawns and wine.

*

It was a relaxed afternoon as they talked, picking at the spread of food and drinks. It struck Dominic that while there was a lot of laughter and chatter, no one actually shared anything personal or said anything about their lives. Some told anecdotes relevant to what was being discussed, but it was all very light and humorous. They were work colleagues, he remembered; perhaps they didn't really know each other all that well.

As they packed up to leave, Alicia turned to Rob and Dominic.

'Would you like to come on board *Tamsin* for a sundowner?'

Dominic turned to Rob, who was already smiling and nodding. 'Sounds great, thanks. We're not far from home, but we'd better leave before dark,' Dominic replied. Getting lost on land was one thing, but he wasn't going to risk getting lost on the water.

One couple headed off in the canoe and the others piled into the speedboat to return to the cruiser. The tide had come in; Dominic and Rob found their tinnie bobbing in the water, thankfully held in place by its anchor.

'Just as well we didn't stay here any longer, the tinnie would have floated home by itself,' said Dominic.

'So tell me, how the heck do you know the luscious Alicia?' asked Rob, once the others were out of earshot.

Dominic smiled and shrugged. 'She's the one I told you about on the phone, the girl who gave me a lift after I got lost that day. Why? Do you want her phone number?'

'Do you have it?'

'I do.' Dominic smiled.

'You sneaky sod!' Rob chuckled.

They were welcomed aboard the *Tamsin* by a crew member wearing a white shirt and shorts with *Tamsin* embroidered on the pocket and the front of his cap. He showed them the way to what he called the top salon, where a group of nine were lounging with drinks. Alicia introduced everyone by their first names, with the exception of the boat's owner.

Harold Marchant looked to be in his eighties. He wore smart shorts and a half-buttoned Hawaiian shirt exposing a grey-haired chest. He was deeply tanned and had a firm handshake and a smile that flashed expensive, brightly white teeth. He waved them to the cushioned seats near him.

Alicia perched nearby, curling her legs beneath her rather like a young deer folding its long legs, thought Dominic.

A smartly dressed woman in a similar outfit to that of the crewman, with a nametag reading *Katie*, passed around a tray of glasses of champagne.

An older woman weighed down with jewellery asked Dominic where his boat was moored.

'At the stern just there,' he replied.

'Oh, the runabout. So which is your cruiser?'

'No big boat, just the tinnie,' he said with a smile. 'I'm living locally at the moment.'

'Oh, I see. How divine. Lucky you.' She turned away, focusing on another guest.

Rob was leaning over talking to Alicia when Harold interjected, 'Say, Rob, what's with the frog?' He pointed at Rob's T-shirt.

Alicia smiled. 'Yes. I was wondering about that too. I only noticed it when you put it on as we left. Smug-looking toad.'

'It's a smart-as frog, Alicia. Toads are nasty,' said Rob smoothly. 'It's the logo of my business.'

'And what is your business?' asked Harold.

'IT. I've done a lot of things over the years, but now I just do things that interest me,' said Rob easily.

'How do you make money out of that?' asked Harold.

'Do you work for a media group?' cut in Alicia.

Knowing that Rob was not the type to blow his own trumpet, Dominic jumped in. 'Rob is being modest. He's an ace communicator. If you've got something to say, sell or save, he's your man,' he said. 'I wish we'd had him on our team at the last election.'

'Please, no politics! House – well, boat – rules,' Alicia said cheerily. 'Now how about some food?'

The crewman and Katie who, it turned out, was his wife, reappeared with a platter of lavish hors d'oeuvres.

People got up to get food and moved about the boat, some joining another group below deck. Rob and Alicia were talking. A short buxom blonde girl in her twenties handed Harold a plate of food.

'Thanks, Tiffany,' the older man said. 'I'll have another champagne too, if you don't mind.' He started eating as the young woman fetched a fresh glass and handed it to him.

'Do you spend a lot of time on *Tamsin?*' Dominic asked him politely.

'Why wouldn't I? Look at the company.' Harold chuckled, pointing his plate to where Tiffany was leaning over to hand the food platter to someone on the ladder below. It looked to Dominic as if she was deliberately pointing her pert backside in revealing shorts towards Harold.

Harold took another bite of food and refocused his attention on Dominic.

'So what's your pal working on?' he asked bluntly.

'To tell you the truth, we haven't caught up for a while, so I'm not entirely sure. What I do know is that whatever Rob does, he's pretty shrewd and smart. Right on top of things.'

Harold brushed Dominic's remark aside. 'So he's a spin doctor, salesman, good on media, right? A classy hustler. I'm looking for someone to flog a deal I'm putting together. Tell him to leave his number. And what do you do?'

Remembering the no politics rule, Dominic settled on, 'I'm writing a book.'

Harold gave a hearty chuckle. 'Wish I had a dollar for everyone I know writing a book. If you decide you want a proper job, let me know. I have contacts.'

Dominic nodded politely, but he thought he'd already seen enough to know he'd rather not work for this man.

Harold continued, 'Listen, get your frog buddy to call me. I can throw something in the pond if he's interested . . .'

'Dominic?' Alicia came up the internal forward ladder. 'Everything okay? You need anything, Harold?'

Harold waved a dismissive hand as he drained his glass. Dominic felt he was also about to be despatched. He gave Alicia a relieved look and she returned a quick smile.

'I think we should leave before it gets too dark,' said Dominic.

'Okay. Harold, I'm going to see that Dominic and Rob head off safely.'

Harold turned away. 'Get Tiffany up here with a bottle and leave us alone for a bit.'

*

Rob was already in the tinnie. Alicia steadied the bow rope as Dominic stepped onto the transom and turned to face her.

'Been a nice afternoon. Thanks for including us.'

'It was good to have some new people around.' She waved to Rob. 'Take care! See ya!'

As Dominic stepped into the tinnie, she coiled the rope and threw it into their bow.

Both men glanced back as they slowly chugged through the clutter of boats. Lights had come on in several and the smell of a barbecue drifted over to them. Laughter rang out; voices were louder. One or two boats remained in darkness save for navigation lights, the flicker of a lantern or the glow of a cigarette.

They didn't speak until they'd rounded the headland and begun bouncing over the choppy, darkening waves.

'That turned out to be an interesting day,' said Rob finally. 'I thought you said you were living the life of a recluse?'

'I thought I was. Now I see how the other half lives. So, did you arrange a date with Alicia?'

'No. Well, not really. I don't think she was so much interested in me,' he added quickly with a grin. 'However, she said the old boy, Harold, wants to meet me. Talk business.'

'Yeah, he said as much to me too. And are you going to? Do you know where his money comes from?' asked Dominic.

'Nope, but Alicia said they're in the "lifestyle" business.'

'That could mean almost anything,' said Dominic. 'I'm not sure – I got a strange vibe from him.'

'He's old-school, for sure. I'll do a little checking.' Rob paused, then returned to the subject that really interested him. 'Sadly, Alicia wasn't paying attention to me because I'm a sexy handsome dog. She said now she knew she was a neighbour she would probably run into you again. Figuratively speaking.'

Dominic smiled in the deepening darkness as Rob turned away and faced the wind and refreshing spray.

3

THE FOLLOWING AFTERNOON DOMINIC and Rob were sitting at the end of the jetty, swinging their legs as they held fishing lines, a beer close at hand.

'This has felt like a real break yet I've only been here a bit more than a day.' Rob sighed contentedly. 'I see why you're not exactly slaving over a laptop as I imagined.'

'Yeah. It's peaceful and addictive here, but I'd really like to be bashing out something meaningful. I've deleted just about everything I've started.' Dominic shook his head in frustration.

'Ouch. I couldn't do that. I keep everything I write or record. Well, in my case it's useful information – interviews, files and so on. I tend to hoard my codes like journos. Never know what bit of old info can come in handy when I'm really digging for a source or information.'

'You sound more like a sleuth than a salesman.'

'I don't flog stuff,' protested Rob. 'I'm an IT specialist! I'm into more innovative, groundbreaking, future-thinking stuff. Things that at the time seemed a trip too far, but are now being accepted as the way to go. For example, everyone I know listens to podcasts now. They're every-where. In the car driving to work, mowing the lawn, doing housework, walking the dog. You can do almost everything while tuned in.'

'Podcasts? They're not new,' said Dominic.

'True. But the new platforms and interlinked networks are expanding all the time. Whether you're listening or participating in forums to exchange views and ideas. You have to sift the chaff from the wheat, be open to new ideas and viewpoints, but some discussions I've had have changed my view on certain matters.'

'Maybe I should abandon the book and just listen and chat,' joked Dominic.

'That's not a silly idea. The trick is finding a subject that grabs people's attention!' agreed Rob.

'Hi, Dominic!'

They turned to see Gloria walking along the wharf. 'Anything biting?'

'Yes, actually. Gloria, this is my old friend Rob. He's caught a couple of decent bream.'

'Well done. Do you want to stick them in our freezer till you need them? Dominic, I came to ask you up to dinner, just a barbie. You too, Rob, of course. I have some neighbours coming over. Thought you might like to meet a few more locals.'

'That's kind of you,' said Rob, who had jumped to his feet and was shaking Gloria's hand.

'We can bring Rob's fish,' said Dominic.

'Thanks, that'd be lovely, if that's okay with you, Rob? Wander up whenever you feel like it, any time after six. We'll just be hanging out on the deck.'

'Will do, thanks, Gloria. By the way, I've been meaning to tell you that I met CeeCee's friend Snowy the other day,' said Dominic, reeling in his line. 'Bit of a character. I was surprised to find him tramping around the hills.'

'And just as well he was,' added Rob with a laugh.

'What happened?' asked Gloria.

'I got lost,' Dominic admitted, 'but he just turned up out of the blue and brought me down to the track that leads to the road.'

'Really? You never know with Snowy. He's a bit of a loose cannon in some ways. Sometimes he ignores people and other times he can ramble on to them. Did he show you the cave of Aboriginal paintings?' asked Gloria. 'He thinks it's his secret.'

'Yes, he took me there. Swore me to secrecy,' said Dominic.

Gloria smiled. 'Actually the cave is listed as an attraction on the national park's brochures and website.'

'I thought it was odd that he'd show a stranger such a place. He seemed pretty together though he made a few off-beat remarks, but he seems, well, a volatile type. Like the smallest thing could set him off,' said Dominic.

'Snowy is very protective of this place. He knows where there's some very old carvings and some shelters but he keeps those to himself. He's part of the old community and we keep an eye on him,' Gloria explained. 'Tonight you'll meet some of the others who've been here for ages, too.'

'We'll bring some wine,' said Dominic, and Gloria waved a hand in acknowledgement and headed back along the jetty.

'Hope you won't find it boring. They're nice people,' said Dominic to Rob.

'You know me, go with the flow. Never miss an opportunity to get out and meet the locals,' said Rob. 'I'm not antisocial like you.'

'Oh, God. Am I? Maybe I'd better invite Alicia over,' Dominic joked.

*

Later, as the sun set, chatter from the group on the deck wafted down to them as Dominic led Rob around to the front door of the Sutherlands' house, where they took off their shoes and stepped inside after rapping on the open door and calling out.

Gloria came to greet them. 'Hello! It's all very casual. Sam is glad to have some more male company.'

Out on the deck, Sam stood and shook both men's hands. 'Welcome, welcome. How're you finding the boat-shed life?' he asked Rob.

'Excellent. I see now why Dom has embraced it.'

Sam turned to a tall young woman who looked to be in her late thirties.

'Dominic, Rob, this is Josie Harris and her husband Riley, and that's Maggie Gordon, Josie's mum. This is Marcia Donaldson. She lives around the corner in Fowler's Inlet.'

There were hellos and handshakes all round.

'Now, let me get you a drink,' continued Sam.

'And I'll bring some nibbles,' said Gloria as they both headed to the kitchen.

Josie was a cheerful redhead with intense blue eyes, while her mother Maggie had fair English skin that seemed long weathered by unkind Australian wind and sun. Riley had a pale complexion and a friendly demeanour. Marcia was plump, probably sixty-something, with greying curly hair in a wispy plait down her back. She had a frank, open face, bright brown eyes and a big smile. She was dressed in a long skirt, soft boots and a shawl.

Maggie smiled. 'Hello, hope you're settling into the old boatshed.'

'Not so old any more, Mum,' said Josie. 'Nigel's done it up.'

'Oh, how nice for you, Dominic,' said Maggie.

'Come by anytime,' said Dominic.

Sam and Gloria returned laden with drinks and a cheese platter and they all made themselves comfortable in the last rays of afternoon sunshine.

'Glad you could make it, Rob,' said Sam. 'How've you two fellows been down there? Saw you come motoring back in your boat late yesterday. Fishing trip?'

'No, we went to the pub for lunch and got picked up by some girls,' Rob said with a laugh.

Sam chuckled. 'Half your luck.'

Dominic added, 'We ended up in Torpedo Bay on a big cruiser owned by Harold Marchant.'

Gloria turned to them. 'I've heard of him. He owns some luxury lifestyle places for over fifty-fives. Very posh.'

'What, you've checked it out?' said Sam. 'I'm not going anywhere.'

'Don't be silly. We couldn't possibly afford such a place,' Gloria snorted.

'I hope you're not thinking of moving! We'll just get

a flying fox or a hoist to get you up and down the hill,' exclaimed Marcia. 'Mind you, those places look pretty amazing. I've seen their ads on TV.'

'Well, none of us is going anywhere,' said Sam succinctly. 'Okay, I'm going to check the barbie.' He strode away as Gloria returned to the kitchen.

'I hear you're settling in well, Dom,' said Josie. 'Gloria said you've adopted old Woolly.'

Dominic chuckled. 'More like he adopted me.'

It was an easygoing, friendly gathering. Dominic and Rob found Marcia a bit of a hoot as she regaled them with stories of some of the characters who'd lived in the area since she had moved into a little cottage in the adjoining bay thirty years before.

'You must have been a toddler,' said Rob. 'What did you do with yourself?'

She pooh-poohed him but looked pleased at the compliment nonetheless. 'I came here to stay and heal myself a bit after I lost someone I loved. I couldn't face the world then, needed to take some time for myself, but I never left. It's a special place with special friends. I travelled overseas a few times with my bags, but this is my home and this is where I'll stay.'

'Bags? What's that mean?' asked Rob.

Marcia smiled. 'I make handbags. For special gifts. Not so many nowadays, though, as my fingers and hands are a bit arthritic.'

'You mean like leather handbags?' Rob couldn't imagine making a living from one-off handbags.

'No, raffia. Look, here's an old one of mine.' She leaned over and picked up a plaited strap hanging on the back of a chair and showed him the tightly woven cream handbag. It was like a compact, firm lunch box with a shell as a clasp. The natural strands of raffia were woven into a complex pattern and then lacquered. She opened it up to show him the pretty silk lining and a mirror glued inside the envelope-style flap.

'Wow. It looks new. I'm not a handbag expert, but this is a knockout,' said Rob admiringly.

Sam returned bearing a huge platter of steaks and fish. 'Right. Let's eat, folks.'

Drinks were poured and people helped themselves to food and settled along the table on the deck.

Later, as a cool breeze came up, they moved indoors for dessert, chatting companionably.

Maggie was the first to leave and Josie rose, saying, 'I'll see you back home, Mum.'

'No, no. I have my torch. I know the way blindfolded, thank you, dear.'

'I'm happy to go over with you,' said Riley. 'Better safe than sorry in the dark, Maggie.'

'All right, thank you, Riley. It's been a nice evening, thank you, Gloria, Sam.' Maggie nodded and waved cheerfully to the group as Sam saw Riley and Maggie to the door.

'How far away is her place?' Dominic asked.

'Oh, not far,' said Josie. 'You can see it from the boatshed, in fact. She can be very independent sometimes. But I'd rather Riley go with her when it's dark.'

'We keep an eye on her,' said Gloria. 'Now, who's for coffee? Another drink?'

'And who's for more dessert?' interjected Sam.

Rob and Marcia were in a deep discussion and Sam joined them, passing more plates of chocolate cake and ice-cream.

As Dominic carried his empty plate into the kitchen he saw Josie filling the sink with hot water.

'You're washing up? Let me help. No dishwasher?' he asked.

'Oh, it's on the blink. Gloria and Sam haven't got around to getting it fixed. Normally it's just the two of them.'

Dominic picked up a tea towel. 'So you've known Sam and Gloria for a long time?'

'Yes . . . They've been like grandparents to me. We never really got to know our real ones. Mum's family stayed in England. With five kids it got a bit costly to go back there to visit.'

'Of course,' said Dominic. 'And your dad's family, where are they?'

Josie hesitated then handed him a dripping plate to wipe and turned back to the sink. 'Have you heard about the man who went missing here years back?'

Dominic nodded, trying to recall the offhand remark Snowy and the Sutherlands had made about a man who'd gone missing. 'Gloria and Sam mentioned something about that last time I was here.'

'Well, that was my father. He just disappeared.' She was very matter-of-fact. 'We have no idea what happened. His family were in England, too. We never got to know much about them.'

Dominic was speechless, managing, 'How awful for you all. So you know nothing about what happened?' He put the dry plate to one side and reached for the next one in the drying rack.

Josie was silent for a moment as she rubbed at the dishes.

'My father's disappearance is always the elephant in the room. No one acknowledges it or talks about it.' She sighed. 'But of course, it never goes away. If anything, it gets worse.'

'Sorry. I didn't mean to be nosey.'

'It makes everyone uncomfortable so it's never discussed,' said Josie. 'Especially in our family.'

'Oh. Would you like to talk about it?'

She shrugged. 'It won't change anything, but I can't help feeling that not enough was done. I mean, well, there wasn't anything to be done, I s'pose . . .'

'What happened, exactly?' Dominic asked carefully.

Josie dumped a soapy saucepan onto the rack. 'I wish I could tell you. That's the whole thing in a nutshell. One day my father just disappeared. End of story. There was no reason, no clues, and he was never found, never heard of again,' she said bluntly.

'Nothing? They did all the searches, investigations . . .?'

Josie wiped her hands on the tea towel Dominic was holding.

'Of course. But they never found any sign of him. A loving father and husband, a caring, decent man everyone respected and liked, just vanished into thin air. Go figure.'

'I'm so sorry.' Dominic was lost for words.

'Don't be. It was a long time ago.'

'Hey, you chaps! Enough of the cleaning up. Come and join us. We'll do the rest of the dishes later or in the morning,' said Sam cheerfully as he came in and put the dirty barbecue tools on the bench. 'Your pal Rob is a card, Dominic. Very entertaining. C'mon, we're having last drinks, then we'll throw you out. Or you can sit on the deck in the dark without us.' He chuckled. 'Wouldn't be the first time. We can't stay up as late as we used to.'

'Thanks, Sam.' Josie excused herself.

'It's been a lovely evening. I'll go drag Rob away or he'll chat all night,' said Dominic.

'No worries. Riley's back and I think he's enjoying Rob's company. He's generally such a quiet fella.'

Dominic followed Sam into the living room.

'We might make tracks, eh, Rob?' said Dominic. 'Let these good people go to bed.'

Riley got to his feet. 'C'mon, Josie, us too. We haven't got far to go.' He turned to Rob. 'The kids have a sleepover so we're staying with Maggie tonight. Thanks, Sam, Gloria, we enjoyed the evening.'

'You fellas all right? Need a torch?' asked Sam.

'Thanks, we're fine, we have one,' said Dominic.

*

Back at the boatshed Rob and Dominic settled on the little deck in the calm dark, listening to the lapping of the night tide, talking quietly.

'Nice evening,' said Rob. 'Nice people. Marcia is interesting and fun. Fancy her making bags that sell around the world.'

Dominic nodded. 'They are all very genuine people. Josie is certainly a no-nonsense woman. You won't believe what she told me in the kitchen, though. I was really taken aback.'

'Why? What was it?'

Dominic repeated Josie's brief story.

'Is that all she said, no details?' asked Rob.

'There aren't any details, apparently.'

Rob stared at Dominic. 'How come?'

Dominic shrugged. 'No answers, I guess. The man's never been found, and no one seems to know what happened.'

Rob blinked, looking out into the darkness. 'Wouldn't be the first time a bloke has taken off, I suppose,' he said.

'She didn't make it sound like that. But who knows?'

They sat in silence for a few moments.

'The wind has dropped. It's so still. I like it like this,' said Dominic.

'It's certainly still. I could hear Woolly purring on your bed last night. Being here is the first time I've ever heard water move. A quiet tide . . . Hey, that's a good title for a book! You can have that one for free.' Rob chuckled. 'But listen, this Josie thing. Could be a book in it.'

'About what? How's it end?' asked Dominic.

'You're the writer! Look, I'm not one to criticise, especially your work ethic. But I hate to see you so . . . unfocused.'

'Thanks for the vote of confidence.' Dominic shrugged. 'I just don't feel that surge of adrenalin, now that the pressure is off.'

'But how long will that last? Look, why not try something different?' He paused as Dominic stared at him. 'That family! Maggie and her missing husband and no idea what happened, how or why? The disappearance no one will talk about? It's the classic cold case! Doesn't that strike you as rather extraordinary?'

'Rob, people go missing every day.'

'Yes. But eventually they're found, be it a body or the persons themselves turning up. Someone talks, a clue comes to light, or police reinvestigate a cold case and offer a reward which sometimes brings in the missing piece of the puzzle. We might not hear the details, but generally, there's a reason for everything. Did Josie give any hints at all as to what might have happened?' asked Rob.

'No. She seemed genuinely puzzled. Upset. How on earth would you begin to unravel such a mystery? There're no clues! Nothing! So, no story,' said Dominic.

'Which is what makes it so intriguing.' Rob grinned. 'Don't you agree?'

Dominic looked at Rob's quizzical, expectant expression, then shook his head.

'It's not that easy, Rob. It isn't a matter of just "showing up"! I've been trying to get on with it, get things going. I've been mulling over notes I've made for ages . . . and getting nowhere.'

'So change tack. Do it as a podcast!' Rob suggested suddenly, looking pleased.

'I'm no detective or crime writer, so where does that leave me? Do I make it all up?' said Dominic a bit exasperatedly.

'Start with Josie.' Rob's tone was calm and reasonable. 'She sounds ready to talk to someone. See what you end up with . . . a book, a podcast, a thesis of some kind. It won't do any harm to have another look into this, and you never know, maybe you'll solve a crime!'

Dominic hesitated, chewing his lip. 'The issue is, if I talk to Josie, that's only one viewpoint.' He looked at Rob. 'I'd have to talk to all of them. And they might not want to. It's a massive undertaking. And anyway, even if they did, we may not uncover anything new . . . and then what . . .?'

'Up to you. Depends what you find,' said Rob. 'They'll be no worse off than they are already.'

'I've never done anything like that. I'm not sure I'd have any idea where to start.'

'You're a smart guy, you'll work it out.' Rob leaned back in his chair. 'It's a gift, mate. And it's all just sitting out there. I think you should at least consider using it.' He stood up. 'I'm hitting the sack. Back to the office tomorrow. This has been such a nice break. You know you can come and stay at my place in town whenever you want, right?'

'Right. Thanks,' said Dominic, adding absently, 'See you in the morning.'

Alone on the quiet deck, Dominic sat deep in thought, Woolly rubbing against his ankles. He leaned down and stroked the cat.

Dominic thought of his own family, how he and Cynthia might have dealt with growing up missing a loving father and living with so many unanswered questions. Maybe Rob had a point. There could be a story in it. But at the moment it was all questions and no answers.

*

Early the following morning, after downing a coffee and toast standing up, Rob dashed off back to work in revved-up city mode.

Dominic was still debating whether he should make contact with Josie Harris. After strumming away at the guitar for a while to clear his head, he tidied up the boathouse, threw on a clean T-shirt and decided to walk up to the general store for some exercise.

He chatted with Daphne and Deidre as he picked through the fruit and veggies locals had left in a big basket by the door and pulled out a bag of lemons.

'My mate Rob has gone. Loved it here. He left this morning,' he told the women.

'We know. He dashed in here to get a coffee for the road. Made us feel as though he'd spent the weekend in the boondocks.' Daphne laughed.

'So what are you up to this week, Dom?' asked Deidre.

'I have a bit of a plan. Might be lining up some interviews,' Dominic said slowly, realising that the plan had crystallised in his mind as he'd been walking. 'But I'm around.' He held up the lemons and a newspaper. 'I'll take these, please.'

*

Back at the boathouse, Dominic took off his shirt and sat out in the sunshine while he made notes on a pad. A little while later, he heard someone calling his name.

'Hello there! Can I come in?'

Surprised, Dominic turned towards the track from the driveway to see the unmistakable figure of Alicia in shorts and a bikini top making her way towards the boatshed.

'Hi. This is a nice surprise!' he called as she came down the steps. 'Where'd you spring from?'

'The shop. I thought you might be lonely now that Rob has left.'

'No secrets around here!' Dominic laughed, reaching for his T-shirt.

'Oh, don't get dressed for me,' she said, smiling. 'I brought you some treats from the store.'

'I was up there this morning.'

'I know. The two Dees told me that too. How are you?' She lifted her cheek to be kissed as she handed him the bag of treats.

He peered into it. 'My favourite ice-cream. The girls told you that as well, I s'pose! Rob and I got some the other day. We'll have to share it. Want some before it melts?' He turned inside and Alicia followed.

'Wow, this is rather smart,' said Alicia. 'You're not exactly roughing it. Compact, cosy and classy. I approve.' She turned slowly, taking in the main living room. 'Oh, and don't tell me, you have a fluffy cat to complete the picture. To show your soft side, right?'

'Woolly chose me.' Dominic couldn't help smiling as the cat ignored Alicia's outstretched hand, and with its tail erect, marched from the room.

They had coffee and ice-cream out on the deck and chatted easily.

'Do you work every day or not? This is Monday, so . . .?' asked Dominic.

'It's a bit erratic, but that's the way Harold likes it. I have to be on call so there're no real office hours. He's always looking at possible projects and I have to be ready to follow up on them if needed. People keep approaching him –'

'Because he's considered a wealthy entrepreneur?'

'He prefers businessman. Developer. He's not up with new technologies, R&D. He's more a bottom-line kind of person. But I like that he's a self-made man. He's in business and open to ideas, provided the numbers stack up. He started as a builder, then a developer, then entered the lifestyle/retiree market. He seems to be torn between doing some last grandstand project or else retiring in a grand manner. All depends on where the cards fall,' explained Alicia.

'Must make for interesting days at the office,' commented Dominic, wondering exactly what Alicia's role was in all this. 'What's your work schedule?'

'Whatever I arrange on the day, depending on what's happening,' Alicia said evasively.

'C'mon, be more specific. What exactly do you do there? I'm interested,' said Dominic curiously.

'Why?' For the first time, Alicia sounded cautious.

'I don't know, really. You don't seem the type to sit behind a desk and type up reports.'

'Actually, I'm very good at reports,' she retorted, but

then seemed to relent. 'I keep tabs on all the details of Harold's projects. I have a specific interest in two of the businesses, and do overall checks on other stuff,' she said casually.

'So what are your special interests, then?' asked Dominic.

'The retirement village out here and two lifestyle complexes. One is an hour from here, one is proposed for near here.'

'Whereabouts around here?' asked Dominic. 'My neighbour mentioned there was a good village in the area.'

'It's one of ours, on its own grounds beside the golf course.'

'So why do you need another one here?' asked Dominic. 'The population doesn't seem quite big enough to sustain a second one.'

She shrugged, then gave a little smile. 'It's not set in cement. Harold might change his mind. Alter the plans somewhat. He's unpredictable.'

'Can he do that? Switch plans for a development for one thing and make it another?' asked Dominic. 'I'd have thought there'd be red tape galore.'

'Harold has friends in high places and lots of ideas. Like I said, he's unpredictable.'

'So where is HQ? You said you live around here. So you don't have to drive into the city each day to work?' He wondered why he'd never seen her about the place, as it was a small tight-knit community.

'I only go to Harold's HQ in the eastern suburbs every few weeks. I have my own office less than half an hour away in The Vale.' She smiled then spread her arms. 'So I can hang out around here most of the time. We're practically neighbours!'

'So what's your work schedule like at the moment?' asked Dominic.

'I have today and tomorrow off. Busy on the weekend. My life has no set schedules. Whatever Harold wants, really. That's why I don't often plan or make dates.'

Alicia lifted her arms towards the sun. 'Let's have a swim. The tide's in.'

'Yes. Looks nice.' Dominic hesitated. Before he could say any more, Alicia dropped her shorts and pulled off her top, revealing full firm breasts, and, wearing only her thong briefs, she skipped along the jetty and dived into the water.

Dominic was wearing his swimsuit under his shorts, as had become his habit. He pulled off his shorts and dived in after the laughing Alicia.

They raced each other through the water, then, as she tried to dunk him, he grabbed her and their faces drew together. She pulled him beneath the water and kissed him.

As they broke the surface, laughing, she wrapped her arms around his neck and pushed her body against him, arousing him instantly.

She stayed the night.

*

The following morning they lingered over a late breakfast.

'So. What are your plans for today?' Dominic asked, hoping she was staying.

'I have errands to do. Next time I'll bring my toothbrush with me.'

'Next time? There'll be a next time?' he teased.

'Of course there will be.' She reached out a leg and curled it around his.

'Okay. Great.'

'Don't tell me you want times and dates,' she pouted. 'I like surprises, don't you?'

'I guess so,' said Dominic.

'I'd better get home and change.' She leaned down and kissed him lightly. 'You're sweet.'

Dominic reached out and held her wrist. 'You sure you have to leave?'

'Yep. Tell that sulky cat he can come back now.'

Dominic stood and looked around for Woolly. 'He's jealous. C'mon, I'll walk you to your car.'

'I have to stop at the general store to top up the petrol,' she said.

'Then I'll come with you. Just to the shop, and I'll walk back,' said Dominic.

*

As Dominic was in the shop paying for his milk and paper, Alicia came in from the petrol bowser.

'Okay, I'm all filled up.'

'This place has the cheapest fuel around,' said Dominic.

'Does it? I just get it when I need it. Morning, ladies,' said Alicia.

'Morning, Alicia.' Daphne and Deidre exchanged knowing smiles as Alicia paid.

'Well, I'll be off.' Alicia waved breezily and headed out the door just as Josie came in. The women greeted each other briefly before Alicia continued out to her car.

'Oh, hi, Dom. My, small world!' said Josie, coming over to him. 'I've just finished my shift, so I'm popping in to see Mum.' Josie's hair was pulled back and she was wearing a white shirt tucked into black slacks, a name badge pinned to her pocket.

'Nice to see you, Josie. You know Alicia?' asked Dominic.

'Yep. I work in a nursing home nearby and Alicia sometimes calls us when a resident in their lifestyle place needs care. I'm a nurse. Alicia has a place somewhere around here, I think. Never been there, though. I didn't realise you knew her.'

'Oh, I met her the other day, and then Rob and I spent some time with her at Torpedo Bay over the weekend,' Dominic explained. 'Hey, Josie, would you and Riley like to drop in to the boatshed sometime for a coffee or a drink?' he added.

Josie smiled. 'Thanks. If we have a moment we'd love too. The kids can visit Mum. I never have enough time. A job, kids, you know how it is.'

'Actually, I don't.' He said it lightly, but it did occur to Dominic then that he didn't have the obligations and commitments of a family like Josie had, and also his sister Cynthia, who spent a lot more time with their parents dealing with small domestic issues than he did. 'Well, whatever suits you, Josie. If needed I'm happy to pop up and check on your mum while I'm at the boatshed,' he said. He took out his mobile and they exchanged phone numbers.

'Thanks. We'll take you up on your drink offer,' said Josie.

*

Later that day Dominic received an email from an online news site that he respected asking him to give them a quote for five hundred words about the government's latest welfare plan for women workers, especially single mothers. It had been a key issue for his former boss, Julie, so he was pleased to respond.

Dominic had had a few other requests in a similar vein. He had accepted some of the smaller, easier jobs, because it kept his hand in and his name circulating, but he felt oddly reluctant to take on anything that required too much commitment. He knew this was because a small but loud part of him still wanted to give his book idea a go.

*

Two days later Josie called to him from the bottom of the steps outside the boatshed.

'Dom, you there? It's me, Josie. Can I come in?'

Dominic leapt up from the little table out on the deck where he was at his laptop.

'Hey, great timing, I was about to make a coffee. Come on in.' He opened the back door. 'Is Riley with you?'

'No, he's working. He's a builder, has a job to finish. I just came from seeing Mum, so thought I'd say hi. Oh, wow, this place is so cute. Nigel must have spent a bit on doing it up. It's charming.'

'I think most of the credit goes to his ex-wife. I'm enjoying being here,' said Dominic. 'Tea or coffee?'

'Tea if you're making a pot. Or just a teabag, thanks.'

They sat in the sun on the deck. Josie looked at Dominic's laptop. 'Busy at work?'

'Just writing a short article.'

'Who do you write for?' She sounded curious.

'I'm not a journalist. Or an author – yet! I was a policy advisor so I get asked by various publications for my opinion on political matters. I'm one of those political animals who wants to write a book about his experiences.' He smiled. 'Actually –' Dominic sat forward.

Now or never, he thought. 'I'm glad you stopped by, Josie. I've been meaning to ask you something. Please feel free to say no, or just to tell me to mind my own business.'

Josie raised her eyebrows, looking intrigued.

Dominic explained how he'd been trying to get his ideas for a book down on paper and that inspiration had eluded him.

'But then after our dinner the other night, Rob suggested that perhaps I should look into your father's disappearance as a potential idea for a book. I'm not an investigator or even a crime writer, of course, but it seemed to me this mystery deserves some attention . . . and you never know, maybe we'll end up with more answers than you have now.' He took a breath. 'I would never write anything without your family's say-so. The idea would simply be for me to look into things initially.'

He sat back nervously, trying to gauge how Josie felt about the idea.

She sat silently for a long moment, sipping her tea, then put her mug down and looked at him. 'When we talked in the kitchen the other night . . . it was the first time I'd mentioned my dad in ages.' Dominic nodded and waited, unsure whether to prompt her or jump in, but Josie continued, 'Funnily enough, since then I've been thinking about what I said, and it seems to me it's time I kicked the elephant out of the room.'

'Good for you,' said Dominic cautiously.

'It's not just me. It's about the whole family. None of us talk to each other about what happened to my father. So your offer just now – it feels sort of serendipitous. Like it could potentially lead somewhere good, whether or not you get any answers. But I think, first, you should speak to my mother – if she'll agree.'

Dominic tried not to look as surprised as he felt. 'Would she? Speak to me? About your father?'

'We can ask. If she knows I've talked to you, she might be open to it.'

Dominic nodded. 'I wouldn't want to do anything without her agreement.' He pulled his laptop towards him. 'Do you mind if I take some notes? Force of habit from my life in the political government sphere.' When Josie nodded, he went on, 'Can you give me a bit of background about the family? What happened around the time of the disappearance?'

'I'd rather Mum told you what happened. As much as we know. I was only a kid at the time. I can fill you in on the family, though.'

'Okay. How many of you are there?'

'Five children altogether. My elder brother, Simon, he's married with a son. Then there're the twins, Paul and Jason. Paul's divorced, no kids, and Jason has a lovely partner. Then there's me with the two kids, and Holly, who's the youngest.'

'Where do you all live?'

'Simon lives on Sydney Harbour with his wife and son; he's done well for himself. Paul is a surfer, never settled to a career, currently runs a surf shop but never left this area really. Hardly ever comes to help Mum.' She shrugged and rolled her eyes. 'Jason is a landscaper, works all over the place. He and his partner Rory live down on the South Coast. And Holly is working in Perth.'

'That's a big family. Yet none of you talk about what happened?'

'It's been such a long time, and we were all kids back then – well, Simon might have been just eighteen. But every so often something comes up and the wound re-opens. I think it's time now to rip off the Band-Aid and sort this stuff out properly. I know you may not be able to do anything, but . . .' Josie stopped and drew breath. 'Maybe it's time to try.'

'I can listen,' Dominic said quietly. 'Give you a fresh perspective, if nothing else.'

Josie let her breath out.

'Can I ask why? I mean, why bring it out in the open now?' asked Dominic.

'Up till now my children have been too young to ask the hard questions, but recently my daughter asked me why she and her brother don't have a second grandfather like their friends do. I'd like them to understand and accept what happened. I don't want it to be this dark family secret any more. Plus, I think it would be worth having someone outside the family talk to Mum about it all. I think she suffers some sort of guilt that she can't explain and she won't talk to any of us.'

'It must be a terrible thing to live with all these years,' said Dominic.

They both sat quietly for a moment.

Then Dominic ventured, 'It might be helpful if I spoke – privately, individually – to all of you. What do you think?'

Josie put her mug down. 'Look, I'm not sure. I do like the idea, but I don't know what the others will think.' She paused for a moment. 'Let me think about it, and start with Mum in the meantime. I'm still not sure about all this, if the timing is right . . .'

'Instinct, perhaps? Wanting answers?' suggested Dominic gently. 'Perhaps I picked up on your feelings. I mean, apart from the sheer pain of not knowing, the always wondering – even subconsciously – must eat away at you. Especially for your mother. Do you think she's ever shared this with anyone?'

'Gosh, I don't know! She's always had that English reserve,' said Josie.

'Then why would she talk to me?' asked Dominic.

'She told me she liked you. I'm just following my gut here. Maybe she won't agree to talk – but maybe she will.'

'I guess it's worth a try.' Dominic smiled. Then he gently probed, 'So why did your parents come out here, or did they meet here?'

'They emigrated not long after they were married. Dad was a teacher and Mum was a nurse. She loves it here. She tells us she warmed to the place pretty quickly, although I suspect it took a little while. Whereas Dad missed England more, often talked about going back.'

'He stayed in Australia because she wanted to stay?' asked Dominic.

Josie nodded. 'Yep. They built that house. Mum hasn't lived anywhere else. Doesn't want to move.'

'Okay. I'll try to talk to her soon. What would you like me to say about why I'm asking her about her painful past?' Dominic asked.

'You're a writer, of sorts. People talk to writers, as opposed to journalists! Just tell her what you told me. I think Mum will understand that having someone new look into the whole case can only be a positive thing. Oh, and –' Josie paused. 'I can't always get over to Mum's when I want to. If there's any chance you could check if she needs any shopping done, groceries, that sort of thing, I'd be very grateful. Might be another way to touch base with her, too.'

'Sure, that's easily done. And writers are nosey, I s'pose. Everyone always thinks they have a story to tell,' said Dominic. 'Leave it with me.'

'Thanks, Dominic. That would be great,' said Josie, a look of relief on her face as she stood up. 'I'd better go. Thanks for the tea.' She looked out across the water. 'I can't believe I've done this. But I've learned to follow my instincts. I don't think anything will come of it, but I think it's something Mum really needs to do. So thank you again. Oh – I'd rather you kept this just between Mum and me at this point, but I'll tell the others later if need be.'

'Of course,' said Dominic. In spite of it being his idea, he felt a trifle run over and the prospect of investigating a cold case loomed large before him. Had he actually agreed to all this?

'I don't think the others could add any more than what I know anyway. Thanks again, Dominic.' Josie hurried around the side of the boathouse and disappeared.

Dominic sat down and stared at his laptop. Gathering his thoughts, he saved what he'd been doing and brought up his internet browser.

It took some searching as there was little to find: just a short few paragraphs about a missing man, Joseph Gordon. Another story snagged his attention: a body had been found around the same time, but that man had later been identified as a hiker who'd sustained a head injury and drowned in the creek. Although it was a sad coincidence, the events seemed unrelated to Joe's disappearance. There was no other follow-up that Dominic could find.

He looked at the dates of the press cuttings: twenty-five years ago.

Dominic felt a wave of tiredness wash over him. So little was known. What was the point of dragging all this up again after a quarter of a century? Then he remembered the relieved look on Josie's face at hearing his offer. Even if he discovered nothing new, he had agreed to speak to Maggie. Perhaps she would simply want to let sleeping dogs lie – but he had said he would try, and so he would. Starting tomorrow.

He closed his laptop, picked up his fishing rod and headed along the jetty.

4

DOMINIC WAS SITTING IN Maggie's living room, having just finished his carefully prepared speech over a cup of tea, when Maggie suddenly stood up. For a moment he thought she had changed her mind about inviting him in and that he was being dismissed, in a nice way. But she gave a slight smile.

'I'll just put the kettle on, for a refill. I know that Josie has spoken to you about her father's disappearance, but I'm not sure yet how much I want to tell you about it. I need to think about what you've said.'

Dominic leaned back. 'Great, thank you. I'd love another cup.' He was in no hurry to go anywhere. He had thought, when he'd gently broached the idea of taking another look at her husband's disappearance, that he'd seen a spark of interest in Maggie's eyes. She hadn't said anything, but she hadn't stopped him, either.

Dominic watched as Maggie refilled the pot and pulled the tea-cosy onto it.

She sat down and poured more tea into his cup, then said matter-of-factly, 'I'll need to think about what you've offered. But if you're interested, I'll tell you something about my background.'

Dominic nodded eagerly as he reached for his cup.

Maggie settled herself across from him. 'I come from a working-class family in Bristol.' She grinned crookedly. 'You can't get away from your background in England! We weren't really poor, but every penny was counted. Looking back, I can see I was a bright kid and very determined. I knew education was the key to my future. I passed my Eleven-plus and got a scholarship to Colston's Girls' School, a very good school in Bristol. In my final year I decided that nursing would be a good career so I applied and was accepted at the Bristol Royal Infirmary where I did my training.'

'Where did you meet your husband?' Dominic asked.

'In Brighton. I was on holidays with two nursing girl-friends. Joe was from there, visiting his parents. It was a bit of a holiday romance. But then he ended up coming to Bristol to do a special course for his job and, well, he looked me up and that was that.' She gave a soft smile. 'I was lucky. I met the love of my life. We were young but we just knew we were right for each other. And we were,' she added.

'When did you decide to come to Australia?' asked Dominic.

'We couldn't afford to travel so when Joe came home one night and told me about the teachers' exchange program, it sounded very exciting. Times seemed hard in the UK even in the seventies, but for young people like us, the teaching exchange was a means of travel paid for by the government, a bit of an adventure. You had a job and accommodation but you had to stay the full contract.'

'So it wasn't like the ten-pound Pom scheme?' asked Dominic. 'I remember my dad worked with English friends who'd come out here on that scheme but then decided to go back.'

'Similar. Some families or couples went back to the UK as they couldn't adjust to life here. Or else they went back and then wished they hadn't and returned, if they could afford it.'

'It was a big step, I suppose,' said Dominic.

'I felt like a fish out of water when we first arrived, though it wasn't long before I loved it.'

'It must have been a big change. So what was your plan when you got here?' Dominic asked.

Maggie shrugged. 'I don't think we had much of a plan, really. We hadn't been married long and it seemed an opportunity . . . something new and exciting.'

'And was it?' Dominic leaned back in his chair.

Maggie's gaze slid away from him, unseeing, and Dominic knew she was thinking of that long-ago time.

The 1970s . . .
'Maybe it was easier coming all this way by ship in the sixties.' Maggie sighed.

'I'd have gone mad trapped on a boat for weeks on end. Lord knows who you'd be stuck with, too,' said Joe.

'Probably people like us.' Maggie tried to smile but she was simply too weary. The long flight from London already seemed a blur. Now, in the fading light of day as passengers fumbled for belongings, the long low grey buildings of Sydney Airport across the tarmac looked forlorn and unfamiliar.

'Do you think we've done the right thing?' she whispered.

'Bit late now.' He gave her shoulders a quick squeeze. 'We'll be okay, darling,' he said fondly.

He was right. It was too late. Here they were, on the other side of the world, committed for a minimum of a year. Even if they loathed Australia and the job, they were stuck here for the next twelve months.

Maggie straightened up, trying to ease the stiffness in her body, the result of sitting on a plane or uncomfortable chairs in airports for what seemed like days.

*

Later, after passing through immigration and customs, Maggie was seated in the back of a car as her husband and the English teacher he was replacing nattered in the front seat.

'How much further, Mr Lilley? This seems a terribly long way out of Sydney,' said Maggie nervously.

'Please, call me Andrew. Yes, West Water is over an hour away from the city centre.' He glanced over his shoulder at her. 'Plenty of things to do around there, though. Lovely spot; we'll miss it. But we're looking forward to visiting England. So glad you wanted to change places for a year. You'll be working in a great school.' He sounded cheerful and reassuring.

Maggie glanced out the window and commented more to herself than either of the men, 'There're hardly any cars on the road. There're no lights anywhere. People can't be in bed this early.'

'We're going through bushland, kind of a short cut down to the coast. Won't be too much longer,' said Andrew.

'How far is the school from your house?' asked Joe.

'It's about a twenty-minute drive. The nearby centre with shops is called The Vale. But most of us WestWater residents use the general store at a spot called The Point, which also has a petrol pump and post office. All rolled into one, and all that's near us, actually. So, Joe, what's your place in England like?'

'We live outside Brighton in a village called Holminster, a short drive to the beach,' Joe replied.

'So it was a nice surprise to know we'd be near the water here too. We thought it would feel familiar,' put in Maggie.

'Do you surf, then?' asked Andrew.

'No. Brighton doesn't have real surf. Oh, I see some lights dotted out there!' said Joe. 'How much further?'

'Not long now. Our house is old but comfy. We've moved in with friends before we fly out on Wednesday but we've left you some basics – milk, cereal, bread, eggs and bacon ready for breakfast. There are important phone numbers by the telephone in the hallway. My Colleen will take you round the traps in the morning, Maggie.'

'That's nice of your wife, thank you. Is she looking forward to your move?'

'Yes, she is indeed,' said Andrew.

*

After unloading the car in the dark and thanking Andrew, Maggie sank into a chair in this strange house they'd call home for a whole year.

'We made it. Australia really *is* at the bottom of the

world. A long way from what we know.' She suddenly worried that in her exhaustion she was being negative. Joe had been so excited by this adventure – as had she, but she was feeling the distance from home in an entirely new way. Maggie tried to rally.

Joe opened the refrigerator. 'Oh, there's some beer in here. Nice of them. Want one, sweetie?'

'No thanks, love. I want to unpack and go to bed and start our new life tomorrow. I'm absolutely done in.' Maggie yawned and headed to the bedroom.

Joe shut the door of the refrigerator and followed his wife, putting his arms around her as she stood in the middle of the main bedroom.

'Good idea. Let's sleep naked and unpack tomorrow.'

Maggie chuckled, turned and wrapped her arms around him. Thank goodness for Joe. He was her strength and the light of her life.

In the middle of the night, they were awakened by an unfamiliar noise, and Maggie clutched her husband.

'What on earth is out there? Some animal? It sounds horrible.'

They held each other as the rasping, shrieking grunts dissipated. 'Must be some weird kind of night bird,' said Joe.

'No. That sounded like something big. Wild.'

As Joe tried to soothe her, Maggie muttered into his shoulder, 'Have we done the right thing, Joe? I'm scared now.'

In the dark, the rustle of tree branches sounded close, and there were no friendly lights anywhere. Maggie felt miles from civilisation. No sounds of cars, or people murmuring as they walked past, even the clash of rubbish bins would have been comforting. It felt like they'd come to the end of the world.

She waited for Joe to tease her and say again that it was all too late now, but instead he said tenderly, 'It'll be an adventure for us. You'll see. We said we'd be brave and try new things. It'll be fine, Mags. You're safe with me.'

Joe kissed her ear and Maggie snuggled closer to his warmth. 'We'll always have each other,' he whispered.

*

In the morning, they stood on the narrow deck trying to absorb where they'd landed in their great leap to a new life, as Joe called this challenge.

In the warming light, Maggie began to be seduced by the view.

It was a clear day. Early sunlight glinted dazzlingly off the blue water below, which was dotted with moored boats, seen through a thick screen of gum trees.

'You'd pay through the nose for a holiday place like this, I'd say,' said Joe appreciatively. 'It is certainly private.'

'I suppose there are neighbours nearby?' Maggie wondered, looking to either side of them.

'Yes, I caught a glimpse of the roof of a house through the trees.'

They were eating toast when Andrew arrived calling out cheerily, 'Good morning! Sleep well, or are you jetlagged?' He strolled through the house to greet them.

Maggie was glad she was dressed. Had they not locked the front door? Even acknowledging that this was Andrew's house, she found the casual Australian friendliness a bit unnerving.

'We crashed out. Though some awful animal noise woke us up at one stage. What would that be?' asked Joe.

'Ah, should've warned you. It's koala mating time. The big old boy is doing his romancing rounds.' Andrew grinned.

'A koala? It sounded like a – well, I don't know what. Scary. The poor females,' said Maggie. She was about to turn inside when two brilliant birds swooped and landed on the railing, cocking their heads expectantly.

'Oh my goodness! Look at them. The colours!' she exclaimed as the large emerald bird and its mate with a scarlet head and throat peered back at her.

'King parrots. Colleen feeds them. They love sunflower seeds. Just don't encourage those white cockatoos, they'll rip half the wooden railing off or anything else if they're not happy,' advised Andrew. 'Well, when you're ready, we'll start the day, eh?'

'Where does one buy sunflower seeds?' asked Maggie as they went inside.

*

For Maggie those first days were a blur. Colleen, a friendly, chatty woman who had set Maggie at ease immediately, gave her a quick tour of The Vale and its limited shops, as well as the schools and the general area.

'Everyone is certainly friendly,' commented Joe. 'Smallish community, and there's always interest in a new teacher, I suppose. Especially one come on an exchange.'

'This place is not quite what I expected,' said Maggie. 'But in a good way. It's not exactly rural, but it's not the suburbs or a formal town, either. It's just like houses have sprung up in the bush after rain, like mushrooms!'

'Maybe we should explore a bit more tomorrow. Shall we go for a drive, find a nice café? Where do you want to go?' asked Joe.

'Not towards the city. Maybe we could just follow the upper road Colleen showed me, see where it goes?' suggested Maggie. 'Shall I pack a picnic?'

'Let's wing it, eh?' Joe smiled. 'Has to be some civilisation out there.'

So the next day, they drove along the upper road and into the national park. Half an hour later Joe pulled onto a small dirt track with a sign – *Lookout 4 km*. 'Shall we?'

'Of course.'

They followed the dirt road, which was more of a one-way track, until they came to a cleared area with words painted on a rock: *Lookout 1 km*.

'Got your hiking boots on? This is pretty bushy,' Maggie joked.

They got out and gazed around. 'There's a sort of path,' said Joe as he locked the car.

Maggie burst out laughing. 'Why are you locking the car? We're in the middle of nowhere!'

The scrubby bush thinned as they followed the path between large rocks, noticing the different species of plants in this area. There was no wind and the sun was hot.

'We're up high on a headland, I think,' said Joe, and then they both stopped, mouths agape.

They were indeed on top of a high headland which ended in a sharp drop a short distance away. Spread before them was a panorama of WestWater and its environs. Welsh Island was a small speck amid the bays and coastline stretching into the far distance, another island hunched into the window facing the open sea.

'I don't dare go closer to see what's under the cliff here,' said Maggie. 'Thank goodness there's no wind, I'd hate to be blown off this cliff! But it's certainly spectacular.'

'Not a fence, a warning sign, nothing,' Joe said in surprise. 'Be dangerous at night.'

'I guess not many people come here, night or day,' said Maggie.

'It would be a fantastic place for a building, appropriately anchored, with these views. Imagine a restaurant here,' said Joe.

'It'd never happen, this is a national park,' said Maggie. 'Still, it's incredible. I've never seen anything like it.'

'Too bad we didn't bring the camera,' said Joe.

After another few minutes, they turned and headed back to the car. Suddenly, Maggie screamed, leaping backwards.

Joe grabbed her, pulling her to him. 'What, what?'

Maggie pointed to where a long black snake was slithering across the path ahead of them. They stood frozen to the spot till it disappeared into the grassy bushes.

'Do you suppose it's venomous?' she whispered.

'Of course. Other than koalas it seems most Australian wildlife is,' said Joe. 'Okay, it's gone, it won't attack,' he added.

Maggie was still loath to pass by where the snake had disappeared, but she did, keeping to the opposite side of the path. She didn't speak again till they reached the car, then let out her breath.

'Phew. Who knows what else is out there,' said Joe, and Maggie could hear the relief in his voice. 'You know, our nearest neighbours are probably snakes and funnel web spiders and who knows what else. You should hear Roger the science teacher go on about the local wildlife.'

'No thanks,' said Maggie, hurriedly closing the car door.

'Okay, let's find civilisation and some sustenance,' said Joe.

But as they wound their way back through the lonely sunlit bushland, Maggie felt uneasy. She gazed at the benign landscape, seemingly untouched for millennia, and felt she was an intruder.

Forty-five minutes later they were driving along the waterfront towards the end of the peninsula when they saw a turn-off marked *The Link Road*.

'Hey, let's go that way,' said Maggie. Joe signalled quickly, making a sharp turn.

'What's down here?'

'Looks like sort of a secret backwater. Everyone seems to have a boat.'

'Not much of a backwater – look at the cars parked up there,' commented Maggie.

Joe slowed as they both saw a long low building with a wide entrance and people standing around it.

'What is this? Too big for a restaurant.' Maggie noted the gardens and the wide glassed-in verandah at the back of the building. 'Joe, let's stop.'

'Let me find a park.' Joe looked around carefully, then whooped. 'Hells bells, Maggie, it's a pub! Look at those people, they're holding glasses of beer!'

Delighted, Joe pulled onto the grass verge behind another car and got out.

A young man carrying a surfboard was walking past.

'Hey, excuse me, do you mind telling me what this place is?' Joe asked him.

'Where're you from, mate?' the lad answered. 'It's the Rangers bloody Tavern.'

'Okay, thanks,' said Joe, shrugging at Maggie.

'It's the local pub, Joe. I can smell food.'

'A barbecue? Well, let's look around.'

Walking inside, Maggie's immediate impression was of space, ugly carpet, noise, laughter, a lot of glass and light. A huge expanse of lawn and gardens spread out in front of the building, and all around them were the calm waters of an inlet where dozens of boats were moored. Along the waterfront smaller boats were tied to a long jetty with a large boatshed. Obviously these were visitors to the Rangers Tavern.

'Must be a marina,' said Joe. 'What a setting. You want to sit in here?' He indicated the long glass-fronted room filled with small tables and chairs set by the windows. Stand-up tables smothered in glasses were surrounded by casually dressed locals, some barefoot. 'Or out there in the garden?' asked Joe.

Maggie took his hand. 'The garden area, please.'

They went down the steps into the grounds where shrubs and plants sectioned off the gardens and low wooden tables and chairs were grouped. There was a small covered outside bar and a cleared area where a jazz group was playing.

'Wanna table? How many?' asked a strapping fellow in a half-open Hawaiian shirt and shorts with a hand towel tucked in his back pocket. He was carrying a tower of empty dirty glasses. 'Or do you want to wander round and please yourselves?'

'There's just the two of us,' said Maggie.

'Pop over there behind them flowers. There's a table there. Order up at the top bar, or at the bottom bar here. Same with the grub. Barbie specials on the menu today.'

While Joe headed off to get drinks and discover what was on offer food-wise, Maggie amused herself taking in the scene.

It was a sunny Saturday afternoon. Kids ran around, people were eating and drinking in groups, their legs stretched out in the sun, all casually dressed, many as if they'd just come from the beach. There were young couples like themselves, with dogs on leashes, babies in prams and strollers, small children playing close by. Maggie thought many of them looked like they belonged to the surfing culture she had seen in the media back in the UK; the men were lean and suntanned with long bleached hair, and they were accompanied by bronzed girls in bright tops and shorts, some in swimsuits with a flimsy cover-up thrown over the top.

Maggie admired the clutter of boats; simple half-cabin wooden launches, a classic Halvorsen cruiser, and yachts of varying sizes. Everyone seemed clustered together very informally, like a large picnic.

As Maggie watched Joe carrying their drinks, weaving through the scattered groups, she looked at him fondly. Somehow he just looked so . . . English, she thought. Joe was very fair-skinned, his light brown hair neatly cut, and he wore casual slacks and a short-sleeved shirt tucked in with a belt. No thongs, as the Australians called flip-flops, no loose, half-buttoned shirt with bright flowers or funny pictures printed on it.

Maggie wore loose slacks and a peasant blouse that showed her shoulders, but she felt overdressed as she looked at the bare, cropped and tight-fitting outfits even the young mums were wearing.

Joe put their drinks on the little table. 'Go have a look at the menu up the top where you order. Here's my wallet; order me the fish and chips, please. The fish were caught right here. Well, so they claim.'

'One of those girls had an amazing-looking hamburger.

I'll get that.' Maggie wandered through the beer garden, looking at the boatshed, the jetty, the gardens and the park where the children had been sent to play, and marvelled again at this magical setting the locals seemed to take for granted.

When it came, the food was delicious. Juice from her burger dribbled along her fingers. Maggie closed her eyes in the warm sun as the mellow sounds of Brubeck mingled with distant laughter and the murmur of voices.

Life was good.

*

It didn't last.

The following week she stood alone on the deck waiting for Joe to come home. Her life felt somehow temporary. Was she homesick? No. But much as she loved this view, the novelty of these new experiences was wearing off and reality was setting in. She missed the familiarity of their home in the UK, the reassuring quality of the pattern of her life there.

Their house back in the village was so cosy. Thick stone walls, a pretty little garden behind a low fence, neighbours snuggled on either side and the sounds of life going by outside: the whirr of cars on a wet road, the snappy click of heels or boots on the footpath outside the front door.

At the end of their street was the Coachman, a compact, cosy pub where they could always find a friendly face. From her house she could walk to the local shops or drive a little further to the new supermarket and hardware store Joe liked.

It was a small world, a short drive from Brighton where the beach, famous pier, outdoor entertainment, hotels and guesthouses, shops and tearooms were spread along the seafront. It was all so . . . organised, Maggie thought.

While WestWater might be beautiful, it felt remote and eclectic – like living in the wilderness. She loved the gentle green woods near Holminster where it felt safe to ramble and pick mushrooms. Here . . . while she hadn't strayed far from the house yet, the trees and brooding hills looked inaccessible and scary and a world away from the famous Sydney Harbour Bridge and the new Opera House. The snake she'd seen had given her a healthy fear of the bushland, too.

Suddenly Maggie could feel herself sinking into a bit of a dark hole. She missed her friends. Joe had settled into a circle of people he worked with at the school, and Maggie had hoped to make friends and explore and learn about their new home, but the days seemed to stretch long and empty ahead of her each morning. She knew there was a hospital near The Vale; perhaps she should enquire about nursing work. That was one way to find her own niche.

I need to get out, she thought. *I can't just sit here and feel sorry for myself*. She decided to go for a walk to get to know the neighbourhood better.

She headed down to the foreshore where there was a small track along the waterfront. The wooden jetties; moored boats; small open motor launches, some with half-cabins; shiny aluminium runabouts and a compact ferry boat chugging past gave her the impression that the locals seemed to prefer to travel by boat rather than drive.

A slight breeze ruffled the surface of the water and she saw that the tide was out. She walked down onto flat rocks studded with small oyster shells exposed by the tide. A crunchy, scratchy sound on the sand behind her made her turn. She stopped and watched what at first seemed to be a huge knobbly blue rug slide towards the water's edge. She stopped to wonder at it when a voice from behind her made her turn in surprise.

'Soldier crabs. Local phenomenon,' came a wry remark.

Maggie saw that the speaker was a youngish man in shorts, boots and a shirt with a badge sewn to the top of his sleeve and a worn leather hat. He was unshaven and his face was creased from a lot of sun exposure, making his age difficult to judge. He had strands of white hair, but didn't seem that old. He lifted a hand, shading his eyes as he squinted towards the avalanche of marching blue.

'You should see 'em up close. Not like other crabs; they walk forwards, not sideways, and they're round like a blue ping-pong ball. Live in the mud and the mangroves up there.'

'Really! And why are they leaving all those footprints or funny marks behind them? Don't they have claws, regular legs?' Maggie squinted, wishing she'd worn shoes that could get wet and sandy for a closer look.

'Sand balls. They scoop up mouthfuls of sand as they move and eat any organic stuff and spit out the sand. Clever little buggers.'

'An army marches on its stomach.' Maggie grinned. 'Do you live around here?' She tried to make out the badge on the sleeve of his shirt, which looked to have a bird on it.

'Sorta.' He caught her looking. 'I'm Snowy. I work for the National Parks.'

'I'm Maggie. Do you patrol around here?'

'Always keep an eye open wherever I am. Are you new to the area or just visiting?'

'Just arrived a week ago. My husband is an exchange teacher at The Vale school.'

'Ah, right.' He nodded as if he knew all about it. 'You from the Old Dart, eh?'

'England, yes.'

'This is a good place here. Might see you round then.' Snowy nodded and strode away.

Maggie watched him go with a bemused glance, thinking he probably spent too much time on his own in the bush as he didn't seem to bother with small talk or meaningless niceties. But all in all, she felt much better. Now she'd be able to tell Joe all about the soldier crabs.

*

She walked around the curve of their bay, noting that the rocks were bigger at this end as she peered around into a larger bay scalloped out of the dense bush. Up on the hillside she could see several large homes. The sun flashed on glass windows and sloping tin roofs. She could hear a car winding down the hill. Maggie decided to walk back along the path where steps and tracks led to the tree-screened houses.

It seemed such an isolated existence. No chatting to a neighbour over the back fence here. How did one meet and get to know one's neighbours? She'd heard of the isolation of Australia's outback, but here they were only an hour from the centre of Sydney!

She arrived back at their house to find Joe was home early, sitting in the sun on the deck, his feet up on the edge of the railing, eating from a tub of ice-cream. He turned and grinned at her.

'It doesn't get much better than this, eh?'

'Sunshine and local full-cream ice-cream! I'd say not.' Maggie sat down next to him.

'Were you out walking?'

'Yes. I met someone who works in the national park and I'm now an authority on soldier crabs!'

'Oh, nice to know they keep an eye on things,' said Joe with a laugh. 'The rangers, not the crabs!'

'The park ranger was a bit of an odd bod, in a way. I think he must live around here too. Had that kind of proprietary air and local knowledge. Not like someone from outside just doing the monthly rounds or whatever.'

'Be careful meeting strange chaps out in the bush,' said Joe, and Maggie couldn't quite tell if he was joking or not.

'Joe, he was a park ranger! I'd say I was as safe as could be. Anyway, we were down on the mudflats. So many boats around there. Do you suppose everyone who lives here has money?'

'It's not exclusively rich people,' said Joe thoughtfully, 'at least that's the impression I get from the staff at work. There are ordinary people like us, too.'

'I miss our neighbours and friends.' Maggie sighed. 'I didn't mind rubbing up against them, knowing what was going on in their lives, bumping into them every day. The people here seem to like to keep to themselves, or maybe it's just that nobody runs into anyone else around here because everyone is so isolated.' Maggie reached over and took the spoon off him, helping herself to a bite of ice-cream. 'I've been thinking that maybe I should go back to work. I haven't been out of the workforce very long and it might be a way to meet people, make friends.'

Joe listened quietly, nodding as she talked, then said, 'It's up to you, Mags. We can manage on my salary. But I can see it's a bit lonely out here for you. Maybe we need to make an effort to look up the neighbours, introduce ourselves.'

Maggie nodded in agreement.

Now she had a plan, Maggie visited the local hospital with its dramatic views out to sea, situated twenty minutes outside The Vale. The sister in charge was helpful and said they always needed nurses, and gave her the phone number of the medical office to ask about the state requirements for registration. 'Mr Whitlam, our prime minister, has made it very easy for nurses to return to work these days, and we'd love to have you,' she told Maggie.

Two weeks before she was due to start work Maggie visited a local doctor in The Vale for a check-up. He was delighted when she told him she was planning to join the staff at their local hospital, but pointed out that there was a potential fly in the ointment. She was, he said, almost three months pregnant. Maggie was stunned.

When Joe got home from work that day, she broke the news and he held her cautiously. Maggie giggled and said, 'You can hug me, you know. I won't break.' Then she added quietly, 'I had no idea about this, with all the excitement and changes . . .' She rested her head on his chest. 'It's going to be all right, isn't it, Joe? A baby won't upset our plans?'

'What's different? Other than that you'll be taking on a different job, as a mum! Of course it's wonderful. I'm excited. Maybe a bit earlier than we planned, but now you have something to keep you busy.' He kissed the top of her head as she hugged him. 'But will you manage with no family here to help you?'

Actually, in this case, Maggie felt relieved they were far from home. Her in-laws were difficult. Joe's mother seemed to resent Maggie's intrusion into her close relationship with her son, and perhaps unconsciously, Joe overcompensated for that, catering to his mother's every whim, spending money following her hints and sighs for this and that. Maggie had a sneaking feeling that he was pleased to be getting on with his own life, their life, without his mother's overbearing presence. Maggie's own parents lived modestly but were independent and boasted of tossing the kids out of the nest as soon as they could fly. She suspected they would not be a great deal of help either.

The pregnancy went smoothly, and Maggie spent a lot of time out walking. Over time, she met the neighbours and a few other locals, and she and Joe began to feel settled and contented. When the time came, Maggie gave birth to a healthy boy. They called him Simon. Suddenly a new world opened to her.

She joined a local mothers' group and made friends immediately. And as Joe was now coaching the school cricket team, they socialised with the parents of those children. Summer with water and beaches at their doorstep was a joy. They picnicked in the national park, where one time they ran into Snowy, who showed them a secret waterfall and creek. A neighbour invited them to use his jetty whenever it suited them to fish, swim or use his dinghy.

The year was passing quickly, and their return to the UK loomed.

One afternoon, Maggie looked down at chubby, happy Simon, wearing only a nappy and jiggling in his bouncinette in the sun. It suddenly occurred to her that she'd come to appreciate the calmness and peace of the setting. Now, the idea of neighbours living slap up against the sides of her home didn't seem as appealing as the warmth, the space and the quietude of WestWater, save for rustling trees in the gentle breeze that ruffled the blue bay.

'So how do you feel about going back to the UK?' she asked Joe when he got home that afternoon.

He didn't answer for a moment, then turned to her. 'Gosh, the time has gone so fast. How do *you* feel about going home?'

Maggie looked around her and down at the healthy little baby in the sunshine, then said quietly, 'You know, Joe, this feels more like home now.'

Both were quiet, watching their baby kick.

Joe broke the silence. 'Actually, I hadn't mentioned it to you yet, but I've been offered a permanent job here. The only thing is that we'll have to find a new home, as Andrew and Colleen are coming back and will want their house back, of course.' He looked at her. 'So what do we do, Mags?'

'Build.' She smiled broadly. 'Take the job.'

Joe's mouth dropped open. 'Build? What would we know about doing that? And how much would it cost?!'

Maggie shrugged. 'Just an idea. We'll have to look for somewhere to rent in the meantime.' But her mind was ticking over. Their new friends Sam and Gloria seemed to know a lot of people around the place. Maggie decided she'd mention to them that they were looking to move within the WestWater area.

In her mind's eye she was visualising a house surrounded by trees where koalas, lizards and birds lived, where she could walk to the water and fish or swim, and where from her home she could see a vista of water, dark hills and endless blue sky. She wasn't even sure how far their savings would stretch. But they'd been putting away what they could from each pay packet. This was money which had no label on it, though while each had their own ideas, she suspected Joe might have been thinking of a trip back to the UK.

More and more, this place, specifically WestWater, had been worming its way into her soul. What sort of a person might she have been if she'd grown up here? She wanted their children to know this place. The seduction of its beauty, of nature and adventure-around-the-corner; the freedom and healthy living made her realise she wanted to put down roots in this new land.

So Maggie invited Gloria over for morning tea and shyly explained that they were thinking of staying and settling in the area. 'Though finding a house we can afford will be tricky. I'd love to build a place. Make it just as we want. I so love WestWater's setting,' said Maggie.

'Yes, we all do. It's why we live here too,' said Gloria. She looked at her new friend thoughtfully. 'You know, there's a terrific block of land around here owned by an old lady who is getting on and doesn't have kids.'

'Would she sell, do you think? Is it expensive?'

'I don't know. She'd want the going rate, I suppose. Would you like Sam to sound her out? We have her phone number somewhere.'

For Maggie, it was an agonising time. She and Joe met with the older woman after Sam's introduction, and now they were waiting to find out whether they had managed to negotiate the sale of the land.

As soon as Joe walked in after meeting with the woman and their conveyancing lawyers, a huge smile on his face and arms open, Maggie flew to him and Joe waltzed her around the room. The old woman was happy to sell and know that a young family would settle there.

Joe said he had to keep pinching himself that they had bought the land so easily and so reasonably.

'It was meant to be,' said Maggie, trying not to look smug.

*

In her spare time, which was limited, Maggie spent hours in The Vale library, looking through books, architecture and home magazines.

One afternoon the librarian, a kindly older woman, smiled at her as Maggie put back the magazines, gently rocking Simon in his pram by her side.

'Are you studying? Or building?' she asked.

'Both, I suppose. Not formally. Just looking for ideas. My husband and I are going to build. I have some concepts but the setting is all very new to me.'

'Compared to England? This area is a bit more rugged than the green fields of home, I suppose.'

'Try the cobbled streets and semi-detached houses of Holminster.' Maggie smiled. 'The block of land we have here is like a nature park in comparison.'

'I imagine so. You should drive around and have a look, as there are some stunning houses tucked away in WestWater, quite simple designs, in a way, but they blend into their setting, taking advantage of the light, embracing the warmth in winter, cool breezes in summer, with views and privacy. In fact, there's a rather famous architect who lives up at Saunders Creek. He emigrated here from Berlin after the war. He's built a stunning place on Welsh Island and won some awards for his contemporary homes. He's been written about. I can find some newspaper cuttings about him if you'd like.'

'Oh, that sounds wonderful, I'd love to see some of his work.'

After dinner that night, Maggie spread out photo-copies of several articles the librarian had done for her.

'I don't know, Mags,' said Joe dubiously. 'These places look a bit plain, no trims or fancy windows, you know, no decorations on them.'

'They don't need it, Joe. Look at these *Home* magazine articles.'

He flipped through the photocopies, pausing to read the captions under the photographs, then looked up.

'Why would anyone want a sunken living room?' He shook his head.

'I've been reading at the library. Mrs Rowley, the librarian, told me there are some very modern homes in WestWater, *and* there's a famous architect, Sergei Malnic, who's built places around here.'

Joe looked a little alarmed. 'We can't afford such things! I thought you said we'd have a *simple* house. It was the *setting* that made it,' he mimicked her. But he did sit down and look again at the articles.

*

Maggie walked down to the main jetty with Simon snug in his stroller to get the 10 am ferry over to The Point and then the bus into The Vale.

She loved the leisurely chug around the various bays, dropping off parcels and packages, bottles of milk, beer and food in boxes which were slung into a waiting crate at the end of each jetty. The captain, their new friend Sam, gave a hearty toot as they pulled away.

As they headed around Welsh Island, Sam let his assistant take the wheel while he collected the fares in his old leather conductor's pouch bag.

'Doing some shopping, Maggie?' he asked.

'Yes, and a trip to the library. I say, Sam, you get around a lot of the bays here. I've heard about some homes a famous architect designed in this area.'

Sam nodded. 'Yeah, there's a few prize-winning houses tucked away. If you walk a mile or two from The Point along Saunders Creek, you'll see one. You and Joe getting ready to build, eh?'

'Yes. We can't afford anything too fancy or complicated, but we don't want to have to rent for long.'

Sam looked thoughtful, glancing over his shoulder at the young man in the wheelhouse.

'You should talk to Terry, there. He's been doing courses in something to do with building and design. Works for me part-time. I'll send him back to have a chat.'

Terry sat on the wooden seat beside Maggie as she explained, over the thumping of the diesel motor, that they wanted to build a timber house to take advantage of the location and views of their new site.

'I just love it there,' she said. 'It's got a pile of lumber on it as the previous owner was going to build but never did. The locals call it the graveyard because of all the abandoned timber!'

'That's a bonus. About the timber. Hope it hasn't been attacked by white ants or weathered badly,' commented Terry.

'I'm not sure; I hope not,' Maggie replied. 'Sam said you were a builder or studying . . .?' She looked questioningly at his earnest expression.

Terry nodded. He seemed a rather serious young man.

'Yes. I have my builder's certification. I've done a few small jobs on my own and worked with other builders. I've been mentored by a wonderful architect called Sergei Malnic.' Maggie's ears pricked up as she recognised the name. 'I've learned a lot about light, space and the harmony between a building and where it sits within the landscape. Sergei introduced me to the concepts of the Sydney School . . . it's an architectural style, not an actual school. Have you heard of it?'

As Maggie shook her head he explained, 'A decade or so ago some architects set out initially to improve the quality of housing for Australians by designing places that weren't imposed on the setting but fitted into the landscape. Quite different from England and Europe.'

Maggie nodded her understanding and he went on, 'Many of these homes were built on difficult slopes, so they were designed to be sympathetic to the site, almost invisible in their bush setting with split levels and sloping roofs. Made for interesting interior shapes, too.'

'No box-like rooms,' said Maggie, and Terry nodded.

'They tried to use natural materials so they became "organic", allowing light and airiness. Sergei went to Japan and studied their use of space,' he added. 'Anyway, there are some very wonderful places tucked away around here.'

'I'd love to see them, even from the outside, to get some ideas,' said Maggie eagerly.

Terry glanced at the wheelhouse. 'I only work part-time for Sam. I could give you a bit of a tour sometime, if you like? You should meet Sergei, he's so inspiring. I'd be happy to look at your land and give you some ideas.'

'Really?' Maggie stared at him. 'That'd be wonderful.'

Terry glanced ahead. 'I'd better relieve Sam, we're coming in to The Point.'

That evening Maggie recounted her talk with Terry to Joe, who looked dubious.

'How much is that going to cost, though? Terry sounds a bit green to be talking about designing and building some avant-garde house.'

'No, modern doesn't have to mean way out there. Sympathetic is how Terry described it.'

'You mean people will feel sorry for us living in some crazy house? Just joking,' said Joe quickly.

'Look, Sam says Terry's really bright and decent. Just because he's young doesn't mean he doesn't know what he's doing.'

'People say that about me.' Joe laughed. 'But I can be trusted! Seriously, Maggie, these houses you've read about – sunken living rooms, floors of wood and tile, shag rugs, no carpet or wallpaper . . .' He looked sceptical.

'What about a built-in bar? They're popular. And the pub is a long way away, not a walk down to the olde-worlde Coachman on the corner, Joe! Anyway, Terry has offered to take us around the area and show us these homes, so let's just do that to start with.'

'Okay. Can't hurt,' he said placatingly. 'But I don't want to spend more than we can afford, nor do we want to rent for long after Andrew and Colleen come home and want their house back.'

The present . . .
Maggie's unfocused gaze settled on Dominic and her eyes sharpened again. He had hesitated to interrupt her story; she'd seemed miles away. She shook her head slightly as if to clear it, and just then, there was a call from the hallway.

'Hello, Maggie? It's me, Marcia . . . you there?'

'In here, come on in,' called Maggie, standing up. As Marcia came into the room Maggie continued, 'You remember Dominic? You met at Sam and Gloria's.'

'Oh, of course! Lovely to see you again, Dominic. Sorry, am I interrupting?' Marcia looked from one to the other somewhat curiously.

'Not at all. Oh, it's book club!' exclaimed Maggie. 'Where has the time gone? I completely forgot. Sorry, Dom . . .'

'Please, don't let me hold you up. We can catch up again. Have you got your shopping list for me?' he asked.

'Yes, I'll get it. Appreciate you getting the groceries for me, Dominic. Just leave them on the verandah table if you're back before I'm done with book club.'

'How often does the book club meet?' Dominic asked Marcia as Maggie bustled through to the kitchen.

'Only once a month. Most of us have other things on our plate,' said Marcia.

'Or are slow readers,' Maggie called back to them with a chuckle.

Dominic rose with a smile and carried the tea tray back into the kitchen, where Maggie handed him her shopping list and some cash.

'I'll catch up with you later, Maggie. Nice seeing you, Marcia. Enjoy yourselves!'

'Oh, we do,' said Maggie. 'We all love a good argument!'

As he headed down the hill, Dominic thought of the excitement in Maggie's voice and face as she'd talked of planning their home. No wonder being here meant so much to her. She certainly seemed to have happy, fond memories of settling in WestWater with her husband Joe; building their home together with such passion would make it very hard to move away.

But as he reached the boatshed, he knew very well he was going to try to sit down with Maggie again and attempt to ease her back into talking about her past. While she hadn't specifically agreed to his offer to look into Joe's disappearance, she hadn't said no, either.

Deciding there was no time like the present, Dominic climbed into his car and drove to the general store for Maggie's shopping and to pick up a few things for himself.

He dropped the groceries back at Maggie's then spent the afternoon out on the deck typing up notes on that morning's conversation.

As the shadows began to lengthen, Woolly rubbed around Dominic's legs. He always seemed to know when it was dinnertime. Then, suddenly, there was shouting and hammering at the front door before someone yelled his name. Whoever it was sounded angry.

'Who's there?' called Dominic, hoping whoever it was didn't come around to the deck where the doors were open.

'It's Simon Gordon, Maggie's son. I need to speak to you!'

Dominic went through the house and pulled the front door open.

The furious man seemed to engulf the entire doorway, twisting his huge shoulders to thrust himself into the room. His face was flushed with anger.

'What do you think you're doing upsetting my mother? My family is *none* of your business . . .!' he shouted.

Dominic held up his hands placatingly. 'Hang on, Simon, what's happened? I don't understand. Please, sit down and we can have a chat –'

'I'm not sitting down for a *chat*!' Simon hissed. 'You keep away from my mother, do you understand? What gives you the right to come and pry into her life, get her all upset about stuff that's in the past?' he demanded. 'How dare you!'

Dominic was stunned. 'You're upset that I spoke to Maggie? But we were just chatting . . .'

'Why? What are you doing this for? Are you some nosey reporter or what?' demanded Simon, still towering over Dominic like a fuming mountain.

'Simon, please. None of those things.' Dominic did his best to explain. 'I'm new in the area; Sam and Gloria introduced us. Maggie was very welcoming, and Josie asked me to pick up some groceries for her if she ever needed anything, which I'm happy to do. We had tea and she began talking about her life in England and moving out here and –' Dominic wondered if Maggie had mentioned the idea of looking into Joe's disappearance. Now didn't seem like a good time to bring it up.

'That's enough. You just keep away from her. I don't want strangers talking to my mother. Understand? It's none of your damn business!' Simon was still shouting.

'I think you should discuss this with your mother,' said Dominic quietly. 'She'll explain that –'

Simon cut him off. 'I told you to *leave my mother alone*!' He hissed the last few words, then turned on his heel and plunged through the doorway before turning and looking back. 'Keep away, you hear me?'

Dominic stared at Simon, seeing a large, strong man in his forties but one who, beneath the anger and bluster, looked somehow fearful.

5

DOMINIC WAS STILL RATHER rattled the next morning after the verbal attack by Simon Gordon. He had seemed to be so overprotective of his mother, and for no rational reason. Really, Maggie and Dominic had only talked about Maggie's early days in WestWater, and the planning of the house, over a cup of tea.

Dominic was sure that Maggie seemed to have positive and loving memories of her husband, though she had only talked of their early days. He had the feeling that if Marcia had not arrived and dragged Maggie away to her book club, Maggie might have talked on and on, reliving her happy early years in WestWater. Had the marriage perhaps faltered in later years? he wondered. But even if it had, she held no grudge, or so it seemed.

He was loath to bring up Simon's frightening outburst with Maggie, but decided he would mention it to Josie when he ran into her again. He wondered if Josie had encouraged her mother to share her story, as she'd suggested she would. She had seemed a little reluctant to involve her siblings, though, he recalled. Perhaps Simon's volatile nature explained that.

Dominic couldn't stop thinking about the family, so he picked up his phone and called Rob to update him. Rob suggested they meet for lunch, and in the absence of anything better to do, Dominic agreed.

They met in a quiet beachside restaurant Rob had discovered. 'Food is sensational, it's being written up soon, so let's enjoy it before the gourmet crowd get here and book the place out for the next three months.'

They ordered and Rob leaned back in his chair. 'So, Dom. How goes life in the backwater – sorry, WestWater! Seen the delicious Alicia recently?'

'Life's good. I keep busy enough. I saw Alicia in the local general store the other day. Still have no idea where she actually lives, though. She just pops up out of the blue occasionally. But the reason I rang,' he pressed on, 'is that I had a bit of a chat with Maggie Gordon.'

'Wife of the mysteriously missing husband?'

'Right.' Dominic explained how Josie Harris had dropped in to the boatshed and that he'd brought up the possibility of his looking into her father's disappearance with fresh eyes. 'I was expecting her to shut me down, but she actually said she felt it was time someone outside the family talked to Maggie about it. Well, an opportunity came up and I dropped in to see Maggie and pick up some groceries for her. We had a cup of tea, and she started reminiscing . . .'

'Good or bad?'

'Very warm and fuzzy. About when she and her husband first arrived, settled in, how they loved it here. Their first baby Simon came and they decided to stay and build a home.'

'So no sinister overtones?' Rob interjected.

'Nope. I think she would have gone on, but we were interrupted by Marcia arriving to take her to their book club.'

'Bummer. Well, sounds like you've made inroads there, anyway,' said Rob cheerfully.

'Hang on. There's more.' Dominic described the wild-eyed visit from Simon. 'So I'm not sure what that was all about.'

'Seriously? What on earth . . .?'

'Why would he be so angry? What did he think his mother might tell me that could be so awful? I certainly didn't upset her,' said Dominic.

'And you're not going to stop chatting to her, right?' said Rob.

Dominic hesitated. 'Well – no. But I mean, I don't want to distress her. I can't look into this story any further without her agreement. I thought she seemed pretty open to talking to me, but Simon seems to have got the opposite impression.'

Rob shrugged. 'I suppose something like this must be awkward for all concerned. And better brains than ours have already looked for answers and come up empty-handed. Besides, who knows what really goes on in a marriage?' He paused and looked at Dominic with a quizzical tilt of his head and faintly bemused expression. 'But bloody hell . . . what *did* happen? Wouldn't you like to know? I mean, what a fucking mystery! Better yet, *what if* – just saying – what . . . if . . . we . . . solved . . . it? Hey? Hey?' he persisted with a smile and raised eyebrows.

Dominic tried to keep a straight face. 'What's this "we"? You're incorrigible. As if. Besides, I don't want to exploit Maggie.'

Rob leaned over and touched Dominic's arm. 'Don't be too modest . . . or polite, my friend,' he said gently. 'Go to Maggie directly. It's no one's business but hers if she wants to speak to you.' Then he picked up the menu. 'Let's order and stop filling up on the starters.'

Dominic pushed the delicious platter to one side. Rob had struck gourmet gold again, he thought. Always one step ahead of the pack.

*

The following morning, Dominic's phone pinged and he found a message from Alicia.

What're you doing? Are you up to getting together?

She arrived in tight white capri pants, a clinging top outlining her bare breasts.

'Let's go to lunch at the hacienda!'

'I thought that place was derelict?' said Dominic, recalling the strange old building nearby set back from the road.

'It *is* derelict.' She grinned. 'It was once a grand mansion, but now it's haunted by ghosts of Spanish dancers and gypsies. Anyway, come with me, it'll be fun. I can meet you there.'

'Well, who could resist, with that description?' said Dominic, succumbing to her flirtatious mood.

The strange old building was set behind stone walls and ornate iron grille gates and screened by old trees. Only the red-tiled roof and crumbling upper floor with whitewashed stucco and wrought-iron balconies could be seen from the road.

The gates were held closed with a chain, which Alicia unhooked. She then signalled for Dominic to follow her up the rutted driveway and park outside the house. Dominic was immediately struck by the graceful archways and carved wooden doors of the building, with their elaborate ironwork and decorative tiles.

'Follow me.' Alicia went around one side of the building where there was a walled garden, sagging, twisted fruit trees, a stone well and rotting outdoor furniture on a patio. A rugged hillside rose steeply behind.

Suddenly Dominic had left the bush, beaches and bays of WestWater behind and was in a sun-drenched court-yard with a neglected empty fountain, the air heavy with the scent of orange blossom.

Alicia ducked through an archway, disappearing into the cool shadows of the house.

'What is this place?' said Dominic wonderingly. 'Should we be here?'

'Why not? I brought lunch. Look!' She gestured to a picnic set out on a marble table in the shady loggia, looking out to the tangled garden and an empty cement swimming pool surrounded by columns.

Dominic glanced at her with a wry smile. 'You were sure I'd be available?'

'I hoped so.' She gave a throaty laugh. 'Otherwise I might have had to find someone else to share this with.' She waved at the large picnic basket where Dominic could see a bottle of wine and a baguette poking from under a tea towel.

'Did you make all this?' he asked as Alicia set out an array of delicious spreads, pickles, cheese, fruit and dainty sweetmeats.

She smiled. 'Maybe.'

'So how come you know about this place? How did you come by a key?'

Alicia shrugged. 'Oh, I have ways and means. It's been empty for years and years. A cleaner and gardener used to look after it, but they died and after that no one bothered to care for it. It's been forgotten about, or written off.' She gave him a saucy look. 'There's a bed and a bathroom.'

Dominic looked suddenly shocked. 'Don't tell me this is where you live!' he asked as she handed him a glass of wine.

Alicia bit into a strawberry. 'No. I wish.' She flung out an arm to take in the surrounds. 'But if I did, there'd be room for a sauna and a gym as well as a hot tub. The gardens, pool and the tennis court need redoing, but they're there,' she said.

'You have expensive ideas.' Dominic tried to calculate what the rambling building and grounds could be worth if renovated and styled, the gardens restored.

'Finish your wine. I'll give you a tour.'

The interior smelled musty. It was dim and cool, the walls thick stone and white-washed bricks. Light filtered through high windows and down from the balconies. And when Dom stepped out onto a balcony with a small black iron balustrade he saw that the grounds of the building sloped away into a deep gully, perhaps even as far as the water's edge, and steep hills rose behind, giving him a sense of being marooned.

Through the rest of the house there were a few bits of ornate furniture, possibly too heavy to move. A huge entertaining room had a small stage for a band.

Alicia twirled in front of him, hands on hips, head thrown back, and stamped her feet in a brief, coquettish flamenco dance pose.

They wandered through the halls, rooms and suites. Dominic paused in the great stone kitchen with its massive heavy iron oven and open fireplace, but Alicia hurried him upstairs. Here bedrooms opened onto balconies and bathrooms were cold, echoing tiled chambers, some with sunken baths.

'This is my favourite space,' said Alicia, turning a corner on the landing. She pushed open a heavy arched wooden door into a white-washed room that was stark but clean. There was a low bed with clean bedding and a cotton blanket, and on the floor a jug filled with orange blossom branches. A silver bucket sat on a carved and ceramic inlaid side table. A bottle of mineral water rested in melting ice beside a candle.

Alicia looked at Dominic with a smile, her head to one side, then pushed him gently onto the bed and lay on him, pinning his arms to his side as she smiled down at him, her fair hair framing her shadowed face. Slowly she lowered her body onto his.

*

Dominic stirred. He'd fallen asleep. He had no idea how long they'd been in the room. It was cool and dimly lit as he rolled onto his side to find the narrow bed empty.

The candle was out, and as he turned to the arched window he saw that the sun was setting. He sat up with a jolt.

'Alicia?' he called softly. When there was no answer to his echoing voice, he jumped up and hastily threw on his clothes.

Slipping his feet into his shoes, he hurried along the musty hallway and down the massive staircase to the tiled ground floor. The front door was still shut but the side door Alicia had brought him through was ajar. He hurried outside to the loggia.

'You out here, Alicia?'

There was no answer. Nothing remained of their picnic. He felt for his phone and saw that he had a message from Alicia.

I've never shown anyone the hacienda before. Just you. See you soon.

His car was where he'd left it at the front of the building, and his keys were in his pocket with his wallet.

He got into the car and turned on the ignition. For a moment he felt a chill as he switched on the headlights in the dimming day.

The beam of light shone on a ragged vine that clung to the surface of the front of the building. For the first time he saw the elaborately carved nameplate arching above the heavy front doors: The Hacienda.

Alicia had struck again. The placidity of life in the boatshed with his simple routine had been upended as he was swept into the vortex of the perfumed whirlwind that was Alicia.

Dominic didn't know whether to smile or sigh. He'd taken the bait, if not the hook.

*

Dominic decided to let Josie know about Simon's visit, so he sent her a text so as not to put her on the spot. A few days later, Josie called to say she was coming by to see him later that day.

Josie arrived with a man Dominic didn't know, who Josie quickly introduced as her brother Jason.

Dominic shook hands with the smiling, good-looking man he took to be about forty. He was tanned and dressed casually in a checked cotton shirt, a brand Dominic recognised. Dominic sensed straight away that Jason and Josie were close.

Josie plunged right in. 'Dominic, I'm so sorry! When I found out what Simon said to you, I was furious. And Mum is very embarrassed.'

'Oh, it wasn't that bad,' Dominic reassured her. 'Please, come and sit down. Would you like a coffee?'

'Whatever's going, thanks,' said Josie, and Jason nodded.

'Hope you don't mind me coming along,' he said, 'but Josie is concerned.'

'So just what did you and Mum talk about?' asked Josie as the three of them settled in the main room facing the water.

'Well, nothing dramatic. Mostly she seemed passionate about building the house. She certainly loves her home. A lot of the time she just reminisced about WestWater and how much they liked it here, once they'd settled in. But I can't imagine what would cause Simon to have a go at me,' said Dominic.

'He's moody,' said Josie.

Dominic looked at Jason who said, 'Oh, Simon is . . . well, unpredictable sometimes. I was so happy that Mum talked to you about the early days with Dad,' he went on. 'She doesn't really talk about the past with any of us. I guess because it gets too close to later events.'

'She does occasionally mention things about building the house, though,' said Josie. 'It was her pet project. And it's one of the reasons she's so attached to that house.'

Jason added quietly, 'There're a lot of memories there, of course.'

There was silence for a moment, then Josie said, 'I'm so pleased that Mum opened up to you, Dominic. I could tell she liked you.'

Jason glanced at Josie. 'You have some arrangement with Dominic? To talk to Mum?'

'Nothing as concrete as that,' said Dominic quickly. 'Did Josie explain to you that we just got talking over the washing-up one day?'

'Yes, she told me, and I was surprised.' Jason paused then said, 'The rest of the family never talk about my father.'

'Jason is the only person I can speak to about what happened,' said Josie quietly.

Dominic waited, then Jason went on in something of a rush, 'If he'd died and we knew what happened, I think eventually we could have talked about it.' He stopped. 'We just have no answers.'

Josie looked at Dominic. 'It's painful living with unresolved questions.'

'Your mother never specifically mentioned the loss of your father to me,' said Dominic. 'But she was enthusiastic about this place back in the seventies. I got the feeling she wanted to keep talking about living here, but Marcia came in and interrupted us.'

'I guess I'm surprised that Mum and Josie both opened up to you,' said Jason, looking at Josie. He gave a slight smile and turned to Dominic. 'You're not a therapist, are you?'

Dominic shook his head, smiling.

Josie broke in, 'It's feelings, Jase. I've never stopped wanting to know what happened. I don't know why, but recently I feel like the stopper has come out of a bottle. I need to let some things out, clear the air.' Her voice faltered.

'It's okay, Josie,' said Jason. 'I know how you feel. I was the same until I was able to share how I felt with Rory. Another reason I love him so much.'

Josie nodded. 'Well, once I'd let that stopper out, I decided it couldn't hurt to let someone with fresh eyes have a look for answers. Maybe there aren't any, but Dominic is here on something of a sabbatical with time on his hands and was willing to talk to Mum, so . . .' She threw up her hands. 'I saw no harm in it. Simon obviously doesn't agree.'

'I wish I could help,' said Dominic gently, leaning forward. 'I do think your mother rather enjoyed reminiscing with me, for what it's worth.' He looked at Jason, who nodded.

'I agree with Josie. Generally I've found that if people don't know your history or story, you tend to chat less cautiously,' said Jason. 'Then if you realise they do know, there's a sort of careful tiptoeing around, not mentioning anything that might acknowledge that they know. People are nervous of upsetting us, and we're nervous about how to deal with that and what to say. It's very uncomfortable for everyone and the conversation comes to an end as we each desperately look for someone to intervene, for the phone to ring, or we suddenly remember an appointment.'

Dominic decided to take a risk, and the question was out before he could change his mind. 'So what *did* happen that day?'

Jason looked away, but answered quietly. 'My twin brother Paul and I were fifteen and away at a weekend football camp. Mum had taken Josie and Holly to a kids' eisteddfod on the Friday evening; I think Holly was in it.' He glanced at Josie, who nodded. 'The first we knew was when Mum and Sam arrived at our camp on Saturday afternoon. Simon was eighteen and he was away camping with some mates; no one knew where they were.' He stopped and the silence stretched out.

Then Josie said quietly, 'Maybe that's why Simon is the way he is. He didn't find out that Dad was missing till he got back on Sunday evening, so he was the last to know.'

Dominic looked at Josie. 'And you and your sister? When did it register that your father was missing?'

'We were so tired that night after the eisteddfod. Mum kind of rushed us to bed, telling us Dad must be visiting a mate. In the morning Dad still wasn't there and when Uncle Sam came over and they started searching, I knew something bad must have happened. Holly was running around crying, "Where's Daddy . . .?"' Josie trailed off.

'After that it was just waiting . . . and we're still waiting,' finished Jason.

'I'd never seen my mother cry like that,' said Josie, looking through the glass doors out to the water. 'Though she tried to hide it from us. Friends searched the bays, the hills, everywhere, for days and days. The police assumed he'd turn up, so we waited. Holly and I slept beside Mum at night, and Mum tried to hold it together for us but it must have been so hard for her. There seemed to be a lot of people in the house, but not at night. In all that time, Mum never said anything, never really mentioned him, just tried to carry on for us kids, telling us he would turn up.'

'She's been a terrific mother. Strong, caring. She did everything for us. I wonder now, did we do enough for her?' said Jason quietly.

'Kids are selfish in their own way. Maybe it's a survival thing. Looking back I think I just took my mother for granted,' said Josie. 'That she'd love us, care for us, protect us. Which she did. Only now with my own kids do I realise what she must have gone through. And wonder how she's survived the way she has . . .'

'Not knowing . . .' added Jason softly.

They were all silent a few moments then Josie went on, 'But you know, Dom, the worst part after that is that among the family – Mum, the twins, Simon, Holly and myself – we all go on as if it never happened. There's just a gaping hole in our lives that we ignore. It's like Dad never existed! I'd like to be able to talk about him if something comes up – you know, memories, his birthday, the Christmas when he gave me a little bike . . .' She glanced at Dominic, blinking back tears. 'But thank goodness, Jason and I have started to share with each other.'

Jason didn't speak but his expression was tight, as if he was trying to bear a deep-seated pain. Looking at the furrows in his handsome face, Dominic sensed that he, like Josie, was one of the walking wounded.

'Whereas Simon blows up?' said Dominic, and brother and sister nodded.

'Simon won't talk about Dad at all,' added Jason. 'Never has.'

Dominic shared a look with Josie, who nodded gently, then steepled his hands in front of him and turned to Jason. 'Look, full disclosure, Jason. When Josie and I spoke, I mentioned that I'm interested in writing a book. I don't know yet what it will be about, but I found your family's story very compelling and I was hoping that by looking into it I might be able to shed some light on what happened, and perhaps get ideas for my book in the process. Maybe not, of course, but Josie and I felt it would do no harm to try. I would never write anything without the family's blessing, if it came to it.' He paused, letting the idea sit between them for a moment. 'Would you like to sit down and go through things with me?' he offered. 'It might do you good, maybe bring some clarity, balance, acceptance, finality . . . I don't know.'

Josie drew a long breath. 'This is why I think it would be good for Mum to talk to Dominic, Jase. I think it's time to get some things out in the open.' She tried to smile but it was more of a choked hiccup.

'Maybe I'd be a good person to do it because I'm outside your family,' continued Dominic.

Jason broke in, 'Yes. Yes. I'll have to think about it, but I don't hate the idea. You seem to be a decent and likeable person, and I understand your reasons for taking it on,' he said.

Josie looked at her brother. 'Thanks for being open to it, Jase. Let's let Dominic ask a few questions, dig around . . . see what he comes up with . . .?'

'I don't want to distress or upset your family, though,' said Dominic quickly.

'I suppose it's a risk we'll have to take. But if we could find some answers, some clue, some closure,' said Josie, 'I think it would do Mum a lot of good. And no matter what Simon says, Mum liked talking about the old days with you, I could tell. Maybe it did dredge up the memories of Dad's disappearance too, but that's not your fault, Dom.'

Josie and Jason both looked at Dominic.

'I'm happy to talk to her again if you think it'd be helpful,' said Dominic. 'As long as Maggie is all right with my popping in to see her occasionally, of course. I know you're working, Josie, so I'm happy to help out whenever she might need anything, too. And if she wants to chat, I'll listen.' He looked at Jason. 'What do you think? I don't want to overstep a line or anything.'

'It can't do any harm,' Jason agreed.

'I'm happy to help. You do sometimes hear of cold cases being solved decades later,' said Dominic, hurriedly adding, 'not that we can expect that, but, well . . .' He shrugged.

'You never know,' finished Josie.

'Will you tell the others or just keep it between ourselves for now?' asked Dominic, hoping Simon would be kept in the dark for as long as possible.

'Let's wait and see if you find out anything first,' Jason suggested. 'But I'd like to try talking to Paul – he's my twin. I don't know how he'll react, but I'd feel weird not running this past him. Plus he's a local. I could take you to him now, if you're free.'

Dominic hesitated, but having committed himself, he could find no reason not to agree. As they all rose Jason reached for his car keys and said, 'I'll drive.' He headed towards the door, then paused and looked over his shoulder at Dominic. 'You know, not having to walk on eggshells, bite my tongue when we're all together, it would make such a difference. So for whatever reason you've turned up and fallen into our lives, Dominic, I'm grateful. Let's just see where it goes.'

Dominic nodded in acknowledgement, then followed Jason with a faint sense that events were moving faster than he'd anticipated.

*

Paul lived near WestWater on the ocean side at Dingle Beach, a small village between two larger, more popular beaches where the wealthy and socially connected elite had homes, though some were only used in the summer.

As Jason drove down the steep and winding road

from the highway to the village on the oceanfront, Dominic commented, 'Bit of a goat track! I thought the link road along the waterfront where the boatshed is was bad enough.'

'The locals here like it that way; don't like the terrorists having easy access!' Jason chuckled. 'That's what we call tourists. It's pretty laid-back here, used to be known as Nimbin by the sea.'

'I remember Josie saying Paul's a surfer. Is he a hippy type?' asked Dominic with a smile, thinking the twins sounded like opposites.

'Kind of. At one stage he smoked dope but he had a mate die from a drug overdose a few years back so that kind of pulled him up. He's single – divorced – seems to have a different girlfriend every time I see him. He gets by okay, he's very easygoing, works for a mate who owns a surf shop. Paul makes some pretty spectacular boards out the back,' said Jason. 'My partner Rory says we're chalk and cheese.'

'You're not a surfer then?' asked Dominic.

'Oh, I used to surf a bit when we were young, you couldn't avoid it living out here. The beach is where everyone met and hung out. I was never as into it as Paul, though. I considered doing an Agriculture course and maybe going on the land, but without family connections or friends with a property and having no contacts, I fell into landscape gardening instead, which I love. I work with several architects on the design side. A sidebar passion is plant conservation and protection; you know, seed banks, biodiversity, food security.'

'Wow, that's interesting,' said Dominic.

'I think so. And it's becoming a necessity, I feel. I'm working with a group through the Botanic Gardens.'

He pulled up in front of a small cottage behind a screen of Norfolk pine trees.

'This is Paul's place; he lives out the back. He's been here ever since he dropped out of uni, apart from some surfing safaris overseas over the years.'

'Certainly a stunning location right on the beach,' said Dominic, noting the cluttered chaos of surfing paraphernalia all over the verandah and front yard, from wetsuits, flippers and diving gear to a trailer loaded with surfboards. A shed to one side was obviously a workshop. Several cars and two restored Kombi vans were parked on the grass. A barbecue with seats and a long table were set to one side.

'This is the HQ of SeaMen.' Jason grinned. 'I did offer the owner of the place a good price to do a bit of basic landscaping for him, but he hasn't taken me up on that.'

They walked across the grass and Dominic could hear a Jimmy Barnes soundtrack over the noise of a sander.

A man bearing a close resemblance to Jason spotted them and came out, wiping his hands on a towel. He wore a paint-splattered T-shirt and colourful board shorts. He was barefoot, with long tangled hair greying at the temples. He looked younger than his twin and was smiling broadly. 'Hey, hey brother,' he called.

Jason introduced Dominic, who said, 'Great set-up you have here.' Then, spotting some elaborately decorated boards leaning against the building, he added, 'Spectacular artwork.'

'You in the market for a new board, or a classic? Gotta ripper Zest here, just been done up,' enthused Paul.

'Ah no, Paulie, he's a mate. We just wanted a word with you, somewhere quiet, private,' said Jason.

'What's up? Anything wrong?' asked Paul, frowning.

'No, no, it's all fine,' said Dominic quickly.

And before he could say more, Jason wrapped an arm around his twin's shoulders. 'Let's have a coffee. Dominic is living in Nigel's boathouse for a few months. He's been keeping an eye on Mum, not that she needs it.'

Dominic smiled at Paul. 'I pick up some groceries for her now and then. Sometimes it saves Josie a trip.'

'Nice of you,' said Paul as he led them to the old outdoor table, calling out, 'Tammy? You there? Bring us three coffees, will you, please?'

A pretty girl in her teens came out and waved acknowledgement, then disappeared back inside. 'That's Tammy, the owner's daughter. She hangs around here all the time. Bloody good surfer, she's in line to nab a title or two at the rate she's going.'

'She must be good,' said Dominic.

They made small talk until Tammy returned with three mugs of coffee, then Paul folded his arms on the table and stared at Jason. 'Okay, what's going on?'

Jason took a breath, then started telling Paul the story of how Josie had met Dominic and talked to him about their father's disappearance.

'Josie just opened up to me a bit, as you do,' Dominic put in, but stopped as he saw Paul scowl.

'What do you mean by "open up"?' he said tightly.

'She talked about Dad's disappearance,' Jason said calmly. 'Well, only briefly. But then Mum also started talking to Dom over tea one morning. Not about Dad specifically, but about their early days here.'

'Hang on. What the hell for? What are you, a psychiatrist?' said Paul loudly. 'And why now?'

'Maggie talked about how much she loves WestWater, and especially the house she and your father built,' said

Dominic, feeling at rather a loss as to how to explain everything to Paul.

'Where's this going?' demanded Paul, looking from one man to the other. 'Why are you here telling me this?'

'Paul, just listen for a minute,' Jason tried. 'Josie and I have asked Dominic to see what he can find out about Dad. Mum enjoyed reminiscing with Dominic, and God knows she can't do that with her family!'

'What happened is our business! We don't discuss it with strangers,' said Paul firmly.

'But Mum seems to want to, and Josie does too. You know it did me a lot of good talking it through with Rory. What's wrong with that?' asked Jason reasonably. 'In fact, Josie and I thought it would be good for all of us if Dominic can maybe find some answers.'

Paul thumped the table, saying loudly, 'Simon has always said it's no one else's business. And he's right. We don't need outsiders poking their noses in! And for what? To end up exactly where we already are?'

'Steady on, Paul,' said Jason grimly but quietly.

'No! You listen to Simon. We've all had enough to deal with! We don't need a stranger stirring things up. Upsetting Mum.'

'She wasn't upset when I spoke to her,' said Dominic quietly. 'Paul, I mean well. I only want to help.'

'Finish your coffee,' said Paul dismissively. 'I have work to do. I'll talk to you privately later,' he said to Jason, and strode off in the direction of the shed.

Dominic turned to Jason. 'I'm sorry if I've caused any friction.'

Jason shook his head. 'Don't worry about it. Nothing new. He goes along with whatever Simon says or thinks.'

*

Two days later Rob called.

'I got your message. I've been hung up in meetings. So what's happening?' Rob asked.

'Full steam ahead!' Dominic filled Rob in. 'Though it's not all smooth sailing with the family. And this is a sad story potentially with no ending,' he added.

'Oh ye of little faith,' answered Rob. 'Look, start with talking to Maggie and the family again. Later, if there are some leads or inconsistencies, follow up the people who knew him, who were around when he went missing. Get more of a handle on the family life. Sure, Maggie is an affable lady, but maybe twenty-something years ago she was a dragon lady? What do the kids recall? What do locals think? What gossip was there? Talk to that Snowy, I bet he has something to tell. I mean, even if we don't find out *what* happened, we might find out a *why*. People are always interested in gossip, in what goes on in other people's lives,' Rob concluded.

'But who would care now? It's not their business. Old news –' Dominic started, but Rob cut him off.

'You think so?' he interjected. 'Everyone is curious about a disappearance into thin air. The thing is, whatever you find out, we get to know this family. Love 'em, hate 'em . . .'

'And then what?' asked Dominic.

The line was silent a moment, then Rob answered, 'We're invested in this family. Will justice be done, will they move on? Is there a villain in the family, or not? Do we ever know? It's the journey, man,' he concluded. 'Don't forget your book in all this.'

Dominic had to smile. 'Seriously Rob, I get it. I guess just chatting to people is the way to go. I do have a slice of time to invest with few expectations. And if I'm helping them all move forward, well, I get a gold star somewhere down the line.'

Rob was quiet a moment, and Dominic imagined him rolling his eyes.

'I think the family is the key, Dom. Outsiders are just that – distant from the story with their own interpretation. Who really knows what goes on behind closed doors, to use the ol' cliché. The heart of the tale . . . unravelling those threads . . . It won't be easy, some of the kids were pretty young.'

'That's well and good, but so far at least two of them won't talk to me.'

'So start with the two who will! On that note, I gotta go. Hey, you seen Alicia lately?'

'Oh, here and there,' said Dominic guardedly. Then he wondered why he was being oblique and not wanting to mention the old hacienda.

'Okay, see ya, mate.' The line was disconnected.

*

Dominic kept to himself for a few days and finished an analysis of a proposal to increase workforce participation by increasing education opportunities and raising universities' standards, as well as outlining his thoughts on immigration policies for a political magazine.

After submitting the latter, he pushed his laptop to one side and walked onto the little deck, debating whether to get the tinnie out and go for a fish, take a walk or call Alicia. She hadn't been in contact since their visit to the old hacienda. The run-down place intrigued him.

'Hey, Dominic! How's it going?'

He turned to see Sam and Gloria heading along the track towards him.

'Oh, hello!' Dominic waved, pleased to see them.

'We've been out walking and as we haven't heard from you or seen you lately we thought we'd just drop by.' Gloria smiled a greeting. 'How are you?'

'Good, good,' said Dominic enthusiastically, realising that he'd missed good company the past few days. 'Come on in.'

They sat in the sun on the deck chatting for a few minutes until Sam cleared his throat and said, 'So, what's with Simon Gordon having a go at you?'

'Oh, you heard,' said Dominic.

'Word gets around,' said Gloria wryly. 'What do you think set him off like that?'

'Apparently just the fact that Maggie chatted to me about her life when she and Joe first came here,' said Dominic.

'Maggie mentioned to me that you'd kindly got her groceries and saved her a trip. And just as an aside, really, she said she'd had a lovely yarn with you,' said Gloria. 'I got the impression from her that Josie had spoken to you about what happened with Joe.'

'Yes,' Dominic replied. 'It's a bit of a long story, actually . . .' and he filled them in on events since Josie first spoke to him, ending with Simon's unwelcome visit.

'Well, that's Simon for you,' said Sam. 'A bit of a firecracker, goes off the deep end sometimes. Takes everything so seriously. Please don't feel you've upset Maggie. Far from it.'

'She doesn't get much of a chance to look back and chat about the old days, I s'pose. We know it all, we were there.' Gloria chuckled. 'You're a new audience for her.'

'Oh, that reminds me,' Dominic jumped in, 'I noticed

that old place on the hill behind the trees, the place that's like a hacienda? What do you know about it?'

'Ah, yes. It's been through several lifetimes and reincarnations,' said Sam.

'We had some lovely evenings there when Monsieur Reynard had it. Remember the night we went with Maggie and Joe for Joe's birthday, the time he got the promotion?' said Gloria, her eyes lighting up.

Sam nodded. 'Couldn't forget that. We were lucky to get in that evening. Remember there was some local politician celebrating something there rather than at the surf club at Pine Tree Beach where all the rich people had homes?'

'Don't forget Hero's up on the hill, that was a pretty swanky place, a restaurant with guest rooms. Had been a big old home that overlooked WestWater,' added Gloria.

'It could have been in Europe, really. It's where all the older bosses took their young secretaries for a weekend!' Sam laughed. 'They had a lookout on the crow's nest thing on the roof to watch for suspicious wives turning up.'

'Sounds like the area was quite a swinging place back then.' Dominic chuckled.

'We didn't frequent those places; mostly we went to the casual old Rangers Tavern where the kids could play in the beer garden,' said Gloria. 'But we rarely go there any more as it's too trendy and expensive now they've got that marina there.'

'I know. I went there with Rob when he came to stay,' said Dominic.

'Mostly we made our own fun back then,' continued Sam. 'You know, going to each other's homes to play Five Hundred or have a barbecue, have a local little jazz group come and entertain or play disco music.'

'I loved the Bee Gees.' Gloria sighed happily and Sam winced.

'Too high-pitched, went straight up my sinuses,' he said.

Dominic laughed. 'So what's the history of the old hacienda? Seems a shame it's not still going.'

'Oh, there're a lot of stories. It had been abandoned for some time I think, then in our time it was resurrected by a French chef who'd had a fancy place in the city then found it and turned the ballroom into a restaurant. He went into partnership with a fellow who had a rather colourful history.'

'An underworld figure?'

'Apparently he was hugely jovial and loved his food. He had private rooms for gambling or just serious card games. We never knew what went on in some of them.'

'We did have some wonderful special occasions there, before as well as after our kids came along. It was known locally as The Hacienda . . .' Gloria turned to Sam. 'Remember Maggie's thirtieth birthday party there?!'

Sam rolled his eyes. 'Oh man, what a night that was!'

'Oh, do tell me,' said Dominic.

'Would Maggie mind, do you think?' Sam grinned.

'Why not, she's told the tale before herself. It's good for her to remember the fun times we all had.' Gloria settled back, ready to recount the story. Then, seeing Dominic's bemused expression, she added, 'You mightn't think it to look at us now, but our era was pretty free and swinging. Aquarius Festival, alternative thinking and living. Joe introduced some new concepts at school and Maggie was very happy-go-lucky.'

Sam rolled his eyes. 'That song she called her mantra . . . the group was the Masters Apprentices, wasn't it?'

Gloria suddenly burst into a song, which Dominic vaguely recognised, with a clear strong voice. She looked at Dom, her eyes sparkling.

'Sounds like you all had fun.' Dominic hesitated for just a second as he felt Rob mentally tap him on the shoulder and give him a nudge. 'So, Maggie and Joe had a happy marriage?'

Gloria and Sam were smiling and their expressions didn't change as they both gazed back at him.

'Oh, indeed yes,' said Sam gently.

'They loved each other to pieces,' said Gloria. 'Anyone could see that.'

Both stared at Dom, their expressions open and soft, their smiles lingering as they nodded, reflecting on happy times.

Dominic hesitated, but then decided he might as well take the plunge. He said quietly, 'Can I ask, what do you remember about the night Joe disappeared?'

6

DOMINIC REALISED HE WAS holding his breath as everything seemed to flip into slow motion. Sam and Gloria's expressions appeared to melt. Their smiles faded.

'I'm sorry . . . this must be painful. I just thought . . .' Dominic began in an apologetic rush.

But Gloria reached over and squeezed his hand, giving him a small smile. 'It's all right. It's been a long time now. Anyway, sad as it was, and still is, Maggie did a great job with the kids. Got on with things.'

'Still a bloody great question mark in one's life, though,' said Sam.

'Yes, indeed. I understand.' Dominic was starting to regret having raised the issue.

But Sam straightened and looked him in the eye.

'It's all right, son. If Josie wants you to help her, then it's only right we tell you what we know. Or rather, don't know.'

Gloria nodded and sighed. 'I wish we did know more. It's hard to think about it; I used to get angry as well as sad. We lost such a good friend, someone we'd had a lot of fun times with. I know Maggie had dark nights over the years . . .' She looked at Sam. 'You start, love.'

Sam patted her arm, then turned to Dominic. 'We were home that night and had just finished dinner when Maggie rang, terribly worried. She'd come home quite late with the girls; they'd been at a concert of some sort. The boys were all away that weekend and Joe wasn't there. No message on the answerphone, no note, nothing. I went straight over just in case he'd had some sort of accident about the place. Maggie said she'd searched everywhere but I still had a good look around.' He shook his head. 'His car was there. He'd quite recently bought a little second-hand Beetle. A mug was in the sink where he'd made himself a coffee. His wallet and car keys were there. Nothing seemed to be missing. A magazine he'd been reading was on the coffee table . . .' He paused.

Gloria went on, 'Maggie had put the girls to bed. She pretended their dad was just at a mate's place for a game of cards or something. Maggie just hoped he'd turn up in the morning. I offered to stay the night, but she said no.'

'We were up at daylight the next day, wondering if he'd turned up. Didn't like to interfere, but by seven I rang Maggie. She'd been sitting up all night. So I suggested I come over and we'd call the police. Which I did,' said Sam.

'I suppose the police hear these things all the time, but they said to give it forty-eight hours or so then get back in touch if he hadn't come home,' said Gloria. 'Made me so mad, because Joe just wasn't the type to disappear! But we had no choice but to wait.'

'As the morning rolled on we decided to go to the football camp and get the twins. I went with Maggie and Gloria stayed with the girls. By the time we got back and there was still no Joe, everyone became very concerned,' said Sam.

'Maggie showed how strong she was. We could see how she was feeling, how scared she was, but she put on a brave face for the kids.' Gloria sighed. She paused and added, 'It just became a slow process of getting through every minute, every hour.'

'There was a bit of a false alarm, though,' said Sam. 'A day or so after they started searching in earnest, the cops called to say that a body had been found and Maggie had to go and identify it.'

'I don't know whether it was a relief or not,' put in Gloria. 'To at least have an answer of some kind. Sam and I stayed with the kids while Maggie went with the police to the morgue.'

Sam shook his head. 'But Maggie came back not long afterwards, quite overwrought. I remember she said, "It's not him! It's not Joe!" Then broke down sobbing, "Joe, Joe, where are you . . ." Bloody dreadful it was. Still is.'

Dominic drew in a breath. 'God, how awful for her. But isn't that a bit strange, that they found a body and it wasn't that of the man who was missing?'

Sam nodded. 'Yeah, we thought it was weird at the time, but it ended up just being a dreadful coincidence. Turned out the bloke was a hiker, often went on solo treks in the national park. They worked out he'd slipped, hit his head and drowned, then got washed down the creek, which is where they found him. He wasn't due back for another day or two so no one had reported him missing. Thing was, they called off the search for Joe when they found the body and wasted valuable hours thinking it was him.'

Dominic shook his head. 'Do you have any theories about what could have happened to Joe?'

Sam flung up his hands. 'We've gone over and over it. None of it makes sense and there's no evidence of anything, let alone anything untoward.'

'And so many unanswered questions, I guess,' said Dominic. 'Did the police have any theories? Any ideas at all? You hear of people going missing but rarely about them being found, unless it's a sensational case.'

'I got pretty angry. It didn't seem possible a good man like that would just drop off the planet. The police were calm about it all but eventually they stopped looking. Said there was nothing to find, until something turned up. That made Maggie furious. She isn't one for holding back,' said Gloria.

'She speaks her mind. Polite, but firm. No-nonsense,' said Sam with a small smile.

'Yes,' continued Gloria, 'she asked me to help, so we had a photo of Joe printed on a missing person flyer asking for any information and we went for miles around sticking them up in shop windows, sports venues, on noticeboards, telegraph poles. Everywhere we could think of. The local paper printed it too.'

'And you heard nothing?'

Gloria shook her head. 'Nothing. Though Maggie did have someone mention that a friend of a friend thought they saw him in Cronulla. So I went there with Maggie. That was a big deal then, as we went by public transport – bus and then train – to the other side of Sydney. Took hours and hours. I wouldn't even go that far for

144

my holidays. Maggie certainly hadn't been there before. Sam looked after the kids. We stayed in a little motel and we spent days walking everywhere with flyers, went to all the shops and businesses. Walked up and down along the beachfront and everywhere we could. Looking, looking, at every person we passed. But no luck.' She paused. 'Y'know, it took me years to stop searching for Joe's face in the crowd everywhere I went.'

'Do you still feel that he's . . . well, that he might be found?' asked Dominic.

Sam and Gloria looked at each other. It was Sam who replied.

'Not really, no. I don't believe he's ever going to walk in the door. I suppose we hold out hope that one day we'll find out what happened, though. He really was the last man on earth you'd think would disappear. It's inexplicable. Whatever happened is way out of the norm.' Sam sighed. 'We felt so helpless for a long time. All we could do was step up and be there for Maggie and the kids. She had it so tough, alone with five children, and suffering too.'

'Maggie must be very grateful to you. What good friends you are. Almost . . .' Dominic hesitated.

'Like family. I know.' Sam nodded. 'Neither her family nor Joe's in the UK came out to see Maggie. I'm not sure why. I know Maggie tried to keep in touch as time went by, sent them updates and photos of the kids. I wouldn't say it to Maggie, but I guess they harboured some sense of blame.'

'Well, Maggie and the kids are very lucky to have had you as neighbours,' said Dominic kindly.

'I hope so. Our kids and theirs ended up a bit like cousins, I guess. They're grown up now of course, but they still keep in touch.'

'Maggie is very independent, though. She tried not to impose then, and still does,' said Gloria. 'When we were young and Joe was around, she was so bubbly and such fun. The four of us were just the best of friends.'

'I hate to ask, but did you ever think that Joe . . . had some problem, or perhaps was seeing someone else . . . anything?'

'No. But naturally we asked ourselves that, even though it seemed totally far-fetched. In the end I just couldn't imagine it. No way,' said Sam firmly.

Gloria hesitated, then said, 'But at the end of the day, I s'pose you really don't know what's going on in someone else's head, or life. Joe seemed like an open book. Cheerful, fun, caring, loving . . .' She wrung her hands in her lap. 'Everyone liked him, took to him straight off. It's just so hard to picture anything being really wrong in his life.'

Dominic was about to say that he seemed too good to be true, but bit his tongue. 'What was Joe like? What sort of a fellow?' he asked instead.

Sam and Gloria both smiled.

'He and I always had a lot of laughs together,' said Gloria. 'He was fun, Maggie too, but Joe and I had a particular rivalry – loved to beat each other at cards. He was always teasing me and telling me things which I believed as he was so educated, but then I'd realise he was pulling my leg. He was a wonderful dad, and teacher – the kids at school all seemed to love him. He used to coach the sports teams and the parents always praised him to the sky.'

'He looked out for the stray kids, too,' Sam added. 'A few of them he recognised as being vulnerable, often with single parents, so he took extra time with them. He was a real family man and a good neighbour.'

'Indeed he was. And don't forget how he and Snowy became friends,' said Gloria.

'Snowy seems a bit of a character,' commented Dominic.

'He's a good man. Strikes some people as a bit abrupt sometimes, and he doesn't suffer fools gladly,' said Sam. 'I think it's a disposition that has some clinical name these days. He's a loner. Doesn't share anything personal, but from what I've observed over the years he's had some tough times that he won't talk about. Never been married, though I think there was a sweetheart in the early days. He keeps to himself but has a knack of just turning up. He became friends with Joe and Maggie, really opened their eyes to what the Aussie bush is all about when they first arrived. That started their friendship, I guess.'

'When Sam says friendship, it's not what you think of as being friends, you know, socialising and such,' added Gloria. 'Snowy comes to you, and by that I mean he just appears when you're out somewhere around here. It's all on his terms. But if you need him, he somehow senses it and just turns up. Didn't that happen to you, Dom, when you first arrived and went astray in the bush? I know it sounds peculiar, but we just accept him, and well, that's Snowy.'

Dominic nodded. 'Yes, I know what you mean,' he said, thinking of how Snowy had just appeared seemingly out of nowhere when he'd got lost in the hills.

'Ever since Maggie's been on her own he keeps an eye out for her in his own discreet way,' added Sam. 'He and Joe had a bit of a bond which, when you think about it, was rather quaint. Joe, the bright, outgoing English teacher who loved literature, animals and sport, seemingly without a care in the world. Snowy, the reclusive

147

naturalist, a loner who kept to himself and ran his own race.'

'You don't make friends with Snowy, he makes friends with you?' suggested Dominic.

'Very perceptive,' said Gloria.

'So that's about it, Dom. Can't tell you much more.' Sam rose stiffly. 'I'd better get back up to the garden and do a bit of weeding.'

'Thank you both for telling me what you know,' said Dominic as he waved them off. He had a lot more questions, but slowly, slowly, he told himself.

*

It was two days later that Maggie rang Dominic and asked him to drop in sometime, as she wanted to apologise for Simon's behaviour.

'Oh, there's no need, Maggie, but I'd love to pop over to see you. Do you need anything?'

'I'm fine, thanks, Dom. Josie was here yesterday. She mentioned Simon had blown his stack because we'd chatted about . . . the old days. He's actually a rather sensitive fellow.'

Dominic rolled his eyes but kept his tone neutral. 'No worries, Maggie.'

'Fine, well come over for a drink if you'd like. Say five-ish?'

*

The day was melting slowly in the sunshine. Dominic dipped the oars into the glassy water, trying to make as little splash or disturbance on the surface as he could. It was a game he played with himself, now that he was quite pleased with his rowing ability.

He turned and glanced over his shoulder, checking ahead, when on the shoreline he recognised CeeCee skipping from rock to rock. He paused, calling, 'Hey! CeeCee, want to race to the jetty?'

She lifted an arm and waved, then leaped onto the mudflat and sprinted towards the boathouse. Dominic dug the oars in and the little dinghy skimmed forward.

She was waiting on the end of the jetty, panting and laughing, when he tossed the painter rope to her.

'Well, that's my exercise for the day! You visiting or staying over?'

'I came down last night. My parents are here for the weekend to do some odd jobs for my grandparents. You been fishing?'

'Look – my new thing.' Dominic reached over and handed a bucket up to her. 'Mud crabs. Four beauties. I reset my crab pots.'

'Oh, you've been up the creek Grandad often takes me.'

'Yep. And with paddles.' He chuckled when he saw that his comment didn't register with the teenager. 'You know the saying, up a creek without a paddle.'

'Oh.' CeeCee didn't look convinced. 'Have you gone up all the way to the falls? It's really beautiful. Be careful of the leeches, though. Grandad uses them for bait. Ugh.'

'So you go fishing with your grandad then?' Dominic asked.

'Not so much any more. I did when I was little, but I can go on my own now. Sometimes I go with Grandad on the boat, though. He likes to keep some of his fishing spots secret.'

'What a great grandad you have,' said Dominic as he stepped from the boat onto the exposed step. 'Tide's coming in.' They walked back along the jetty, Dominic pulling the dinghy back to where it was kept tied to a tree by the old boat slips.

'Would your grandad like a couple of muddies?'

'I'm not carrying them while they're squirming around. Put them in the freezer to go to sleep,' said CeeCee. 'But thanks, I'll tell him you offered. See ya, Dom.' She gave a wave and headed along the track to Sam and Gloria's.

Dominic watched her disappear among the trees, wondering if she knew how blessed she was with family, security and loving grandparents in a magical environment with freedom and safety. All doors were open to her, just as they had been for him and his sister. Again his mind turned to Josie and her siblings. While they seemed to have had a secure and stable upbringing, thanks to Maggie's dedication and the support of good friends, neighbours and community, there remained a gaping hole in their lives that apparently none of them had really come to terms with. Each suffered and reacted in their own way.

Why am I so interested? Dom wondered suddenly. Why did he care so much about these people? Curiosity over a strange disappearance, perhaps, or the challenge to solve a mystery as in the plot of a book or the finale of a TV crime show? Or was it merely the prodding of his mate Rob, the opportunist?

In a way Dominic felt he was living in a parallel universe, or leading a double life, where he was becoming enmeshed in the lives of these people as much as his own. But there were no shadows haunting his life or the lives of his loved ones. Dominic felt a faint twinge of guilt at his own position of stability and security. Sure, he could fret about some things, but he knew well that he was more than okay.

Dominic was still deep in thought as he walked to Maggie's house later that afternoon.

Maggie greeted him warmly, reaching out to squeeze his arm.

'Come out on the deck, it's going to be a lovely sunset.'

Dips and salt crackers were laid out beside the chilled wine.

'I have some cold beer if you prefer?' she said.

'A glass of wine would be lovely, thanks,' Dominic replied.

He joined her and sat down and she dived in. 'I'm so sorry about Simon; Josie told me what happened. He's not normally so unpleasant. I don't know what prompted such an overreaction.'

'Do you think he will sanction this get-together, or should I expect another visit?' Dominic smiled.

Maggie brushed the remark aside. 'It's none of his business. Besides, I invited you.' Her bright expression softened. 'It's hard, you know. All the children have had . . . issues with each other, at one time or another. Simon has thin skin and just seems to wear his pain on his sleeve. He is mostly thinking of me, I suppose, but I do wish he'd move on with his life. Mind you, he and Judy seem happy and young Ritchie is happy and well adjusted.'

'Were your three boys ever close to each other? I met Jason and Paul the other day. They are like polar opposites,' said Dominic with a smile. 'Unusual for twins?'

'All the kids are very different,' she said. 'Always have been. And they've taken different paths in life, too. Maybe that's good as they've never had to compete in the same arena. Simon, I think, has always carried a sense of responsibility, being an adult . . . at the time.' Maggie sipped her drink.

It struck Dominic that Maggie couldn't bring herself to say the actual words, *when his father disappeared* . . .

'I'm sure he's been a great support to you,' said Dominic.

'I just wish he'd feel less responsibility for me. I'm doing fine. I love this house, I have good friends and neighbours and, well, I'll never leave here.'

Dominic glanced around, looking at the house properly for the first time. It was a beautiful building, married perfectly to its setting. Much thought, work and love must have gone into it.

'It's a stunning house in an amazing location, for sure. But Maggie, it's awfully big for one person . . .' Dominic hesitated as he saw Maggie's expression begin to change. 'Though with five children and grandchildren I guess it must be perfect for Christmas, family gatherings . . .'

Maggie nodded.

'So you'd never consider downsizing?' asked Dominic softly.

Maggie was shaking her head before he'd even finished the sentence. 'No. No way. I will never leave here,' she said again firmly. Then before Dominic could speak, she added, 'Joe will expect me to be here.'

Dominic caught his breath. 'Maggie . . . do you believe Joe will just turn up one day?' he asked gently.

Maggie gave him a frank, calm look. 'I hope so.'

Dominic was rather lost for words, so he turned the conversation back to the house. 'Last time I was here, you were telling me about how you and Joe designed this place and had it built,' he prompted.

'Yes. I did a lot of reading and research. We wanted to shake off the cold formality of England. We felt so blessed to be here. Immigrants always look at a new country through aesthetic eyes, in a way. For us it was the light, the sunshine, the space and peacefulness. Joe was easy-going and friendly, but there was more to him than just the English teacher at school who coached the cricketers and footballers. He ran the debating club and was involved in raising funds to expand the library. He was open-minded, but I still had to persuade him to agree to my ideas about the house.'

'Oh, really?' said Dominic.

'I told you how I read about Japanese design and all manner of architectural thinking,' she enthused again. 'That meeting with Sergei Malnic opened my eyes. Fortunately our local builder, Terry, was young and interested in doing something different when he heard our plans, even though we were on a tight budget. We were lucky that friends like Sam and Gloria, and Colleen and Andrew, helped us with some of the easier jobs like painting, to save money.'

'Colleen and Andrew . . .?' Dominic tried to remember how these friends fit in.

'The couple we swapped with on the teachers' exchange program. They're still good friends.'

'Oh, right.' Dominic mentally added them to his list of contacts to interview.

She smiled at Dominic. 'You have to live in this house to really appreciate its design.'

'I've really only hung out in the living room and on this deck,' he said with a grin.

She nodded. 'This was Joe's favourite spot.' She waved an arm to embrace the deck.

'And it's lived up to what you dreamed?' he asked, seeing her enthusiasm.

'Yes . . . why don't you come and have a tour?'

Maggie stood and Dominic got up to follow her, curious to see the home after hearing so much about it.

Maggie first pointed upwards where, under the pitch of the roof, glass panels framed the tops of the eucalypt trees outside like a long mural.

'The panels can be opened in the summer as they're screened. We wanted open spaces for light and air, but in the winter, see here . . .' Maggie reached out and drew across a sliding screen that partitioned off the rooms between the living and bedroom sections. 'Warmer, more private and cosy in winter. Spacious with cool through-breezes in summer. The verandah wraps around but the glass doors all slide open. In a way it's a bit like a ship: you can feel the house relaxing against the elements. The wood breathes like a musical instrument and you feel you know where all the family is, not boxed away from each other.'

'Amazing,' said Dominic. 'I love it.'

'There're four bedrooms, such a luxury compared to the tiny semi-detached home we had in the UK. Josie had her own bedroom until Holly came along . . . as a bit of a midlife surprise . . .' she added. 'Simon had the smaller bedroom and the twins shared the larger one. Joe and I had the big one at the end overlooking the view to the water. Mind you, Jason used to like to sleep out on the side verandah a lot with his dog. Now, here are the bathrooms, which always surprise people.' Maggie chuckled. 'They're doubles.'

She slid the door open to reveal two large adjoining bathrooms with twin showers and a bathtub that faced onto a shared open-air courtyard planted with tubs of lavender and screened by a tidy forest of rhapis palms. These were sheltered on each side by widely spaced louvred cedar shutters. Above the showers a huge skylight opened to the sky.

'We love the breeze in summer, and in winter the sun dries the bathroom quickly after a shower.'

'The courtyard would be a great spot for a hot tub spa,' said Dominic.

'They weren't common then and, anyway, we couldn't afford one. We liked the bath opening to the outdoors. This was all considered rather bohemian back then.' Maggie smiled. 'A bit like swimming nude at the beach.'

Dominic breathed in deeply. 'Wow, smell that lavender.'

Maggie inhaled, a slight smile curving at her lips, her eyes closed.

*

'Hmmmm . . . what smells so nice? There's magic in the water,' said Joe softly as he lowered his face and kissed Maggie's shoulder beneath him.

Their wet bodies slid further into the oily warm bubbles, causing water to slosh over the rim of the tub.

'Only lavender. I thought it would be relaxing.'

Joe chuckled. 'Relaxing enough.' He wrapped his arms around her slim body, pulling her to him once more and kissing her throat.

She wrapped her legs around his hips and pulled him to her . . . then her buttocks slipped and their entwined bodies skidded beneath the water.

They sat up, spluttering and laughing.

'Well, at least we've christened the tub!' Joe laughed.

*

Maggie opened her eyes and smiled at Dominic. 'Yes, lavender always brings back happy memories for me.'

Dominic looked at her weather-beaten, tanned face and suddenly glimpsed the creases softening, her eyes wide and sparkling, a mischievous curve to her mouth and saw for an instant a young woman, deeply in love.

Maggie turned away. 'Come and see the rest.'

The house was very much a home, filled with photos, paintings, books, colourful rugs on the polished wood floors and memorabilia all around. Dominic had the feeling little had changed since Joe was there.

Even the laundry was spacious and bright, with a skylight that also revealed treetops.

'See,' Maggie pointed to the notations beside the doorway, 'we marked the children's height as they grew. Always a lot of competition between the twins.'

'The whole house is stunning, Maggie. Be worth a lot of money now, you know,' said Dominic, but Maggie lifted her hand.

'I know. But this is my home. Our home.'

Dominic followed the straight-backed woman, wondering if 'our' meant her children or her husband. The kids had moved on. He felt that, no matter how understandable it was, Maggie was somehow stuck in a time warp, and he felt sad for her and realised this was not the time to probe into Joe's disappearance. They chatted amiably about gardens before Dominic thanked her and headed back to the boatshed to catch the last of the sunset with Woolly.

*

Several days later Dominic was standing in the general store flipping through a magazine when he heard Deidre exclaim, 'Marcia! Haven't seen you in our shop for months! Who're you visiting?'

'You girls! I've been craving your honey, the one with the honeycomb, so I thought I'd stop in and stock up on your goodies. Shopping in the supermarket near me is so boring.'

Dominic stuck his head around the corner of the newsstand. 'Hi, Marcia!'

'Hello, Dominic. How lovely to see you. Have you seen Maggie lately? We never have enough time to chat properly at book club. Sam and Gloria sometimes drop in to see me but generally only when they're out on errands. How are things with you?' She tilted her head, giving him a faintly quizzical look.

'Going along okay, thanks. I had a drink with Maggie recently.' Remembering something Maggie had said, Dominic continued, 'Actually, she mentioned her old friends Andrew and Colleen. Do you happen to know if they're still in the area?'

'Sure I do. They live at the village in The Vale. Would you like to meet them?'

It took a second for Dominic to work out that by 'village' Marcia didn't mean a small quaint English town but the over-fifty-fives lifestyle village a short distance away. 'Oh, right. That'd be great, if it's not too much trouble.'

Marcia looked at Dominic curiously, and he explained, 'It's a long story, but I've been having a bit of a chat to Maggie about the past. I think it would be good to talk to Andrew and Colleen about their memories of the time.'

'Is this the honey you want, Marcia?' Deidre reappeared, holding out a fat jar of local honey.

'Yes indeed, that's the one, thanks, Deidre. So yummy. Smells like wattle after a spring shower.' Marcia turned to Dominic. 'So, would you like me to organise a visit? I could ask Andrew and Colleen, if you'd like? I could come too, introduce you.'

'Thanks, Marcia, I would. That would be great. I know the place – pretty buildings surrounded by trees and gardens?'

'That's the one. How about Thursday? That's between Tuesday book club and Friday tennis. Say three-ish? I'll let you know if that doesn't work for Andrew and Colleen.'

'Wonderful. See you then. Let me know if I can bring anything.'

*

The low buildings of the retirement village had a lot of windows and were embraced by greenery and lawns. Many shrubs were in flower, sheltering twittering birdlife. Bees buzzed. Established shady trees gave privacy, coolness and a sense of security, though a discreet dark-green metal fence around the perimeter was an additional safeguard. It looked safe, stylish and comfortable. *If you had to live in a multi-complex community, this was better than most,* Dominic thought. However, it struck him that although he lived in a compact space, he preferred his surroundings of wild natural bushland, the expanse of water and the privacy, all of which gave him a huge sense of freedom, spaciousness and independence.

Dominic met Marcia at the main reception and they set out together through the complex. Andrew and Colleen lived in a low block of single-storey units, sensitively positioned among three-floor units with balconies. Each building was designed so everyone had a choice of view, shade, sun, garden, lawns and privacy.

When they reached number 10, Marcia knocked and the door was flung open to reveal two smiling faces. Andrew had thinning grey hair, a silver moustache and a hearty manner, whereas Colleen was sweet-faced and much shorter than her lanky husband.

'Welcome!' said Colleen, ushering them in.

Following Marcia inside, Dominic saw that the interior was airy, modern and compact.

'Good to see you, Marcia, and lovely to meet you, Dominic. Marcia has told us all about you. I'll get us some tea – why don't you head outside? It's a lovely day,' said Colleen.

Through the back doors there was a small covered patio with a portable barbecue and table setting, surrounded by flower beds. A hammock swung between two trees while a fence of shrubbery divided the garden from the neighbours on either side.

'This is very well designed,' commented Dominic. 'A greedy developer would have jammed in a lot more floors and units.'

'This place costs a lot, but it's worth it,' said Andrew. 'We're allowed small pets, too. We look after our neighbour's dog if they go out or away, so we don't need one of our own.' Andrew smiled. 'We used to live in WestWater, and sometimes we do miss the privacy and the bush, but, well, we felt we should make the move while we were fit enough and had the opportunity to buy in here. The neighbours are great, and we don't invade each other's space, but they're there for a cuppa or if we need a hand. At least there's no traffic or city noise. Plenty of birds.'

Before he could say more, Colleen bustled outside with a tray covered in tea things and biscuits. They all settled comfortably at the little outside table in the afternoon sun.

'So what brings you down this way, Dominic?' asked Andrew.

'Oh, taking time out professionally, making one of those life adjustments, I guess. Where to now, that sort of thing.' Dominic smiled, wondering if Marcia had filled them in on his whys and wherefores.

Colleen nodded. 'We know what you mean. We were at that stage when we were young, before we had the children. That's really why Andrew decided to do the exchange program. I'm so glad we did, it was very interesting. Certainly gave us a taste for travel. But we were glad to come back home after our twelve months. We did make a trip back to England a few years ago, though.'

'We've done a few cruises – easy way to do things – but frankly we prefer independent travel. What about you? At your age you should be out seeing the world,' said Andrew.

Dominic couldn't help smiling at his schoolteacherish tone. 'I agree. And I plan to do so one day. I've been to Asia and Hawaii. But I'd rather like to explore my own backyard first. I just feel I need a reason, a purpose to it. Be inspired in some way.'

Andrew nodded approvingly. 'When you go, keep a diary. You'll find it very useful later on. One tends to forget things. Very interesting to read one's notes later in life.'

'Young people don't keep diaries any more,' said Colleen. 'They take photos on their phone instead. Did you keep a diary, Marcia?'

Dominic was surprised when Marcia nodded enthusiastically. 'I did. I was an only child of a single parent. It was a habit I kept for years, even as an adult. Haven't looked at them in yonks.'

Andrew intervened, taking over the conversation. 'So, Dominic, I believe you wanted to meet us?'

Dominic was a bit taken aback at his directness, but he replied, 'Actually, it's because of Josie. We were at Sam and Gloria's one night and out of the blue she opened up to me about her father's disappearance.'

'Really? That's unusual,' said Colleen. 'No offence, dear. It's just something that family never mentions. Or so I thought.'

Dominic nodded. 'So I believe. Josie told me after-wards she just hit a wall and wanted to start clearing the air about the whole thing. Not just the not knowing what happened to their father, but also because it has been such a taboo subject in the family. None of them ever mention it, never talk about him. I have some time on my hands, so she asked if I could help in some way, maybe gently look into it. So I've been chatting to people who knew Joe.'

'It was a dreadful, dreadful sad business. Most puzzling.' Andrew shook his head.

'Were you close friends?'

'Good friends, yes. Joe was a wonderful teacher, quite gifted. Inspired students to go that extra mile. Cared for every student no matter their ability. I moved to another school in the area some months after we came back from the UK but Joe stayed on, and I could have stayed at that school too but I was offered a position with more admin-istrative duties which I rather liked. We kept in touch, though, and we did socialise with them every so often. We were all busy with young families.'

'Those were the days.' Colleen smiled fondly. 'Remember the time we went to the races with them?'

'Horseracing?' Dominic raised his eyebrows. He'd never been to a race meeting in his life. Watching the

Melbourne Cup on TV each year was as close as he'd come.

'Oh, it was so popular back in the seventies!' put in Andrew. 'Still is, of course, but back then there were hardly any overseas horses except for New Zealand ones. Anyone felt they could have a go, whether by being part of a syndicate or picking a winner. The Saturday races was a fun day out for people back then; Randwick, Rosehill, Warwick Farm and Canterbury racetracks were always busy. We went with Joe and Maggie a couple of times to Randwick. We couldn't afford to be members, but had an enjoyable time on the flat, you girls in your maxi skirts – eating Chiko rolls and burgers!' Andrew laughed.

'Oh, we had some posh picnics too, on occasion,' Colleen reminded him.

'Did you ever win much? Or keep an interest in the horses?' asked Dominic. Marcia was leaning forward, looking intrigued.

Andrew and Colleen chuckled and looked at each other. 'No! We picked the horses by name association or lucky colours and numbers. But that Joe . . . what a character. He loved the horses,' said Colleen.

'Remember the Silvermaster's Cup?!'

*

'It's a sure thing,' whispered Joe when Maggie found him in the queue waiting to place a bet with the bookmaker Clarry Sturgess.

'There's no such thing, Joe! Colleen and I will be on the flat. Andrew is in the line for the food.'

'I thought you brought a picnic?'

'We did. But Andrew wants those horrible fried things.'

162

Joe grimaced and turned his attention to the bookie's board and the changing betting odds.

Maggie and Colleen were seated on the grass 'flat' encircled by the racetrack. They faced the stands and while they didn't have the overview of the race from up high, they were close to the rails at the finish so that sweat and dirt flew into their faces as the winner pounded across the line. It was exhilarating and they found themselves jumping up and down and pummelling the air even if they hadn't had a bet on that race.

In between the men placing bets and buying drinks, the women packed up the picnic and were sitting in the sun when Joe and Andrew returned.

'Having a good day, girls?' asked Andrew.

'Certainly are. What have you boys been up to?' asked Colleen.

'We had a beer, chatted to some interesting fellows.' Andrew grinned at Joe. 'Joe has the bit between his teeth now.'

'What's that mean?' asked Maggie, raising an eyebrow at her husband.

Joe sat down on the grass, stretching out his legs. 'Mags, we met these chaps – Arabs they call themselves –'

'You mean they had robes and turbans? I heard they're getting into the racing here,' said Colleen.

Joe laughed. 'Not at all, they're Aussies who belong to the Australian Racing and Breeding Stable. It's a scheme to help people like us battlers get into racing. Take an interest in, as in owning, a racehorse – or at least, part of one!'

'Are you mad?!' exclaimed Colleen as Maggie laughed.

'No, seriously, dear . . . it doesn't have to cost much, depending on how many are in the syndicate,' explained Andrew.

'Imagine watching your own horse win!' exclaimed Joe. 'Let's look into it just for fun!'

'Who gets to name the horse?' asked Maggie, playing along.

'I think it has a name by the time it's been trained,' said Joe seriously.

'C'mon, you two big-time racehorse owners, let's put the stuff in the car and go mingle in the paddock for a bit. See who's swanning in the birdcage,' Colleen said cheerfully.

'Can't stay too much longer, I'm afraid. Sam and Gloria are looking after the kids. It will have been a long day for them,' said Maggie.

'All right. I wouldn't mind a glass of bubbly to finish the day,' said Colleen. 'Then we'll head home.'

'With our huge winnings,' joked Maggie.

'No joke,' said Joe with an arch look as he dug in his pocket and pulled out a fistful of bills which he stacked on the grass.

'Hells bells,' exclaimed Andrew.

'Joe! You won this?' Maggie tentatively leaned out to touch the notes. 'How much is here? These are hundred-dollar bills!'

'Long odds on Champagne Glory in the Silvermaster's Cup,' said Joe proudly.

'Not bad for a two-dollar bet,' said Andrew.

'And the rest,' remarked Joe.

'There's got to be a couple of thousand dollars here,' said Andrew quietly.

'I've never seen so much cash at one time before,' said Colleen in awe.

'Oh my, now we can have a proper holiday like we've been promising the kids,' said Maggie.

'Maybe.' Joe smiled. 'Come on, let's go and mingle with the rich and famous,' he said, stuffing the wads of bills into his jacket and pulling Maggie to her feet.

*

'I remember that day so well,' said Colleen.

'So did they go on a holiday?' Dominic asked.

A shadow flitted across Andrew's face. 'Not really. I seem to recall the money diminished as Joe lost a heap on the last race.' He glanced at Colleen. 'Perhaps an omen of things to come.'

Dominic caught his breath. 'Joe gambled? Did it become serious?'

'I don't think it was the betting so much as that he kept joining syndicates and there were endless expenses. We stuck to betting matchsticks on Monopoly and card games.'

'For a smart man, Joe did have a silly streak when it came to horses,' said Colleen.

'I see,' said Dominic thoughtfully, wondering if he could raise the issue with Maggie next time they met. *Had Joe's gambling been a problem?* he wondered.

Possibly this issue opened a door into new dark and dangerous territory.

*

Back at the boatshed, Dominic sat down to update his notes, which he saved in a folder he called *Maggie, Joe and Co*. He'd also started a list of questions awaiting answers, which was now growing longer. The scenario of the missing man was all very puzzling and confusing, but he had to admit, it was becoming more intriguing by the minute.

Just as he was reading through the documents a second time, his phone pinged with a text message from his sister.

Kids have a school event over your way tomorrow afternoon. I'll drop by for a coffee for an hour . . . 2 pm OK? Cyn x

*

'You've made yourself quite at home,' said Cynthia as she gazed around the main room, seeing Dominic's books, the small, cluttered desk, fresh greenery and flowers from Sam and Gloria's garden – a thank you for the mud crabs – as well as a beach towel and fishing rod at the ready on the deck. The cat was curled up in the new fluffy bed Dominic had bought him.

'It's compact but very comfy,' agreed Dominic as he carried the tray with coffee things and a plate of biscuits to the table on the deck in the sunshine.

He poured their coffee. 'So how's the family? Have you seen Mum and Dad lately?'

'Yep, they're fine. They wish you'd visit more. They don't like to interrupt you too much. I think Mum is expecting you to produce something amazing.'

'What, like a hit novel or something?'

'Well, no. But that would be acceptable. Come over for dinner on Sunday. Bring a nice girlfriend. That'd make them happy.'

'Okay. But it'll just be me.'

'You're not lonely down here? What about your mates, friends?'

Dominic shrugged. 'I've seen Rob a bit. But since I left my job I don't have much in common with them and I'm too far out of town to meet for a quick drink. I've been hanging out with some of the locals here, though.'

'Like who?'

'Well, there's a bunch of nice women here. A gay couple run the general store, and Marcia makes amazing handbags . . .' Dominic paused suddenly, making a mental note to ask Marcia if he could buy one for Cynthia. 'There're the locals who've lived here most of their lives. An interesting bunch. One of their grand-daughters is about fifteen, a really nice kid. She's not here often, though. And an eccentric guy who lives alone in the hills . . . .' He stopped, seeing Cynthia's face, and laughed. 'Yes, I know what you're thinking. It's a bit of a parallel universe compared to the city.'

'It is awfully pretty here. A world of its own, really. If you didn't turn off the road down here you'd never really know how beautiful, how secret it is. Very different from the vibe of the trendy influencers and obscenely rich out at the beach.' Seeing Dominic nod in agreement, Cynthia added, 'But you can't stay here forever, remember.'

'Well, no. Not here . . . Nigel will be back in a few months, anyway.'

'But . . .?' Cynthia looked at him searchingly and reached for a biscuit. 'You'll have to make plans even-tually, Dom.' And before he answered, she bit into the biscuit, exclaiming, 'My God, these are divine! Where'd you get them?'

'Gloria up the hill made them. Maggie does cakes.'

'Those women are spoiling you. Seriously, just what *are* you doing here?'

'You mean apart from my writing gigs? Actually, I'm digging around into a twenty-five-year-old mystery.'

Dominic started to explain, setting out as clearly as he could the facts of Joe's disappearance, the effect it had had on friends and especially the family, the sheer mystery of it all. Then he described how Josie had spoken to him, and Rob's suggestion that Dominic might find ideas for a book in it. Finally he said, 'Well, now that I've got this far, I'm not sure where to go with it next.'

Cynthia was staring at him, intrigued. 'It seems so utterly . . . strange. Especially given what you say about this guy's wife and family. But if the police or detectives have never found anything, why are you persisting? What's your mate Rob have to say about it?'

'He thinks there's a story to sell in it. But I'm not sure how, or if I even want to . . .'

'There isn't a story if you don't have a finale, is there? I mean, everyone will want to know what happened, so how do you solve the mystery?' asked Cynthia.

'Well, that's just it. I don't know. Anyway, I'm just following my gut instinct for the moment, and this has been a welcome distraction. Imagine the good it could do if I found any answers?'

Cynthia nodded. 'Thank goodness your mortgage is being paid by your tenant,' she added.

'True. Anyway –' began Dominic, then stopped as he saw Alicia walking towards the boatshed. She lifted a hand and waved.

Cynthia raised her eyebrows. 'Is this another distraction?'

Alicia was in brief shorts, showing off her long legs, and a shirt loosely knotted under her breasts, revealing her tanned midriff. Gold chains glinted and a gold snake bracelet with ruby eyes coiled around an arm. She wore heeled white sandals that appeared to have colourful jelly beans glued to them. She was empty-handed. She strolled around the side of the boatshed as Dominic quickly murmured, 'She lives locally. Just a friend.'

Cynthia shrugged. 'Okay.'

'Hey, Alicia. How are you?' Dominic stood up, gesturing to an empty chair.

Alicia came to him, kissing him on the cheek and pressing herself against him as a bemused Cynthia rolled her eyes behind Alicia's back.

Pulling away, Alicia turned to Cynthia. 'Hi. I'm Alicia. I'm a neighbour.'

Dominic couldn't help but note the faint challenge in Alicia's bright smile and cold eyes.

'Hello. I'm Dom's sister, Cynthia.' She held out her hand.

'Well, how nice to meet some of your family at last,' said Alicia brightly as she sat down, crossing her legs and reaching for a biscuit.

'Do you want a coffee, Alicia?' Dominic asked.

'Oh please, yes. I'm exhausted.' And as Dominic moved to go inside, she smiled. 'You know how I like it. The coffee, that is.' She winked at him before he turned away.

'So you're a local too,' said Cynthia calmly. 'Where's your place? It's such a lovely area.'

Alicia waved vaguely. 'Over the hill, down the road. I'm out walking. By boat, it's nine minutes.'

'How convenient,' said Cynthia politely. 'Do you work around here?' She paused a beat. 'Or not?'

Returning with the coffee, Dominic jumped in, recognising what the family called Cynthia's smiling assassin tone. 'Alicia works for a big lifestyle village company. They're doing some innovative contemporary installations in the area.'

'Retirement homes?' asked Cynthia, her eyes flicking over Alicia's scanty clothing.

'Cyn,' said Dom quietly, shooting her a warning look.

'You mean the glam retirees who can afford to opt out of the rat race and walk barefoot along the beach, holding hands in a muslin dress and half-buttoned shirt, hearing in the distance their share prices clicking happily upwards?'

Alicia laughed lightly. 'I like your sister's sense of humour, Dom dear.'

Dominic swiftly directed the conversation back to general chitchat, then politics, where he was on firmer ground, and the latest abhorrent proclamation from the PM. 'Really, he has to go, he's a total embarrassment,' he said.

'That's putting it politely,' said Cynthia. 'I'm glad you're still keeping up with the issues.'

'Easier to criticise when one isn't directly involved.' Dominic grinned. 'Besides, criticism of the PM sells as it has a big receptive audience.'

Alicia kept quiet through their talk, munching on a third biscuit.

'Do you follow politics at all, Alicia?' asked Cynthia.

'I don't need to,' she said breezily. 'I work in private enterprise and my boss is pretty happy with the current state of play.' She unfolded herself and stood up. 'I'll leave you and your sister to catch up, Dom. See you later, Woolly,' she called to the cat lazing in the sun. Woolly ignored her. Alicia gave Cynthia a smile that failed to reach her eyes.

Dominic jumped to his feet, but she waved him to sit down. 'Bye, Dom, I'll drop your things in later.' She sash-ayed away down the side of the boatshed.

There was silence for a few moments until Alicia was out of earshot.

Cynthia looked at Dominic and raised her eyebrows. 'Things?'

Dominic shook his head. 'I have no idea what she's talking about. I don't even know where she lives.'

'I wouldn't trust her for love or money. I'm assuming you know that? A go-getter, as Mum says, and not in the complimentary way. A user, I would say.'

'That's a fast judgement call,' said Dominic.

'Just be careful, Dom. I know the type. The jewellery is real and she hasn't walked far in those heels, which, by the way, are Louboutin.' Cynthia put down her empty mug. 'I gotta go get the kids.'

'You don't have to treat me like a kid brother, although I know you mean well. Woolly loathes her.'

Cynthia stood up with a parting shot. 'Lifestyle living? Whatever. Big bucks business. Anyway, she doesn't seem your type.' Her voice softened. 'You need to come back to the big smoke for a bit. Get grounded. Have a night on the town with Rob, or some other pals.' She leaned over and kissed him. 'Come and spend time with your family. We miss you. See you for dinner Sunday?'

He watched Cynthia walk back to her car. Good old Cyn, ever the big sister. Telling him how it was.

But the memory of Alicia's legs and braless breasts escaping her shirt was hard to shake.

7

Dominic was standing in the wheelhouse beside Sam as his ferry chugged towards Welsh Island.

'Just got one more stop before I call it quits, Dom,' said Sam over the noise of the engine. 'Some mail for the Hoffmans. Poor old buggers don't get out a lot, they're getting on. Ralph used to go to The Point every day a few years back. But Glenda, his wife, never liked going in their little boat. Besides, the old runabout is a devil to start. That's why I drop off their mail and milk. This is the last run of the day and I've got no passengers, so we can pop up and see them if you like. They've got a very nice place.'

There was a young boy fishing beside a motor launch tied to the broad jetty as Sam expertly pulled alongside and tossed the painter rope to the boy.

'Can you throw the loop over the pylon, please?'

'Sure, Sam. Will I put the milk in Mr Hoffman's box?' replied the boy, grabbing the rope.

'She's right, thanks, son. We'll just take it to their door and say hello. Can you please keep an eye on things here?'

'Sure thing!'

Sam and Dom climbed onto the broad steps of the old wharf, walking through a shelter which had two old benches either side and a couple of boxes with surnames painted on them.

'This is the public wharf for the island, unofficial mail and message centre. A place for the kids to wait for the school ferry when it's raining,' explained Sam.

It was a pretty walk around the waterfront across lawns to where a large white house with a red tile roof and gracious gardens faced Crouching Island that marked the entrance to WestWater.

'This is like a park, how lovely,' exclaimed Dominic.

'The Hoffmans have been here decades, just as long as we have. This was a weekender until they retired, all bush with wallabies in the front yard. The family used to own several jewellery stores that have long been swallowed up by a big international mob.'

'So I take it they live here permanently now?'

'Yes, they have help. Wendy comes in every day. She and her hubby live on the other side of the island, so that's handy. The Hoffmans hardly leave here now, but all their family troop over regularly to see them. Their son keeps their beautiful old Halvorsen cruiser at Hunters Hill and brings it here every so often for family events.'

Dominic heard a friendly call as an elderly man came towards them from the side of the house. He wore a straw hat and carried a walking stick which he lifted in a genial wave. 'Ho there, Sam!'

They shook hands and Sam said, 'This is my neighbour, Dominic. He's housesitting Nigel's boatshed for a few months. We're just doing the last run so you get door-to-door delivery today, Ralph.'

'Kind of you. Glenda is having a bit of a kip or I'd ask you in for a beverage. Maybe next time, eh? So lad, how do you like WestWater now you've found us?'

'I like it very much. I must say this area is a well-kept secret,' said Dominic.

'Secret is right. We try not to broadcast what we have here. Oh, I say . . . here's the champ!' Ralph turned as a large dog raced towards them with a friendly bark.

'This *is* the champ.' Sam grinned. 'Raffles has won the Island to Point race three times. Haven't you, old fella,' he said, patting the black and white dog.

'Does Raffles compete in dog trials?' Dominic asked curiously.

'He wouldn't win anything on dry land! He's a Heinz 57 mix. Thinks he's a fish,' said Ralph cheerfully.

'The Island to Point is an annual swimming race wharf to wharf. They start the dogs and get them to follow the lead boat,' explained Sam.

'What about sharks?' asked Dominic.

'Ah, there's a bit of a flotilla around them, a lot of banging noises. Dogs must think it's to egg them on.' Ralph chuckled. 'Raffles outswims the lot.'

'Well, then you are a champ,' said Dominic, scratching behind the dog's ears. He straightened up. 'I understand you've been here a long time, Ralph,' he continued.

'Guess you could say Glennie and I are almost locals.' He smiled. 'Coming up for forty years soon.'

Dominic hesitated but Sam broke in.

'Dom here is a writer of sorts. He's interested in the area, its history.'

'What do you write? Fact or fiction?' asked Ralph.

'A bit of both, I suppose. I'm still researching and thinking, really,' said Dominic.

'A lot of good stories around here, that's for sure,' said Ralph.

'You and Glenda could be a story. About how your family escaped from Europe in the thirties,' prompted Sam.

'Yes, I can imagine there are a lot of interesting stories around here,' said Dominic. He paused then asked, 'Did you know Joe Gordon, by any chance?'

Ralph nodded. 'Sadly, most of us back then came to know his name whether we actually knew him or not. I think Glennie knows his wife, a nice woman apparently, still lives over in Flounder Bay.'

'Yes, I've met Maggie,' said Dominic. 'Strange business; Joe's disappearance is certainly a mystery.'

'It's only a mystery until it's solved, lad,' said Ralph with a slight smile.

'Be a miracle if anyone ever finds out what happened to Joe,' said Sam. 'Well, best be getting on. See you, Ralph. Say hello to Glenda for me.'

'Charming man,' said Dominic as they walked back to the wharf. 'I bet he has a story to tell.'

Sam nodded. 'Like he said, lots of stories around here if you wanted to dig them out.'

*

Dominic was in the supermarket in The Vale the following day when his phone rang.

'Hiya, Maggie. How're things? Hey, I'm in the supermarket. Need anything?'

'Not really, but thanks for asking, Dom. Could you drop by on your way home? I want to ask you a favour.'

'Sure. I'll see you soon.'

*

'So how can I help you, Maggie?' Dominic asked as Maggie ushered him inside. 'I'm happy to do any digging in the garden or whatever might be required that meets my capabilities,' he smiled.

'Oh, nothing to do with my garden,' said Maggie. 'It's about our book club.'

They moved through to the lounge room and sat down.

'A group of my friends get together once a month to stretch our minds. We like to talk about things you wouldn't normally chat about, you know, not just politics and personalities. We all read the same book and analyse and talk about what we think of it. Of course, it's all very informal, and members can invite a friend or two. So I'd like to ask you to be our guest speaker at the next meeting.'

Dom was quite taken aback. 'Me? I haven't written anything! I mean, I haven't had a book published. And I'm not sure your club would be interested in the sort of papers and opinion pieces I tend to write.'

Maggie looked at him. 'I thought that was why you'd taken six months off? To break out and write a book?'

Dominic shrugged, rather at a loss for words. 'I'm not very far along,' he managed.

'Well, you could talk about what your plans are, or what you've done so far! Everyone in the club dreams of writing something. It'd be interesting to follow your progress, Dom,' said Maggie enthusiastically.

'I don't know about that, Maggie . . .' began Dominic, starting to feel guilty that he had written so little, and that his motivations for writing were becoming more entangled in Maggie's own story by the day.

'You could pop in every few weeks or months and let us know where you're up to!' said Maggie.

Dominic hesitated. 'Oh. I would just do it as a one-off, I think. I wouldn't like to commit to something regular.' He shifted in his seat.

'Thanks, Dom. I know Marcia and the others will be thrilled if you pop along.'

'Of course. Love to meet them all,' he said.

'Well, I think you'll be wonderful,' and the matter was settled. 'We'll so look forward to your talk.' She turned and stared out the window. 'I do love getting out each month with the girls.'

'Do you get out much other than that, Maggie? Do you ever get lonely?' asked Dominic gently.

Maggie was quiet a moment. 'I wouldn't say this to the kids, but I tell Joe everything, every day. Just in my head.' She gave a small smile. 'I like to think that I know what he'd say. Sometimes we have a few laughs at silly things.'

Dominic nodded, feeling at a loss for words, but before he could think of anything to say, Maggie went on, 'It's like Joe is with me, just in the next room. Or out in the garden.'

'That must be comforting. I understand why you're so embedded in this house.'

'Be like losing a part of me if I ever had to leave here.'

*

Several days later, Dominic called in to Maggie's again to borrow the book that everyone was reading for the book club.

'You got time for a coffee, Dom?'

'Always,' he answered.

As she put the kettle on and got out coffee mugs, the doorbell rang.

'I don't know who that can be. Everyone I know just sings out and doesn't bother with the doorbell.'

Dominic heard Maggie greet someone and bring them inside.

'Dom, this is Leo Banks, an old friend of the family,' Maggie said as she re-entered the kitchen with a stranger in her wake. 'Went to school with Josie. A couple of years below, was it, Leo? He and his dad lived up the back for years – not sure if you've seen the place, Dom? – right at the top of the steep stairs above our property. Leo owns a local real estate agency and has done very well for himself. Haven't you, Leo?'

'I do all right.' The man smiled but to Dominic he looked smug.

Dominic nodded politely at Leo, noting he was in his mid-thirties, very tall and thin with jutting cheek-bones and no doubt a sharp and bony body. His hair looked slimy with some substance gluing it in place. Leo peered at Dominic through owlish glasses and gave a bright professional smile which looked as genuine as a shark's – *too many teeth in too big a mouth*, thought Dominic.

Maggie fussed, taking out another mug and insisting they sit at the kitchen table as she put a plate of biscuits in front of them.

'Been a while, Leo. How're things?' asked Maggie.

'All good. Work is keeping me busy. The real estate business is very buoyant these days. You're looking well, Mrs G. The garden looks terrific.'

'Oh, you haven't seen the half of it. You wouldn't recognise it now. Jason has helped me over the years. He's designed a nature forest for me using all native plants and trees. It looks wonderful. Feels like you're in a magic forest.'

'I didn't realise this place was so big,' said Dominic.

'Our land runs into the boundary to the national park, a bit rugged to build on, but we liked that,' said Maggie. 'I love the wildlife, especially the koalas. Though when we first moved here we had wallabies coming down to eat the garden. Which for a week we thought was exciting, then we put a fence up.'

'Bushfires must be a concern, though,' said Dominic.

'We have a very good volunteer fire service at The Point. Snowy keeps an eye on things, too,' said Maggie.

'This place would now be worth a large sum,' said Leo carefully. 'What if you were made a fantastic offer for it?' There was that professional smile again.

'And pigs might fly. There's not enough money in the world, Leo, for me to sell,' Maggie said firmly.

'There could be. I thought I saw a pig fly past on your driveway.' He gave a strange giggle which was meant to be a chuckle, Dominic assumed.

Dominic remained silent, unamused.

Then, as Leo gave a slight shrug and looked down and sipped his coffee, Maggie's eyes narrowed.

'Just a minute, young man. You aren't trying to size me up, are you?' she said evenly.

'C'mon, Mrs G, we've been friends a long time,' started Leo.

'I haven't seen much of you since your schooldays. So it seems a little bit odd that you'd turn up now like it was only yesterday and start talking about how much my house is worth.'

And then, when Leo didn't answer immediately but gave a cocky half-smile, Maggie slammed her mug down, making the two men jump.

'Leo, I will make it very clear: I will NOT leave this house no matter how much money I am offered. This is my home! I designed this place. Joe and I helped build it with our own hands. I know every nook and cranny, every blade of grass on this land, and I will not leave it. I will die here!' she shouted.

'Steady on, Maggie . . .' Dominic tried.

'Who sent you here, Leo? Who's after my place? What makes you think I'd sell? Are you mad? As if I would. This is our *home*!'

Maggie got up and poured her mug of coffee down the sink.

'Mrs G, just hear me out . . . there's a buyer, Harold Marchant. He's prepared to give you heaps for this place. I was approached to see if you'd be interested. I mean, time goes by, you're on your own . . .'

Maggie stood gripping the edge of the sink, her back to the men. 'Well, the answer is no. I won't do a deal. Go tell your buyer to buy somewhere else. This house is not for sale.'

'Well, I had to ask, didn't I!' Leo threw up his hands. 'You can't blame me for trying to do you a favour. Harold Marchant wants to offer you a really good price for this place. You won't get a better one.' He ran his hand over his head and crossed his arms, his greasy palm leaving a smear on his shirtsleeve.

'I think Mrs Gordon's mind is made up,' said Dominic firmly.

Leo gave him a cold look, shrugged, and stood.

'Thanks for the coffee, Mrs Gordon. You know where to find me if you change your mind,' he said stiffly, and left the room.

Maggie didn't move as Leo's steps echoed on the polished wood floors. As the car drove away, Dominic quietly pushed back his chair and went and touched her shoulder.

'You okay, Maggie?'

'No!' She turned to face him. 'Vultures. Starting to hover before my body is even cold!' she snapped. 'We tried to help that kid and his wretched father. Thank goodness my kids moved on and had nothing to do with them.'

'C'mon, Maggie, sit down. You said no very clearly, so that should be the end of it. Shall I make you another coffee?'

'No. Forget it. But thank you, Dom. I'm glad you were here.'

'I suppose you could say it's hardly surprising you'd be approached by real estate people, given what's happening in the property market,' said Dominic. 'This is an enviable site, with its beautiful bushland setting, water views, and a unique home –'

'That Marchant man would cut down the trees, spoil our paradise . . . our hideaway . . .' Tears ran down her cheeks.

Dominic reached for her hand. 'It's okay, Maggie. It's your house, and no one can change that.' He paused. 'But you know, if you did sell, you could do anything you wanted to be comfortable in the decades to come. Money no object,' said Dominic reasonably. He didn't want to

181

upset her any further, but he was coming to suspect that Maggie's attachment to the house might not be entirely healthy.

'I am doing exactly what I want already, Dom,' she said, but she sounded calmer now.

'Fine. Then don't stress. It's your decision.'

'It was always Joe's and my decision. To stay here. Till the end,' she said quietly, then turned away. 'I'll just go wash my face. Excuse me, Dom.'

'I can stay if you want, Maggie.'

'I'm fine. But finish your coffee.'

*

Dominic left quietly and once back at the boatshed, he pulled a cold beer from his fridge and sat sipping it, mulling over the odious Leo.

Finally he rang Alicia.

'Nice to hear from you,' she said as she picked up.

'I've just been with my neighbour, Maggie Gordon. A realtor guy called Leo Banks dropped by while I was there and told her Harold Marchant wanted to buy her place. Do you know about this?'

'Tell me again how you know Maggie Gordon?' Alicia asked, and Dominic could hear the guarded note in her voice.

'She's a neighbour. And pretty upset, actually. She has no intention of leaving her home.'

'She'll come round. They always do. It's hard to resist the big bucks,' said Alicia dismissively.

'What do you know about it?' persisted Dominic.

'Just that Harold wants her place.'

'Really? I can't see Harold moving into Maggie's house,' said Dominic.

'No, of course not. He'll pull it down, it's far too small.'

'What! You're joking! Why would he want to build a place in the solitude of WestWater? It's not ritzy and glamorous,' Dominic exclaimed. 'Anyway, Maggie won't sell and that's that.'

'We'll see,' Alicia said easily. 'When am I going to see you?'

Dominic hesitated. It was hard to say no to Alicia, and he wanted to find out more about Harold Marchant's plans.

'Want to come over? Sunset drinks sound okay?'

'I'll bring some fruit for breakfast,' she said, and hung up.

*

First light seeped into the shadowy room, now so familiar to Dominic as he heard the gurgling of the full tide on the turn beneath the boatshed.

He rolled onto his side to reach for Alicia's naked body but found he was alone. It was a double bed against the wall; how had she climbed over him without him noticing? he wondered. Normally Woolly was stretched out at the foot of the bed, but whether from jealousy or some feline intuition, Woolly always disappeared when Alicia was around.

Dominic threw back the covers, reaching for his swim shorts and pulling them on as he smelled coffee.

'You've started the day?' he asked as he saw that Alicia was dressed, though her blonde hair was still attractively pillow-mussed and without make-up she looked softer, gentler.

She poured herself a coffee. 'How do you drink this crap?' She lifted her cup. 'Get a decent coffee machine.'

'Plunger does me. I don't tend to hang out with up-themselves super baristas in trendy cafés like you do.' He smiled. 'So what plans for the day? I thought you liked to laze around when you first woke up? But today you're up and at 'em!'

She shrugged, eyeing him over the rim of her coffee mug. 'I am.'

'Is it something to do with Harold's interest in Maggie's house?' Dominic asked casually.

Alicia raised an eyebrow as she took a sip and then put her mug down, folding her arms.

'Harold says he wants her place. He's used to getting his way. It's a great location. All this area is.' She nodded her head out towards the deck. 'That's all there is to it.'

'Yes, the area is beautiful. Which is why the locals want to keep it like this. A bit of a backwater, a secret setting. Not flash and pretentious. Real and natural,' said Dominic, with a bit more passion than he intended.

'Harold isn't planning any mega developments, no resorts, no luxurious facilities or lifestyle units here.'

'Thank goodness for that. So what *does* he want to do?' asked Dominic suspiciously.

'He wants to live here. He has a dream house he wants to build. A legacy for his family,' she said calmly.

Dom snorted. 'C'mon! His kids and grandkids are grown up. Do they care?'

She shrugged. 'Sure they do. So long as it's a good investment. Besides, it's not just your friend Maggie's house, he wants the two blocks on either side as well so he has all the land from the top of the ridge sweeping down to the bay. The house he builds will be an absolute show-stopper. One neighbour is ready to sign and the other is well on the way.'

'*What!* Surely not.'

'Money talks. He's offered more than the market value. He wants the three blocks for his estate.'

'*Estate?!*'

She shrugged. 'The usual – pool, bathing pavilion, tennis court, summer house, staff quarters, lift, the lot.'

Dominic was almost speechless. 'And of course that mega cruiser moored off the jetty,' he said sarcastically.

'No, I think his grandkids want speedboats for skiing.'

'Oh, so he's got it all planned out. Fait accompli,' said Dominic. 'Surely the council won't allow such a structure here.'

Alicia smiled. 'Oh, council planning is all taken care of, don't you worry.'

'I just can't see it happening if Maggie digs her heels in, though, will it?'

Alicia threw up her hands. 'Dominic, why do you care? She's not a relative of yours. You say you only just met her and you don't live here. You didn't know these people or the area a few months ago!'

'Well, I care *now*,' said Dominic with some heat. 'Can't you see that? I don't like how people like Harold just expect to get their way . . . no matter what. Putting pressure on her through Leo? That was not okay. What do you know about Leo? What's your connection?' He stopped, staring at Alicia's slightly bemused – no, *smug* – expression. 'You don't get it, do you? You actually don't care, either. Why do you work for Harold, Alicia?' Dominic shook his head despairingly. Then held up his hand. 'No, don't tell me. I don't want to know.'

'Fine. Are you going to spend the rest of your life like this, Dom?' She flung her hand around the boathouse.

'Unfocused, big dreams, all talk, no ambitions? Drifting along until someone rescues you? Props you up?'

'That's unfair, Alicia,' he said evenly. 'I do my own thing. I don't use people.'

She shrugged. 'Whatever. Listen, I have to go. I have a breakfast meeting.'

'You don't want to have any fruit?' Dominic lifted an eyebrow and gave a small smile.

'Sorry, Dom. I forgot to bring any.' She kicked back her chair and stood, picking up her shoulder bag from the floor and moving to stand by him. She leaned down and kissed his cheek.

'Be careful, Dom. You're too soft. Especially for the likes of me,' she said quietly. She headed to the door, calling out to the skulking cat, 'See ya round, hey, Woolly.'

*

After breakfast, trying to distract himself from his unsettling conversation with Alicia, Dominic returned to his file on the Gordon family. Then he called Josie.

'Hi, Dom! Funny, I was just about to call you!'

'Ah, great minds and so on. I wanted to let you know I saw your mum yesterday. A real estate agent was sounding her out about an offer on her house. Leo Banks? I gather you know him?'

'Oh yes, Leo grew up just up the hill from us. Anyway, I'm sure Mum made it clear to him that she won't sell. She doesn't want to move,' said Josie.

'What about your siblings?' asked Dominic. 'What do they think?'

'To be honest, we've never discussed it. It's Mum's house, and we all know she wants to stay there.'

'Well, I just heard some rather unsettling news. The

interested buyer – Harold Marchant – has already made offers to the adjacent neighbours which apparently they're keen to accept. Your mum's in the middle. The buyer wants all three adjoining blocks sweeping down the hillside.'

There was silence as Josie caught her breath. 'I didn't know that. Good grief, what's he going to build that spreads over three blocks? Listen, Dom, I'll come down there tomorrow. Can I see you? Then I'll drop in and tell Mum about the neighbours.'

'Of course.'

'I'll come by after work, say three thirty?'

'Would you rather meet somewhere closer for you?'

'That would be great, actually. I have to pick up some school things for my daughter. There's a coffee shop at The Vale called Pinocchio's, do you know it? I could be there at three fifteen.'

'Fine. See you tomorrow.'

*

Josie looked concerned as she greeted Dominic. He signalled the waiter as he sat back down.

'Sorry, have I kept you waiting? I was late leaving work.' She ordered her coffee.

Dominic frowned. 'All good. You look upset, is everything okay?'

Josie tried to smile, struggled a bit and then ran her hand through her hair and sighed.

'Not really. One of the residents in the nursing home where I work passed away. It was not unexpected. Nancy was in her nineties, but I liked her immensely. She was one of those people who never wanted to be a bother to anyone. I used to find books she was after, bring her a sweet treat occasionally and take a bit of time to chat. Her mind was very much still in the present, but she did like to reminisce. Her family were scattered so rarely visited. She just slipped away quietly in her sleep, making no demands on the staff. Some people can be very demanding and difficult, but Nancy certainly wasn't one of those.'

'Losing people must be one of the harder parts of your job, I suppose,' said Dominic.

Josie nodded. 'It's the ones who don't want to make a fuss, who just die quietly alone, that I particularly feel for.' She hesitated, then said softly, 'Just like a withered leaf flutters to the ground and no one notices.' She sniffed. 'Sorry, I don't want to sound melodramatic. She was so lovely, such a contrast to some of our people who can be really difficult – like Leo's father, Dean Banks.'

'Why is that?'

'He's in a fairly early stage of dementia, but even before that he was demanding and illogical and created hell for everyone at the home. Mum says he's always been a difficult person.'

'It must be hard for older people who've had to leave their home just because they're frail,' said Dominic. 'Not everyone can move into an upscale lifestyle village like Colleen and Andrew have.'

'I've long thought there are better options and improvements that could be made as aged care expands as a market,' said Josie. 'Privately owned establishments tend to run on a tight budget, cutting corners and staff to save costs, and government-funded places have their budgets whittled away or left at the bottom of the "to do" lists of limping projects.' She shrugged and tried to smile. 'Not everyone likes to plan for the day they can't manage in their own home.'

'You're thinking of your mum?' Dominic hedged.

Josie nodded. 'She is adamant about not moving. But how much longer can she manage in that big house? Ten years or so? And then what? The longer she leaves it the harder it will be to move.'

'Her mind seems made up,' said Dominic. 'But it could be difficult if both sets of neighbours want to sell to Marchant.'

'She mustn't know about the neighbours yet or she would have said something to me. Not that she'd change her mind even if she did, and that could make life difficult for everyone. All the same, I can't blame Leo for encouraging her to sell. He wants his fat commission.' Josie looked distraught. 'Dominic, you know the real reason she won't sell? She thinks Dad is going to walk in the door one day!'

Josie dropped her head in her hands, her elbows on the table.

Dominic reached over and touched her arm. 'I can believe it. Maggie implied something similar when we spoke.'

Josie looked up, tears glinting in her eyes now. 'It's because she *needs* to believe it. She'll never accept that Dad's dead unless we know for sure. She's lived her life in limbo for years! She could have started a new life, but she didn't. She lived for the memory of Dad. It's as though she's stuck in a time warp!'

'Maybe making a move might be a good thing for her,' said Dominic. 'Give her a fresh start. Maybe you should talk to your siblings?'

'I could mention it to them; they might agree that the money would make her life easier and more comfortable. But we can't force Mum to sell – she's perfectly fit and sane. I just don't know what would be best.'

'Maybe Sam and Gloria could help?'

'Yes. I'll chat to them.' She straightened up, trying to smile. 'So, tell me what you've been up to. How's the writing coming along?'

'Just making notes, thoughts and ideas, though I am going along to Maggie's book club as a guest! My mother is in shock after I told her,' he said with a chuckle.

Josie smiled. 'It will be good practice. Wait till you're a published author, you'll be in high demand. Please don't let Mum boss you around. But we're all so grateful to you for keeping an eye on her. Sam and Gloria are great, but you're a breath of fresh air for her.'

'It's no trouble as I'm right there in the boatshed.'

'You're not neglecting your own parents, are you, by keeping an eye on Mum?'

'Of course not. I feel lucky that my mum and dad are happy and busy. Dad has retired but plays a lot of golf. Mum does some volunteer work, but she helps Cynthia, my sister, with her kids a lot. And she's still trying to matchmake and introduce me to a "nice girl". She's highly suspicious of online dating,' Dominic laughed.

'I tried that too, had a few okay encounters, but in the end I met Riley at a charity function and we just clicked. What about you?'

'I've worked with a lot of women so have had plenty of female company, but after seeing and hearing about my friend Rob's disastrous online encounters, I was turned off the idea,' Dominic said. 'I'm meeting him for a drink tonight, actually. I might pick his brains about Harold's offer as Rob is across the wheeling and dealing. Is that okay?'

'Go for it. I have no idea how to deal with this situation, especially as Mum's neighbours could make things so uncomfortable for her.' Josie sighed.

*

Rob was late, with the usual apologies as he sat down at a local bar near Dominic's parents' home.

'Sorry, mate. Got a last-minute call and had to chase up some info for them. Where're you off to, then?'

'Going round to Mum and Dad's for dinner. I'd like to run a few things past you first.'

'Sure. How're things down there with all your gang?' Rob grinned. 'Seen Alicia?'

'Yep. A few nights ago.'

'And . . .?'

Dominic frowned. 'We had a bit of a discussion over breakfast. Nothing unpleasant. But we decided to agree to disagree.'

Rob raised his eyebrows. 'You're sleeping with people for information? Shame on you. So? What'd you find out?'

He listened intently as Dominic outlined Harold's plans for a grand estate.

Rob shook his head. 'That'll be the end of WestWater.'

'Maggie won't sell.'

'What do Maggie's kids have to say? She could sit it out for a higher offer, I guess,' suggested Rob.

'An offer like Harold's only comes along once, I'd say. He's not going to hang about. He'll look elsewhere, and if he does, Maggie's neighbours will be really pissed off.'

'And Alicia is on board with the idea? I mean, what's her role in his business? I don't quite get it. Maybe Marchant keeps her around to look at. She's very fetching,' said Rob.

Dominic shook his head. 'True. But she's also very smart. Marchant might have money but he runs a tight fiscal ship by the sounds of things,' he said.

'When a man like Marchant makes up his mind, he doesn't like to lose. And there's not much either of us can

do about it. Could be a rocky road ahead for Maggie . . .'
Rob trailed off. 'So what other news? Have you found out
any more about Maggie's lost husband?' he asked.

'You make her sound careless! Seriously, she's still
waiting for him to come home. It's part of the reason
she's so set on staying in her home. It's really sad.'
Dominic sighed. 'Josie and Jason are keen for me to dig
around, but Paul isn't too fussed on the idea, and Simon
is downright hostile. I haven't spoken to the younger
sister, Holly, and the others tell me she was probably
too young at the time to remember much. However I did
meet Andrew and Colleen, their friends from the teacher
exchange who knew Joe well. He and Andrew stayed
pals when Andrew came back to Australia. Actually, one
thing they did tell me was how they all used to go to the
races every so often. Apparently Joe was super keen on
horses.'

'Betting on them?' asked Rob with interest.

'Yes, as well as owning them, it would appear.'

'How could he afford a racehorse on a schoolteacher's
salary?'

'Andrew said he used to buy into syndicates,' said
Dominic. 'A few hundred dollars a share, maybe. Gave
him the chance to be part of the world of racing. Mix with
the rich and famous in the saddling enclosure.'

'Did you see any framed photos of racehorses or a
prize cup or anything in Maggie's house?' asked Rob. 'I
know a racing guy. I'll see if he can find anyone who may
have known Joe.'

'That's a long shot, isn't it?' said Dominic.

Rob shrugged. 'You never know. Did Andrew say if
he ever won big? Or lost big?' he persisted.

'They told a story about a big win Joe had one day,

but apparently he frittered it away on the other races. I don't know if there were other times.'

'Maybe he did lose money. You're too trusting; you take everything at face value,' said Rob, finishing his wine.

Dominic gave a wry smile. 'I wouldn't say that. It's my cover. How else do you think I dug out the deals and dirt about some of our less illustrious politicians? Everyone liked me and trusted me. Thought I was their best friend.'

Rob had to smile in acknowledgement. 'Same with the women, huh?'

'Not really. See how they flock to me?' Dom chuckled, gesturing around him at the lack of any visible partner.

'I'm weeping into my beer,' said Rob.

'No you're not, you've downed two glasses of red. Look, I have to go. Can't be late for dinner with Mum and Dad. This is my treat.'

*

As Dominic pulled on a pair of cotton chinos, he was amused about having to wear trousers twice in two days. It seemed like he'd been living in shorts for months. It had been a lovely evening with his parents, Cynthia, Jeff and the kids, and he'd suggested they come to the boatshed for a barbecue sometime with Maggie, Gloria and Sam.

It had surprised him when Maggie had told him the book club was meeting for dinner at a small restaurant in The Vale.

'So how does this work, Maggie? I thought you'd meet at each other's houses or the library?' said Dominic as he helped Maggie into his car.

'A restaurant is a lot more fun. When I meet my trivia friends at the pub, it's too noisy. We have to hear what everyone has to say at book club, not just shout an answer.'

'What about bingo?'

'Lordy no, wouldn't play that in a fit,' declared Maggie. 'That's for old people!'

They were seated at a long table in the rear section of the little restaurant where it was quieter. Dominic was surprised to find he knew most of the women there – Maggie, Colleen, Deidre from the general store and Marcia. He was introduced to Suzanne, who was very skinny and serious, and Nola, who was chubby and jolly, making their names easy to remember. They were about Maggie's age; Suzanne lived at The Vale and Nola at The Point. Dominic thought if he was casting a dignified retired schoolteacher in a movie, she'd look exactly like Suzanne. Noticing his gaze, Colleen leaned in and whispered to him, 'Suzanne used to teach with Joe.'

'We've pre-ordered nibbles and food, just order and pay for your own drinks,' said Maggie to everyone.

'Here, let me,' said Dominic, but was gently pulled back to his seat.

'You're our guest of honour,' said Nola.

It was certainly informal. Maggie lifted her wineglass and welcomed everyone, introducing Dominic.

'Welcome to my new young friend and neighbour, Dominic. He is not only a helpful and kind friend to myself and other neighbours, but he has had an interesting career in the corridors of power witnessing the shenanigans of our pollies. He is writing a book, possibly a "tell-all shocker", eh, Dom?! Maybe he will tell us more about all that a bit later on. For now let's go around the table so everyone can give a comment on our book of the month.'

Dominic listened with interest, sometimes nodding and laughing at the funny, acerbic and thoughtful comments.

He looked at his notes and when it was his turn, gave a brief overview of the book and why he'd enjoyed it.

'You sound surprised you liked it,' said Marcia.

'Don't give us that line about "you don't normally read women's books,"' said Deidre.

'I certainly won't! I liked that it was set in Australia, in a place I've never been to and now want to go and see for myself,' said Dominic.

'Me too,' chimed in Nola. 'Harry and I want to do more travelling in Australia. He wants to buy a fancy caravan. We are so over cruises!'

The waiter brought their starters and there was more conversation about travel as they shared suggestions, ideas and anecdotes. Dominic went with the flow, as this seemed to be how they chatted. Colleen commented that she loved Paul Theroux's travel books. Dominic agreed, surprised at how much he was enjoying the company and conversation.

Next to him, Suzanne gave him a slight smile and leaned towards him. 'Our meetings are always like this – free-ranging chat. I hope you didn't come prepared with notes to address a hushed audience.'

'This is refreshing. Now I know why book clubs are so popular,' he said with a smile.

'Oh, some clubs take themselves terribly seriously and are full of pretentious bores,' she replied. 'But not us!'

'You're a teacher too, Marcia tells me? Are you still teaching?' asked Dominic.

'Kind of you to ask. No, I retired a few years ago. I was principal at The Vale School. I taught with Joe; that's how I know Maggie. Actually –' She lowered her voice a little. 'Colleen mentioned to me that you were curious about his case. We all are. But like life itself, his death will remain a mystery, I fear. Hard, of course, for Maggie to accept,' she said quietly as they glanced towards the end of the table where Maggie and Marcia were talking.

'Would you be willing to meet with me? I'd be very interested to know a bit about Joe's life as a teacher,' said Dominic.

'He was a natural teacher and leader. A great loss to us. Can't see that I can shed any light on anything personal, but I'm happy to reminisce about our time at the school.'

'Thank you, Suzanne. Can I have your number? I'll be in touch,' said Dominic, and as she recited it, he tapped her number into his phone.

Maggie called the table to order.

'Okay, everyone . . . let's hear from Dom. Tell us a bit about yourself, why you've stepped away from your career to . . . what? Pursue a dream?' said Maggie with a small smile.

Dominic put down his glass and drew a breath. 'There's not much to tell about myself that's terribly interesting. I come from a loving family, my parents are retired. I have an older sister who's a great pal, happily married with two kids. I graduated from uni with a degree in history and political science. I was interested in current affairs and was advised to do journalism. But it didn't appeal to me; I am a more retiring sort of fellow. I considered journalism to be a similar career to acting and politics.'

The women chuckled.

'However, I did like writing. And I did follow current affairs. And like a lot of things in life, I fell into a career when I met a friend of a friend who suggested I apply for a job attached to the office of a local MP. Luckily it was a woman I admired, and I agreed with her thinking and attitudes. Not always, of course, but in principle. So after a few years I moved up the ranks, writing speeches, policy portfolios, researching future initiatives, that sort of thing. There was a lot of pressure and long hours. Eventually I realised that I was living in something of a "bubble". Then in the last election, my MP lost her seat in the turmoil of our current times. And, well, I felt I needed to take a step away, move outside that pressurised life and do something for me.' He paused.

They were looking at him, listening attentively. Suzanne was nodding appreciatively, as if to a pleasing student. Maggie was smiling. All were watching him with warmth.

Dominic went on, 'I realised the thing I liked doing best was writing. Researching, analysing, finding the right words to express something I cared about. Occasionally attempting to influence public opinion . . . but through another person's voice.' He hesitated, then continued, 'I thought it was time I used my own voice to write about things that interest and concern me. I'm interested in other lives, other histories. Everyone has a story. I'd like to hear all of yours one day. Thank you.' He finished and they all clapped, causing some people in the restaurant to glance back at their table.

Marcia leaned across the table. 'Dom, I have a story or two for you! Might be X-rated, though!'

Everyone laughed and there was general chat as they debated about dessert.

During the dessert and coffee, Dominic moved along the table, sitting between different women for a personal brief chat, and smiled inwardly when he heard Colleen turn to Maggie and say, 'We have to find him a special girl. He's lovely.'

Maggie tapped her spoon on her coffee cup and all fell quiet.

'Now, Dom, as I mentioned to you earlier, we have a long-standing tradition that the guest chooses the next book for the club to read.'

Dominic nodded. 'I looked at travel, history, romance and crime. But since coming to live at WestWater I have a new awareness of place, identity and belonging. I also have a new longing to travel more in our own country. But I rather wish I could do it in the "olden days" of the 1950s and sixties. Like George Farwell. I find him to be a wonderful travel writer, apparently a charming and dashing Englishman who came out to Australia as a young man and stayed. He was a journalist, broadcaster and travel writer. He's published a heap of books with great old black and white photos of his travels around outback Australia and some of the Pacific Islands. I read *Australian Landscapes* and it brought the country – as it was then – to life.'

'You sound so enthusiastic about him. Why don't you write about WestWater?' said Nola.

'No! Don't do that! You'll have every man and his dog wanting to move there,' said Marcia.

'Well, we can all go travelling through books. Let's all do a favourite travel book for our next club . . . and share the stories. That way it will be like we've taken a trip,' said Maggie. She turned to Dominic. 'Thank you for coming and being such a sport and sharing your thoughts with us, Dom.'

'My pleasure. And thank you all for your company.' He smiled.

*

'You were a big hit,' said Maggie as she got out of the car. 'I so appreciate it. We don't get a guest very often, especially someone interesting and young. I'm going to search out George Farwell.'

'The library, eBay or second-hand bookshops are best, Maggie. I enjoyed the evening. Thanks for asking me. See you soon, eh?' He walked her to the front door and waited till the light went on inside before turning the car up the driveway and circling down to the waterfront.

He reached in his pocket for the door key, hearing a complaining meow from inside. Dominic glanced at the bit of paper he pulled out with his key, which Colleen had pushed into his hand as he'd said goodbye. Scribbled on it was a note – *Call Nola on this number. She could be helpful too . . .*

*

It was late morning. Dominic stood up and stretched his back. He'd been hunched over his laptop for several hours. As he got up he heard hurrying footsteps. Maggie called to him as she reached the deck.

'Dom, oh dear, something terrible has happened . . .'

'What! What is it, Maggie?' He hurried to meet her.

Maggie was in the doorway looking distressed.

'It's Paul! He's had a terrible accident at the beach . . . in the surf. The girl from the shop rang, the paramedics are there. I'm too upset to drive . . . Could you take me down there, please? Gloria and Sam aren't home. I'm so upset.'

Dominic took her arm and sat her on the sofa by the doors. 'What happened?'

'Some idiot kid on a surfboard speared across the wave and hit Paul in the neck as he was paddling out. They're scared to move him . . . Josie is on her way to him . . .' Maggie dropped her face into her hands. 'Oh dear heavens, what if he is paralysed for good . . .?'

'Maggie, it will be okay, the paramedics will know what to do,' said Dominic, trying to sound positive. 'Let's hop in the car and I'll drive you to wherever they take him. I'll just throw some shoes and a shirt on. I'll meet you outside.'

Maggie looked at him, her face twisted and distraught. 'I can't believe this has happened . . . I try so hard . . . to look after everyone, keep them safe . . .'

Dominic put his hands on her shoulders. 'It's not your fault, Maggie. Paul will be fine. C'mon, let's go. I'll call Josie and let her know we're coming.'

But his heart twisted as he saw her shoulders slump and hands shake. *Poor Maggie*, he thought. She'd been through so much.

8

DOMINIC WAITED IN HIS car. Within ten minutes Maggie called him.

'Hi, Dom. Paul has seen the doctor now and is in a neck brace. He's been very lucky. He has to recuperate slowly, so we'll get him sorted and he'll stay with me till he's back on his feet. Or back on his board, I should say!'

'That's a relief! Anything I can do, Maggie?'

'Thanks, Dom, we're fine. Josie can take me home. Paul should be let out in a day or so. I really appreciate your help.'

'No problem, Maggie. Any time. Give Paul my best and let me know how things are, or if you need anything.'

*

Dominic made contact with Suzanne from the book club but she was busy for the next week, so he looked through his papers for the note containing Nola's number instead, but couldn't find it. Annoyed with himself for misplacing it somewhere in the growing piles of papers and note-books that were heaped around the small boathouse, he turned his focus to his paid work instead. He kept his head down for several days, catching up on delivering a political opinion piece which a financial newspaper had commissioned.

He typed with some force as he tried to remain restrained and objective about yet another government rort. His informant in parliament had been blunt: 'Voters in the 'burbs and the bush have no idea how they're being ripped off.' At least he could bring this one scandal to light.

He finished the piece late one morning but decided to take a break before checking the article with fresh eyes. And at that moment he heard someone calling his name and CeeCee popped her head around the open folding doors.

'Hi, Dom! How's things?'

'Not bad CeeCee, how about you? C'mon in. I was just about to take a break. So, are you visiting your grand-parents for the weekend?'

'Yep. I have a break before my exams. I heard about Paul; he was lucky, eh?'

'Indeed. Do you surf? Ride a board?'

'Sometimes. Just to show off – if I can! Hey, can I please borrow your dinghy? I was going to go down the bay to the poet's house. I have to do a project for school.'

'Poet? Who's that? Don't think I've met him.'

CeeCee laughed. 'It's a her. And she's long gone. Dead, that is. Like, decades ago. I think she was sort of famous in her day. Anyway, she built an interesting old house up by the creek. I've only seen it through the trees from the water.'

'Who's living there now?'

CeeCee shrugged. 'I don't know. Thought I'd go round and knock on the door.'

'Don't your grandparents know them?'

'Grandad said it's only a weekender now and the owner hardly ever comes down; he hasn't taken anyone there in the ferry for ages.'

'Maybe they have their own boat,' suggested Dominic. 'You can't just trespass.'

'Just looking. Getting a feel for it. The poet wrote a lovely poem called "A path among the trees". I thought I might find it. The path, that is.'

'Well, sure. I'm happy to take you in the dinghy, if you don't mind me coming too. I'll check my crab pots while I'm at it,' said Dominic.

He held the boat steady as CeeCee settled onto the wooden seat. He pushed the oars into the oarlocks and stroked deftly away from the jetty. CeeCee sat facing him in the stern, watching the shore as they glided quietly towards the end of the bay. Her hair blew across her face, which was free of make-up, and she wore denim shorts, a T-shirt with the logo of some music group he vaguely recognised, and sneakers with hand-painted flowers on them which she must have done herself.

'Do you like poetry, then?' Dominic asked.

She shrugged. 'I guess so. Anyway, it's on the curriculum. I figure if I've gotta do the project, I might as well try to make it interesting.'

'Good idea. Being positive means you look at all the angles rather than just deciding it's boring and a pain. You never know what you might find. Don't accept everything at face value, I've learned.'

She nodded and kept watching the hillside above the shoreline. There were few houses to be seen as the trees were thicker and the hill steeper at this end of the bay. A boatshed had been converted into a double-storey house at the water's edge. Another house, seemingly all glass, glinted in the bright sunlight above. *Someone with money had found this idyll*, Dominic thought to himself.

But as they turned into the wide mouth of the creek, the trees closed in and Dominic wondered if there were wallabies and koalas still to be found in this thick tangle of swamp mahoganies and gum trees rising up the hillside.

'There's the jetty.' CeeCee gestured.

'Oh, so it is. Easy to miss. Where's the house?'

'Higher up to the right, see?' She pointed.

Dominic stopped rowing and gazed up through the trees, finally spotting the reflection from the sun on a roof – or was it a glass window? He wasn't sure. 'Looks like a bit of a hike up the path from the wharf. So, tell me what you know about this poet,' said Dominic as he stroked towards the small jetty.

'Not much. She grew up in the country on a big property. The family were pretty rich. But back then girls weren't allowed to run anything. And if they married, they had to live on the husband's property. But when her father and brother were killed in World War One, she took over the property as her mother never recovered from grief.'

'So she never married? What happened to her?' asked Dominic.

'She was swindled out of her home when she fell in love with some stupid man who cheated her. So she moved to a boarding house in the city and hated it.'

'That's looking like a pretty big home up there,' said Dominic as they drew closer. 'How'd she afford that?'

'Well,' CeeCee said with a quick smile, 'she ran away with a married man. But he'd left his family a long time before. And they came here, my grandmother says, but they didn't mix with the locals. This was long before Nan and Grandad arrived. The man was much older and when he died, he left her the house. So she stayed here the rest of her life. But she wrote lots of poems which were published. She was sort of famous but now she's forgotten.'

'Well, you've found out about her, and you're interested and like her poems, so doesn't that make her still famous?' asked Dominic as he angled the little dinghy towards the wooden steps alongside the stone landing.

CeeCee shrugged, then stood up and inched past him as he leaned to one side so she could get to the bow and grab the rope.

'Hey! Be careful on those steps, CeeCee, they look slippery!' Dominic warned as she jumped from the bow of the dinghy to the old steps.

But she kept her balance and Dominic shipped the oars as she tied the little boat to the old pylon. 'Just as well the tide is in; be a bit tricky getting out at low tide,' he said, following her along the short jetty.

A small rusting tin shed by the wharf was surrounded by a few old empty kerosene drums, ropes and indiscernible paraphernalia piled at the back. Cracking flagstone steps wound around the rise and up towards the house.

As they got to the crest of the path they saw that the house had large sandstone foundations and fading green-painted wooden fretwork around the verandah railings. Some windows had shutters.

'Grandad's right. Whoever owns this place mustn't come here very often,' commented CeeCee as they walked towards the front stone steps.

Dominic was looking around. 'I don't know about that . . . someone is cutting the grass occasionally, by the look of it.'

They stared at the lawns, which, while in need of a mow, were certainly not neglected. They walked around the back of the house, where a stone terrace under a vine-covered portico had sagging lattice on three sides. It faced the hillside which stretched beyond, thick with trees and undergrowth.

'Is that a wallaby?' asked CeeCee.

'No. It's a large stone boulder.' Dominic smiled.

'I thought it was keeping still, hiding in the grass,' she said with a laugh.

'I think that's the national park right on the back doorstep,' said Dominic as they turned and walked around the other side of the quiet old house.

Then suddenly from behind them came a voice calling, 'Hey there!'

CeeCee and Dominic swung around in surprise to see Snowy strolling towards them from the bush.

Dominic shook his head in amusement. 'How does he know . . .?'

'Hey, Snowy! What're you doing here?' called CeeCee. 'Do you know the people who live here?'

'Yeah. I keep an eye on the joint for them. Clear around it and check on things.'

'Shame they don't live here. It's a beautiful house,' said Dominic.

'Solid as a rock. Big rooms, great views from the verandah. Could have a lovely garden if someone bothered.'

'So who does live here?' asked CeeCee. 'It belonged to a poet, y'know. I'm studying her at school.'

Snowy grinned and tipped his hat back on his head. 'Well, that's good to know. This place is still in her family. Some great-nephew, I think he is. Lives in the country somewhere.'

'Can we have a look inside?' asked CeeCee.

'I don't think Snowy can allow that, CeeCee. I assume you only do the grounds, Snowy?' said Dominic.

'I've got a key as I have to check no vermin have got inside,' he said. 'You could help have a look with me,' he added casually.

CeeCee skipped onto the verandah and attempted to peer through a window, but heavy curtains were pulled across it.

'So what did you learn about this place?' asked Snowy, following her. Dominic hesitated, then joined them, staring through the trees to the wonderful water view.

'She wrote here and loved the animals and serenity. She used to walk in the bush along some special path . . . I s'pose that might be all overgrown now.' CeeCee sighed.

'Depends. What's so special about the path?' asked Snowy.

'Well, you could say the trees represented guardians, sheltering a special world. It's a path with no end in sight or at least, no one knows where it ends up. It's a metaphor for life's journey. That sort of thing,' said CeeCee, suddenly looking shy.

'Sounds a good way to travel to me.' Snowy smiled, glancing at Dominic. 'So. You wanna come in and have a squiz around? No touching anything, eh?'

'Really? Are you sure it's okay?' started Dominic, but Snowy was already walking around the side verandah to a door at the far end, CeeCee on his heels.

'Woah, it's dark in here,' whispered CeeCee as Snowy opened the door.

'Musty, too,' said Dominic. 'How often do you come in here, Snowy?'

'Every few months, just checking for storm damage, vandals, and that no wildlife has come down the chimney, that sorta thing.'

The room was suddenly awash with sunlight as Snowy yanked back the heavy curtains nearest him.

Dominic caught his breath.

'Wow,' exclaimed CeeCee.

'Reckon it's pretty much as the old lady had it. No one really lived in the place after she died; they just kept it for holidays, I think,' said Snowy.

The front room ran the length of the house where long glass windows and French doors opened onto the verandah. Bookcases lined one wall, and a large sandstone fireplace was at the far end. The room was furnished with several old-fashioned and bulky aged leather chairs, an oblong table, a drinks cabinet and shelves which held a few carvings and ornaments. A large Chinese vase sat in the centre of the table. Faded oriental rugs were scattered on the deeply polished but worn wooden floorboards.

They followed Snowy in awed silence.

'The kitchen hasn't been changed since the fifties, I'd say,' said Dominic in hushed tones. 'Nor the bedrooms; look – iron bedsteads, pressed metal ceilings, painted wood panel walls, even a picture rail. I bet there's horse-hair mattresses under those crocheted quilts.'

'Yuck, that sounds awful. I like the big windows, though,' said CeeCee. 'The rooms must all have lovely views.'

'Here, you'll like this little room back here, CeeCee. It's a sorta study which is kept locked,' said Snowy.

He unlocked the door to show her a room with a desk, a small fireplace, compact settee and walls of heavy bound books. One wall had photos and paintings, but with the curtains drawn it was hard to make them out. CeeCee looked at the desk, which had a bottle of ink and a case of pens and pencils beside a smudged blotter in a leather holder. As she looked at the shelves she saw on a bottom shelf a very old-fashioned upright manual typewriter. She turned to Snowy.

'Do you suppose this is *her* stuff?'

Snowy shrugged. 'Must be. Old-fashioned, out of date, who'd use it? The family don't seem interested. Last person who seemed to know about her was Joe Gordon. Being an English teacher and so on.'

'You mean Maggie's husband, the man who went missing?' asked CeeCee, and when Snowy nodded, she went on, 'Did he ever come here? Meet her?'

Snowy shrugged. 'Not possible. She died in the late 1960s before Joe and Maggie came here. C'mon, let's lock up. I'll just check all the curtains are down and nothing open. See you at that side door.'

As they walked back into the gardens, Snowy looked at CeeCee. 'Come with me.'

Dominic followed as CeeCee and Snowy headed up the garden to where a wire boundary fence sagged, a barrier between the cropped grass inside and high bracken and bushes beyond, which stretched to the edge of the thick bushland and trees.

'See what I see?' said Snowy.

CeeCee peered into the undergrowth then exclaimed, 'I see it! A path! Where does it go?'

'This goes up to the waterfall that feeds the creek. There used to be a bit of a track to the neighbours round the bay, but that's grown over now.'

'How did you get here, Snowy?' asked Dominic curiously.

'I know my way about,' Snowy said casually. 'Just thought CeeCee might like to know there's a few old paths in the bush around here.'

'I'll have to come and explore,' said CeeCee excitedly.

'I bet there's snakes and who knows what in there,' cautioned Dominic.

'Maybe the old lady never went anywhere. The path could've been made by wallabies,' said Snowy. 'C'mon, I'll walk with you back down to the water.'

*

As they headed down the hill, Snowy asked Dominic, 'How's that young fella Paul doing? Had a surf prang, was it?'

'Yeah, another surfer slammed into him while he was paddling out the back. He was very lucky. He's resting up at Maggie's,' Dominic replied.

'Certainly lucky. Better take it easy. S'pose Maggie'll like looking after him. She was a nurse,' said Snowy as they reached the cluttered old boatshed. 'Well, I'll be off. G'luck with your school paper, CeeCee.'

'Thanks for letting us have a look inside,' she said with a grin. 'I feel I know more about her now.'

As they got into the dinghy, CeeCee said, 'I might ask Maggie if I can visit Paul.'

'Good idea. I might pop up to see them too. Funny, though, it's only been a couple of days. I wonder how Snowy knew about his accident?' mused Dom.

CeeCee shrugged. 'Everyone knows everything round here. Can I row back?'

'Sure, let's check my crab pots first.'

*

Later that afternoon, Rob called.

'Hey buddy, how're things?'

'Moving along,' said Rob cheerfully. 'Anything new over there?'

'Not really. Did a political report, nothing too exciting. What about you?'

'Well, I do have a bit of interesting news. That friend in the racing industry I mentioned has come up with some info.'

'Yeah? About Joe? Like what?'

'Turns out our friend Joe was quite the racing aficionado.'

'Well, we knew he was keen on horseracing.'

'This was more than a friendly day or two out at the races. Remember we know Joe took an interest in horse syndicates?' said Rob.

'Owning shares in a horse doesn't sound so serious. Unless he was backing it and betting heavily . . .?' Dominic mused.

'I don't think Joe was a problem gambler per se, but he was involved in more than one syndicate. And he was into horse breeding stats,' added Rob.

'Hmm. That's an advantage when it comes to placing a bet,' said Dominic. 'If Joe made serious money, maybe Maggie didn't know about it. But I don't think Maggie was holding back anything in any way, and she didn't mention money troubles either, apart from the usual saving to buy their land and build the house. You're making Joe sound like he had a secret life . . .' Dominic let the words hang. 'What else did your mate have to say?'

'He mentioned certain insider names,' said Rob slowly. 'It might be hearsay and gossip, but according to my source, Joe was hobnobbing with some serious person-alities. Heard of Maurie Richards?'

'I've heard the name; he was a notorious crook, wasn't he?' exclaimed Dom.

'Sure was,' said Rob.

'Does that mean anything, though? It's not like Joe was *involved* with them, was he?' said Dominic.

'Well, it means racing people are a bit of a closed shop. Legit or not, if someone has a hot tip, inside knowledge, or is a big spender, they don't big-note themselves. Especially if certain insider names are mentioned,' explained Rob.

'Certain names?' Dominic prompted.

'Let's call them by the cliché – "colourful racing iden-tities", if you know what I mean,' said Rob.

'C'mon, a Pommy schoolteacher with a good reputa-tion and nice family wouldn't be mixed up with those sort of people! WestWater is a world away from metropolitan racetracks,' objected Dom. 'I think that's laughable. Your mate must have the wrong fellow!'

'Joe Gordon. Seems like it was definitely him,' said Rob firmly. 'I told my contact that Joe had been missing for decades and he suggested he might've been bumped off! That's the world of Maurie and his mates for you.'

Dominic shook his head. 'It just doesn't fit the picture I have of Joe. He had a fulltime job, other activities and a family.'

'Maybe, but people can always surprise you. Did Joe have any connection to racing in the UK, do you know?'

'I don't think so. I'll have to talk to Maggie,' said Dominic, still feeling bewildered at this possible connection.

'I'll be keen to hear what the old girl says,' added Rob.

'Yeah. Me too,' said Dominic thoughtfully. 'I'll let you know.'

*

The following day, after calling ahead to check she was in, Dominic headed up the hill to Maggie's place in the early afternoon sunlight.

Maggie greeted him at the door. 'Good timing, Dom. A few of my kids have dropped in, so we're having something of a family reunion!'

'Oh – I hope I'm not intruding, Maggie,' said Dominic.

'Not at all, you're very welcome,' said Maggie cheerfully, and ushered him in. 'I think you know most of the family by now.'

Dominic headed into the living room where he found Paul propped up in a chair, wearing a neck brace and clutching a ginger beer. He could hear voices in the kitchen.

Dominic said hello and shook Paul's hand gently.

'So how are you feeling, Paul?' he asked as he sat down opposite.

'Getting there, I guess. Feel bad that Mum is waiting on me all the time.'

Josie came in with a big smile. 'Good to see you, Dom. Mum's doing a great job of caring for Paul.'

'You're lucky you have a trained nurse looking after you,' Dominic said to Paul.

'And the rest of us waiting on him hand and foot,' added a voice that Dom didn't recognise. He turned to see a stunning girl with creamy skin, thick brown hair and dark eyes that reminded him of melting chocolate. She was casually dressed and gave him a sort of wave-cum-salute. 'Hi. I'm the other one. Holly. Maggie's other daughter.'

213

Dominic suddenly felt a bit confused. 'Oh. Holly. The sister from Perth!'

'Not any more.' She smiled. 'From Perth, that is.'

'I thought you'd rushed across the country to visit your devoted brother,' said Paul with a bit of a grin. 'Instead she's just moved house.'

'Not quite true, Paul! I came much earlier than I planned, just to see *you*.' She ruffled his hair affectionately and turned back to Dominic. 'So you're the good Samaritan in the boathouse?'

'Much more than that,' exclaimed Maggie, emerging from the kitchen. 'Dom is very kind and generous. Now, there's some cheese and biscuits and nibbles on the buffet.'

Maggie sat casually beside Paul, but Dominic could tell she was keeping a weather eye on him.

Dominic turned back to Holly. 'I've always liked WA. To me Western Australia means pearl shell and boab trees, red anthills and Aboriginal art . . . So is this a permanent move back to Sydney for you?'

Holly nodded. 'There's a lot more to WA, of course, but yes, it's a beautiful place. I love Perth, and being in the west; Broome and Denmark were my favourite places. But I started to feel a bit claustrophobic, emotionally as was well as physically. I've been managing the same luxury hotel for five years and I was offered a promotion of sorts, I guess, to move to a sister hotel overseas or a new one in the Northern Territory.'

'Well, that sounds exciting, and a nice change,' said Dominic politely.

Holly grimaced slightly. 'Not really. Once inside the place you could be anywhere in the world. The hotel chain has got the same style, service and setting down pat. When I started counting the stars in the carpet and knew how many windows and drapes the place had, I wasn't ready for more of the same. Time for a change!'

Dominic couldn't help chuckling. 'Maybe that familiarity is what customers who can afford it like. It's not my taste, if I'm honest.'

'So what's your idea of a holiday then?' Holly asked him.

He shrugged. 'I've mostly combined holidays with work. Meetings, conferences, accompanying pollies on tour. I arranged extra days for myself to sightsee afterwards.'

'Doesn't sound like much of a holiday,' said Holly. 'Although Mum said you're on a kind of a holiday now?'

Dominic laughed. 'I s'pose it looks that way. I'm working on my own stuff. But it is a bit like a holiday being in the boatshed . . .'

'So Paul was just an excuse to come home, hey, Hol?' said a hearty voice, and Dominic looked up to see Jason joining them.

'It was planned, Jase. I had given notice but when I heard about Paul's accident they were okay with me leaving a bit early. But you didn't have to go to quite these extremes to get me home, bro,' Holly said to Paul with a small smile.

'Yeah. Right,' said Paul rather glumly.

'Well, it's lovely to have my family all within hugging distance, and of course you here too, Dom,' said Maggie, beaming around at them all. 'Well, Simon is within hugging distance, just not in the room.'

Holly turned to Dominic. 'So you're part of the family now?'

'Just a neighbour,' he said calmly.

'You're more than that, Dom! You know you can't move away now!' said Josie in a jovial tone.

'Well, I only have the boatshed for a few more months, so I'll have to join the real world again pretty soon,' said Dominic.

'I've put the kettle on. Could you make the tea, please, Holly?' asked Maggie.

Dominic jumped to his feet. 'Let me help.'

'Thank you dear,' said Maggie, so Dominic followed Holly to the kitchen.

'Sorry, I didn't mean for Mum to treat you like the scullery maid,' said Holly as she passed him the teacups.

'Not at all. I'm happy to lend a hand.'

Holly paused and looked at him. 'So what do you do, exactly? Seems unusual for someone like yourself to just be hanging out in this . . . hideaway place.'

'Backwater?'

'Some people might think so. You have to know it, grow up here, to appreciate it,' she said as she opened the cutlery drawer and began pulling out teaspoons. 'So why are you here? What kind of work are you doing? You don't seem the type to just hang out and fish.'

'I'm cat-sitting,' said Dominic lightly. Then, as she flicked him a wry look, he added, 'To be honest, I'm doing a bit of writing; maybe even a book. I like it here. It suits me for the moment. I enjoy being part of this pocket of the community.'

Holly poured the boiling water into the teapot. 'Simon said you were asking lots of questions. We're not that sort of a family.'

'What sort do you mean?'

'We don't talk about ourselves.' She looked at him, then turned away. 'Could you please take the cups in? I'll bring the teapot.'

'Sure,' said Dominic affably. But he wondered why she seemed so wary all of a sudden. Maybe Simon had said something to her.

Dominic sipped his tea slowly, looking around the room at Maggie and her family. They chatted with warmth and familiarity.

As they all finished their tea and rose from the table, Josie drew Dominic aside, walking him out onto the deck and saying quietly, 'Don't mind Holly. She can be protective, and maybe she feels a bit out of things, having lived away from us for so long.'

'I thought perhaps Simon had been in her ear,' said Dominic.

Josie nodded, glancing back inside. 'Yeah, it's possible. He thought you were too nosey.'

'So maybe she won't talk to me about your father?'

Josie shrugged. 'Like I said, Holly probably doesn't remember our father much at all anyway. She was only five when . . .'

Dominic nodded, noticing that Josie appeared to share her family's habit of not being able to say any words like, 'since he disappeared' or 'died'. Perhaps Maggie had forbidden them to acknowledge the fact out loud.

*

The following morning Dominic headed over to the general store for the paper and a few supplies. As he was standing at the freezer looking at pizzas and sausages, Deidre walked past with a box of canned goods which she started stacking on a shelf.

'How you doing, Dom? Haven't seen you for a bit.'

'Oh, just been working, socialising occasionally. Went up to Maggie's yesterday to see how Paul is doing.'

'Nice. How is he? Terrible accident by the sound of it; he was lucky.'

'He's improving. I also met his sister Holly. She's moved back here from Perth,' said Dominic.

'Yep. She brought her mum in this morning. Maggie's thrilled she's back.' Deidre smiled.

Dominic laughed. 'I can't beat you with the breaking news.'

'Have you heard that Steve and Sheila are moving? Well, selling up. No idea where they might go. Just grabbed the offer when it came along. That millionaire Harold Marchant who builds the retirement villages is the buyer.'

'Is that so?' said Dominic mildly, not wanting to spoil her scoop. 'I don't think I know them.'

'They're a young couple, just scraping along, working hard. They want to start a family. Can't blame them for taking a good offer when it comes on a silver platter, I s'pose.' Deidre sighed.

'Anybody else selling up?' asked Dominic, figuring that if Harold had made another offer, Deidre would know.

'Locals all hope not. The last thing everyone wants is to turn this area into a trendy place like some of the beaches around here.'

'Would be good for your business, maybe,' said Dominic with a smile.

'Are you joking? More likely we'd be steamrolled by some big fancy supermarket chain and before you know it there'd be a shopping centre here. Then apartment blocks. Imagine the traffic!'

'There goes the neighbourhood! That's how it happens,' said Dominic.

'Development would spoil what we have here and love about the place. Well, I'd better get back to work.'

*

Dominic made arrangements to meet Suzanne from the book club.

'Come to my place in The Vale. I'm in a ground-floor apartment and have a lovely little garden patio where we can sit and chat over a coffee.'

She welcomed him warmly. As he remembered, Suzanne was tall and fit-looking with a firm, strong voice and blonde hair faded to a soft pale grey which was braided and wound on top of her head. She wore sensible shoes, a linen dress and bright pink lipstick. She ushered him into the small walled garden, pointing out favourite plants.

'Tyson, our local carpet snake, hangs out here near the little water feature, so don't be startled if you see him.' She smiled. 'Sit down and I'll bring you out a coffee. How do you like it? I can make short black, cappuccino, a latte . . .'

'A plain flat white will be fine, thank you. No sugar,' said Dominic. 'Sure I can't help?'

'No, enjoy the fresh air. I won't be long.'

Dominic reached over to several books on a chair, *No doubt book club homework*, he thought.

'These look like a good selection,' he said as Suzanne returned and put his coffee in front of him, then settled herself in the other chair.

'Yes, I'm enjoying the biography of a nineteenth-century lady botanist. I do hope you can find time to come to book club again; we had such a good time. So, how are things with you, Dominic?'

'All good, thanks. Time slipping away too easily.'

'You wanted to talk about Joe Gordon, you said?' She was direct but friendly, giving him a warm smile.

'It's such a sad and tragic story, and such a mystery. Were you surprised at what happened? His disappearance?' Dominic asked.

'Totally shocked. Would have been the last person I could imagine in such a scenario. I thought I knew him quite well from school and social occasions. I had the twins in one of my classes, and I saw the family at school functions. Maggie was working as a nurse then so I only saw her during after-school events. I got to know her more closely once I retired.'

'But you knew Joe well?'

'I believed so. I admired him tremendously; he was such a good and caring teacher. He volunteered and put in so much time with the children, weekends and often after school. He ran some of the sports programs in his spare time.'

Dominic nodded. 'So I've heard. Sounds like he kept busy.'

'Very much so. Certainly not a clock-watcher. He was always available for the kids if they needed to talk to him.'

'He sounds almost too good to be true,' said Dominic lightly. He sipped his coffee, waiting for her quick denial or a shaking of her head. But to his surprise, she daintily picked up her cup, wrapped both hands around it, and stared into her coffee.

'I did occasionally wonder . . . but I'm not one to gossip or take any notice of rumours and innuendo. I shudder at how social media spreads misinformation.'

'But . . .?' prompted Dominic.

220

'I've never said anything, but in retrospect there was some chatter, whispers, gossip, among some of the staff. Nothing like the trolling and faceless accusations nowadays . . . I doubt it went further than the staffroom.'

Dominic leaned forward expectantly. 'Do you think whatever it was might have had anything to with what happened . . .?'

She put her cup in its saucer, looking faintly embarrassed. 'You understand this is for your ears only. I value Maggie's friendship and admire her staunch loyalty to Joe very much.' She drew a breath. 'There was speculation that Joe could have been having a relationship with another of the teachers, Lizzie Lyons.'

As Dominic stared at her, quite stunned at this unexpected news, Suzanne went on, 'Lizzie was a young new teacher, very pretty and sweet-natured. She was always asking Joe's advice about this and that. She went overseas a few weeks before Joe disappeared. Perhaps a strange coincidence?'

Dom drew a deep breath. 'Where did she go, I wonder?'

'Maybe the usual, Europe and the UK.' She gave him a frank stare. 'I can't remember, to be honest.'

'Do you think Maggie ever knew? Suspected anything?'

She shook her head firmly. 'Goodness no. I don't believe so. When you saw them together . . . they looked to be such a happy, loving couple. Lovely children. A model family,' she finished. 'I've watched the pain and angst Maggie has lived with all these years, just not knowing what happened.'

'So you didn't believe the gossip and rumours? Did Maggie ever discuss how she felt?' asked Dominic.

'Goodness no, on both counts. It was such a long time ago now. But something makes me think Maggie probably gets up every morning praying today is the day Joe might walk in the door.'

'Do you have any theories about what might have happened to Joe?'

'Of course, there was intense speculation everywhere when he went missing. People who didn't know him or the family were jabbering their theories. No one knew anything, it was always just wild stories.'

'Did you ever mention this Lizzie Lyons to the police?' asked Dominic.

'I thought about it. But no, I did not,' said Suzanne firmly. 'It was only rumours. I had no evidence of any kind,' she added.

Dominic could tell the subject of Lizzie Lyons did not sit comfortably with Suzanne.

'Now, let me show you these books. Feel free to borrow one if you like, Dom.'

*

Dominic mulled over the conversation as he drove back to WestWater.

Joe might not be around, but he was emerging as a complex and challenging character. *Almost some kind of chameleon*, thought Dominic. Was it possible that he was the perfect family man and a popular teacher, but also someone who might have had an affair and hobnobbed with crooks?

Dominic couldn't help slapping his hand against the steering wheel.

'What the hell, Joe!'

*

Dominic watched the sun go down over the hills as Woolly rubbed against his leg. He'd been practising a new song on the guitar, and was pleasantly surprised how quickly it was coming back to him. He found the guitar an excellent way to relax and clear his mind. Just then, footsteps echoed around the side of the boathouse and he craned to see who it was.

'Well, hi, Jason. You still here?' Jason, dressed in linen shorts, an expensive T-shirt and leather sandals, looked stylish.

'Stuck around for a few days to do some work in Mum's garden. Ah, you busy?'

'Nope. Was just going to open a beer. Like one? Pull up a deckchair.'

'Sure. Thanks.'

Stowing his guitar inside, Dominic returned with two chilled bottles of beer and settled himself in the chair next to Jason.

'Good to see Paul starting to move around,' said Dominic.

'Yes. It's been a bit of a trip. Scary.'

'And infuriating for Paul when it wasn't his fault,' added Dominic.

'He was talking about suing and trying to find the kid – some clueless teenager – but he's letting that go now. He just wants to be better and get back in the surf.'

'I bet. Well, that's good. You don't surf much yourself?'

'No. I like swimming but I suppose Paul and I tend to do different things, sometimes unconsciously. We hated being dressed alike and having to do things together at school. Then we had a cool teacher who separated us. That way we got interested in different things. The competiveness wasn't so heated then.' He smiled. 'We hardly saw each other through the day, made friends of our own. But we always walked home together. By the time we went to high school we were following our own interests.'

'Well, you do have quite differing passions it seems,' said Dominic with a grin. 'How did you get into landscaping?'

'My dad, actually. I used to help him in his veggie garden. He loved that we had the space to grow our own vegetables, and flowers for my mother. Looking back I realise how special that time was . . . just the two of us. We all had special things we did with Dad, one on one. He and Paul went fishing. Josie had chickens and together they built a big safe run for them. Simon was an engine freak, always fiddling with the boat or the car.'

'And Holly?'

Jason looked thoughtful. 'She was so little. I don't know. We were all into our own things. I know the girls did music and ballet and stuff. We all played sports, cricket and soccer at some stage.' Jason glanced away. 'Dad used to quote poetry to the plants, sometimes sing . . .' His voice trailed off and he looked down, his expression filled with sadness.

'He sounds like a special person,' said Dominic quietly.

'Yes . . . Dad had a knack of making you feel you were the most important person in his world. When you were with him, he was totally focused and listening to you. Yet as I got older I realised everyone else felt the same way about him.'

'That *is* special,' said Dominic. 'Your father seemed to be involved in so much, I wonder how he found the time to keep all the different people and activities in his life without dropping the ball?'

Jason nodded emphatically. 'Yeah, I know. He had us kids, his job, he was always there for any schoolkid who needed him, the after-school stuff, home stuff. Yet he and Mum always had time for each other. They would often sit out on the deck with a sundowner drink, watch the birds, talk about their day.'

'What about his own interests? Did he have time for himself?' Dominic asked conversationally.

'He and Mum had friends. They'd play cards, do social things as well as being involved in the community. Dad liked the races, and of course, he was always reading.' Jason paused, then said, 'He was very sensitive, very understanding and fair. He was a schoolteacher and much more in tune with kids than other parents. I was so nervous when I came out to him and told him I thought I might be gay.' Jason looked at Dom. 'But he was so loving, and fair and rational. No lecture, just warmth, wanted me to be happy, to never feel unworthy. Follow my dreams. It was his idea that I do an architectural degree and then, if I was still keen, branch into environmental and land-scaping courses.' He paused and lowered his head. 'I told Dad about being gay shortly before he . . . disappeared. Sometimes I blame myself . . . maybe he was actually ashamed of me and couldn't face people?'

Dominic shook his head forcefully. 'It really doesn't sound like it, Jason. Seems like he was very proud of you.'

'It's been shit growing up without a father, Dom,' said Jason suddenly and vehemently. 'Everyone feels sorry for you! And they're nice because they think they have to be. It's not like he got sick and died. There's no closure, and there are always whispers behind your back. I just hate not knowing.'

'I can understand that.'

Jason rubbed a hand over his face. 'Yeah. Sorry. I hardly ever talk about it.'

'That's okay. Do the others feel the same?' asked Dominic quietly.

'Well, you know Josie does. The others – I don't know, really.'

They were both silent for a moment or two, Dominic at a loss as to how to comfort the grown man in front of him.

'I just wish he could see what I'm doing for Mum, especially around the house.'

Dominic nodded as Jason took a sip of his beer. He decided to change the subject; this conversation was too painful.

'Did Josie tell you about Harold Marchant's offer to buy your mother's house?'

Jason nodded. 'Oh, yes. And I heard the rumours that the neighbours are selling. But Hell will freeze over before Mum would ever move. Why would she?'

Dominic shrugged. 'The usual reasons: it's a big house, she's not getting any younger, the steep drive, the garden –'

'I'll look after the garden. Dad said it was my job.'

Dominic tried not to react. 'Your job? . . . Like, if he wasn't around . . .?'

'No! He didn't mean it like that!' Jason looked shaken. 'I was just a kid. I think he was just giving me responsibility, a way to help out. Dad was always patient and calm. Mum was more the boss and organiser.' He paused and his face crumpled slightly. 'I miss him. And I'm angry at him . . . If we only knew why . . .' He drained his beer. 'I'm just so annoyed at Leo, pushing Mum to sell when he knows how much our place means to her.'

'Yeah, I met Leo,' said Dominic. 'Didn't know quite what to make of him.'

'Leo didn't get on with his father,' Jason said, glancing across at Dominic. 'His parents were divorced and when Leo stayed down here with his dad, he used to come up to our place a lot, hang around. I got the impression he didn't like being at home. My parents were good to him – which makes it all worse. He's just after the money. It makes me so angry!'

He thumped his empty beer bottle on the table, then his shoulders slumped. 'Sorry. I didn't mean to dump on you,' he said in a low voice. 'It's like Paul's accident and us all being together again has brought it back to the surface, rattled everyone.'

Dominic got up. 'I'll get us another.'

'No, thanks. It's okay.' Jason stood. 'Sorry to bother you with my problems . . . old hurts.'

'No, no, mate. It's fine.' Dominic reached out and touched his shoulder. 'It's good to get things off your chest.'

'Look, thanks for keeping an eye on Mum. She likes you a lot, as her friend. She enjoys talking to you – I hope she doesn't bore you silly!'

'No, Jase, not at all.' Dominic hadn't analysed why he liked Maggie. She was a woman who was living the past and present entwined. Occasionally he had those glimpses of Maggie as a happy young bride, but he'd also seen her present pain, as well as the strong and forthright woman she'd become in between.

And, he had to admit, her story and the circumstances around Joe's disappearance was like a fragile spiderweb beginning to cling to him.

9

'Hey, Rob . . . I have a meeting on the North Shore and I'm seeing my folks afterwards. I wondered if you were available for a coffee or a drink later . . .?' Dominic asked.

There was the barest fraction of a pause on the line. 'Aw, sorry. I have a meeting too . . . with Harold Marchant.'

Dominic tried to hide his surprise. 'You're mixing with Harold these days?'

'Nah, not really. Business. Could be a job deal in it for me.'

'Doing what? Anything to do with him buying up land at WestWater?'

'Don't think so . . . but as far as I know, Harold still wants the land out there. I'm just networking, making a few introductions. Remember Terry, the builder who did the retreat for my folks at my sister's farm?' said Rob.

'Yeah . . . but "builder" is gilding the lily a bit, isn't it? Isn't he the one who has no qualifications but is a genius at design and telling tradies what to do?' Dominic laughed. 'Surely Harold wouldn't hire someone who's talented but not qualified. He'd be getting a bigtime architect, wouldn't he?'

'Harold asked Alicia to find a designer so she called me for ideas. I showed her some photos of the jobs Terry's done over the years. You'd be surprised, he calls himself a "design creator for future living" or something. Alicia showed them to Harold and he wants to meet Terry. Now Harold thinks I can hook him up with anybody.'

'You are the star spin doctor! But it seems nothing will divert Harold from buying at WestWater.'

'Well, as Alicia says, whatever Harold wants Harold gets.'

Dominic wondered privately how often Rob had spoken to Alicia.

*

'My! Well, look at you, Dom! Long pants, good shoes and a smart shirt tucked in. Where're you off to?' Deidre said with a chuckle as Dominic picked up his newspaper and some milk.

'I had a meeting with a former client. Wants me to write something.' Dominic grinned.

'Oh, secret pollie business?'

'Nope. Boring economic piece for a political audience.'

'So – boring pollie business.' Deidre laughed.

'Pretty much. Involves a lot of digging, though. Seems the country's not in such good shape as some people like to make out.'

Deidre wrinkled her nose. 'That's no surprise to me. And there, Daphne and I thought you were writing a book.'

'It's still on the cards,' he said casually. 'You never know.'

'Plenty of subject matter round here, I reckon.' Deidre rang up his items and handed him a receipt. 'By the way, we haven't seen Alicia for a while. Have you?' She gave him an arch look.

'No. I think she's staying in the city.'

Deidre looked surprised. 'Oh. I thought she was your girlfriend.'

'No. Alicia is her own boss. She calls the shots.' Dominic smiled.

'Talking of friends, have you seen Snowy lately? He hasn't been around for some time. We wondered if he might be ill.'

'I saw him a week or so ago, maybe more, when CeeCee and I ran into him up at the old poet's house. I'll see if someone can check on him. Although I don't know where he lives precisely,' said Dominic.

'Yeah, he's a bit vague about where his shack is, and he likes it that way. Daphne said she thought he lives around the Morning Rise track. Bit of a trek to get there.'

'I don't know that area. I'll have to take a hike,' said Dominic.

'There's a lot of hidden secrets in these hills. Daph and I go skinny-dipping at protected coves that haven't seen a footprint in years,' said Deidre.

'Sounds fun. Although what happens if you get into strife with no one around?'

'Oh, we stay in the shallows. Might look like the

secret sea but I always wonder what's lurking in those coves,' said Deidre. 'And there's no phone reception.'

'I'll keep that in mind. See you, Deidre.'

'Let us know if you hear how Snowy is,' she called as Dominic headed out the door.

*

In the twilight the water around the boatshed was still and silent. Dominic sat at his office desk – the little table and folding chair – on the deck. He kept an occasional eye on his set rod, hoping for a decent bite.

He rifled through his notes to find the phone number Rob had given him for his racing friend, then rang it. The call was answered with a curt, 'Hello. Who's this?'

'Hi, Gareth. My name's Dominic Cochrane. I'm a friend of Rob Talbot's. I know he spoke to you recently about a guy called Joe Gordon who went missing twenty-five years ago. I'm a researcher and I'm interested in Joe's links with the well-known racing identity Maurie Richards.'

'Oh, right. Yeah, I remember Rob asking about him. Why do you want to know? It was decades ago.'

'I'm just interested in what might have happened to Joe. You mentioned to Rob that he might have been "knocked off". I'm just wondering what you meant by that,' said Dominic.

'Well, people who got in Maurie's way or messed up had a habit of disappearing. Breeding stud racehorses is a big-money business, and Joe knew all the bloodlines.'

'Breeding? Rob mentioned that Joe was part of syndicates and interested in racing stats. I gathered he liked the races and placed a bet or two, as well . . . but he was just a schoolteacher –' began Dominic.

Gareth interrupted him. 'Yeah. But smart, had the knack, apparently. He wasn't in the business per se. That's what made him stand out to me; seemed like he was a rank amateur. It was a sort of hobby for him. What's it all to do with you?'

'I'm a friend of the family. They've been living in limbo since Joe disappeared. No one in the family ever mentioned that he was interested in horse breeding and thoroughbred stud farms, though! Just that he liked the races. When was all this?' Dominic asked.

'It was back in the seventies, I think, round the time of the Magic Millions, before The Everest race started,' said Gareth. 'Maurie was the go-to guy for the form – which horse was likely to place and who was definitely going to win . . . wink, wink. Didn't always work out, of course, but the odds were generally in his favour. If you knew where Maurie put his money, you knew it'd be a pretty sure thing. 'Course, knowing was another matter. Maurie played his cards close to his chest, so to speak.' He gave a slight laugh. 'Joe Gordon was just a name mentioned in passing as being knowledgeable about thoroughbred genealogy.'

'The fact Joe's name is even remotely linked to such a character is a bit of shock,' said Dominic, thinking that was actually a massive understatement.

'Yeah, well, he wouldn't have been the first to get into trouble with horses and big money. But I can't help you any more than that, sorry, mate.'

'No worries. Thanks for this. Cheers.'

Dominic rang off and sat staring at his phone.

It simply didn't make sense. None of this matched his impression of the sensible, inspiring schoolteacher, loving father, husband, friend and neighbour.

He went to his contact list and hit the number for Andrew and Colleen.

*

'Lovely to hear from you, Dom! How're things?' said Colleen.

They exchanged pleasantries then Dominic asked, 'I was wondering about the old days, when you and Maggie and Joe went to the races . . .'

'Oh, we didn't go too often, just occasionally for the festive days,' broke in Colleen.

'Did Joe place biggish bets or seem to know a lot about the horses?' asked Dominic cautiously.

'None of us had much money to throw around back then! Joe was interested, though, typical of him; he studied the form. And he always liked to walk around and "check out the horseflesh" as he put it. Maggie used to roll her eyes. But none of us took it very seriously. Andrew is out at the moment but he'd say the same, I think. Why do you ask?'

'Oh, Joe's name came up in a conversation about racing, that's all.'

'He had small shares in horses; a lot of people did at the time. Mind you . . . he was a thorough person. He used to always say if something's worth doing, it's worth doing properly. But bigtime gambling? No way. Did you mention this to Maggie?'

'No, I haven't. Didn't want to upset her.'

'Oh, she'd probably laugh at the idea of him being a gambler. By the way, what's happening about her house, do you know? We heard she could get a substantial price,' said Colleen. 'I don't want to pry, it's Maggie's business. But, well, we all know she says she'll never leave there.'

Dominic was tempted to comment about Maggie hanging on to the idea that Joe would walk in the door one day, but he held his tongue. 'I understand how attached she is to this place. It's a magical area,' he said instead.

'I agree. But there comes a time when a house can get too much, especially on your own. I know her kids help her but that's a lot of land around her place. My Andrew stopped mowing lawns and kept hinting about four flowerpots on a balcony being the perfect-sized garden! So we downsized. Have to say, though, we're busier than ever – but doing fun things. Moving here took a lot of worry off our kids' shoulders.'

'Sounds like it was the right decision for you. Thanks, Colleen. Say hi to Andrew for me.'

*

In the next hour Dominic was lost in the internet world of the life and times of Maurie Richards. It was a shocking read – of lawsuits, arrests, gangland murders, front-page reports of trials, the dark world of illegal gambling dens, betting and racehorse frauds and scandals. And Maurie and his associates were everywhere in the world of high-stakes racing: the glamour and money of mistresses, socialites, trainers, jockeys and strappers presenting the façade of the rich, the powerful and the crooked.

Some of the stories were horrific: slaughtered stallions, murdered minders, small-time criminals, bags of cash and the bigtime players wanting to get on Maurie's bandwagon. Others sounded simply stupid, in one case painting a horse to pass it off as a different runner.

What was shocking to Dominic was the subsequent headline trials and newspaper exposés of some police (referred to as 'the bent coppers brigade'), lawyers, flamboyant businessmen, movers, shakers and politicians going back decades who were involved in Maurie's web of activities. And the infamous Maurie Richards always slipped through it all unscathed.

That was, until a severed arm was found on a popular beach: leftovers from a shark's feeding frenzy. Maurie's 'cement boots' were finally caught in a trawler's drag line. Seems there'd been no lock on the chain wound around the body, and Maurie, wrapped in a tarpaulin, floated to the surface, his feet protruding. The captain called the water police to say a pair of sneakers had been found in 'unusual circumstances'.

A forensic officer explained to the press that *these weren't just any sneakers, these were alligator Louis Vuitton running shoes belonging to the infamous Maurie Richards*. His luck had run out.

Maurie never ran a yard in his life, a close associate commented. *But he had taste, man. Only the best for Maurie*.

Dominic shook his head and shut his laptop after checking the date Maurie died, which was five years after Joe disappeared. This connection with Maurie Richards just didn't add up. Why would the Joe Gordon who Dominic had come to know be mixed up with a man like that?

Dominic stood up. 'Lot of questions, Woolly,' he commented to the cat, who was looking at him expectantly. 'Okay, I'll give you dinner, and then I just might pop up and have a word to Maggie.'

*

Dominic found Paul sitting outside on Maggie's deck. 'How you going, Paul?'

'Okay, I guess. Getting a bit bored with no action. Jason offered to drive me down to the beach.'

'What? To just look at the breaks?' asked Dominic in surprise.

'Yeah. How dumb. Last thing I want to see when I can't get on a board,' he said grumpily.

'Your mum around?'

'Nope. She went over to Sam and Gloria's.'

'Ah. Okay then.' Dominic hesitated.

'Want a beer? Don't think she'll be long.'

'Sure. Why not. Thanks,' said Dominic. He was about to offer to get his beer but paused as Paul was already on his feet. Dominic suspected Paul was probably more than a bit over being watched and waited on.

Paul handed Dominic a beer and they both sat down. 'Mum is talking to Sam about the house offer. Leo keeps bugging her. I think he's taking advantage, just because he knows us. Y'know, pushing her. After his percentage.'

'What do you think your mum should do?' Dominic asked.

Paul shrugged and sipped his beer. 'Her business.'

'What's Jason think?'

'He knows this place will get too much for her one day and much as he loves looking after the garden and land, it's time he's got to find.' Paul put down his beer and ran his fingers through his hair. 'Josie's starting to think she should take the offer. But we all know Mum won't move. I'm not going to argue with her.'

'Because of your father?' said Dominic quietly.

'Guess so. The decision is hers.'

'What would you say if your father did walk in the door one day?' asked Dominic, hoping Paul wouldn't take offence.

Paul glanced away. Then he looked back at Dominic. 'Probably – "*What the hell took you so long?*" Because if he came back, it would mean he left by choice. What do you say to a man who left his family to wonder what happened to him for twenty-five years? Thanks a lot, Dad?' Paul looked bitter as he drained his beer. 'No one can replace your old man, whether he was good or bad. Anyway, it ain't going to happen.' He stood up, 'Another beer?'

Dominic hesitated, then heard footsteps. 'Sure, thanks. I think I hear your mum coming back.'

But it wasn't Maggie. Holly strode into the room in shorts and a T-shirt.

'Hey, Paulie . . . oh. Hello, Dominic. Where's Mum?'

'She's over with Sam and Gloria. Dom just dropped in to see her.'

Holly turned her gaze to Dominic. 'Can we help?'

While she wasn't abrupt, she wasn't welcoming either. Dominic felt a bit like he was marking time, holding up a queue. He put down his beer.

'It's okay. It can wait. Not important . . .'

'What's not important?' asked Maggie, coming into the room. 'Hi, Dom. What are you three cooking up?'

'Dom just dropped by to see how I was. We were having a beer,' said Paul.

'How're Gloria and Sam? I haven't caught up with them for a bit,' said Dominic.

'Been busy with rellies, grandkids. Glad to be back home with no plans,' said Maggie.

'What about you, Mum? Have you any plans?' asked Holly rather bluntly.

'Not at the moment. Well, yes. I'm going to put the kettle on.' She gave Dominic a smile.

'Well, I'll head back to the boatshed,' said Dominic, fairly sure now wasn't the time to have a chat with Maggie about Joe's involvement in horseracing. 'Oh, by the way, Maggie, have you seen Snowy lately? Deidre and Daphne are a bit concerned, said they hadn't seen him around at all lately.'

'How's his health? I haven't seen him since I was last here,' said Holly, sounding concerned.

'Well, he's getting on even if he does seem fit,' said Maggie worriedly.

'Doesn't he have a phone?' asked Paul.

'He doesn't have good reception at his place and he hardly ever looks at his phone,' said Maggie.

'No one seems to know where his place actually is,' said Dominic. 'Otherwise I'd be happy to go see him.'

'I know it,' said Holly. 'I'll go.'

'I'll come with you,' offered Dominic.

'Oh, Dom, that would be terrific, thank you both,' said Maggie quickly as Holly went to say something but closed her mouth after her mother interjected.

'Yeah, thanks, Dom. Sorry I can't help you guys,' said Paul. 'I'll stay by my phone, so call if Mum and I can do anything.'

'You don't have to come . . .' started Holly, glancing at Dominic. 'Snowy can be a bit funny about his privacy . . .'

'Nonsense,' said Maggie briskly. 'Snowy liked Dom from the moment he first met him. He told me so. Holly, go first thing in the morning. I'll make up a small bag for you with water, some biscuits, and some food, milk and such to take for Snowy.'

'All right,' said Holly, but she still looked unconvinced.

'Good idea. See you, Paul, Maggie. See you early in

the morning, Holly,' said Dominic, and he was out the door before Holly could raise another objection.

*

Not long after daybreak, Dominic grabbed a bottle of water, put on his hat and sneakers, thrusting his phone in the hip pocket of his shorts. He left the doors to the deck ajar so Woolly could come and go and walked briskly up the hill to Maggie's house.

Holly met him outside the house as she pulled on a small, crammed backpack. She had a light jacket tied to it and a baseball cap pulled over her thick hair, her eyes screened behind sunglasses.

They headed up behind Maggie's house through Jason's plantings and well-tended native garden. As they came to the narrow bush track, Dominic fell in behind Holly, following her neat figure as she strode purposefully along.

At one stage she glanced back at him. 'Not going too fast for you?'

'No,' said Dominic pleasantly.

'How come you're staying in Nigel's boatshed? You between jobs? Got divorced, or moving somewhere?'

'Two out of three. Sort of. I worked in politics. Was at a bit of a loose end after the last election and out of a job when my MP lost her seat. The boathouse fell into my lap, so I decided to take six months out and see what happened.'

'Midlife crisis?' she said a little snidely. 'So, what are you going to do? Writing, was it?'

Dominic looked at the back of her head. 'I could ask you the same thing. Except you're not at midlife yet.'

She turned, giving him a bemused glance over her shoulder. 'No. I'm not.'

The wallaby track they were following began to peter out into tufted grass mounds between lumps of flat, protruding rocks. Dominic caught up and walked beside Holly, watching where he stepped.

'There're a lot of Indigenous rock carvings around here; don't step on any,' said Holly. 'I feel it would be discourteous.'

Dominic nodded. 'I agree. First time I went exploring up here I got lost and Snowy turned up –'

'As he does –'

'Yeah. He showed me the cave with the wonderful paintings. Wish I could get in there for a decent look around . . .'

Holly stopped and stared at him. 'Snowy showed you the dreaming cave?'

'Yes. He did.'

Holly studied him. 'Interesting. Snowy likes to keep that a secret. Only shares it with select people.'

'I thought it was listed on the visitors' map on the park's website?'

'That's a different spot. More accessible. Not far from the old fire trail car park. The places around here he only shares with certain people.'

Dominic leaned in slightly and peered at her, trying to see her eyes through her sunnies. 'So, does that mean I get a tick of approval?'

'From Snowy, yes. I don't know you yet.' She set off again.

Dominic was about to say that Snowy hadn't really known him when he shared the cave with him, but he stayed silent.

They had walked for some time when Holly stopped and reached for her water bottle.

'Take a quick break. We have to head through the scrub over there.'

Dominic unscrewed the top of his water, staring ahead. 'Where exactly? It's just bush.'

'See the big angophora? That marks the way to his shack.'

'Wow, a beautiful tree, must be old.'

'Yes. A rusty gum. You can see it from the water. We could go back along the waterfront if the tide's out. Slower going over the rocks, though.'

'Let's see how Snowy is, eh?' said Dominic.

As they went into the canopy of shady trees, Holly picked up the pace, seeming familiar with where she was going. Trying to see ahead, Dominic missed his footing and stumbled. Holly glanced back at him.

'You okay?'

'Yeah, I'm fine, wasn't watching where I was going.'

'Sorry, should have warned you it was rough going. I know this area well, been coming here since I was about ten.'

'Who brought you here?' Dominic asked.

'Mum the first time. Then I used to come check on Snowy, like CeeCee sometimes does. Occasionally he came to our house. Snowy's not much of a social person.'

'I noticed. How come your family care about him?'

'I'm not sure. He's just always been in my life.'

'Was he an old friend of your father's?' ventured Dominic.

'I don't know. I never asked Mum. You ask a lot of questions, though – Simon was right about that.' She said it matter-of-factly.

'Sorry. Does it bother you?' Dominic stopped. 'Look, if I were you, I'd be wanting to know things . . . about Snowy, and about a father I never knew,' he said gently.

Holly paused and looked at him. 'Why? I hardly remember my father. A few fleeting memories. I never got to know him.'

'Do you feel you know him a bit from what your siblings have told you?' asked Dominic quietly.

'No. Not really. We've never really talked about him. Too painful for Mum. My father's never been part of my life. C'mon. There's Snowy's place.'

She hurried forward through the thinning trees to an old fence surrounding a wooden slab shack with a sloping rusted tin roof curving in a bull nose above a small front verandah. A large brick chimney was to one side and a water tank on the other. Windows were pushed open, propped on wooden sticks. There was a lot of paraphernalia about, from an outdoor stone barbecue to a woodheap, an old vehicle and a small storage shed. A netted vegetable patch struggled at one side.

To Dominic this first impression looked a bit like a scene from an old American TV show. *The Beverly Hillbillies* came to mind.

Holly hurried ahead calling out, 'Snowy, Hey, Snow . . .?'

She disappeared indoors as Dominic looked around, but in a few moments she came outside again. 'He's not here. His phone is, though.' She waved an old mobile in the air.

'Well, he can't be far away.'

'He could be anywhere. Like Mum said, he doesn't bother with his phone much as there's no reception here. You have to walk up the hill a bit to get it.' Holly looked worried. 'It just doesn't feel right. He's left milk on the table and it's gone off. Must have been left out for some time.'

'How long ago was his phone used?'

Holly picked up the phone and tried to turn it on. 'It's flat,' she said with a shrug.

'Well, let's look around the place. I'll do that side, you go the other way; we'll work in a circle back down to here,' said Dominic. 'Does he have any animals, pets or anything?'

'He has a few chooks.'

When they met back at the house, Holly looked concerned. 'The chooks had no water and the eggs haven't been collected. That's not like him.'

'Okay. He's got to be around here somewhere,' said Dominic firmly. 'Let's do this in an organised manner. How far does his property go?'

Holly explained quickly, pointing as she spoke. 'There's a track up the hill where there's a spot he can get phone reception. There's a bit of a creek up there too; he runs a pipe from it to the vegetables. Plus he has a spare tank.'

She looked deeply worried now. Dominic touched her shoulder. 'He'll be okay, Holly. He's a tough old bugger.'

'I know.' She nodded. 'Okay, you go up the hill. I'll do a circuit further down.'

'Let's meet back here in, say, twenty minutes. Holler loudly if you find him. He wouldn't have gone fishing, would he? You know how he just seems to turn up anywhere,' said Dominic, but this sounded unlikely even to him.

Holly shook her head. 'He wouldn't leave everything like this.'

They separated and each hurried through the scrubby bush around Snowy's fence line, calling and whistling. Dominic also started shouting 'cooee', figuring it might carry further.

As he headed back to the house, he saw Holly's worried face as she hurried towards him, shaking her head.

'Nothing. I think we'll have to get some help, get people to search.'

Dominic glanced around the hillside. 'This is pretty inaccessible . . . the fire trail must be some distance up the hill and this place is a good way from the water.'

'That's why he likes it here. Look, we could phone Sam. Get him to come up here and see what he thinks.'

'Okay, where up the hill is the reception? I'll go, you stay here in case he comes back,' said Dominic.

'All right. Follow the fence on that western border and you'll come to a rock shelter. Above it is that rusty gum you saw. Stand about a metre away from it and face east and you should get a signal,' Holly said. Dominic could hear the tension in her voice.

'Try not to worry, Holly. I'll be as quick as I can,' said Dominic as she hurried back down the slope. She lifted her hand in acknowledgement, her fingers crossed.

Dominic followed her instructions to the phone reception spot. He jumped from a flat rock, landing on the twigs of a dead tree branch which snapped and crunched under his weight. Stumbling slightly he caught his breath, and then he heard a sound like a moan.

'Snowy, Snowy . . . is that you, mate?' he called.

Straining to hear anything, Dominic froze, waiting.

And then he heard it again. A low groan and, this time, a mumbled voice.

Listening intently, he crept to his left and the voice became louder. And then, by the shade of the rock shelter, he saw the crumpled figure of the old man.

'Snowy, mate . . . what the hell? Snowy, can you hear me?'

Dominic reached the hunched man who was pale, his eyes closed, breathing shallowly in short breaths. Dominic looked down and saw that Snowy's leg was bloodied, swollen and twisted awkwardly. He was pale and weak but managed to shakily raise a hand. Dominic grabbed it.

'I got you, Snowy, help will be here soon. Holly Gordon's coming.'

At the mention of her name, Snowy seemed to relax slightly. Dominic clambered up onto the rock shelter, cupped his hands and shouted as loudly as he could.

'Holl-eeeee! Holly! He's here. Found him . . .!'

Dominic was bending over Snowy, supporting his head and trying to help him swallow water from his water bottle when Holly appeared.

'Oh Snowy, Snowy, are you okay?' cried Holly as she reached Dominic and leaned over the old man, feeling his forehead and lifting his wrist to take his pulse.

'It's his leg. Looks like he's taken a bad fall and been here a while, I'd say. That's not good.' Dominic pointed at the twisted leg.

'His pulse is fluttery, and he's got a fever. Damn and damn,' Holly muttered as she carefully rolled down Snowy's bloodied sock and gasped.

Dominic caught his breath at the sight of the ripped flesh oozing blood and pus surrounded by shredded skin that was bright scarlet. There was an open wound on the old man's ankle. And as Holly pointed, he saw movement, and to his horror, realised what Holly was showing him – several small white maggots were moving on Snowy's wound.

'It's badly infected. Should we pour some water on it, flush it out?' Holly murmured.

'It needs a lot more than that, I think. He has to go to a hospital.' Dominic pulled out his phone and waved it around. 'There's no reception. Are you sure this is the place?'

'Yes! But sometimes it depends on the weather. Snow . . . Snow . . .' Holly leaned close to the old man's sunburned face which was covered in grey patches of stubble. 'Snow . . . can you move?'

Snow opened his eyes and tried to smile. 'Hol . . . glad you come. We're going . . . picnic, remember . . .' His eyes closed.

Holly looked at Dominic in alarm.

'He's delirious. I'm going to run back. We need to get help right now,' said Dominic.

'You don't know the way . . . I'll go.' Holly started to get up.

Dominic gently pressed her shoulder. 'No. I'm sure I can find my way back. It's more important that you stay with him. He trusts you. Keep giving him sips of water . . . not a lot. Thank goodness he's in the shade.' He looked around grimly. 'It's going to be hard for a chopper to pick him up from here but we'll have to figure something out.' He patted Snowy's arm. 'Hang on, mate. You'll be okay.'

Holly looked up at Dominic, tears filling her eyes. 'You think so . . .?'

'As soon as I get to phone reception I'll call triple zero. Can you give me the location . . .?'

As Dominic sprinted away, memorising her directions as best he could, Holly called after him, 'Don't get lost! And call Sam!'

There was only one point at which Dominic faltered. Did he follow the track to the left uphill or down to the right? He headed to the right and in a few moments heard a ping on his phone and it rang. Relief flooded through him as he saw it was Sam.

'Hey, Dom, Maggie . . . told me . . . we're all worried . . . have you found Snow?'

The reception was patchy but Dominic broke in quickly, 'Snow's in a pretty bad way. He fell and can't move. He has an infected leg and I think maybe concussion. I'd say he's been like this for a day or so. I don't see how a chopper or ambulance can get to him.'

'Where is he?'

'Up the hill behind his place, the rock shelter . . . where the phone reception is supposed to be. But there's no reception at the moment . . .'

'I know it. I'll handle things. Is Holly with him?'

'Yes.'

'Okay, stay in phone reception till I get things sorted.'

Taking a deep breath Dominic looked for somewhere to wait in the shade. The sun was overhead and the air was stiflingly hot. He headed for the nearest tree, then glanced down at his phone and saw there were no bars on the screen.

'Damn.' Slowly he turned and retraced his steps, watching his phone. The minute he had reception he placed the phone on the ground, then moved to sit under a tree in semi-shade.

The next thing he knew, his phone was ringing as if from a great distance. He realised he'd dozed off. Lurching up, he stumbled across to answer it.

'Hello . . . hello . . .? Hi, Sam. What's happening?'

'Sorry it's taken so long. I've borrowed a decent launch from my mate on the island. I'm coming over now.'

'Where will you come to? How do we get Snowy to a boat?' broke in Dominic.

'You and Holly will have to figure that out. Take too long for us to get up the slope to the house or where he is and then back down; we'll miss the tide. And the fire trail road is blocked. This is our best bet. Listen, there's an old landing at the end of the bay below Snowy's place. Pretty rugged, but there was a track somewhere when the landing was in use. A bushfire took out the old place that used to be there. Holly will know it; she grew up rambling around these hills.'

'Okay. I'll head back. Where are you going to take him then?'

'To the jetty at The Point. The ambulance is meeting us there. Go easy with the old man.'

'Right,' said Dominic.

*

Dominic was panting, red-faced and dripping perspiration when he returned to Holly and Snowy. He saw that as the sun had moved across the sky, Holly had rigged up some shade for Snowy's head under her rain jacket tied between sticks.

'What's happening?' She stood up.

Dominic quickly explained Sam's plan. 'We have to somehow get him down to the old landing. You know it?'

'Yeah. Far out.' She thought for a moment. 'That landing's tidal. Did he say he'd checked when the tide was high?'

Dominic nodded. 'Yep. But we have to get Snow down there as soon as possible. So how do we carry him?'

Holly bit her lip. 'Okay. You stay here with him and catch your breath. I'll go down to the house, see what I can find.'

Before Dominic could answer, she took off at a sprint.

Dominic sat beside Snowy and felt his forehead. It was warm, whether from the heat of the sun or because his temperature was still up, Dominic couldn't tell. He glanced longingly at the water bottle, knowing they needed to keep it for Snowy. Dominic wiped sweat off the old man's forehead.

'Hang in there, Snow,' he said softly.

In what seemed like no time, he heard Holly racing back up the hill. She was carrying a blanket and a paper bag.

Panting, she dropped the blanket and pulled a small hacksaw from the bag along with a large roll of heavy-duty duct tape.

Dominic saw instantly what she had in mind and reached for the hacksaw. 'I'll do it.'

Holly pointed at a nearby cluster of young trees. 'Those look strong enough. Here, have some water.' She handed him a warm bottle.

Dominic drank thirstily. 'Thanks.'

He hurried over to the tree and cut two long branches, shaving off the twigs along its length. He tried bending them over his knee.

'They're strong enough, pretty green.' He handed them to Holly.

'This is going to be tricky,' said Holly.

'No choice. We can do it,' said Dominic.

Together they doubled the blanket over the poles, and Dominic wove the strong tape back and forth between them to secure Snowy's weight on top of the blanket.

'We have a stretcher. Now the hard part,' he said.

'Yep. And you haven't seen the way down to the water,' said Holly.

'We'll have to be as gentle as we can,' said Dominic.

Holly smoothed a flat piece of ground and laid the stretcher on it. They both looked at Snowy, who was unresponsive, eyes closed.

'Okay, let's lift him,' she said.

Dominic leaned down, picking up Snowy under the arms. 'Holly, you take his feet,' he said. 'It's okay, he's not heavy.' Together they lifted Snowy's slight figure, Holly supporting his injured leg, and laid him on the blanket. Folding it over him, they taped across the blanket to secure him in the makeshift stretcher.

Holly slung her backpack on, saying, 'You take the weight in front as it's downhill. I'll tell you where to go. We'll have to take it easy.'

After some initial stumbles, they worked out a system of shorthand warnings from Holly about where to step and what to avoid. Once or twice there was a soft moan from Snowy, but he seemed to have drifted into unconsciousness.

Time seemed suspended as each put one foot carefully in front of the other. Dominic had no idea how long they staggered downwards, till Holly finally muttered, 'Here's the old path.'

It was narrow and overgrown, but the grass was flattened enough for faster and easier walking.

'This is better. It's quite smooth,' puffed Dominic.

'Wallabies,' said Holly.

At that moment, they heard the shrill blast of a horn of some kind.

'Sam. He's there,' said Holly with relief.

'Ahoy. Coming down,' yelled Dominic.

Suddenly they could see water through the trees, and then a large launch moored by an old wooden landing at the edge of the water, the tide swishing around the muddy pylons.

Sam was standing staring up at the hillside and suddenly caught sight of the two figures cautiously inching down the slope and waved. He raced to meet them, catching his breath at the sight of Snowy's pale face. Silently he took Holly's end of the stretcher and she hurried ahead to the launch.

At that moment Maggie stepped onto the landing.

'How is he?' she called.

'Hanging in there. Where can we put him?' called Holly.

'On the floor, we have a blow-up mattress,' answered her mother.

Dominic and Sam manoeuvred Snowy on board and onto the mattress.

Maggie immediately felt for his pulse and touched his face. Snowy's eyes were closed, his face pale, his breathing shallow.

She caught her breath as she looked at his leg. 'He's not too good. And if the infection gets away . . .' Maggie muttered.

Dominic stood beside Sam as he drove the boat at full throttle across the water towards The Point. Occasionally Dominic glanced back at Holly, who seemed never to take her eyes off Snowy as she held his hand.

As they pulled in towards the jetty, they could see the ambulance waiting for them. Holly stood up and waved and the two paramedics hurried down the wharf with a stretcher.

'Who's going in the ambulance?' asked Sam.

'Me,' said Maggie.

The paramedics took over swiftly and efficiently.

'Right. We'll take care of him, don't worry. You can call The Vale Hospital to check on him.'

Holly squeezed Snowy's hand as they slid him into the rear of the ambulance and then she turned and gave her mother a quick embrace. 'Call me.'

As Holly and Dominic got back in the launch, the ambulance siren wailed in the fading daylight.

They travelled in silence to Maggie's jetty. Dominic watched the flash of movement between the trees from several cars on the top road heading home from work. *Just another day at the office*, he thought. A deep exhaustion came over him, but a feeling of satisfaction, too. They had done their best for Snowy and given him a fighting chance.

'Good work, you two. Let me know how the old boy does, eh, Holly? See you tomorrow,' said Sam.

'Thanks, Sam,' Holly and Dominic said together.

Holly turned to Dominic as they headed along the jetty. 'And thanks so much to you, too, Dom.'

'Happy to help.' He smiled. 'Would you like to come over for a drink after all that?' he asked.

Holly paused. 'Okay. I will. Thanks.'

Dominic was a bit surprised, though pleased, at her reply.

They walked around the bay to the boathouse, and Holly stopped at the door as Woolly came up to her and rubbed himself against her ankles.

'Hello, cat. Who are you?'

'That's Woolly. He adopted me.' Dominic smiled. 'I'll get us a drink before giving him dinner. Red or white wine, or a cold beer? I have light beer. Or just sparkling water?'

'Actually a cold beer sounds refreshing, thanks. Can we sit outside?'

'That's my office, it's very comfortable with expansive views. And no mosquitoes at the moment.'

Holly smiled and sat in one of the deckchairs.

Dominic came out and handed her a tall glass and an opened beer, and poured one for himself. They clinked glasses.

'We did it! I'm sure Snowy will be okay,' he said.

Holly nodded. 'Thanks for your help. It really hit me how much I care about the old fellow. I know he can be rather, well, grumpy, or stand-offish. But he has a caring heart under the gruffness.'

Dominic nodded. 'I gathered that.' He took a sip of his drink. 'If he's up to it, shall we go over and see him tomorrow?'

'That'd be great. But let's see how he goes. He always puts a brave face on things. He won't want us to see that he's unwell,' said Holly.

'I get that. But I'm wondering how he'll get over this on his own. That place of his is no place for crutches, walking stick or a wheelie walker thing,' said Dominic.

Holly nodded. 'You're right. He shouldn't be on his own. Not for a bit, anyway. I'll speak to Mum.'

'And what about you?' asked Dominic gently. 'How long are you staying with your mum?'

Holly shrugged and gave him a small smile. 'Not sure. Haven't had much of a chance to think things through. Seems to have been one thing after another since I got back. I'm going to meet some girlfriends and catch up. They're always happy to give advice,' she added with a crooked grin.

'Will you stay in hotel management?' asked Dominic.

'I am good at it,' said Holly calmly. 'I'm very organised,' she added. 'But maybe a change . . . I'm not sure. Anyway, I'm not rushing into anything.'

'I feel the same. I quit my job, took time out . . . had a few ideas. But then I've been swept up in the magical cobweb of WestWater.' He waved his arm out towards the outline of Welsh Island, a darkening silhouette as night fell. 'I know the road behind us leads to civilisation, but as long as I'm screened by trees and hills, facing the water, well, I could be on a desert island. With a cat for company,' he added, as Woolly began giving him a where-is-my-dinner look.

'So, it seems you've settled right into being something of a local. A new pal, as Sam says.'

Dominic chuckled. 'Does he say that? The neighbours are all such good people.'

Holly nodded. 'Yes, they are. Mum has been lucky to have such good friends. Of course, they all go way back, so they've stuck by her. What about your family?' she asked.

Dominic didn't answer for a moment as Holly's amazing brown eyes studied him.

'My family are great. All doing their own thing.'

'Lucky them. Lucky you,' said Holly.

'Would you like something to eat? I can whip up a bit of a barbecue?'

'No, thanks. Anyway, I'm beat. Aren't you tired?' She paused. 'Pretty amazing what we did today, don't you think?' They exchanged happy smiles.

'Oh yeah, I'm done in. We barely stopped at all, did we? We just "did". You're very . . . capable.' Dominic wished he'd come up with a better word. She was super pretty, smart, and . . . he couldn't put his finger on the word.

Holly yawned. 'I'm going to crash. Thanks for the drink. I feel I'll sleep now. I was worried that I'd worry all night about Snow.'

'Nothing from your mum?'

Holly glanced at her phone. 'No. It'll be a while, I guess.'

Dominic suddenly said, 'Hey, how is she getting home from the hospital tonight? Tell her I'll go in and get her. It's not that long a drive into The Vale.'

'That's kind of you, Dom. But I'm sure she'll stay the night with a friend or else get a taxi or Uber home.'

'Well, call me if you need anything. I'll check in with you tomorrow morning,' said Dominic, getting up.

Holly bent down to Woolly and picked him up. 'Your dinner is coming, Woolly. Here . . .' She reached out to put the cat in Dominic's arms.

He took Woolly in one arm and awkwardly wrapped his other arm around Holly's shoulders. 'Snow will be okay, don't worry,' he said softly.

For a second or two neither moved, then, as Woolly squirmed between them, they broke apart.

'G'night, Dom,' she called as she headed around the side of the boatshed. And then she was gone.

Dominic put Woolly down and the cat promptly marched inside to his dinner bowl. Dominic followed the imperious tail, smiling to himself.

He put the radio on to listen to the news as he made himself dinner of a salad and a sandwich. Then he opened his laptop and skimmed his emails.

One in particular caught his eye, from an ex-colleague of his who he'd thought might be able to help him.

Hi Dom,
You asked me last week if I could find out what happened to a teacher called Lizzie (or Elizabeth) Lyons. My pal at the Dept of Ed. found the woman you

asked about . . . Her name is now Lizzie Chambers.
She retired from teaching some time back, but lives
in Barrow Field on the North Shore. Hope this helps.
Catch up sometime?
  Cheers
  Glenn

*

It took a second for Dominic to register that this was the woman Suzanne from the book club had mentioned in relation to Joe. Yawning, he added tracking down Lizzie Chambers to his mental list of things to do in the next few days.

Closing his laptop, Dominic wandered out to the deck and stood in the still darkness, taking in the familiar sounds of the night tide swishing around the piers, moonlight gilding the water, the glow of lights amid the trees from unknown houses across the bay. The sound of a distant car on the top road drifted down and he thought of the friends he now knew in the houses dotted among the trees.

All was peaceful. He crossed his fingers and waved them to the night: 'Sleep well, old Snowy.'

10

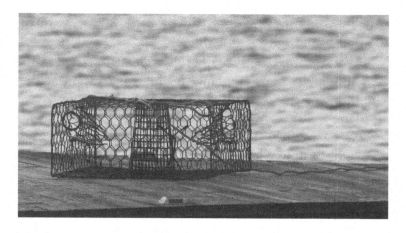

DOMINIC STRETCHED, FEELING SLIGHTLY cramped after hunching over his laptop since breakfast. But the article was finished and he felt he'd done a pretty decent job. He read it through one more time, then sent it to his contact.

He decided he needed some exercise, so he pulled on a T-shirt and laced his sneakers to jog to the general store.

He was halfway there, lost in his thoughts, when he heard someone running up behind him. He slowed and stepped to one side of the grassy track beside the old road. But as he turned to let them pass, he saw that it was Holly.

'Hi.' She waved and slowed to a walk beside him. 'Didn't know you did this little run.'

'It's not so little. But I do generally go at a faster clip. You caught me daydreaming. How's Snowy doing?'

'Mum spoke to him this morning. Said he sounded quite chirpy, but he has to stay in hospital for another day or so. He was pretty dehydrated, and they're monitoring that infection. At least his leg isn't broken.'

'I'll go in and see him later this afternoon. Want to come?'

'Yes, please. Good idea.' Holly smiled, and just as she was about to jog off, she glanced behind at an approaching car. It passed then suddenly slowed and pulled over ahead of them.

'Why are they stopping?' Holly wondered.

'Oh. I know who it is,' said Dominic. 'Come and say hello.'

'I hope they're not offering a lift. That's cheating.' She grinned. 'But I'll race you to it . . .'

They both ran to the big four-wheel drive and reached it side by side, laughing.

Alicia leaned out the driver's window with an amused smile.

'Want a lift?'

'No thanks, just heading to the store,' said Dominic.

'Good, don't think you would have fit anyway.' Alicia grinned as she pointed a thumb towards the back seat, which was stacked high with boxes and paraphernalia.

'What's with all the stuff?' Dominic asked.

'I'm moving. Into the city . . . I'm too busy to be this far out. Of course, I'll still be doing my rounds every month or so.' She leaned out and reached for Holly's hand. 'I'm Alicia Pickering.'

'Holly Gordon.'

'This is Josie's sister,' said Dominic.

'Nice you're keeping fit. Keep it up, Dominic.' Alicia winked. 'By the way, Rob and I are working on a few ideas. Nice to meet you, Holly.'

The car pulled back onto the road and sped away.

Holly looked sideways at Dominic as she started jogging. 'Friend of yours?'

'I'm not sure what I'd call our relationship. She's quite a . . . character.'

Holly raised her eyebrows before speeding up. 'Race you to the shop!'

*

The hospital corridor was quiet save for the low voices at the nurses' station. They found Snowy sitting up in bed sipping a cup of tea and eating a shortbread biscuit.

'Hi, Snowy! Wow, a room to yourself,' said Dominic, noting that the bed beside him was empty.

'Yeah. Moved me in here yesterday. When can I get out of here? I'm dying for a rollie and they won't let me smoke in this place.'

Holly sat in the chair beside the bed. 'When they say so. How's your leg?'

'Right as rain.'

Holly looked at Dominic, who winked.

'Take it easy and make the most of being waited on,' said Dominic. 'Everything is okay at your place.'

'What about the chooks?'

'Sam is looking after them. Everything is fine,' said Holly reassuringly. She exchanged another glance with Dominic and both decided not to mention that Sam had carted the chickens back to his house to keep an eye on them.

'Bloody stupid thing to do. Don't know how I fell off the damn rock shelter,' muttered Snowy.

'You were lucky we came along,' said Dominic. 'WestWater needs better phone reception.'

'My TV is crook too,' said Snowy. He put his cup down and leaned back against his pillow. 'Dunno how much longer I can stay in this damn bed.'

'You'll do what the doctor says,' said Holly sternly. 'And Mum will eat you alive if you get up before you're allowed,' she added.

Snowy drained the last of his tea. 'How'd you get me in here?' he asked suddenly.

'Dominic and I carted you down the hill in a blanket stretcher and Sam and Mum took you to The Point in a launch and popped you into the ambulance. Easy peasy.' Holly smiled.

'Piece of cake,' added Dominic.

'Cripes, I must have been out of it, all right. Don't remember any of that. Thanks,' Snowy said quietly.

'You've done a lot for people around here over the years,' said Dominic. 'Anyone would have helped you. Just lucky we came along.'

'Well, we won't wear out our welcome,' said Holly, pushing his tray table to one side. 'You need anything, you let us know.'

Snowy lay back on the pillow. 'Righto. Cheers.' He lifted his hand as he closed his eyes.

Holly looked at Dominic as they headed to the car.

'There's no way he can go back to his place from hospital.'

'No,' Dominic agreed.

*

Dominic was hosing down the stone steps beside the boatshed where he'd cleaned some fish the night before when Maggie came down the track and called to him.

'Hi, Maggie. Ready for a cup of tea? I was just going to put the kettle on.'

'Always ready. I went in early to see Snowy and pick up a few things in The Vale. Normally Snowy avoids doctors like the plague. He won't tell anyone about his accident. I'm glad he's getting a proper check-up in hospital. Especially as he has no close neighbours,' said Maggie.

'Yes, his place seems very isolated. And no reliable phone reception. You should get a group together to lobby your MP about that,' said Dominic as they headed inside. He flicked on the kettle.

'We're neighbours in that we check on him, but it's not the same as being able to yell over the back fence,' said Maggie. 'There are houses near-ish to him, but no one living there, or rarely. The old ritual of people coming from the city each Friday night to their little fibro holiday shacks doesn't happen like it used to.' Maggie sighed.

'Those weekenders have been totally overhauled in so many places. Suddenly they're glamping sites or trending on Airbnb. I'd hate to see that happen down here,' said Dominic.

'Me too. That's one reason I'm not leaving my place,' said Maggie firmly. 'No matter how much money they throw at me.'

Dominic hesitated, then said, 'Maggie, are you sure? In years to come, it all might get a bit much. It's a big house and garden . . . I know your family are worried about you.'

'I can look after myself, and I can always get someone in to help me. The house is all paid for. I won't be imposing on my kids. Now, let's change the subject.'

'Can I just raise one point?' began Dominic, who saw her lips tighten but decided to press on. 'I know that the offer Harold Marchant has made isn't just for your place, it's a package deal for the other two places adjoining yours. Word is that both sets of neighbours are keen to accept his offer. They won't be happy if they lose this opportunity.'

'I can't help that. We built here first. We said we'd never leave.'

'Maggie . . . I know it's not my business –'

'No, it's not.'

Dominic sighed. 'Are you sure it's not because you and Joe built that house?'

Maggie's head snapped up and she stared at Dominic. She hadn't been expecting this. She seemed frozen for a moment, and then her face crumpled slightly, perhaps fighting off tears. Dominic thought she looked like she'd been punched and he felt a wave of guilt.

Slowly Maggie drew a deep breath. 'I don't know. I just don't know any more.'

Dominic went to her and touched her shoulder. 'Maggie, I'm sorry. I didn't mean to upset you. I'm trying to help you see both sides of this situation. Really I am.'

She patted his hand. 'Of course you are. I do appreciate it. I love my house. And I miss him. I miss Joe so much.'

They were both silent, and Dominic was unsure what to say next. He moved away to pour the boiling water into the teapot.

Reflectively, Maggie looked out at the water. 'We had a good life. We were always so busy . . . the kids, work, the house and our garden. I gave up work again after Holly came along – I think I told you, she was a bit of midlife surprise. Joe tried to make time for everybody . . . the family, the school, all the school projects and kids, plus our own kids.'

'Did you have much time to yourselves, or did you all do your own thing?' asked Dominic.

'We tried when we could. Of course, he spent a damned lot of time at night studying all his books.' Maggie rolled her eyes.

'What sort of books, was he doing a degree or something?'

'Ha! No. I guess we all have our passions and interests. He was obsessed with thoroughbreds. Genealogies, breeding lines. He said it was his hobby. More like an obsession,' she said tightly.

'Did he share this with horseracing people, or just follow his own hunches? Did he like betting?' asked Dominic cautiously.

Maggie spoke slowly. 'It was a game of skill, he said. He followed certain breeders, even got to know some of them. He bought into a couple of share syndicates. I thought it a waste of money, but he was so enthusiastic, I didn't like to give him a hard time about it.'

'Did he have friends in this group? Did you know them?' asked Dominic.

'Oh, I went once or twice to the racetrack when he talked with the trainers and other racing people. Bored me rigid and frankly they weren't my kind of people. A fun day out with friends at the races is different. The behind-the-scenes stuff is not my sort of thing. I told Joe I didn't like him mixing with such types. We had a bit of a row about it. But when I met another couple in the owners' syndicate, they were charming. Lived over the other side of the city, so we rarely saw them.'

'Was Joe paid for his . . . research? Did he win much?' asked Dominic casually.

'Oh, I wouldn't think so!' said Maggie. 'Sometimes he'd come home with a win, like fifty dollars or so. We weren't rolling in money! I ran the household. Joe was the more gregarious one. Always helping people.'

'So you both had separate interests outside the family. And the neighbours?' asked Dominic.

'Dominic, wait till you're married.' Maggie sighed and held out her mug for him to pour the tea. 'There's that mad passion at the start, where you can't bear to be apart, you want to know what the other person is thinking, how they're feeling . . . But after a while, all that wild passion turns into, "Did you feed the dog? Where're the children's schoolbags? Don't forget to call the dentist!" There's no time even to ask, "When are we going to have time together – just the two of us?" Life is full, complicated, busy . . . but when you look back, it was happy.' She looked at him. 'You don't always realise it at the time.' She glanced away, her lip trembling slightly as she added in a low, tight voice, 'And now I feel so angry with him. How dare he . . . just leave us . . .'

She lifted her mug and took a deep swallow.

Dominic waited a moment as he sipped his tea, rather at a loss for words.

Then, as Maggie seemed to straighten up and gather herself, she said, 'Joe and I had good friends in Sam and Gloria and Andrew and Colleen. The people who knew him best. Marcia befriended me; she's on her own. Joe and I had such a busy life . . . I had the kids, and worked when I could. Then . . . my life went on hold. Still is,' she added quietly.

Dominic wondered about her finances, but he

refrained from probing further. Instead he asked, 'What about your future, Maggie?'

She stared at him. 'My kids still need me. And my grandchildren.'

'Do they? Really?' asked Dominic quietly. 'Of course they love to be with you. But do you make any decisions on their behalf? Do you tell them what to do? Would they wait for your advice or approval before doing anything in their lives? Of course, I'm sure they share and discuss things with you. But if my mum or dad tried to run my life . . . I mean, I ask for advice on occasion, and I tell them my plans. But they really have no say in my final decisions. I'm grateful they raised me the way they did and I've learned from my mistakes, but they let me run my own life. They trust they've brought me up to do the right thing. I'm sure your kids feel the same way.'

'I hope so. It hasn't been easy. I've made mistakes . . .' Maggie straightened up and put down her mug. 'But that's what being a parent is all about. It's just harder on your own.'

'I can imagine. Do you ever get lonely, Maggie?'

She held up her hand, as if to stop him. 'Of course I've felt lonely. And you can feel lonely in a marriage too . . .' She stood up. 'I know what you're implying, but I'm not leaving here, Dom. Would you?' she suddenly asked.

He paused, looking across the deck to the quilt of glittering morning water. 'To be honest, I think I'd stay here too Maggie,' he said quietly. 'You know that some of your children think that this place has just got too big for you. Too much for you to look after. Maybe they're right. I just think these big decisions are worth thinking long and hard about.'

She stood up. 'I agree with you, Dom, but rest assured,

I've done my thinking. Thanks for the tea. Holly and I will go in and see Snowy again tomorrow, I think. Much as he won't like it, we'll have to get him some sort of respite care. I'll talk to Josie; she'll know what to do.'

*

It was a quiet street. Dominic drove slowly, looking for number twenty-four.

The houses sat on neat lawns in an avenue of large shady trees.

Lizzie Lyons, now Mrs Chambers, had agreed to see him, though she'd sounded puzzled as to why.

'Tell me who you are again?' she'd repeated when he rang her.

Dominic had given something of a fumbling answer, saying he was a friend of the Gordon family, doing some research, and knew she had worked with Joe Gordon.

'Oh indeed, I did! Such a sad loss. I don't know how I can help, but I'm happy to chat to you.'

He rang the doorbell of the attractive house and a friendly, smiling woman opened the door almost immediately.

'Hello! Right on time. Come in, come in,' she said, stepping back into the hallway. 'I'm Lizzie.'

A man came up behind her and stretched out his hand. 'Hi. I'm Phillip. Come in.'

As Lizzie led the way into a sitting room, Phillip said, 'So you're a friend of my wife's old pals?' He looked slightly wary.

'Not exactly. I know the family now as I'm living close by.'

'So, you're doing some sort of research or something,' Lizzie said?'

'Phil, stop pestering Dominic. Let's sit down and hear what he has to say.'

Dominic felt a slight rising panic. He felt he couldn't ask personal questions if Lizzie's husband was there.

But as they came into the lounge room and sat down, Lizzie shooed Phillip away good-naturedly. 'Phil, scoot. Stop hovering. Would you make us a cup of tea, please, darling?'

Phillip didn't look thrilled, but he shrugged. 'Right, milk and sugar?'

'Just milk. Thanks,' said Dominic.

When he'd left the room, Lizzie said, 'Don't mind Phil. He's a bit curious about someone turning up out of the blue. It was all such a long time ago.' She sighed. 'And such a shocking thing to happen.' She looked at him. 'So what did you want to know? How can I help?'

'You and Joe worked together quite closely, I believe. So you knew him fairly well, I guess? Would you have any idea why he might disappear? What could have happened to him?'

'Oh my goodness, no! I didn't even know about the tragedy at the time as I had gone overseas a short while before it happened. I met and married Phil in Scotland – he was an Aussie travelling around like me. It wasn't till years later when we moved back to Sydney that I heard about Joe . . . just disappearing. I couldn't fathom it. I didn't know Maggie well – I'd only met her a few times at school functions – but, well.' Lizzie sighed. 'I really felt for her. What a thing.'

'But you were close to Joe before you left? I mean, I heard you were very involved . . . in school projects together,' said Dominic politely.

'Ah, yes, we were. Joe and I had such fun together

doing the school plays.' She raised her eyebrows and gave him an amused glance. 'I know what you're suggesting. I suppose there was a bit of gossip as we stayed late doing rehearsals and such. But I can assure you there was never anything untoward between us. Joe adored his wife.' She suddenly looked distressed. 'Oh my goodness, I hope Maggie doesn't think there was ever anything between us! That would be devastating.'

'No, no! Of course not. You know how people throw out casual remarks. I apologise for getting the wrong end of the stick,' said Dominic quickly.

'Here's the tea. Lizzie . . . Dominic . . .' Phillip put the tray down on a small table. 'So, who's grabbing the wrong end of the stick?' He looked from his wife to Dominic.

'Me, I guess,' said Dominic. 'It's such a mystery as to how and why Joe Gordon went missing. I'm trying to chat to people who worked with him, knew him well, neighbours, anyone who might be able to shed any light on it all.'

'And what theories have you come up with?' asked Phillip coolly.

'None, really. Total blank. Lizzie, did you know Joe was into racehorses?' asked Dominic, glad to be able to steer the conversation onto safer ground.

Lizzie looked stunned. 'No way! What, you mean . . . betting on them?'

'Actually he studied their breeding, went through their genealogy, working out what were possibly the best combinations to result in potential winners. Apparently he was very good at it.'

'How peculiar,' said Lizzie. 'I had no idea.'

'He must have made money from it, then,' said Phillip.

'They never seemed to have extra cash,' said Lizzie.

'I do remember Joe saying that he was trying to save up to take a trip back to England to his parents when they were getting on.'

'And did he ever make the trip?' asked Dominic curiously.

'I don't know. I was away six or seven years before Phil and I moved back. We stayed in Adelaide near Phil's family for a couple of years then came back here as my parents missed seeing their grandchildren. I ran into Andrew and Colleen one time and they told me about poor Joe.' She shook her head. 'It doesn't make sense; it never has. He was such a happy-go-lucky sort of fellow. Very caring.'

'Sounds like it'll stay an unsolved mystery, eh?' said Phillip. 'What do they call them . . . a cold case?'

'I'm so sorry I can't help you,' said Lizzie. 'Joe was a lovely, decent man. I hope he didn't have some awful . . . accident. Are his children doing okay? I remember the twin boys quite well.'

'Yes. Maggie has been a devoted mum. She's still in the same house, but on her own now.'

'Oh, please give her my best wishes,' said Lizzie.

'And good luck with your enquiries. You just doing this as a favour for Maggie, then?' asked Phillip.

'Not entirely. Her daughter Josie asked me if I could help. The family were hoping for some answers,' said Dominic. 'Anyway, lovely to meet you both; appreciate your time. And thanks for the tea.'

*

Dominic was checking the pots he'd planted with tomatoes which sat on the deck where he could wave off snooping predators. Woolly had become the official watch cat, giving a death stare to any bird or beast that approached the precious plants.

'Wow, they're coming on nicely,' came Josie's voice as she walked around the corner to his deck. 'What are they?'

'Tomatoes. They're not ripe yet.'

'I can see that.' She looked at the label stuck in the dirt. '"Grosse Lisse". Nice. Oh, I see they have cute "dresses". Is that to stop the vermin?' she asked, lifting up the 'skirt' of strong netting draped around the pot.

'I cover them at night. Had a possum sitting on the railing eyeing them off.'

'Can I sit down?' asked Josie, pulling out one of the deckchairs.

'Of course.' Dominic smiled. 'Have you seen Snowy?'

'Yes. He's doing okay.'

'That's good.'

'Well, it is and it isn't. He can't go back to his place yet,' said Josie.

'Yes. He has no family at all?' Dominic asked.

'Not that we know of. He never married. Said he was an only child. He once said he had an uncle he was fond of as a kid.'

'That's not much of a family history. So what's the plan?'

'I've managed to get him into The Glades where I work. It's got a respite care centre. He'll be able to have good care and physio to help him get back on his feet. He'll whinge and object, of course. But it's the only way to get him fit enough to go back and be on his own. If he didn't live in the middle of nowhere, he could have regular home visits,' said Josie.

'He'd shoot himself before he'd move into a retirement home, I'm guessing,' said Dominic.

'Don't say that!' exclaimed Josie, looking alarmed.

'Oh, sorry, I didn't mean that like it sounded. Snowy wouldn't be that stupid. He's still got all his marbles,' Dominic apologised. 'So long as he knows the respite care is only temporary. I'll be able to visit him every few days,' he added.

'Yes. That would help. It's so sad and difficult when you see older residents who are left to their own devices with families who rarely visit.' Josie sighed. 'There're residents in there who must feel so abandoned. Even if they have dementia, sometimes they have moments of lucidity. Situations like that are heartbreaking to see, actually.'

'So you can understand how your mum feels,' said Dominic. 'About selling her place.'

'She's not going into a home! If she sells up she'd have enough money to buy a nice little place, travel and keep some aside for later plans,' said Josie firmly.

'Have you talked about this with her?' asked Dominic.

'Have you?' she asked pointedly.

'Kind of . . . it's clear she really doesn't want to leave. I can understand her point . . .' he started.

'Oh, Dom, I thought you'd talk some sense into her.' Josie gave a rueful smile. 'But I know what she's like. Hey, I also wanted to ask you if you'd found anything out, about my father, I mean. With everything that's been happening, I haven't had a chance to catch up with you.'

Dominic nodded. 'If I had anything concrete, I'd tell you straight away, of course. But actually it's been quite a challenge! There's one avenue that might need some exploring. Did you ever hear your mother talk about a friend – acquaintance, really – of your father's called Maurie Richards?'

Josie thought about this for a moment. 'No, I don't think so. But then I don't know if I ever met all their friends. Who is – or was – he?'

'An unsavoury man who had a lot of nefarious business activities that got him murdered. There's lots of colourful stories about him on the internet. He was also involved in the racing scene with your father, it seems.'

Josie looked horrified. 'What! That's horrible. My parents wouldn't know people like that!' she exclaimed.

'Did you know your father was very clever at researching, tracing, analysing – whatever the term is – thoroughbred horse bloodlines?' asked Dominic. 'Your mother said he'd spend time on it in the evenings.'

Josie stared at him. 'No, I didn't. He liked the races, I remember that . . . How come you know all this?'

'Just chatting with people who remember your mum and dad in their early days here, and doing a bit of research.'

Josie looked away, biting her lip. 'I do seem to recall my parents arguing once. It shocked me as they never fought. It wasn't vicious or anything. I wasn't yet a teenager and didn't pay a lot of attention. It was so strange to hear raised voices, but Mum did sound fed up. I remember Dad used to sit up late at night working in his study and Mum was always complaining about it. I always assumed it was schoolwork. Hmmm, well, that's interesting. But I doubt whatever he was doing was a big issue in their marriage. What did Mum say? I suppose you've asked her?'

Dominic shrugged. 'Your mother told me she had no interest in Joe's obsession with horses, though she didn't seem to mind him having his horse hobby. Your dad also bought into horse share syndicates, but I think that was a peripheral thing and not uncommon then. I gather his knowledge was useful in racing and breeding circles.'

'Really?' Josie was staring out at the water now. 'This is a bit of a surprise. You don't think he lost money on horses? Betting or something like that? I'd hate to find out Riley had some side passionate interest I didn't know about.' She was thoughtful for a moment. 'But you know, I don't think Dad gambled. Mum wouldn't have stood for that. They were careful with money; we weren't spoiled by any means. But I never heard any quarrels or threats about money. Mum is big on budgeting.'

'Well, it's not something I was expecting to find. Horses sound like an interesting hobby. It doesn't seem like money was involved.'

'I suppose there always has been, always will be, speculation about what happened to him,' said Josie sadly. Then she looked at Dominic, her eyes widening. 'Oh – you're not suggesting that he might have been . . . you know, killed by some gangsters, are you?'

Dominic hesitated. 'I wouldn't think so. Though . . . you couldn't rule it out, I suppose. But there was another piece of information I heard, and I was able to rule that out as potentially useful.' He looked Josie in the eye. 'I heard some speculation that your dad might have had a romance with one of the young teachers at his school. She left the school and went overseas just before your father disappeared.'

Josie looked taken aback. 'What? You're joking. Really? I haven't ever heard that,' she said. 'What did Mum say?'

'I didn't feel it was right to mention it. But I found the teacher, a nice woman. She was surprised and a little shocked when I mentioned the rumour and she said she and Joe were just good friends at school, working on the same projects together,' said Dominic.

'Did you believe her?'

'I did. I was never convinced that he'd voluntarily run off, because of all the things he left behind – including his wallet. You can meet Lizzie, if you like.'

Josie shook her head firmly. 'There's no need. If she's prepared to sit down and chat to you about my missing father, then I'm satisfied she had nothing to do with it,' she said. But she quickly added, 'I mean, I really appreciate what you're doing and everything, Dominic.'

Dominic bowed his head in acknowledgement.

'But you're not going to stop looking, are you?' she said anxiously.

'Of course not.' Dominic smiled. 'I'll keep looking for answers while I can, Josie.' The more he got to know the family, the more he could see how deeply the loss of their husband and father had affected them. He realised he felt invested now. But seeing Josie's reddening eyes, he steered the conversation away. 'So. Who is going to break the news of going into respite care to Snowy?'

'Mum will. He'll accept it from her,' said Josie firmly, straightening in her chair.

Dominic nodded, knowing Snowy would trust Maggie. 'How long do you think he'll be there before he goes home?'

'Probably two or three weeks, till he has his strength back. And as long as he does all the exercises. Or else . . .' Josie said with raised eyebrows.

'What's that mean?' asked Dominic.

'Well, maybe getting settled somewhere new now might be easier and better than when he's frailer and can't manage. Snowy would never want to be a burden. I'm just being practical. Mum should be thinking along the same lines, I reckon. But she'll have choices as she'd be getting a terrific price for her place. And all that land!' Josie stood up. 'Thanks for the chat, Dom. Always good to catch up.'

'See you, Josie. Say hi to Riley.'

*

Holly tapped on the side wall as she came around to the deck.

'Hey, Dom, you there?'

'Hi, Holly. How're things? News of Snowy?' Dominic smiled as Woolly stretched and padded over to greet Holly.

Holly squatted on her haunches to pat the cat. 'Bit of a problem, actually. Snowy's refusing to go into respite care. Josie is cranky and Mum can't persuade him.'

'Argh, the old bugger. I guess that's no surprise. He definitely can't manage on his own yet?'

'No way! Not yet.'

'So what to do? Kidnap him?' Dominic asked, only half joking. 'Tell him we'll take him to lunch at the pub and take some beers to the care home?'

'He'd never speak to us again. He's due to be released from hospital tomorrow. I feel so sorry for him,' said Holly.

They were both silent a moment.

'So how bad is he?' asked Dominic, remembering how frail Snowy was when he and Holly had first visited.

'Well, he'll be on crutches for a while, so he can't easily cook or do stuff. He refuses to let anyone shower him. Sits on a stool in the shower. Has to remember to take his medication. And he can fall easily. That kind of thing, according to Josie. His place would be totally unsuitable.'

'Maybe we could persuade him by promising that if he spends time in respite, we'll smuggle him out and take him home and look after him? I'll help,' Dominic suggested.

'What? Live with him in his shack? No way, it's too primitive. But you could,' she countered. 'You just sit at a laptop all day.'

They both laughed.

'What about your mum's house?' Dominic asked.

'She's already got Paul. And how would we get him down all those steep steps on crutches? Anyway, he'd never agree, because he'd hate feeling he was a burden on my mother more than anything.' Holly sighed, then glanced up at Dominic. 'You know, I can see this nightmare repeating itself with Mum one day. I'm beginning to see what Josie means about trying to convince her to sell up while she has a golden opportunity.'

'Yeah, I know what you mean. But at the end of the day, Maggie's fit and agile now and knows her own mind. She'll have to come to the decision on her own,' said Dominic. Then, seeing Holly's glum face he continued, 'I was just heading down to the creek to get the crab traps. Want to come? Throw in a line? The tide will be coming in soon. And by the way, how're Snowy's chooks? Do you know?'

'Sam says they're fine. I think he's getting quite attached to them.' Holly added, 'Maybe we should check on Snowy's place? Do you have time?'

'Sure. But if the tide is low we won't be able to get to the old landing.'

'I know another way . . . we can go to the jetty down from the poet's house and cut through from there on a track over the hill.'

'Okay, if you say so. You ready to go now?'

'Half an hour? I'll just grab a few things, then meet you back here.' Holly waved and hurried away down the side of the boathouse.

Dominic stood still and mentally ran through a checklist.

'I'm going prepared this time,' he said to Woolly. 'I'll leave you some food.'

Holly laughed when she returned to find Dominic's compact backpack, hat, towel, thick gloves and small shears all ready to go.

'Boy Scouts, huh? What're the cutters for?'

'I've been caught out before. Sometimes those crabs can grab and hold on to the pot or have a go at you. Just need a weapon of some description.'

There was little wind and they made good time down towards the creek under the midday sun.

'Let's go to Snowy's place first and swing past the pots after. Don't want any crabs to expire while we're checking out his shack,' said Dominic.

It was hard to talk above the noise of the engine, but neither seemed inclined to chat. It was pleasant just cutting through the calm water in familiar surroundings.

Dominic steered the small launch into the wharf below the poet's house and they tied up quickly and climbed the oyster-covered steps.

'Heavens, the boatshed here is still a shambles,' said Holly as they headed along the jetty towards it. 'There's probably gear and an old boat in there.'

'Yes, I wondered about that when I came here with CeeCee,' agreed Dominic, pointing at nets, old oars, rotting baskets and traps.

Leaving the wharf, rather than head towards the poet's house, Holly followed a faint trail that wound around the hill. As they came over the crest, Dominic saw the roof of Snowy's shack and the mighty angophora behind it in the sheltered gully.

'Did Snowy throw this place together himself?' asked Dominic as they finally reached his outer fence.

'Yes, it started as an old army tent, he told me. Then he got some corrugated iron and a mate gave him bits of timber, and it went from there. I think Mum, Uncle Sam and Aunty Gloria gave him things over the years – tea towels and other basic stuff. Simon says he remembers coming home from school one day and Sam's ferry was weighed down to the gunwale with furniture and boxes. A local, old Mr Flowers, had died and his wife – who was extremely religious – said she was going into a nunnery or something, so had no need of "possessions". Can you imagine it! Simon told us all never to tell Snowy where the stuff came from as he loathed Mrs Flowers. So did Mum. Gloria told me the story of how Mrs Flowers saw Mum over at The Point ferry wharf in the middle of the initial search for my father. She made her get down on her knees in the middle of the general store and pray aloud with her while people were buying their milk and bread and papers next to them. Apparently Mum was mortified.'

'That would have been embarrassing,' agreed Dominic, raising his eyebrows. 'Have you ever asked your mum about it? Or your siblings?'

'Nope. It's always been easier to avoid the subject completely. And you know, I never have anything to add anyway – I was only five at the time and I don't remember anything about it.' She gave a him a look he couldn't quite decipher. 'I thought you knew all our family foibles. Isn't that why you're hanging around?'

Her sort-of smile took the sting from her words but Dominic couldn't help bristling. 'Is that what you think . . .? That I'm just here for the . . . I don't know, sensationalism, of the story? I mean, it is a strange mystery, tragic of course. But is it so hard to believe I'm just keen to help my new neighbours?'

'It's okay, Dominic.' She cut him off. 'I'm sorry. I didn't mean to accuse you. Let's get down and check the house. Thank goodness Sam took the chickens.'

Dominic was happy to let the subject go. 'What's left of the garden sure needs work,' he said as they went through the gate.

'It could be a lovely place.' Holly stopped and looked at the shack. 'Y'know, if you built something proper here and went up a floor you'd probably see the water.'

'What about that nightmare track down to the old landing?' said Dominic. 'And you'd have to build a deep-water jetty.'

Holly shrugged with a small smile. 'Just takes money.'

'Well, Snowy's never going to do it. Nor sell.'

'Of course not. Where would he go?' said Holly.

'Speaking of that, any further thoughts on how to get Snowy to agree to go to Josie's nursing home for respite?' Dominic asked.

'When I was back at the house Mum said she'd just have to give him an ultimatum: if he doesn't go into respite for proper care, he won't go home at all. Don't worry, Josie will keep an eye on him. Maybe we should visit him as soon as he's settled in and reassure him,' said Holly.

'Poor old bloke. I guess it is the only way. If he doesn't get better, he won't get back here,' said Dominic.

'Let's not jump the gun.' Holly put her hands on her hips and looked around again. 'Okay, I'll start inside; you check round the place outside.' She pushed the front door open.

By the time they finished tidying up, the sun was starting to sink.

'I've cleared up as much as I could. Miracle I didn't see a snake,' said Dominic as he came inside. 'Oh, this looks very shipshape. Want a drink of water?' He opened his backpack.

'You can make a black coffee or tea,' said Holly. 'I've cleaned out his fridge.'

'Can I have a look around?' asked Dominic. 'Does Snowy need anything from the house?'

'He could probably do with some clothes. Not much to choose from here; he lives in those khaki shorts and shirt like a uniform.'

Dominic walked through the cottage, which was indeed basic.

A sagging sofa and a chair sat in front of an ancient television, and there were roughly made shelves on bricks that supported books, maps, some files and an unconstructed model aeroplane still in its box. Dominic moved forward to look at some fading photos hanging on the wall.

There was one of a young Snowy in an army cadet's uniform; a photo of yachts sailing with Crouching Island behind them; a photo of a woman – *could it be his mother?* Dominic wondered. And there was a framed award of some kind. It wasn't a fancy frame or prominently displayed, just a certificate for an *Outstanding Citizen's Award for Community Support* awarded to Johnathon 'Snowy' Burns.

'Holly, have you seen this?' Dominic called.

Holly came over and peered at the wall. 'Wow. I wonder what that was for? Must have been a long time ago, it's yellowed with age. I bet if we ask him about it, he'll just brush it aside and say it was nothing, typical Snowy.'

Dominic pulled out his phone and took a picture of it. 'I'll show it to Maggie or Sam, see what they know about it.'

Holly looked around. 'Well, this is the best we can do till he gets back and restocks the cupboards and fridge. We'll have to wash stuff like sheets too, though he's only got an old tub and a copper out the back, can you believe it?!'

'A copper what?' Dominic grinned.

'To wash clothes in! With a fire underneath it . . .' she started, then saw he was joking. 'Oh, you do know what a copper is.'

'Not many today would. I've just read a lot of books! C'mon, let's go. I'm keen to see if there're any crabs in the pots,' said Dominic.

The little tinnie puttered through the last pink and gold light of the day, turning into the darkening creek.

'Tide's coming in,' said Holly. 'Looks very fishy.'

Dominic peered into the water. 'Sure does. Shall we throw in a line before we check the crab pots? There's handlines up under the bow there. With the bait for the traps – mullet frames and fish scraps.'

'I wondered what I could smell,' chuckled Holly as she bent down and took out a mini-esky. 'How deep is it here?'

'There's a bit of a hole I've found. Who knows what might be lurking, resting up, breeding . . .'

As Dominic guided the boat to the spot he knew, Holly pulled out two fishing lines on old plastic reels, a knife and a plastic bag of fish guts, flesh, mullet skeletons and a few prawns.

He cut the motor. 'Grab the anchor. When I tell you, can you please drop it over?' He was looking for his marker among the trees. 'Okay, now. Gently.'

Holly slid the anchor into the water and once it stopped she looped the rope around the cleat on the side. 'I got it, Dom,' she said as she tied it in place with a bit of slack. 'I grew up around here, remember?' She gave him a crooked grin and reached for the bait bag.

Dominic watched Holly expertly strip some of the sinewy skin and meat off the fish frames and twist it onto the hook, then handed him the knife and some of the scraggy fish skeleton. 'Might not be much left for the crabs,' she said as she dropped her line in the water.

Dominic fished in the stern on the opposite side of the boat. They sat in companionable silence, the lines balanced on their fingers, their eyes adjusting to the darkness that swiftly followed the twilight. In the distance a yellow light winked on in a house on a hillside.

'I think I had a decent touch there,' said Dominic softly a short time later.

Holly nodded but didn't answer; she was concentrating, watching her line. Then suddenly she jagged it and start pulling the taut line into the boat, dropping coils at her feet as Dominic watched. He could tell by the tautness and Holly's straining that it was a decent-sized fish.

As he stood, cursing that the net and gaff were out of reach under the seats, Holly sat down with a thump.

'Damn. Lost it. Tackle too, by the feel of it.'

They examined the bitten-through line.

'You need a trace – there should be some in the bottom of that tackle box,' said Dominic. 'Can't let that one get away.'

He was about to offer to help tie on the trace and

new hook and sinker, but bit his tongue when he saw that Holly had found what she wanted and was expertly tying the wire between the line and hook. She checked the weight of the sinker, rebaited the hook and dropped it back over the side.

'Who taught you to fish?' said Dominic with admiration.

She didn't look up from the line disappearing into the still water. 'Snowy, actually.'

'Of course he did,' said Dominic.

'Oh, I got a few tips from Sam, too,' Holly added. But she didn't look away from the water.

Dominic had a bite then and pulled in a decent little bream. 'Well, that's legal size. Woolly's dinner for a day or three.'

They sat comfortably, sometimes chatting, sometimes enjoying the stillness. Dominic had no idea how much time passed. Holly's silhouette was motionless save for occasionally lifting her hand slightly, testing the weight of the line.

Dominic was rebaiting his hook when suddenly Holly jerked, stood up and began pulling her line in hand over fist. At first he thought she was making a bit of drama out of it, but then he dropped his line and scrambled for the net lying to one side under the middle seat.

Holly was straining against the weight, then the fish angled around, so she moved to the other side of the boat.

'Keep hauling in, Holly. I've got the net,' he called as he moved next to her.

'No. No. Too big. Got a gaff?' she panted as the fish made a frantic run away from the boat.

She was slowly making headway, but Dominic could see the line cutting into her finger.

'Do you want me to have a go? Take over?' he asked.

'No way,' Holly panted.

Later neither of them could recall how long it took for Holly to gain the line, inch by inch, until there was a surge beside the boat. Dominic picked up the gaff and, standing close to Holly, leaned down, trying to get the gaff into a massive fish.

'Leave it,' Holly puffed. Twisting away from Dominic she turned, flung her arms and heaved herself back, slinging a massive dark shape into the boat. Instantly they both saw the huge triangular head.

'Flathead!'

Holly had her foot on its lower tail section as Dominic turned the watery beam of the old torch on the fish, which suddenly stopped twisting and lay still, gasping through its gills.

'Wow, that's massive,' said Dominic wonderingly. 'It's, what, ninety centimetres?! It's as big as a kid! Want a photo?'

'No. No. It's a female when they're this big. We have to put it back.'

'You're right. It must be breeding up here. Watch the spike on its head!'

Dominic pulled off his T-shirt and wrapped it around the head of the fish as Holly gently removed the hook and dropped her line. For a moment they both stared at the mottled dark-brown prehistoric-looking creature.

'Sam would say, "You could put a saddle on that lizard!"' said Holly with a delighted grin.

Slowly they lifted the fish to the gunwale and Dominic unwound his T-shirt. The huge animal slid silently into the water, disappearing instantly with a flick of its tail.

Neither said a word as they stared into the water. It was as if the fish had never appeared.

Without speaking, Holly pulled in the anchor, Dominic stowed the gear and started the engine, and they headed for his crab pots.

*

It wasn't till they could see the dim outline of the jetty and the boatshed, where no doubt Woolly was waiting impatiently, when Holly asked over the noise of the engine, 'What do you think she weighed?'

'Close to five kilos, I'd say.'

'I'm glad we let her go.' She turned away.

Together they tied the boat to its mooring by the slips and took out their gear. They'd found four decent mud crabs in Dominic's pots, which he'd transferred to a bucket. As he picked this up he said, 'Fancy a crab salad?'

Holly shook her head. 'I'm whacked. Maybe tomorrow. But I'd love a beer or a wine!'

'Me too.' They looked at each other and smiled.

When they got inside, Holly went to wash up in the bathroom and Dominic threw the bream into the microwave for Woolly.

'My turn to have a wash. Woolly can smell that bream! Help yourself to a drink,' said Dominic as Holly reappeared.

Feeling less fishy and in a clean T-shirt, Dominic returned to find Woolly tucking into his dinner.

'I took the bones out, only took a couple of minutes to cook.' Holly smiled.

'Once he smells fish, he won't settle for anything else.'

'I opened a bottle, hope you don't mind,' said Holly, handing him a glass of wine.

'Cheers. Here's to you! Why don't we sit outside, light the candle.'

It was balmy, mosquito free and quiet. They settled in the deckchairs and Woolly, having scoffed his fish, immediately jumped onto Holly's lap and curled up contentedly. Dominic felt relaxed, maybe because he was tired, but also, he knew, because he felt comfortable in Holly's company. He didn't feel the need to make stimulating conversation.

'You forget how special it is here when you're indoors,' said Holly quietly. 'One of the few things Mum says about my father is how he used to sit on their deck, feet on the rails, "drinking it in".'

'It must have been so different from England,' said Dominic.

'Josie's been to Bristol, where Mum came from. She says it's a nice enough city. But it ain't WestWater. No wonder Mum took the big leap and agreed to stay on.'

'Where do you feel most at home?' asked Dominic. 'Or are you still looking?'

'I could say wherever I am is home. But it's not. WestWater is my home. Always will be. No matter where I end up.'

'So what are your plans?' asked Dominic, then wished he hadn't.

'Same as yours,' Holly said lightly.

'I don't have any.'

'Touché,' she said, reaching over to clink her glass against his.

They refilled their glasses and slipped into an easy conversation.

She was curious about Dominic's family. 'Which seems only fair, as you know everything about mine!'

He was intrigued by the work she'd done in Perth and wondered how she could apply hospitality management to other areas.

After an hour or so Dominic asked, 'Hey, would you like something more substantial to eat?'

'No, I'm fine, thanks. I'll take a raincheck; I'm knackered. Oh, but I hate to disturb Woolly.' She looked down at the cat and smiled.

'He's never fallen for anyone before.' Dominic got up and bent over to lift Woolly off her lap.

Holly looked up at him, her expression soft, her prickly defences absent.

Their faces were close. On impulse, he leaned in and kissed her.

She softly kissed him back, and Dominic was suddenly hit by a torrent of feelings that surprised him. He stood up, feeling confused. Holly uncurled her legs and gave Woolly a quick pat.

'G'night, Dom. See you tomorrow.' And she was gone.

*

Dominic stood on the deck, looking at the full tide lapping close to the top of the jetty, then suddenly pulled off his clothes and dived in.

He wondered if Holly had heard the splash.

For a moment it crossed his mind that, had it been Alicia, she'd be swimming naked beside him.

But then, Alicia would not have thrown the fish back into the water.

He thought of Holly's sweet face as she'd looked at him. And, treading water, he smiled.

II

DOMINIC FOUND AN IRON in a cupboard with a portable collapsible ironing board which he set up on the table to improve his wrinkled short-sleeve shirt and crumpled white shorts.

Sam and Gloria had asked him up to dinner.

'Just a neighbourly thing,' Gloria had explained. 'We haven't caught up for a while and Paul is moving back home now he's well enough, so we wanted to have a get together before he left. Sorry Maggie can't be here as she and Marcia have gone out to dinner. But Holly will be.'

*

As he went through the open front door it occurred to Dominic that it was nice to walk into a neighbour's house and call out, 'Hey, where is everyone?'

'Out here, Dom, help yourself to a drink on the way through!' called Sam from the deck.

Availing himself of a glass of wine from the bar, Dominic came through the doors onto the deck. 'Hi, everyone! Sam, I left a bottle of something in the kitchen. This is a nice drop, though.' Dominic lifted his wineglass.

'Take a seat, Dom. We're only on the nibbles,' said Gloria, passing the grazing plate around. Holly smiled at him and Paul raised his beer by way of greeting.

'You ready to hit the waves again, then, Paul?' asked Dominic.

'Ready to work. Been away too long, have a pile of jobs waiting. But yes, I'll venture out on my board.'

'Are you nervous?' asked Holly.

Paul shrugged. 'Cautious. Now I'm recovered I'd like to find the kid who hit me. The locals know who it was.'

'What for? Are you going to take legal action?' asked Sam.

Paul shrugged. 'Nah, too hard. Just might talk to him, though.'

'How's Jason?' asked Dominic. 'Haven't seen him for a while.'

'He and Rory are busy,' said Holly. 'Mum is hoping Jase can come back and help with some new project.'

'He's overloaded with work,' said Paul. 'If Mum does sell and downsize, he won't have to do so much at her place.'

'But he loves what he's doing and so does Mum,' said Holly.

'If she does move, we'll be very sorry to see her go,' said Gloria carefully.

'We're not moving anywhere,' said Sam. 'And we're older than Maggie.'

'But there's two of you,' said Holly. 'That does make a difference. You can help each other as well as share the work in the garden and stuff. Mum would go nuts without a garden, even if it is hard work for her.'

'Mum'd get enough money from the sale to buy somewhere with a garden plus hire a gardener for the harder jobs,' said Paul.

'Maggie manages very well. We all rely on our kids occasionally . . . and good friends,' said Sam, smiling at Dominic.

'Doesn't she get lonely, though?' said Holly. 'No offence, Sam, you and Aunty Gloria have been wonderful. But that's a big house to be in on her own.'

'But it holds a lot of memories,' Gloria said softly. 'Maggie's fit as a fiddle, and she'll be able to get help if she needs it later on,' she continued, adding calmly, 'It's her decision, after all.'

'Our kids have been saying the same thing to us for years,' said Sam affably.

'But time moves on . . .' said Paul. 'She doesn't have to move too far away; look at all those luxury retirement places Marchant has built.'

'But they're small!' Gloria interjected. 'My friends live in one. They're not like a proper house.'

'And meanwhile Marchant builds a sprawling luxury estate on Maggie's land,' said Dominic.

'Really? Is that what his plan is?' Sam asked, sounding alarmed, and rolled his eyes. 'Well, if Maggie sticks to her guns, Marchant might have to rethink it. No matter how much money he throws at her.'

'An offer like Marchant's wouldn't come along too

often, I reckon,' said Paul.

'But I'd hate it to be our family that ruins WestWater,' said Holly.

'Not an easy decision,' said Sam. 'Pros and cons on both sides.'

Gloria pushed back her chair. 'I'll just go and get the bread and salad,' she said, putting an end to the subject.

'Need a hand?' asked Dominic and Holly together, then laughed.

'No, no thanks, it's fine. Later maybe.'

Dominic smiled at Holly, admiring her dress, which was made from a light summery fabric and tied on her shoulders. Her hair was piled on her head, tendrils falling around her face.

'I popped in to see Snowy today,' said Sam. 'Never seen him looking so frail. He watched you kids grow up.'

'Who's going to look out for him when he goes home?' asked Paul.

'I will, of course, but I can't be there twenty-four-seven. It's the damned phone reception that's the problem,' said Sam.

'Maybe he needs a satellite phone,' said Dominic. 'A shame there's no neighbours living close by.'

'Seems to me we had a lot of friends and neighbours dropping by in the old days,' said Sam. 'I had a lot of great mates.'

Sam leaned back in his chair and began to recount a story of a group of local sailors back in the day who'd started racing their old boats outside.

'That's the ocean in the wild blue yonder past Crouching Island,' he explained. 'Then one bloke challenged the others to race all the way down to Hobart.

291

Their prize was a carton of beer and an Aussie jam tin, shined and mounted with a plaque! And they say that's how the now-famous Sydney to Hobart race started.'

'That's pretty amazing,' said Dom. 'You never know what happened in the old days I guess. Which reminds me ...' He took out his phone and scrolled through it, handing it to Sam. 'I took this picture when we cleaned up Snowy's place. What's the story about this certificate for some citizenship award Snowy was presented?'

Sam peered at it. 'Ah, I'd forgotten that. It was quite a big deal at the time. Snowy discovered and caught some blokes who'd been trapping and then selling wildlife from the National Park. Removing anything from the park is a crime. He knocked that on the head by having them arrested.'

'I love it,' said Dominic, smiling at Holly. 'There must be a million more stories I've yet to uncover down here.'

'Oh, you have no idea,' said Sam.

Gloria put a butter dish and salad dressing on the table.

'Oh, that's so cute!' said Holly, pointing to the ceramic replica of a thatched cottage which held the butter and a wishing well full of salad dressing.

'That was my granny's,' said Gloria. 'I still have some of her pieces, passed down by my mum.'

Paul rolled his eyes. 'Yep, we have "treasures" too, as Mum calls them. Mostly books and stuff. If Mum moves out, she won't be able to take all those things.'

'Maybe your mum should go through them and start writing out who's who and where it was on the back of photos. The stuff we had to toss out when my folks passed on . . .' began Sam, shaking his head.

'Pass your plate, please.' Gloria gave Sam a look as he passed his plate to her.

*

After a lovely meal, Gloria stood up. 'Let's clear the dishes and we'll have dessert. Who's for coffee?'

'I'll help.' Paul got to his feet. 'Stay there, Holly.'

Sam pushed back his chair. 'Nightcap, anyone?'

'I'm fine, Sam,' said Dominic.

'No, thanks,' said Holly.

They were alone on the deck. Dominic turned to Holly. 'You look very pretty.'

'Thanks,' she smiled.

'Can I take you out to dinner one night?'

'I'd love that. My mother says I'm becoming a hermit.'

'Shall we go somewhere super trendy and upmarket? I'll ask my mate Rob what's hot at the minute.'

'It doesn't have to be expensive and snooty . . . just good food and a bit of fun,' said Holly. 'Apart from seeing my old friends here I haven't caught up with the new places.'

'Done. Are you free Thursday night?' said Dominic. He didn't want to rush anything. But he couldn't help thinking his mum and dad would like Holly. He'd hesitated at the thought of taking Alicia home to meet his folks, especially after Cynthia had been so scathing about her. He got an entirely different impression about Holly. *Slowly, slowly*, he cautioned himself.

They sat in comfortable silence for a few moments, then Dominic asked thoughtfully, 'What Paul said, about your mum having a lot of keepsakes, photos and such. Do you know what's in them?'

'No idea. Mum has a lot of favourite things, too: cushions, books, a special vase. Human nature, I guess, hanging on to tangible things rather than memories. That's one of the problems if Mum moves. She'll want to take *everything*,' said Holly.

Dominic got to his feet. 'C'mon, let's clear the last of this. A coffee sounds good.'

*

'Who's the new girlfriend?' asked Rob when Dominic answered the phone.

'I was about to call you,' said Dominic. Obviously Alicia had passed on the news of him out jogging with a brunette. 'I'm taking her to dinner . . . haven't been anywhere smart or fun in too long. I'm out of touch down here, though, any ideas where we should go?'

'A seduction or a keeper?' asked Rob. 'Or both?'

Bemused, Dominic shook his head. Rob was a one-off.

'What if she just happens to be a nice girl I'm friends with? She's down here at WestWater with her family, who are very nice, and she's someone I like, who's easy to get on with,' said Dominic. 'Actually, she's Maggie Gordon's daughter.'

'That sounds intriguing,' said Rob. 'Right. Go to Swami's. It's a mix of India meets Mata Hari . . . exotic, delicious, sexy.' He chuckled. 'So what else is new? What are you doing with yourself?'

'I might ask you the same thing,' said Dominic. 'I've still been digging into the horseracing elements of Joe's story, but there's nothing really new to report. Catch me up on your exciting life.'

'Well, to tell you the truth I'm busy . . . with Harold Marchant. He's impressed enough with Terry – my creative futures designer mate – to hire him for a project. Alicia says Harold doesn't know quite what that's going to be but doesn't want to lose him to another job.' Rob hesitated, then added, 'I think Harold's planning on Terry doing something fabulous with Maggie's land.'

'Well . . . it might not be that easy. I know Maggie's dead against selling, even though her kids seem to be coming around to the idea. And frankly, Rob, I can see Maggie's point of view,' added Dominic.

'But it's a no-brainer, mate. She'd be mad to say no to the money Harold's offering. Has the WestWater plague got to you now? Or just this family?'

'Maybe both. Look, the family are not as sentimental about the house as Maggie is, but Maggie is adamant about staying.'

There was a pause on the other end of the line before Rob said, his voice sounding slightly strained, 'Listen, Dom, you've got to get them to persuade Maggie to sell. *My* future hangs on it!'

Dominic was surprised at the seriousness and intensity in Rob's voice.

'What do you mean? You can always get work!'

'It's Alicia. We're working together and I don't want to let her down. Plus, I can see that hanging around Harold could be profitable. There could be a lot of opportunities for me, as well as him! But he's got a short attention span. Wants to make his mark in some way.'

'So what's Alicia think?'

'She sees it. Harold wants a legacy that's tangible. And she likes us working – well, hanging out – together.'

'And you?'

'I'm a bit smitten,' admitted Rob. 'I see another side to her.'

Dominic bit his tongue, but was wondering what Rob had seen other than the sexy, teasing woman Dominic knew.

'How deep does smitten go? Is this the Rob of easy come, easy go?' Dominic joked, but he was thinking that Rob was sounding . . . well, entangled. 'Listen, Rob,' he continued. 'Maggie's situation is complicated. But she's a strong woman. She could tell her kids to go to hell . . . much as she loves them. There's a pull here for her . . .'

The phone was silent for a few seconds. 'Joe?'

'I guess so,' said Dominic quietly. 'What would Harold do if Maggie's answer was a definite no?'

'He'd be very pissed off . . . at me. So would Alicia.'

'Can't you come up with something else? Another place, another idea?' said Dominic. 'There've got to be other potential sites with great views and workable locations.'

'The problem is the loss of face. It'd be a resounding fail – unless I had something else in play. Anyway, it's not just Maggie's place,' said Rob. 'The young couple up the back have agreed to sell. And the people on the other side aren't far off.'

'So it's just Maggie sitting in the middle? What happens then? You can't very well build around her.'

'No,' said Rob in a resigned voice. 'The huge compound Harold has in mind requires three blocks. If one owner refuses to sell, then the deal is off for all of them. It's all or none.'

'Well, that's a pretty awful situation. Maggie wins and she loses, either way.' Dominic didn't know what to feel.

'It sounds like she's made up her mind – although I don't know how she can still think that the missing husband will just bloody walk in the door one day.' Rob sighed, sounding more disheartened than Dominic had ever heard him.

Dominic felt very conflicted, torn between Maggie's and Rob's different ideas. But before he could say anything, Rob said quickly, 'Listen, don't stress. Not your problem. Enjoy Swami's.'

*

And they did. Dominic sat across from Holly, thinking what a chameleon she was; casual and outdoorsy, with no make-up and looking like a teenager one minute, sweet and demure at Sam and Gloria's dinner, and now sophisticated, elegant and stunning in the glow of the brass lanterns inside the exotic trappings of the restaurant.

'This food is extraordinary,' said Holly. 'Such subtle spices, it's like Indian meets tropical South Pacific or something. I love it.'

'I feel like I'm on the set of a Bollywood movie, though,' said Dominic.

She laughed. 'Bring on the exotic dancers!'

They lingered over the elaborate dishes, talking intensely on many subjects, sharing parts of their lives, making each other laugh.

When they returned to WestWater, it seemed perfectly natural to walk together to the boatshed.

'Shall we share a nightcap with Woolly?' said Dominic.

Holly kicked off her shoes and curled her legs under her on the divan. 'Sounds good.' As Dominic handed her a glass, she went on, 'So. What do I do about Mum? And Snowy. He's still mad as a cut snake about being in respite. I'll go and see him again.'

'I'll come with you as extra support. He just needs to know there are people who care about him. Hopefully that'll help get him through.'

'Thanks, Dom. He likes you. You know how I knew

you were a decent person and I could trust you?' she asked suddenly.

Dominic shook his head.

'The fact that he showed you the dreaming cave. Very few people know about it; Snowy keeps it that way.' There was a comfortable silence before she said, 'So are you writing anything at the moment?'

'I've been doing some articles to keep my bank account happy. Nothing I can really sink my teeth into, though. That stuff doesn't really interest me as much as it used to.'

Holly nodded, looking thoughtful, then shot him a direct look. 'Josie told me that you were looking into my dad's disappearance as a way to get ideas for your book.' She held up a hand as Dominic moved to explain. 'It's okay, I understand you'd never write about it without Mum's – or our – permission. Josie explained that she was just happy someone was trying to shed some light on it all.' She paused, then continued, 'And I am, too. Do you think we will ever find out what happened to him?'

Dominic looked at her. 'I really, really hope so. Do you? Isn't that the real reason Maggie won't sell the house?'

Holly shrugged. 'Maybe. I think on some level she must understand that he's not coming home. But it's the not knowing why . . . how . . . if . . . And the fact she loves the place, that house they built together. I don't think she could ever be happy anywhere else. Perhaps she's worried the memories will fade if she's not there, where those memories were made. Everything from grass to glass means something to her. Oh, we've heard the stories for years.' She looked at Dominic with a pained expression. 'It's the same for Snowy. He'd shrivel up and die if he couldn't be at WestWater.'

Dominic's heart twisted as he saw her expression.

'Holly, we'll go and see him tomorrow. Back him up, explain he's got to exercise in that place. He can't sit and mope or he'll never get out,' he said insistently.

'Yes, good plan. Thanks, Dom.' She looked at him. 'Sam gets it. He'll be carried out on his old ferry. We've all put down roots here. No matter where we go.' She unfurled her legs and stood up. 'We were having such a fun night . . . sorry to get all maudlin!'

Dominic jumped up and wrapped his arms around her, holding her. 'It was fun. Let's do it again soon, find another great place.' He smiled and looked down at her, his heart turning over at the pools of her huge brown eyes, so he leaned down and kissed her deeply. Then, at her intense response, they were suddenly, wildly, reaching for each other.

Breathless, Holly drew away.

'Oh, Holly . . . stay, please . . .' Dominic whispered.

'Not tonight.' She gave a small smile. 'There's no rush, Dom. It's okay,' she said softly, putting a finger to his lips. 'I'm not going anywhere.' She turned and, carrying her shoes, walked softly outside.

He watched her figure disappear up the dark track, knowing she knew every inch of the path. She had so much of this landscape imprinted on her soul.

Out of habit he checked his emails as Woolly made a nest on the bed.

Hey Dominic! Hope all okay there . . . just checking in . . . not sure exactly when I'll be back but will give you a heads-up! Be in touch. Cheers, Nigel.

Dominic stood on the deck staring at the outline of the hills and Welsh Island darkly painted on the silver sea across the bay.

Every shiver from the trees, every swish of the lapping night tide swirling around the pylons to dissipate on the rocks, every smell and sound and sensation was now familiar and reassuring.

It would be hard to leave.

*

Dominic was sitting at the end of the jetty, fishing, when he heard footsteps and turned around expectantly. His heart sank when he saw Simon striding towards him with a dour expression of impending drama. *What will the issue be this time?* wondered Dominic. He didn't fancy a repeat of their first meeting.

'Hey, Dominic! Any bites?' Simon lifted his hand in an awkward greeting as Dominic scrambled to his feet.

'One or two. You visiting your mum?'

'Yeah. Trying to talk some sense into her.'

'Oh, about selling the house?'

'Yep. I keep telling her it's a no-brainer. She'll never get as good an offer again, I'd say.'

Dominic moved his line slightly, wondering whether to pursue this topic. Thankfully, Simon ploughed on before he had a chance.

'But actually, the reason I wanted to speak to you is that I had a talk with Josie the other night.'

Dominic held his breath. 'Oh?' he managed.

'I'll admit I didn't like the idea of you asking around about my . . . missing father, raking up old hurts. But Josie has now filled me in on what you've found. I was concerned about digging up, well – who knows what.'

'Josie asked me to see what I could find,' cut in Dominic quickly. 'She felt the . . . silence had gone on too long. Not that I've found any real answers, but we thought it couldn't hurt to try,' he added.

Simon nodded stiffly. 'I get that now. Well, Josie told me about Miss Lyons, the teacher from the school. I remember her and, well, I always wondered . . .' He trailed off awkwardly. 'She and Dad always seemed very close.'

'I believe any speculation about that can be put to rest,' said Dominic slightly pointedly, looking down at where his line disappeared into the water.

'So I gather. It's a sensitive issue. In the back of my mind I've always thought he might have disappeared with that woman. And now I know he didn't. I – ah – just wanted to apologise for having a bit of a go at you. I was worried you'd find out he *did* run away with her and it would break Mum's heart. But I must say, to now learn he mixed with gangsters and gamblers – well, I didn't see that coming at all.'

'It did seem out of character against the picture I had of the man,' said Dominic.

'Do you think his disappearance might have had something to do with his association with these criminals, even if it sounds like the plot of a crime movie? I haven't broached the subject with my mother. It just seems so . . . unbelievable.'

'I really don't know,' said Dominic. 'It must be difficult for all of you. I guess you never come to terms –'

Simon cut in, sounding irritable and frustrated. 'That's the point! I'm beginning to think that while Mum is in that house it will always hang over us all. She should sell, get out, move on. So we all can.'

Before Dominic could reply there was a tug at his line, so he turned and started pulling it in.

'I'll leave you to it,' said Simon, and he started to turn away.

'Thanks for coming, Simon,' said Dominic, but the other man was already walking down the jetty and didn't turn.

*

Dominic and Holly were directed to a room at the end of the hallway. They tapped at the door and a gruff voice called out, 'Push it open. I'm still in here!'

They exchanged a smile and opened the door to see Snowy sitting in a chair, his leg stretched out on a stool. He broke into a big smile.

'Well, thank my lucky stars! Are you gonna spring me outta here?'

'Not quite yet, Snowy,' Holly said, laughing.

'How're you doing, Snow? We brought you some goodies from the general store,' said Dominic.

'Any beer?'

'Nope. Next time. How's the leg?' asked Holly.

'Aw, getting there. Can't stand on it for long. Have to use crutches or the blasted walker thing. Fat lot of good that's going to be at home,' he muttered.

'Well then, you'll just have to get stronger before you can walk out of here,' said Dominic.

'What do you do with yourself here, Snowy?' asked Holly brightly. 'Can you eat with the others in the dining room?'

'The tucker's not bad. But I'm blowed if I'm gonna play games and watch crap TV in the social room.'

'What do you do instead?' asked Dominic.

'I'm doing the exercises they showed me, that's like homework for me. And then I do the crossword. Well,

302

try to. What's the sum of a nurse's pay?' he asked.

Holly and Dom looked at each other blankly.

'Not enough?' said Holly.

'Nearly!' exclaimed Snowy. He picked up his newspaper. 'See, it fits in here ... M. E. A. G. R. E.'

'Very clever,' said Dominic.

Holly unwrapped some slices of cake and put them on Snowy's side table. 'Do you want tea or something?'

'It's not tea time. Everything runs by the clock here. Sort of. You can go to the tearoom place if you're mobile enough. I tried it once; never again.'

'Why, is the tea that bad?' said Dominic.

Snowy screwed up his face. 'That mad old bastard Dean Banks is always in there. Seems like he's lost his marbles, but I reckon he knew who I was.'

'Who's that? Why is he a mad old bastard?' asked Dominic mildly, though the name rang a bell. 'Banks? Any relation to Leo?'

''Course he is. Leo's nutty father.'

Dominic looked at Holly, who shrugged.

'What's wrong with Mr Banks?' she asked.

'He's always been a cranky old sod,' said Snowy. 'A nasty piece of work. Never liked him. And I don't think his son is the sharpest tool in the shed.'

'Leo went to school with Josie, I think,' said Holly. 'Few years younger, maybe. He was around our place a lot for a while when we were growing up.'

'Money. That's all real estate people think about.' Snowy sniffed.

'Well, it is their job,' said Dominic placatingly.

'Listen, Snowy. This is a local place with local people. There're probably other people you'd know and like living here,' said Holly. 'You be nice.'

Snowy winked at Dominic. 'Maybe if I make a nuisance of myself they'll throw me out early, eh?'

'You can't leave till you can walk and are able to look after yourself,' said Dominic firmly. 'Come on. Finish your cake and we'll go for a wander down the hall, see how you're doing.'

It was slow going. Snowy shuffled as he gripped the handles of his walking frame. Holly and Dominic walked on either side of him as he limped down the empty corridor. They reached a small lounge and Snowy promptly sat down, panting slightly.

'Bugger me, what a pain in the bum this is,' he muttered.

'Cup of tea will fix you up. Black and sugar, right?' said Dominic cheerfully.

'I'll make it,' said Holly, heading to the bench where tea things were set up beneath a sign: *Ring bell for staff to make hot beverages.*

'Aha!' came a friendly voice as Holly was putting a teabag in a mug.

They all looked up as Josie came towards them.

'Well, this is a nice surprise. Visitors, eh Snowy?'

'Hi, Jo, we didn't know if you were working today, didn't want to bother you,' said Holly.

'Yes, I'm working, but I try to pop in each day to see Snowy. How're you feeling?' Josie asked him.

'Crook,' said Snowy grumpily, then corrected himself. 'No. I'm pretty good, Josie.'

Josie tried to look stern. 'You can't fool me, you know. You do your exercises and you'll come good.'

'Thanks for getting him in here,' said Holly quietly to Josie, knowing how hard it was to get respite care at short notice.

Dominic looked over as a woman in a smart but comfortable-looking staff tracksuit with a name badge came in, pushing an elderly man in a wheelchair who peered at them in a slightly glazed way.

To Dominic's surprise Snowy tugged at his arm, hissing, 'That's him . . . bloody Dean Banks. Get me out of here, I can't stand that bastard.'

'Hey, Snowy, it looks like the poor fellow doesn't know where he is,' said Dominic quietly.

Snowy turned in his seat, putting his back to the man in the wheelchair as Holly took his tea over and handed it to him.

'What's going on?' asked Josie quietly.

Dominic shrugged. 'Snowy has some beef with the old bloke over there . . . says it's Dean Banks, Leo's father. Can't stand him for some reason.'

Josie went over and spoke quietly to the carer with the old man and then re-joined them.

'He's a difficult old fellow, been that way for years. Hard for Leo.'

'Does Leo visit him?' asked Dominic.

Josie shrugged. 'Not much. Mr Banks can get aggressive at times, but we can manage him.'

'And he doesn't remember you? Your family?' asked Dominic.

'Yes, but he rarely acknowledges me, even then,' said Josie dryly. 'He never smiles and is fairly unpleasant with the staff. I wonder if he was always so miserable.'

'What about Leo?' asked Dominic.

'I know he had a difficult childhood. His mother left when he was young. Can't say I blame her for leaving her old man if he was such a grump during their marriage,' said Josie quietly. 'Can't have been easy for Leo.'

Snowy sculled his tea and handed the mug to Holly. 'Thanks, love. Now let's get outta here.' With difficulty he stood, holding his head high and staring straight ahead, and walked stiffly out of the room with the help of his walker.

Holly and Dominic followed behind him, glancing back at Josie who gave a shrug and a thumbs-up.

Halfway down the hallway, Snowy sat down on his walker for a rest.

'Snowy, what's got into you, I never thought you'd hold a grudge,' said Holly.

'He's a nasty piece of work. Never liked him.'

'What about Leo? Mum said you took all the kids and Leo fishing a couple of times,' said Holly.

Snowy harumphed noncommittally.

'Leo and his old man lived near you, didn't they?' Dominic asked Holly.

'Yes. They were in the house the young couple have now, up the back. Was rented out for yonks. Banks Senior had some woman living there for a while, Mum says. Don't think she liked the place, or him really,' said Holly.

'No wonder Leo hung around your house,' said Dominic.

Holly nodded. 'And now he wants her to sell. He's after a fat commission. I think he's very ungrateful.'

'Maybe everyone should just let your mum make up her mind,' said Dominic as Snowy eased himself to his feet and set off for his room again.

'I'm starting to feel the same way.' Holly sighed. 'Moving would be a nightmare for me too right now. Got to get serious about finding a job first.'

'You can't leave our neck of the woods, Holly. It's good having you around again,' said Snowy.

Holly smiled. 'I'm glad I'm back too, Snow,' she said with a glance at Dominic.

Dominic held the door open for the old man. 'Well, you'd better get shipshape and fit again so you can get home,' he said firmly.

'Aye, aye, captain,' said Snowy.

*

Dominic glanced at Holly as he drove back to WestWater.

'You're worried about him,' he said.

'Can't help it. He's been around as long as I can remember. Hardly ever came to our house, though. Uncle Sam and Aunty Gloria were always around to do all the nitty-gritty stuff after Dad disappeared.'

'It's sad you never got to know your dad, have some memories,' said Dominic.

She shrugged. 'Don't miss what you never had,' she said stoically, but Dominic thought he heard a small note of bitterness in her voice.

'You're a survivor, huh?'

'Not really. I feel for my mother in one sense, but she has always been strong; she's protected me, loved me. She's never shown her angst or pain to me in the way she has with the others. All this has brought up a lot of pain for her that I've never seen before.'

'By "this" do you mean my asking questions, talking about the past?' asked Dominic quietly.

'That's part of it. But I really mean Mum being pushed out of her house –'

'I don't think that's the case –' started Dominic.

'Yes, it is. I think I should call Leo and talk to him. Just because he knows us doesn't give him the right to pressure Mum,' said Holly.

Dominic thought for a minute. 'There's something I have to tell you. My friend Rob, the one who visited me before you came home, is involved with Harold and Alicia too. He told me that if your mum sits tight and refuses to sell, Marchant won't buy the neighbours' lots. It's an all or nothing deal. Leo hasn't explained that to your mum, it seems.'

'What?! But doesn't that mean that if Mum refuses to sell, nothing can happen? That would be good news, wouldn't it?'

'Well, yes, but if she doesn't sell it might be a case of Maggie winning the battle but not the war. The neighbours may be furious. Harold can be a devious old businessman; I reckon he knows how to get what he wants.'

'That's why he's rich, I suppose,' said Holly. 'How much influence does this Alicia have? Who is she exactly?' She gave Dominic a sideways glance.

'I met her when I first got here and Rob and I spent an afternoon at a party on Harold's big cruiser. She just crops up now and again.'

'So she's just a friend?'

Dominic hesitated. 'I did spend some time with her initially, but to be honest, I'm glad she's gravitated towards Rob now. They're friends.'

'Well, at least Mum can make the decision knowing all the facts now,' said Holly. 'I'm going to talk to her, and, if it's what she decides, we'll ring Leo to officially refuse the offer.'

*

Rob rang later that afternoon and announced he was driving down to see Dominic.

'No ifs or buts, mate. Need to have a chat. Want to walk around a bit and see what's what, let off steam.'

'Sure thing,' said Dominic calmly. But as he put down his phone he knew the news about Maggie's firm refusal of the land sale must have filtered through to his friend.

Rob turned up in shorts and a T-shirt. He hadn't shaved and looked like he hadn't slept, either. He dropped into a chair on the deck. Dominic handed him a cold beer.

'Cheers.' Rob swallowed a mouthful and sighed. 'Man. I see why you like it down here. Hassle free.'

'Maybe you should drop out for a while too,' suggested Dominic with a smile.

'Yeah. I wish. Look, this land deal is turning into a big issue –'

'Is that why you've stopped by?' Dominic cut in. 'To get me to ask Maggie to be reasonable?'

'Well . . . not exactly. I mean, you're not family, though you do seem to have some influence. Everyone likes you, Dom,' Rob said a trifle sarcastically.

Dominic shrugged, dismissing the dig. 'Look, I know the deal would mean a lot to you –'

'And Alicia. It's not the money, lord knows Harold has it in spades, but having money breeds a desire for more, I've learned.'

'And Alicia?'

'Listen, she's ambitious, I know that. But I think she's a straight shooter. We've been working together and well . . . seeing each other.'

'As in . . .?'

'Yeah. *Seeing* seeing.' He looked at Dominic. 'Do you care?'

Dominic smiled. 'Alicia is hard to resist. But good on you. Take care, though. She can be dynamite . . . in a good way, but also unpredictable.'

Rob didn't ask Dominic's reasons for saying this. He got it.

'So how angry is Harold going to be?' asked Dominic. 'Have you or Alicia spoken to Leo Banks? He won't be pleased either. That's a big commission to lose.'

'They'll all be furious, is my guess. The neighbours who wanted to sell won't be happy either.'

'No,' agreed Dominic. He was about to continue when he heard footsteps and Holly skipped around the side of the boathouse to the deck, then stopped.

'Oh. Sorry, didn't realise you had company.'

'It's okay, Holly, this is great,' said Dominic, leaping up. 'This is my friend Rob.'

Rob stood up. 'Sorry, I wasn't expecting to meet a beautiful woman.' He smiled charmingly, tugging at his T-shirt.

Holly wore no make-up and looked fresh and youthful in a simple sundress. She looked slightly taken aback at Rob's greeting.

'Sit down, it's good you're here,' said Dominic. 'Want a cool drink?'

'Just sparkling water, please.' Holly turned to Rob as they both sat down. 'Are you staying, or are you guys planning something? Talking business?'

'You're a very welcome distraction. You're Maggie's daughter, the one from Perth, right?' Rob smiled.

'Half right. I'm from WestWater originally.'

'I get it. No matter where you are, this is always home,' said Rob.

'Might sound like a cliché, but yes, that's true. What's your connection with Dom?' she asked.

'We met at uni.'

'And he led me into heaps of trouble,' said Dominic, handing Holly a tall glass.

They chatted briefly, but Holly sensed Rob was being polite, wanting to talk with Dominic alone. She stood up.

'I'd better go. I was just passing on my way to see Marcia. Nice to meet you, Rob.'

Rob glanced at them. Holly was standing beside Dominic, her hand on his shoulder. Dominic had reached up to cover her hand with his. They were both smiling at him.

Rob was suddenly reminded of a formal sepia photograph of a nineteenth-century wedding with the groom in formal suit, seated, and the modest bride standing by the chair. Were they posed that way to show the status of their union, or for the bride to show off the laboriously stitched gown she would never wear again? *Did she realise her life would possibly be one of hard work, child-rearing and remaining in the background?* Rob mused.

It was just a flash of a thought, but he saw instantly the bond and affection between Holly and Dominic, a connection that possibly they didn't see or know themselves.

He smiled.

'Nice to meet you, Holly. I'm sure we'll see each other again.'

Dominic stood as Holly left and called after her, 'Say hi to Marcia for me.'

Rob looked at Dominic as he sat back down. 'How long has this been going on? She's very sweet.'

'Nothing is "going on". She's just part of Maggie's family.'

'Did you go to dinner at Swami's? How was it?'

Dominic couldn't help but chuckle. 'Nothing gets past you. It was fun. Super place, thanks for the recommendation. I haven't been getting out much. And frankly I don't miss trekking to an office in the city every day,' said Dominic.

'I'm all over the place.' Rob sighed. 'Harold and Alicia have me on the hop. Honestly, I really need this land deal to come off. Is there any way Maggie can be convinced to change her mind? I know of some very cute places that might appeal to her.'

'You sound like Leo,' said Dominic. He paused, then continued, 'I'm surprised, mate. You've always been a free agent, a one-man band. This deal with Harold doesn't sound like your sort of thing.'

Rob leaned back, stretching his legs out. 'Man, it's complicated. Alicia got me into it, and I was happy to be involved . . . both with her and this idea for Harold. But now I feel a bit like I'm down a rabbit hole.'

'You want out?'

'Alicia is addictive.' Rob gave a small smile. 'And the chance of a cut of Harold's development is also alluring. At the moment he thinks I'm some kind of marketing genius, but if the sale for his estate doesn't go through, I'm pretty sure he will blame me.'

Dominic sipped his beer. 'And what about Alicia? Will she dump you too? How do you feel about that?'

'Sometimes I feel like a fly in a spider web. I mean, she can spin you to the moon and back and then you walk in expecting hugs and kisses and she looks up like she's trying to remember your name!'

Dominic burst out laughing. 'That's what makes Alicia so exciting. You won't have a dull moment. But seriously, how entangled are you with her? Combining business and pleasure is never smart.'

'You know me, I get bored easily.' Rob smiled, then became businesslike. 'I think I have a handle on how Harold operates, but his mind is a bit like a Catherine wheel: spins from one thing to another and gets faster and faster as ideas tumble out. Some mad, some way out of left field, and some brilliant. He has the money but not the time. The estate is to be his legacy.'

'Why doesn't he leave money to a bunch of not-for-profit good institutions instead?'

'Just not his style. The trouble is, Harold is into edifices. Alicia says he wants to leave something that is tangible. With his name on it.'

'Yes, I realise that,' said Dominic.

'So come up with an idea for me. Something better than building a massive home and buildings for staff or whatever he has in mind.'

'Like pools and peacocks,' said Dominic, rolling his eyes. 'I mean, can you imagine the locals loving a bunch of screeching peacocks in this nature's wonderland?!'

Rob smiled but Dominic could see he was worried.

'We'll put our heads together. Another beer?'

Rob gave him a thumbs-up. 'Thanks, mate.'

12

THE NEXT FEW DAYS were unexpectedly busy, and for the first time Dominic wished he had more room in the boathouse – an office or study where he could leave piles of notes and reference material. He picked up sheets of paper from the floor before they could blow out through the open doors to the deck and into the water – well, the mud – as the tide was out.

He anchored his notes under two books and headed outside for a breather to clear his head. Seeing his ripening tomatoes, he picked them before the birds descended.

Two hours later he was wearing a shirt and tie and seated at a table in a restaurant overlooking Sydney Harbour.

He smiled at an attractive woman opposite him.

'Hard to believe how the time has flown, Julie. It all seems a world away now,' said Dominic.

'Maybe for you, Dom! Sounds like you're living in paradise. I'm going flat chat. Did I tell you I'm working with Senator Lauder? But I've decided to run for election when it comes up next time. Do you miss it? The politics, the crises, the manipulations and spin?' she asked.

'Oh, you mean the back-stabbing, the outright misleading ploys, the "naked ambition and smiling assassins"? Isn't that what Brian Crumbie wrote in his opinion piece – "24 Hours in the House"?' Dominic said, laughing.

'Another journo who won't be on the premier's Christmas list,' Julie chuckled.

'No. I don't miss it, really,' Dominic replied. 'Sometimes I miss the energy, the friendships, even the deadlines, I guess. But I set my own schedule at the moment, which is rather elastic depending on the fishing, or guitar practice, or whatever else takes my fancy that day.' He smiled.

'I can see the attraction, but it's a waste of your talent, Dom,' said Julie seriously. 'Listen, I asked you out for lunch to ask a favour, sort of. Paid, of course. I need some background on a couple of projects I'm sitting on . . . an investigation into the racing industry.'

Dominic's ears pricked up. 'Funnily enough, I've made a connection there, as they say in the racing business,' he said.

Julie leaned across the table. ''Twas ever thus. Corrupt for years – money changing hands and deals being done between high flyers, money laundered, bribes paid. There are legitimate and passionate people in the industry, of course, but the dark underbelly needs exposing. It needs a clean-out. And Senator Lauder and I want to see it done.'

'Good for you. So how can I help?' asked Dominic.

'I need background info, facts. And written up so that it's clear and logical. I'll send you a proper brief, of course.'

Dominic thought a moment. 'It's a one-off, right? I don't want to slip back into fulltime work just yet. I'm still looking into some things of my own.'

'Dominic, I need this background information. The senator and I don't have the time or the staff to devote to it. You could really help me out,' she said.

Dominic knew his former boss was ambitious and smart and he shared her values.

'Okay. Give me the basics,' he asked as small bowls of chilled cucumber cream soup were served with parmesan crostini.

'Hmm. Gorgeous.' Julie dipped her spoon in the soup. 'The racing industry is multi-layered. Attracts all kinds.'

Dominic paused as he broke his crostini in half and tucked into his entrée. 'There must be dozens, if not hundreds, of businesses attached to such a huge industry. Legal and not-so-legal. So who takes home the money?' he asked.

'Hard to say, but we want to know who's illegally involved or has a conflict of interest.' Julie pointed her spoon at her soup. 'This is divine.' She took another bite. 'Also, there are high-profile people in other fields who are involved and some big racing players you'd never know about. You'll see certain names and companies connected to influential people that are of interest to us.'

'Okay. I'll start making discreet enquiries,' said Dominic as their waiter cleared their bowls and topped up their mineral water.

'You have a good nose for a cover-up, as I've learned. The money involved is staggering. I'll get the paperwork sent to you. There're some recordings as well. Do you think you can get back to me before my committee convenes again?'

'I'll do my best,' said Dominic. 'Holy mackerel!' he exclaimed as their waiter put an overflowing seafood platter in the centre of the table.

'Salmon, sir,' smiled the waiter.

'And the rest. Looks amazing! Good choice, Julie.'

They looked at the lavish platter of salmon surrounded by halved Balmain bugs, tiger prawns, Sydney rock oysters, grapes, strawberries, asparagus, charred lemon halves and crispy golden French fries on the side. Two glasses of complimentary champagne appeared as a second waiter placed finger bowls beside their plates and a jug by the platter.

'Hollandaise. Or any other dressing if you prefer?' asked the waiter.

'The chef's own Hollandaise?' asked Julie.

'Of course, madam.'

'I believe we are just fine then, thank you,' said Julie.

*

Still thinking about his lunch with his former boss, Dominic got out of the car and loosened his tie. As he turned away he heard a toot and looked up to the road to see Alicia waving at him. She made her way down the driveway towards him.

'My, a tie . . . where've you been?'

'I might ask you the same thing.' Dominic smiled. 'I thought you'd moved?'

'Oh, I have. Twice since I last saw you, actually. I came back for some pot plants I left behind. And I wanted to speak to you.'

He watched Alicia's long legs carefully descend the rough stone steps in ridiculously high stiletto heels. She was wearing a green pants suit, the jacket buttoned over her breasts. Her blonde hair was sleek, her eyes screened behind huge dark glasses, her lipstick a burgundy slash.

'That's your gardening outfit?'

She shrugged. 'I was doing a little business on the side. What's your excuse?'

'Same, actually. A business lunch. Very nice it was too.'

'The food or the company?' She reached him and smiled, her familiar perfume drifting across to him.

'Both. My old boss. Well, she's not old. Former boss. Wants me to do a job for her.'

Alicia paused, tilting her head as if to lean towards him. Dominic pulled his keys from the car.

'So, is this business, a coincidence, or do you want to ask me something?' he said pleasantly.

Alicia folded her arms. 'It's about Rob. I need you to persuade Maggie Gordon to sell up. It's a decent offer.'

Dominic sighed. 'And why should I interfere?'

'Because Rob is your friend. And mine. I don't want to see him screw up an opportunity with Harold.'

'What makes you think I can change Maggie's mind? She doesn't listen to her family. She's entitled to decide how and where she lives,' said Dominic calmly.

'C'mon, Dom. You know what I mean.'

'No, I don't. Rob's my mate, yes. But we've never interfered in each other's business lives.'

'You want to see him lose a great opportunity? Harold can be very generous.'

'And very tight, probably, if it suits him,' said Dominic.

Alicia pushed her sunglasses up on her head and gave him a faintly quizzical smile. 'Rob told you that?'

'He didn't have to . . . it's a trait often noted in obscenely rich people. Listen, Alicia. As it happens, I have talked extensively to Maggie about the offer – both the pros and the cons. But I couldn't and wouldn't try to talk her out of staying in the home and area she loves. She has no reason to sell up and move. That's her decision.'

'Harold was hoping to turn the area into something of a . . . landmark.'

Dominic didn't want Alicia to race back to Rob and say he'd refused to listen to her, so he said, 'Alicia, you're smart. You must know no one around here wants a landmark. They want it just as it is. There must be other places, other projects, that would interest Harold.'

'I told him about this land at WestWater. So I need to make it happen. I can smooth out any wrinkles.'

'What do you mean, wrinkles?'

Alicia shrugged. 'Oh, like irksome bureaucratic council regulations.'

Dominic gave a short laugh. 'That'd be right. Look, Alicia, Rob is my friend, and he can be amusing and a bit colourful, but he's actually very stable, sensible, decent and honest . . .' He paused as Alicia pouted and gave an amused scowl. 'I don't want him hurt – financially, professionally, or emotionally. Okay? You look out for him,' he added, to soften his comment.

'Fine. I get it.' She glanced over Dominic's shoulder, then leaned forward and surprised him by giving him a quick kiss on the cheek before turning back to the steps. She paused and looked over her shoulder, blowing him a kiss. 'Glad you enjoyed lunch, sweetie! See ya!'

Slightly bemused, Dominic watched her long legs in

the crazy shoes head up the steps. Who wore a designer linen pants suit and shoes that must have cost a grand, to collect pot plants? Alicia.

He shook his head and turned to go down to the boat-shed, then stopped.

Halfway down the hillside path Holly was standing staring at him. She turned away and hurried back up towards Maggie's house, disappearing into the trees.

'Holly! Wait! Hol–'

*

Dominic changed out of his suit and hurried to Maggie's house.

Jason was out the front holding the hose over his head.

'Hot?' asked Dominic.

'Yeah. How're you, Dom? I've been working up the back, bit of a hike.'

'You're not planning to transform all that bush, are you?' Dominic asked.

'No way. Anyway, it's hard to tell where Mum's boundary ends and the national park starts. Which is what the art is – to make a native garden look like it's been there for generations. You looking for Mum? She and Holly just left. Gone house hunting.'

'Whaaat? Is Maggie considering selling up after all?' exclaimed Dominic.

'Hell no. Holly's looking for an apartment.'

'Oh. I didn't realise she was thinking of staying in the area more permanently,' said Dominic.

'Yeah, I don't know either. Seemed to be a spur-of-the-moment idea. Seeing what's available, I guess.'

'Ah, where is she looking?'

'No idea. Seems silly when she could end up working anywhere. A few times when she was manager she lived on the hotel premises, but she's looking for something a bit different, I think. I thought she was only hanging around until she found the right job.'

'How's Paul?'

'Glad to be back at the beach. Lot of mates looking after him. Though their sort of "looking after" isn't quite the same as Mum's.' Jason chuckled.

'You spend a lot of time here but Paul said the other day you're flat out with work. It's a lot for your mum to look after; how do you feel about her staying on?'

'It's her choice. And frankly I'm glad she's staying. I understand her feelings. I mean,' he paused slightly awkwardly, 'I mean, it's not just because of . . . what happened that she won't leave. This area is a magic circle in a way: the water, the bush, being surrounded by untouched nature. Its history . . .'

Dominic nodded. 'I get it. It either draws you in or not. It takes a certain person to appreciate and fall in love with WestWater. I have friends who just look at me like I'm mad, not for living in a boatshed, but for being away from everything,' he shrugged.

Jason rolled his eyes in amusement. 'Yeah, like the amenities of a shopping centre, cafés, people, entertainment and so on.'

'They're reachable when you need them,' Dominic agreed.

'Hey, how's Snowy? I'm going in to see him in the morning. Is he well enough to talk to about . . . well, serious things?'

'Of course. Just go gently. Is everything okay?' asked Dominic.

'Oh yeah. I just wanted to ask him about a job offer I've had. I'm kind of tempted but I'd like Snowy's advice.'

'I'm sure Snowy would appreciate that. Be good to distract him from where he is. Nag him about doing his exercises. The sooner he's fit, the sooner he'll get out,' said Dominic.

Jason sighed. 'Right. But we're all wondering how he'll cope in his place alone. I'll chat to Holly when she comes back. She went off in a bit of a huff for some reason.'

'Oh. That might have been my fault,' said Dominic guiltily. 'A misunderstanding. I'd like to see her when she gets back and explain. Let me know if you're still around.'

Jason smiled. 'Sure will.'

*

Dominic didn't hear from Holly that afternoon, so he decided he would send her a message to explain what had happened and then leave the ball in her court. He sat on the deck and composed the text: *Holly, I apologise for what you saw. There is nothing between Alicia and me any more – and it was never serious. I'm not sure what her reason was for stirring the pot when she saw you behind me, but that's partly why she and I were not a good fit. I hope you can understand. Dom.*

He hit *Send*. To distract himself, he dived into the work Julie had sent him. He'd been intrigued by his initial research into the racing industry concerning Maurie Richards. But it appeared to be a lot more sophisticated now than when Joe had dabbled in it; the money involved was staggering. No wonder it attracted big business and small punters hoping for a lucky break, although it appeared there were still a lot of 'colourful racing identities' as well as massive business conglomerates involved in the industry. He'd see what more he could dig up for Julie.

He decided to ring Rob's racing contact again, the one who'd first told him about Joe's connection with the racing world.

'Oh, hi, Dominic. How can I help you? You still digging around about that Joe guy?'

'Oh, not really. This is regarding info for an investigation my ex-boss is doing.'

'Good luck with that! What do you want to know?'

Dominic explained some of the issues Julie had raised and they talked of the hidden money, gambling, the politics and the huge sums paid for a thoroughbred before it had even raced.

'Crazy business,' said Dominic eventually. 'And big money. I can see why Joe was intrigued by the breeding side of it. How do I find out more?'

'About breeding? There's an old guy in New Zealand who's a bit of a prodigy pedigree analyst. He's an older fellow but knows his stuff.'

'Pedigree analyst. Didn't know there was such a profession,' said Dominic.

'Works for himself, has some big clients, though he never says who. I reckon he still works with a sheet of paper and his files as he's not too computer savvy. S'pose he has an offsider to do that these days. He can spot a good horse when he sees it, but he says the clues to great horses are in their history. The very intricate mating, breeding of sires and dams going back generations. All the quirks and traits of certain bloodlines. Like how they move, funny little habits, all manner of things their offspring could inherit, which is why he checks them out. But mostly it's all on paper. He's a great believer in following the line of dams, the mares, rather than the generations of stallions.

He's quite an interesting old chap. Frederick Vine is his name, known as Freddie.'

As soon as he hung up, Dominic found Freddie's website and rang the contact number.

An hour or so later, Dominic closed his notebook and stretched thoughtfully. His phone rang. It was Rob.

'Hey, Dom. Any news? Ideas about salvaging my career with Harold?' Rob said flippantly, though Dominic could hear the edge in his voice.

'Not at the minute. But I've just been on the phone for ages with a horse pedigree analyst called Freddie Vine in New Zealand. Fascinating, in a way. It's given me a bit of insight into Joe.'

'Really. More on the gangsters?' asked Rob.

'No. Joe's hobby was in thoroughbred blood-lines – his interest as an amateur analyst was well known, apparently. In fact, when I asked Freddie about Maurie Richards, Freddie said, "That old gangster wouldn't have hurt a hair on Joe's head. Someone like Joe is worth a lot more alive than dead."'

'That sounds a bit deep to me. Unless . . . does he mean that just going by the breeding, he could predict, or even guarantee, a winner from birth?' asked Rob.

'More like from conception. It's pretty amazing, if that's your interest.'

'Well, it would be if I was a breeder – or a horse buyer,' said Rob. Then he paused before adding, 'Be handy knowledge to pass on. Or sell. How does it work?'

'Freddie is hired by certain breeders, buyers and sellers to advise on progeny. His advice can influence the price for top racehorses,' said Dominic. 'According to Freddie, Joe was a natural at spotting good bloodlines.'

'Amazing. Does Maggie have any of his documents?'

'No idea. I'll check with Josie. Doesn't really get us any further in finding out what happened to Joe, though,' said Dominic.

'True,' said Rob. 'Now, c'mon, turn your considerable intellect to thinking about how I can wriggle back into Harold's good books. I need a plan.'

Dominic chuckled. 'I ran into Alicia . . . she said she was collecting some pot plants . . .'

'Right. She's trying to tart my place up a bit. Home décor is not my forte,' said Rob.

'Nice of her. Seeing a bit of Alicia, are you?' said Dominic dryly.

There was a fraction of a pause before Rob answered. 'Yeah . . . er, you said that was okay with you, right?'

'Of course! Alicia and I were never an item,' said Dominic cheerfully. 'Take care, brother,' he added.

As he hung up, Dominic recalled the amused 'gotcha' glance Alicia had thrown over her shoulder as she'd gone up the steps to her car and was tempted to gallop up the track to Maggie's house. He checked his phone: nothing from Holly. With a sigh, he turned back to his computer.

*

Going through his papers the following morning, Dominic came across the note with Nola's number which Colleen had given him after the book club meeting.

'There you are,' he murmured, recalling that Colleen had mentioned Nola could be worth speaking to as she and Maggie had worked together.

After his conversation with Lizzie Lyons, Dominic hesitated, but then realised that as Nola had worked with Maggie she would have a different take on Joe than one of Joe's own workmates would. He dialled her number.

Nola was well spoken and very agreeable. She explained she was living in a nice unit in The Vale. 'Why don't you pop over now for some morning tea, Dominic? If you're free, of course.'

No time like the present, thought Dominic. It would be a nice distraction. Holly had still not been in touch.

Nola greeted him at the door and, as Dominic had half suspected, her first question was, 'When are you coming back to our book club, Dominic?'

'I've been busy.' He smiled. 'What are you reading at the moment?'

They chatted as Nola made coffee from her coffee machine. Dominic flicked through the next assigned novel and decided he must make more time to read for pleasure.

After chatting for a short while, Nola put down her cup and said, 'Have you seen Maggie and the kids recently?'

'Yes, they're all fine.'

'I heard Maggie had an offer from Mr Marchant for her house. He built this place,' said Nola, waving a hand at her surrounds. 'Of course, Maggie wouldn't sell. Not everyone agrees with her, but no one at book club tried to talk her out of it. I know Maggie when her mind is made up.'

'So you go back a long way,' said Dominic.

'Oh yes, indeed. We nursed together for quite a few years. I'm older than her but we were great friends. In those times of emergencies and stress and long dark nights, you share a lot and bond together. I always felt like a sister to her. She has no family out here.'

Dominic nodded. 'When did Maggie quit her job as a nurse?'

'She didn't quit; we both took breaks in our career

over the years for babies, family things, the usual. But she hadn't worked for a while after Holly was born and then Joe disappeared. She had to come back to work then as she needed the money.'

'Do you have any theories about Joe's disappearance?'

'You mean, about what happened?' Nola shook her head. 'It's an utter mystery. I think it must have been foul play; there was no reason for him to leave Maggie and his kids. I don't believe for a moment that he left of his own free will. But as to what happened . . .' She shrugged. 'I guess we'll never know.'

Nola's words seemed innocuous, but Dominic thought he sensed something furtive in her tone. He decided to keep quiet; he could see Nola was struggling with whether or not to say what was on her mind.

She put her cup in its saucer with a clatter. 'Oh, dear. I thought I'd never speak about this. But when you get to my age you just never know when you're going to drop off the perch.' Nola drew a breath. 'I'm sure you understand this is confidential. But I just feel someone else should know . . . other than Maggie. She'll never tell.'

Dominic nodded, wondering if he needed to hear whatever it was Nola was going to say. Nola obviously liked to gossip.

She straightened up. 'As I told you, Maggie and I became very close. Funny, looking back, we were closer than sisters. And you know how sisters can bicker.' She smiled slightly. 'All those long shifts, especially the night ones; the early hours when someone would pass away. We bonded. Yet we rarely saw each other socially or outside the hospital.' She paused. Dominic waited.

'We talked a lot. Knew each other's lives, told each other things maybe we wouldn't normally,' continued

Nola slowly. 'Private things. So I wouldn't like you to think that I am breaking the trust of a friendship. But I believe that some secrets should be shared . . .'

Dominic felt uncomfortable. 'Nola, am I the right person to tell this to? Not someone closer to you and Maggie . . .?'

Nola shook her head firmly. 'No. I have thought about this for years, wondering what to do, who to tell. Because it's not something you gossip about. My children barely know Maggie. My judgement of people has never failed me. So if you'd bear with me . . .' She raised an eyebrow.

'I would never want to see Maggie or her family hurt,' said Dominic quietly.

Nola seemed to dismiss this as she pressed on, 'I knew Maggie and Joe were close, but, well, I s'pose we all have our foibles. She hated him spending hours at night in his study with his horse books. And I guess other small things bothered her, as they do most couples. At one stage they both seemed to get a bit fed up; they needed a break, a holiday away together, just the two of them. But that wasn't going to happen. Then Joe was offered a secondment, just for a couple of months, to fill in at a distant school way out in the bush somewhere. There was a stipend attached so there'd be more money coming in, and he was excited to see the outback, or what he considered the wild outback. It was a small township, a bush school with a dozen kids or something. This was long before Holly was born. Maggie couldn't disrupt the family life, so she agreed Joe should go, and as she was on night shift at the time, she thought she'd manage somehow. Sam and Gloria were a great help to her.' Nola picked up her cup and took another sip. Dominic waited, undecided whether or how to stop this torrent of words.

'It was at that time we had a new Resident come to the hospital, a lovely fellow and a good doctor. Interesting chap, as I recall. I couldn't help seeing that he and Maggie became friendly.' Nola looked at Dominic.

He stared back at her.

'I don't know the details, and didn't want to know, but one night Maggie came to me and told me she had slept with him.'

'The doctor?' said Dominic.

Nola drew a breath, nodded and continued, 'Maybe I shouldn't have said anything. But there comes a time in our lives when we have to share our secrets.'

'Why are you telling me this?' asked Dominic quietly.

'Someone else should know. Not the children, of course,' said Nola, sounding somewhat relieved to have unburdened herself. 'Of course, I'd never mention this to anyone else,' she added modestly.

'I understand.' Dominic paused, wondering why she'd dumped this information on him. He wasn't sure he believed her when she said she hadn't shared it.

Nola held up her hand as if to push away a weight. 'I have written down the resident's name and the dates he was at the hospital . . . just in case.' She sighed and shifted in her seat. 'It's a relief to have got that off my chest.'

Dominic hesitated before asking, 'Do you think Joe ever knew?'

Nola shook her head. 'No. I don't believe so. As I said, he was away at the time. Silly of me, my thoughts have always been for Maggie. Sometimes we do rash things. We all have regrets . . .'

'Of course,' said Dominic quickly, before Nola could share some of her own. 'Nola, I feel privileged that you shared this with me,' he managed. 'Shall we now agree it's a closed book and move forward?' He smiled tightly, anxious now to get out of there.

Nola gave a wistful smile. 'I always close a book with regret. It takes us on a journey, and into other people's lives for a brief time. It's sad to come to the end.'

Dominic stood. 'Quite. Thanks for the coffee, Nola.'

Outside her door Dominic shook himself as if trying to free himself of the whole episode. *What a garrulous old bitch*, he thought. Mentally he erased the last hour from his memory.

*

Dominic pushed back his chair from the little table on the deck and decided to make a coffee and read through the information he'd gleaned from Freddie the pedigree analyst.

It had now been nearly a week since he'd seen or heard from Holly. He had buried himself in Julie's racing project to try to keep his thoughts from meandering back to her, but he was starting to wonder if the incident with Alicia had been a deal-breaker for Holly. It seemed she was unable to forgive him, misunderstanding or not.

He was ready for a break. Cynthia had asked him over to a barbecue that afternoon and he was looking forward to catching up with his own family. He decided to call in and see Snowy on the way.

Snowy's door was open and he could hear the old man's voice.

'Hello, Snow! How are you?' said Dominic as he knocked and stepped into the room to find a pretty woman in a uniform seemingly entangled around Snowy, with one hand under his back and the other lifting his leg.

'Hi, Dominic. This is Amy. She cracks this and then

she cracks that,' said Snowy with a mock groan. 'She's trying to cripple me.'

'Hi, Amy. I'm Dom.'

'Hello. I won't be a minute. It's hard enough to get him to submit to this. I'm his physio.'

'Looks intense,' Dominic said.

'It certainly is,' said Amy at the same time as Snowy groaned, 'Bloody hell!'

'Okay, deep breath and relax. You can sit up now. Slowly,' said Amy.

As Snowy swung his legs over the edge of the bed, rubbing his thigh, Amy smiled.

'His muscles are getting stronger every day. He's been very good with his exercises. I'll leave you with your visitor, Snowy. Drink plenty of water. See you later.'

Amy smiled at Dominic and closed the door behind her.

'Struth, can that little girl throw a punch,' said Snowy.

'Is it working?' Dominic asked.

'I reckon. But I'm not telling her that.'

'It's so good to see the old Snowy,' said Dominic, meaning it.

'Less of the old, thanks. There's blokes in here decades older than me. I want out of here!'

'So have you had many visitors?' asked Dominic, hoping Holly had called in to see him.

'Jason popped in the other day. We had a good old heart-to-heart.'

'That's good. I saw him briefly at Maggie's after he'd been working at her place. He does put in a lot of time there.'

'Yep. He loves that place. Seems Maggie's going to stick to her guns and not sell, and good on her. Seems to be if Maggie doesn't sell, the deal is off.'

'Yes. I suppose that's gone over like a lead balloon with the neighbours,' said Dominic.

'Yeah, but they'll get over it. Jase says they're not too narky; only one couple were dead-set keen to sell. And if that's the case they'll get another offer sooner or later.'

'That's true.'

'Jase told me he wants to change careers.'

'Oh yes, he mentioned he was going to ask your advice about something. But I thought he loved landscaping, gardening,' said Dominic.

'He's passionate about the land. The earth, plants, trees, soil, rocks, water, creatures. Whole box and dice we call the environment.'

'Doesn't landscaping include that?' said Dominic.

Snowy shook his head. 'Jason has come to the conclusion that nature knows best. He's over people wanting shaped shrubs, mowed lawns, clipped hedges, flowers in a row. A rock wall that's fake rocks and cement.' Snowy sniffed.

'I see,' said Dominic slowly. 'So what's he want to do?'

'Work for National Parks. He has a lot of skills. I can put him in touch with the right fellows.'

'Really? What's brought this on?' asked Dominic in surprise.

'Marchant's offer was the tipping point. He didn't like the idea that land like his mum's could be cleared for swimming pools and a mock Italian palace thing . . . what do you call it?'

'A palazzo . . .? Well, none of us want that. But what's that got to do with a change in career?' asked Dominic.

'Marchant's plan got Jase thinking. He says the big picture is preserving and creating green space as much as possible in and around towns and cities. No more clearing

332

every twig and leaf, let alone decent big trees off a block to build on, but leaving big trees for shade and oxygen, plus building in green space on all developments. Cities and suburbs are now frantic to cool those treeless bloody places. Not fit for humans let alone a poor bloody bird or any creature.'

'Wow, did Jase give you the sermon or the other way around? Just joking,' added Dominic. 'I agree.'

'We're on the same page. Anyway, I gave him some contacts. And better still, he and Maggie have worked out a plan for all that wild land up behind her place. She's arranging to sign it over to National Parks, right away,' added Snowy.

'What! That's brilliant!' exclaimed Dom.

'Jase's taking her to see her solicitor.'

'And how's that gone over with the rest of the family?' asked Dominic.

'Dunno. It's Maggie's business.' Snowy shrugged. 'Her house is still valuable and there's more than enough land. Her view can't be built out.' He paused. 'My old place could be worth a few bob too, if someone wanted to go to a bit of trouble. But I'm not going anywhere.'

Dominic knew better than to say anything on this point, so he just nodded.

'When . . . and if . . . I do want to make a change, *I'll* decide,' Snowy said firmly. 'So, what's happening? Holly said she hadn't seen you for a while. What's that mean? She looked a bit po-faced when she was last here, if I'm honest.'

Dominic sighed. 'My fault . . . well sort of. A woman I know stopped to chat and when she saw Holly she gave me a peck on the cheek to cause trouble.'

'Dump her. Holly is special.'

'Oh, that woman is long gone. Wasn't anything serious anyway.'

'Women. I can live without 'em,' said Snowy boldly. 'Though that little Amy is strong as an ox. I'm feeling really good now.'

'Don't overdo it, Snowy.' Dominic grinned. 'Listen, I have to go. Off to see my family.'

*

Dominic was enjoying being with his family and a few of their friends. He had just sat down with a fresh drink when Cynthia came and sat next to him.

'You've been busy, by the sound of it. How're things? How's Alicia?' She raised her eyebrows questioningly.

'She's out of my life. I think Rob's keen on her. So I hope that works out.'

'Big step for Rob, isn't it?' said Cynthia.

'I don't think he's complaining.' Dominic smiled. 'He's much more suited to Alicia than I ever was.'

'And you?'

'I'm treading softly. There's a girl I like . . .' He trailed off, not sure where he stood on that front.

Cynthia took the hint. 'Okay. I won't pry. When is Nigel coming back, must be soon?'

Dominic glanced at his sister. 'Hasn't told me specifically yet. I hate to think of it, actually. I've been bogged down –'

'Settled down, more like it,' Cynthia cut in. 'I never thought you'd adjust so well into that boatshed place. It's cute, but . . .' She shrugged. 'Maybe it's time to move back into your flat and join the real world again.'

Dominic stared at her. The idea of moving back into his small flat in the city suddenly did not appeal to him

334

at all. Yes, the boatshed was small too, but at WestWater he was surrounded by space – sea, bush, privacy, stillness broken by tides, rustling trees, sea and bush birds, the chug of a distant motorboat . . . In his flat he'd have to get used to the sounds of city traffic, neighbours and life going on twenty-four-seven again.

'You know,' he said slowly, 'I don't think I could live in the city again.'

'Do you have a choice?' said Cynthia, sitting up in surprise. 'I mean, you could sell, but what would you buy? Even places in WestWater probably don't come cheap.'

Dominic shook his head. He felt as though he were at a crossroads.

As if reading his thoughts, Cynthia said, 'You're going to have to decide. Where do you go from here, dear brother?'

*

Dominic sat on the end of the jetty with his guitar, picking out a new tune while he watched the ferry come around the island in the distance and head back towards Sam and Gloria's.

He hadn't seen Maggie or Holly for over a week now. He hoped one of them might see him on the jetty and wander down. Jason had returned to his place down south, Paul was busy catching up with his surfboard business and Gloria was apparently out and about while Sam was at work. Marcia had taken a trip rustling up outlets for her handbags which some influencer had spotted. Snowy was still improving.

Dominic had finished his initial report for Julie. While it had been interesting, he wasn't sure whether he wanted to accept more work in the same vein. He wasn't ready to give up on the idea of a book, yet frustratingly, the ideas and plans that were swirling in his mind were still misty and unclear.

Dominic watched the ferry head down to the inlet near the creek. With Snowy away, there was no one living in that quiet corner of the bay. Maybe Sam was checking out the old landing and the poet's jetty?

It was getting dark. He'd hoped to catch up with Sam when he returned, but there was no sign of him, so Dominic returned to the boatshed and put away the guitar.

He usually enjoyed the twilight time as he fed Woolly and watched the night roll in over the hills. But today he felt edgy, and so he was glad when he heard footsteps come around to the deck. The visitor, however, was a surprise.

'Hi, Dominic,' said Leo. 'I've been up with Maggie. I'm heading back; just thought I'd say hello.'

'Ah. How are you, Leo? How do you feel about Maggie not selling?' Dominic asked gently. 'Losing such a big commission must be disappointing,' he added.

Leo shrugged. 'To be honest, I suspected Maggie wouldn't want to leave here. But I had to ask.'

Dominic was surprised to see that the younger man had dropped his real estate speak. 'Makes sense,' he said mildly. 'Hey, I was visiting a mate in respite care at The Glades and saw your father there. Has he lived there very long?'

'Some years now. His health hasn't been too good for a while.'

'You don't live down this way, though?' Dominic asked.

'No.' Leo hesitated. 'I didn't like being a kid down here. I'm happy where I am, but then if a sale does pop up, well, I'm not going to knock it back, am I?'

Dominic nodded. 'I guess not.'

Leo seemed to rally a bit and resume some of his cockiness. 'Ta. Okay. Well, gotta go. Few places to check out. People work during the day so I said I'd pop round to a couple this evening. See you, Dom.'

Dominic watched Leo leave and then decided he might as well shake off his malaise and visit Maggie. He tidied himself up a bit and headed determinedly up the track.

The lights in Maggie's house were on as the night drew in, but Dominic smiled, realising he knew this path so well now he could follow it blindfolded.

'Maggie? You home?' He knocked on the open door. He could hear noises in the kitchen.

'Yes, that you, Dom? Come in,' answered Maggie, bustling out to meet him. 'CeeCee was just here. I was helping her with a school paper. Actually, she should talk to you. She wants to go into public affairs. Politics or something like that, eventually.'

'CeeCee is smart. Very much her own person. I'd be happy to talk her out of it! Just kidding, we need more young women in public office. What's her paper about?' asked Dom.

'She'll tell you. She's going to talk to you before she goes back home on Sunday.'

'Right. I just saw Leo. He seemed pretty philosophical about losing Harold's deal.'

'I think Leo does okay. He might be secretly pleased it fell through; he knew I'd be upset,' said Maggie, heading back into the kitchen and stirring something on the stove. Not looking at Dominic she said, 'I hear you had a chat with Nola recently.'

Dominic felt uncomfortable.

'I know because Nola was quick to mention it to me. I'd rather like to talk to you about it,' said Maggie.

'I didn't take much notice, it was just a lot of gossip,' he tried.

'Yes, and I know what about,' said Maggie, turning to face him. 'She told you about my affair, right?'

Dominic nodded. 'Ah . . . yes, she did. It's none of my business, Maggie, and I certainly wouldn't repeat such gossip.'

'It's not gossip. It happened.' Maggie thought for a moment, then continued, 'I was at a stage in my life where I was feeling very neglected and lonely. Joe was either in his study with those damn racing books or busy, and then he took off on some adventure to teach in the bush for two months! So when I met a nice attentive colleague I was susceptible to his charm and attention.'

Dominic nodded sympathetically as she went on, 'I slept with him once only, and realised it was a huge mistake. I took leave and went to see Joe and we had a wonderful ten days together. After he came back I fell pregnant with Holly.'

'Did Joe ever know about it?' asked Dominic.

'Absolutely not. I could kick myself for ever mentioning it to Nola. I keep in touch with her because she's older and rather lonely. She doesn't have a lot of friends.'

'I can see why,' said Dominic.

'Stay and have dinner with me, Dominic. I'm on my own. Holly is out with Paul.'

*

Maggie was soon her cheery self again, much to Dominic's relief.

He carried the plates out to the table on the deck and lit the mosquito candles to ward off bugs. Over dinner, they talked of different things that had nothing to do with WestWater. It was comfortable and easy as well as interesting.

Dominic mentioned the research he'd done for Julie.

'Would you go back to work in the political arena again?' asked Maggie.

'Certainly not in a public way. I'm a quiet, backroom guy,' said Dominic. 'But the research I'm doing for her is interesting.' He paused. 'It concerns horseracing, actually. Do you know much about the research Joe did into the racing business? The bloodlines, and so on?'

'Not really, no. It must have been a lot, he spent enough time on it.' She gave Dominic an arch look. 'Time I often wished he would spend with me.'

'Well, if it's any consolation, I think Joe might have been pretty good at it. In those circles he was well known,' said Dominic.

Maggie frowned. 'You're kidding. Well, I suppose that's the insular racing world for you.'

'Actually, Maggie, it's a much bigger world than you realise.'

'I guess people do get passionate about odd things.' She collected their plates.

'Did you happen to keep his papers?'

Maggie turned in the doorway. 'Why?'

'Paul mentioned once that you might have kept Joe's old notebooks and things.'

Maggie looked a bit flustered. 'Oh, they're probably around somewhere. I don't think I threw a thing out.' She went into the kitchen.

As she made coffee, Dominic washed up their plates.

'Why are you so interested in Joe's old stuff, anyway?' asked Maggie.

'I was put in touch with a man in New Zealand

who knows all about horse breeding. There are experts who take note of and categorise all the idiosyncrasies of each horse to work out the best matches . . . It's like a family tree going back generations. Talk about arranged marriages!'

Maggie was thoughtful as she handed him a mug and they sat down again.

'Well, if I kept Joe's papers, I think I know where'd they'd be.'

'Really?'

'Do you want me to look?' asked Maggie, and before Dominic could reply she added, 'Come on.'

Dominic followed Maggie as she took a torch from the top of the fridge and went outside. They went around the house, where she unlatched a lattice door that led under the house, then leaned in and switched on a light.

The hanging bulb was dim, but Dominic saw all the paraphernalia of an old lawnmower, boxes, a rake, some tools and an old bicycle. Maggie shone the torch into the far recesses, its beam flicking over stacked boxes.

'We'll be here till dawn looking through all this!' said Dominic.

'No, I remember now. There was an old suitcase I shoved somewhere up the back here. It had a label on it with Joe's name.'

They followed the beam of light as Maggie waved it across the dark reaches under the floorboards of the house.

'Wait! There . . . to the left,' called Dominic.

'That's it! I remember it now. Oh, how to get it out of there!' said Maggie.

'Let me try. If I move those cartons, I can wriggle through enough, I think,' said Dominic.

It took a little time for him to reach and grasp the old suitcase and drag it down towards Maggie, who pulled on the handle and yanked it down to the ground.

Dominic stood back. 'You sure you want to open this, Maggie?' he asked gently.

Maggie nodded and snapped open the latches.

On top was a layer of old newspapers with articles about the tragic disappearance of Joseph Gordon. In a plastic bag were dozens of cards and notes of condolence. Maggie put them quickly to one side.

'I can't look at those.'

'Whoa, look at that!' Dominic leaned over the neatly stacked books. Diaries, ledgers, notes filed, paperclipped folders holding documents. He looked at Maggie.

'Do you remember this?' he asked.

Maggie picked up a book and opened it, slowly turning the pages. In neat handwriting there were columns and columns of racehorse names, numbers of wins, distances, speed, dates.

Another book had diagrams linking cross-references to progeny and bloodlines.

'Going through this would do my head in,' said Maggie.

Dominic was studying a page. 'The detail is extraordinary. Meticulous. It might mean a lot to someone who knows about this stuff.'

'It's all a foreign language to me. I mean really, who cares?'

'Breeders, buyers, trainers . . . any number of people who are into racehorses,' said Dominic. 'Looks like it goes back decades.'

'All be out of date now, I s'pose,' said Maggie.

'These dates are from the 1980s and 1990s. Possibly

someone in racing would be interested in this stuff. Do you think I can borrow one of these?' Dominic asked.

Maggie shrugged. 'Sure. Why not?'

He closed the suitcase. 'I'll put it back up there, shall I?'

They locked the storage area and went back into the house.

'Thanks for dinner, Maggie. I'll look after this.' Dominic waved the notebook.

'No worries. G'night, Dom.'

*

Back in the boatshed, Dominic skimmed through a few pages of Joe's meticulous, neat notes, but eventually he closed the book and shook his head.

'Beats me, Woolly. So the bloke had a hobby. But does it have anything to do with his disappearance? And how or why?' For Dominic, like the rest of Joe's family, Joe's disappearance was just too hard to fathom.

13

DOMINIC HUNG UP THE phone and let out a deep sigh. He'd called Alicia and been talking to her for fifteen minutes or more and he felt like he'd been holding his breath the whole time.

Hearing her businesslike, practical, challenging and then finally enthusiastic tone had been a relief.

He'd woken up that morning with an idea, and as he'd laid in bed thinking about it, inspecting it from all angles, he'd begun to get excited. This plan could resolve several problems in one fell swoop, he'd thought, not least of which was getting Rob back into Harold's good books.

Alicia had grasped his idea immediately and he was confident she would run with it now she understood where he was coming from. However, Dominic sensed she was trying to be laid-back and not show the admiration she actually felt for the plan, in true Alicia fashion.

Before ringing her, Dominic had spent the morning doing some research, finding contacts and getting his idea down on paper. Alicia would look into costs and make a rough business plan. If it came together, Rob could go all out and market the whole enterprise.

Now, Dominic felt relieved and quite excited at the prospect that the whole endeavour might come to fruition. He wished he could talk it over with Holly, but she still hadn't got in touch, so he had to assume she simply didn't want to. He tried to keep busy to ward off the sadness that this thought brought with it.

*

On the way back from shopping in The Vale, Dominic dropped in to The Glades and tapped at Snowy's door.

'Who is it?' Snowy growled.

'Only me. Don't be grumpy,' said Dominic jovially.

'Oh, g'day Dom. Sorry, mate. I just can't wait to get out of jail. I'm going nuts in this one bloody room.'

'You can walk around the grounds; there's a rec room and dining area –'

Snowy waved a hand irritably. 'Listen, Dom. Anywhere I go I seem to bump into old people or that wretched Dean Banks. He snarls at me. Never could stand him.'

'Why is that, exactly, Snowy?' said Dominic curiously.

'It's his personality. Or lack of it. Just a grouch. He's always been like that,' mumbled Snowy.

Dominic smiled. 'Y'know, people could think – just saying – that you can be a bit of a grump too, Snow.'

'Nah.' Snowy shook his head, but gave a slow grin. 'I've just no time for idle chitchat. I get on with things, that's why I'm happy being in the bush, where nothing talks back.'

'Don't you ever get lonely out there? Just sometimes?' asked Dominic quietly.

'Why would I?' said Snowy. 'I can wander round the bay and see Sam and his mob. I keep a bit of an eye on Maggie and the kids . . . well, when they were younger. Young CeeCee seems to like hanging around with me. She's a smart kid, like Holly, and I taught her how to row and fish . . . Look here, I'm talking to you, aren't I? And you're a newcomer!'

'Okay, okay.' Dominic laughed. 'So, what's the verdict on your leg?'

'I'm on the mend. S'posed to take it easy. But I'm not going to creep around being careful. I'll get the girls at the store to get me some good steaks and chops, strengthen me up a bit.'

'Do it your way, Snowy.' Dominic smiled, knowing the circle of neighbours would keep an eye on him. 'Anyway, I have to be going, just popped in with those biscuits you like and some fruit.'

'Thanks, mate,' said Snowy gruffly.

*

Several days later, Alicia rang Dominic back.

'It's on. Well, the idea has got through the first gate. I'll keep chasing it until Rob can take over and we'll pitch it to Harold.'

'Has Rob been there, seen it yet?' asked Dominic.

'You said you wanted to walk him through it all,' said Alicia. 'He asked you for help and ideas and you've come up trumps. Lucky you knew about it, eh?' she commented obliquely, then added, 'How's the girlfriend?'

'She's terrific,' said Dominic stoically.

'Whatever,' said Alicia, sounding disinterested.

'I'll speak to Rob and set things up. Thanks, Alicia.'

'I'll make sure it all works. This could be good for all of us. See ya.' She hung up.

Dominic called and arranged to meet Rob early the following morning.

'Seven thirty. This is the address.'

*

Dominic drove through the elaborate wrought-iron gates which someone – Alicia, he presumed – had unlocked, and up the winding driveway to the mysterious old hacienda. It evoked the same air of mystery, romance and escapism as he remembered, despite its forlorn state of neglect.

He pulled up outside the rambling building and took in the sweep of overgrown grounds. Rob's car was parked nearby. He could tell the leaf-strewn double wooden doors were still locked and possibly hadn't been opened for years.

Dominic slipped through the side gate which was also unlocked, casting a quick glance towards the old pool, the gardens and loggia overlooking the rolling acreage and rising hillside in the background.

'Hey there!' Rob called to him, walking with his arms outstretched as if encompassing the surrounds. 'Get a load of this . . . what the hell! Where am I?'

'Paradise-to-be, pal,' said Dominic, grinning as Rob slung an arm around his shoulders.

'How has this place gone unnoticed? Just quietly fading into the night like an old lady of once-great wealth!' He nudged Dominic. 'Man, what a night. Let you in on a secret . . . Alicia brought me here last night. I couldn't believe this place. It looks like such a dump from the outside. Then . . . candlelit dinner over there . . . hello, romance.'

'You spent the night here?' asked Dominic.

'Yeah. A romantic interlude with Alicia . . . she's known about this place for ages. But she said she's never brought anyone else here. Ever.'

'Lucky you,' said Dominic nonchalantly.

'I am,' said Rob seriously. 'Things are getting pretty serious. I want this to work out, Dom.'

'I hope it will,' said Dominic, and meant it. 'So, to business. Have you looked around? What do you think?'

Rob spread his arms again. 'Genius. Insane. How come no one has taken this place over? It's mega bait for the jet set, Europhiles, anyone with taste! It's the Riviera meets romantic Mexico in secret Sydney! The ultimate classy getaway for thems wot can afford it, eh?'

Dominic smothered a smile. If Rob liked a plan, he tended to get overexcited and wanted to list it on the stock exchange immediately – otherwise he hated the idea and jumped all over it.

'I get the picture.' Dominic grinned. 'But will Harold go for it? Let's step this through, starting from the ground up. How much work and cost is going to be involved to make the vision happen?'

Rob was suddenly all business. 'I did start to make notes after Alicia left this morning. There's the basic luxury, the ultimate romance experience, the European vibe, the décor, ultimate dining, the gardens, the renos. Upgrade the pool grounds, and we could run a golf course down to the beach. That's where we'll have our private retreat, bar . . . not to mention the spa facilities, hideaway bistro . . . Aussie bush experience in the nature reserve which will be set aside, with Harold's name attached, of course.'

'Of course,' said Dominic mildly. 'Okay, you get the picture.'

'Is the owner willing to sell?' asked Rob anxiously.

'The original owner died years ago. His daughter inherited it and is in Geneva and would be happy to have it off her hands . . . for the right price,' said Dominic.

'Do you think Harold will buy this?' asked Rob. 'I know he's feeling a bit cranky after not getting Maggie's place. All too much of a headache. This will be a business venture, a very different proposition.'

'Alicia says he won't be able to resist, but we need to do a bit of set dressing, tart it up like they do in those TV house-selling transformations. Alicia suggested we bring him here for a sunset cocktail party.'

Rob was bubbling with enthusiasm. 'Great idea. It's a no-brainer to sell to the market. But it needs to be managed well . . . up to an international standard. It's the details that count, that make it desirable –'

Dominic held up his hand. 'That's where your expertise comes in. You need to transform this place and find the right people. Train them in the finer points if necessary. Like some of the very exclusive boutique places in Europe as well as here.'

'That I can do,' said Rob happily. 'C'mon, get out your notebook, and let's take photos.'

*

It was a sunny morning. Maggie called Dominic as he was working on his laptop out on the deck.

'Aren't I lazy, ringing you instead of popping down? What are you up to this morning?' she asked.

'Nothing much, why?'

'Well, I have to go out for a few hours. But I've asked Holly to do a job for me, and she'll need a second pair of hands and eyes. I thought you mightn't mind helping her,' said Maggie. Dominic thought he detected a rather knowing lilt in her tone.

'Not at all.' Dominic smiled. Good old Maggie, she had figured out a way to get Holly and him together. He wondered how much she knew about what had happened.

'We have to photograph and check all the boundary posts up the back of my place to where my property ends. You heard I'm donating that land to National Parks? Anyway, it's a bit of a hike. With the measuring it'll take a couple of hours . . .' began Maggie.

'Happy to help,' said Dominic. 'I'll be there in half an hour.'

*

Dominic grabbed his hat and a water bottle and met Holly as she came outside with a small backpack looped over her shoulder.

'You're prepared,' said Dominic.

'Mum's idea. She's famous for always throwing together a small picnic-on-the-run if we went anywhere even for the shortest time,' said Holly a trifle coolly. Without meeting his eyes, she set off up the hill.

It was warm work as they followed the boundary markers in the overgrown grass.

'Hasn't Google Maps found this area?' Dominic sighed.

'Guess not. I can see why Mum sectioned it off. Far too much to look after. She likes leaving it as it is for the wallabies and wildlife.'

'Giving the land to the National Parks is a wonderful idea. Less garden and maintenance work for Maggie into the future, too.'

Holly turned and looked at him properly for the first time. 'Actually, I wanted to thank you for being an objective voice when it came to that business of selling the house. I think we were all pulling her in different directions, whereas you just laid out the pros and cons. Mum appreciates that, I think.'

'Oh, I didn't do anything special, but I'm glad if our conversations helped. And Jason gets the credit for the deal with National Parks. Phew, let's sit in the shade over there and see what Maggie has made us.'

The sandwiches and snacks were welcome. Dominic found that his water was warm, but it didn't bother him. He was enjoying sitting there with Holly as she talked about her job plans when an idea started to take shape. So he was only half listening when she paused, smiling perplexedly, and said, 'I don't have your full attention . . .'

Dominic met her gaze. 'I'm sorry. It's just that I've had an idea. I need to talk to Rob before I can take it any further, but it might be something that would interest you. How would you feel about having dinner with me, Rob and Alicia, to talk it over?'

Holly bristled. 'With Alicia?'

Impulsively, Dominic reached out and took Holly's hand.

'You know, I am so sorry about what happened. Alicia and I did see each other casually a few months ago, but it was never serious and it never felt right. She's going out with Rob now. It's in her nature to tease and I know that's what she was doing when she saw you the other week. She likes creating drama.' He shook his head. 'But I've been miserable not seeing you the last couple of weeks. Can you forgive me?'

Holly looked up and gave him a crooked grin. 'I've been miserable too,' she said quietly. 'Yeah, it's okay. I was just hurt, I guess.'

'I know. I really am sorry.'

'It's all right. And I'm pretty tough. I think I can bring myself to have dinner with Alicia, if you think it will be worthwhile,' she shrugged.

Dominic smiled with relief. 'I really think it will. Rob has a project on the go that will need someone with your skills and experience. There are a few finer details to tie up, but it's going to be exciting.' Persuading Harold to buy the hacienda was probably a bit more than a fine detail, but Dominic didn't want to spoil the moment by saying so.

'Are we talking fulltime, reliable employment?' asked Holly.

'Well, Rob can be rather entrepreneurial, but this time I think he's on a winner. You decide after he explains it.'

'Sure. Why not.'

'Of course, I have a vested interest.' Dominic smiled. 'I'd hate you to move away from WestWater,' he said simply.

Holly gave him a smile that made him catch his breath. He leaned towards her as she did the same, their lips touching.

And suddenly they were wrapped together, entwined as the barriers of the last weeks fell away, and under the shady tree they made love, enveloped by the sky, the warm smell of crushed grass, a slight breeze cooling their naked bodies.

Afterwards, Dominic held her, too emotional to speak.

'The sky is spinning,' said Holly softly.

Dominic nodded, burying his face in her soft sweet skin.

They lay in silence, lost in the wonderment and joy of one another.

'Holly . . .' began Dominic quietly. But she put a finger to his lips.

'It's okay, let's just enjoy this moment,' she said with a warm smile.

Later, they dressed and picked their way back down the hillside, Dominic following Holly, his mind racing and his body still tingling as he looked at her slim figure ahead of him.

As they threaded their way through Maggie's garden towards the house, Dominic said, 'I have to go and meet Rob. Outline some plans. I'll call you when I get back.'

'That's okay, Dom. No demands on either of us. Let's take it one step at a time, okay?' She smiled and Dom felt himself relax. 'Thanks for all your help today. Mum will be impressed she can hand this over to the Parks people.'

Dominic gave a small salute and turned down the path to the boatshed, still smiling.

*

It had been raining nonstop for days. It was as if a solid wall of water reached from sky to land. Rob had postponed their dinner meeting as it was too wet to go out anywhere. Dominic had to keep the double deck doors shut the entire day. Peering through the side windows, he couldn't even see the end of the jetty let alone anything else through the seemingly solid wall of pounding water. He was distracting himself with his guitar, but could hardly hear his strumming through the rain on the tin roof.

The onslaught of water had everyone dismayed. And then concerned. Very concerned.

Sam had valiantly steered the ferry through the sheets of rain for the first few days. But floating debris, even trees and boats that had broken their moorings and were partially submerged, became too much of a danger. He and Gloria had gone over to The Point, left the ferry on its mooring, and their son had collected them to stay with his family for a few days after the upper road was cut off by a landslide. Luckily for Snowy's chooks, Sam had left them enough feed.

Deidre and Daphne kept the general store open for those who could reach it, though supplies were dwindling with no fresh deliveries getting through to them.

Dominic put down his guitar and picked up his phone.

'Hi, Josie . . . how are you doing in this unbelievable weather cell?'

'It's a nightmare. I can still get through to work, but for how much longer I'm not sure. Mum said you're all cut off by road and water.'

'Yep. I'm locked in a box with only my guitar and Woolly to amuse me. Internet is down again. My parents are OK but I keep checking on your mum as Sam and Gloria have gone to their son's place. Have you seen Snowy?'

'Thanks for keeping an eye on Mum. Snowy is Snowy – can't wait to be discharged. He's going crazy being cooped up.'

'Well, he can't come home in this weather,' said Dominic.

'No, I know. I'd worry about him in normal weather. In this weather it's unthinkable. Of course, if he was going home to be looked after, taking it easy, that'd be different.

But you know how he is. I can see him falling and . . . well, I hate to think. Like it or not, he'll have to wait till this rain clears up.'

'I feel for him, but maybe it's a good thing he'll have a few more days there,' said Dominic.

'Normally I'd agree with you,' Josie replied, 'but it's all a bit tense. Dean Banks and Snowy have a spat every time they see each other. It's getting on everyone's nerves. I'm actually thinking that when the weather clears, I might ask Mum if she could stand to have Snowy stay with her for a bit, just to make sure he's right to go home.'

'That sounds like a good idea, Josie. I'll help out as much as I can, too.'

'Thanks, Dom. Appreciate it. I'll let you know when he's ready to be discharged. And I'll talk to Mum and keep you in the loop.'

'No worries, Josie. I'll be there.'

*

The following morning it was still raining but it was less heavy, and, hoping this was a sign of a break in the weather, Dominic threw on the bulky rain gear Nigel had left behind and set out to walk to the general store.

There were several people in the shop, and Deidre looked frazzled.

'Hi, Dom. You okay? And Maggie and the others?'

'We're all just bunkered down. Sam and Gloria are with their son. I'm getting tired of baked beans. Is there any fresh bread?'

'No, sorry, long gone. I've a couple of frozen pizzas left. We've been busy. Daphne is out the back cleaning up as our storeroom got flooded, roof leaked a bit.'

'Need a hand?' Dominic asked.

'No thanks, we already have a couple of mates helping out.'

Dominic picked up a few items and paused. He thought he should call Maggie to see if she needed anything, not that much was left in the shop, but found he'd left his phone behind in the boatshed. As he set off home, he noticed that the sky was darkening with more heavy rainclouds.

It had taken longer than usual to get to the store and back. He shrugged out of the rain gear and made himself a coffee. Then he picked up his phone to check the weather forecast and saw one missed call from Holly and several from Maggie.

Maggie answered the phone on the second ring and started talking. For a moment Dominic couldn't understand what she was trying to say. Something about Holly . . .

'Maggie, Maggie, slow down. What about Holly? Maggie, please, take a breath . . . What's happened? Start again, slowly . . .' Dominic could feel his heart start to pound at the hysteria in the older woman's voice.

'She went to help Marcia. I got a message from Marcia that she was in trouble and then her phone went dead and I can't reach her or Marcia, no one –'

'Holly is at Marcia's? Why? How did she get there?' asked Dominic, feeling a rising panic. 'She didn't take your boat, did she?'

'I'm not sure. Holly just fled out of here. She tried to ring you, apparently. But she just took off, said Marcia was in trouble.'

It was a decent walk around to Fowler's Inlet where Marcia lived which would take time, especially in this weather. Surely Holly hadn't taken the boat out in this sea?

He ran down to the jetty and peered through the misting rain to see that Maggie's little runabout had gone. Sam had said there was a bad current, but Dominic knew the hidden dangers of debris, dead animals and trees were a bigger threat. He glanced at the churning grey water, then turned and ran back to the boatshed.

He pulled a blanket off the bed, shoved it into a plastic bag, grabbed the first aid box from under the sink, and rushed to untether Nigel's tinnie.

Dominic wasn't sure how much fuel he had, but he hoped it would be enough. He struggled into a life jacket as the small boat sped at full throttle, its hull thudding and slapping across the rough waves. He could barely see a few metres ahead, and just hoped nothing big was in the way or partially submerged and out of sight. The slanting rain stung his eyes.

Dominic was trying to recall exactly where Marcia's cottage was. He'd seen it on a few of his walks and remembered it being high on a slope with a lovely view. All he could see through the rain was a blurry entrance to the little inlet.

The sea was the roughest he'd ever seen it, and he realised he'd have to take a slow big curve into it, so as not to have a rogue wave hit him beam on and tip over the little boat. But as he took a wide turn, something loomed ahead, and Dominic swung the tiller, peering through the rain. Suddenly his brain registered what the bulk was and his heart raced.

Like an arching whale or large fish, the grey shape was unmistakably a capsized tinnie. The small boat was wallowing in the heaving sea. Instantly he knew it was Maggie's runabout. He slowed the engine and angled towards it, his heart pounding.

Then he saw the bright orange life jacket.

Dominic edged his tinnie towards the boat as Holly lifted an arm and called something into the wind, and he could see that she was clinging to the boat, one arm grasping the bow and its rope.

How long had she been in the water? How much strength did she have left? But she was alive, and he was here. He circled close as both boats heaved, idled the engine of the tinnie, then got into its bow as the boats threatened to collide and a wave surged. He kept Holly in his sight, praying a wave wouldn't drive the tinnie against her as he tossed his bow rope towards her. Loath to let go of Maggie's boat, Holly reached out with her other arm but missed the rope.

Dominic had no time to do more as he cut the engine, glancing behind to see what was coming, and in those few seconds between surges, the two boats moved towards each other.

'Let go and grab the rope!' Dominic yelled.

Holly hesitated a split second. As they were now only a few metres apart she let go and flung herself towards the rope, this time grabbing it in both hands. Already Dominic's boat was drifting away from her on the next swell.

'Hang on!' Dominic yelled as he began hauling in the rope, dragging Holly towards him. Frantically she grasped the gunwale. Dominic leaned over the side, lifting her by her lifejacket and then her arms as she clung to the side of the boat.

He had no idea how he managed to drag her over the side, but he did, and they both fell into the bottom of the tinnie, breathing heavily. But there was no time even to check how she was. As a wave lifted the boat beam on, Dominic hastily restarted it, flinging himself at the tiller, revved the engine and turned it into the wind.

Glancing down, he saw that Holly was soaked and spluttering, and trying to sit up. Dominic headed towards the little bay in the curve around The Point where he was protected from the full force of the wind and rougher sea. As they got past The Point it was calmer, so he slowed. Yanking the blanket from the plastic bag he flung it over her.

'Are you okay? Holly?' he asked anxiously.

'Okay . . . yeah.' She started to shake. 'Get the boat . . .'

'We'll go back for it when it's safe. It's just wallowing.' He leaned down, quickly stroking Holly's wet hair and face. 'It's okay now. How long were you in the water? Marcia wasn't with you, was she?'

She shook her head. 'No. Was on my way there. Don't know how long . . . Marcia . . .' She coughed. 'Marcia needs help.'

'Okay, don't worry. We're headed there now.'

By now they'd been seen. Two boats were heading towards them from a nearby wharf.

Dominic recognised one of the men and shouted to him and his mate to tow in the upturned boat.

'How's the skipper?' one of them yelled.

Dominic gave a thumbs-up. 'She's okay. Do you know what's happened to Marcia Donaldson?'

'Another landslide,' he yelled back. 'Local SES blokes are there. She's okay.'

Holly was shivering in the stern of the tinnie. Dominic thanked the locals, who said they'd tow Maggie's boat back to their jetty.

'You sure you guys're okay?' called one of them.

Dominic gave another thumbs-up and put his arm around Holly. 'We're all good. Thanks, mate.'

The other fellow waved back. 'Give her a hot rum!'

*

Holly didn't speak on the bumpy but safer trip back. The wind and rain had abated slightly. As soon as he was able, Dominic called Maggie.

'She's okay, Maggie. We're on our way back to my place now. She's safe, dripping wet and cold, but she'll be fine. I'll get her inside and give her a hot drink. The steps are dangerous – you stay where you are. She'll give you a call.'

'Oh Dom, thank God. Let her rest up a bit. Hot shower might help. Just watch her as delayed shock might set in.'

'I'll give her some clothes and I'll look after her, Maggie, don't worry.'

'I know you will, Dom. The rain's easing up, thank goodness.'

*

Dominic picked up Holly's wet clothes from the floor outside the bathroom and replaced them with a pair of his jeans, a belt and a sloppy T-shirt, then went to the kitchen to make a pot of tea.

He opened the double doors to the deck, relieved to breathe in the salty fresh air. The rain was gentle now, the sky still grey but no longer so threatening.

'Hi. That feels better,' said Holly, emerging from the bathroom and rubbing her hair with her towel. 'Sorry I'm so wobbly. I have no idea what happened. I was trying to see through the rain and the boat bumped into something . . . next thing I was in – under – the water. Thank heavens I didn't have boots and raincoat on. I just ran out as I was without thinking . . .' Holly stopped, and began shaking.

Dominic put his arms around her. 'You're here.

You did the right thing putting on that life jacket. Here, have some tea . . .'

She wrinkled her nose. 'That's sweet and strong!' She took a deep breath, then another sip. 'I can feel it doing me good, though.'

'Maggie rang Marcia who sends her love and says she's so touched and grateful to you,' said Dominic as Holly sank into a chair.

'I didn't do anything, just made trouble for everyone . . .' Holly sighed.

'Not for me. I'm just glad I was here,' said Dominic.

She looked over the rim of her cup as she took another sip of tea. 'Me too.'

'I'll always look out for you, Holly,' said Dominic quietly, struggling with the awareness that Holly could so easily have drowned.

'I know, Dom. Now, I really know.' She put her cup down and curled deeper into the curved chair and closed her eyes.

Dominic picked up the mug and pulled a throw rug from the divan, settling it over her.

*

Dominic leaned in the doorway as Woolly poked his head out, but even though the rain had stopped, everything was wet. The cat went back inside. Dominic glanced at the clearing clouds. A faint ray of sun was beginning to shine through.

Holly was safe. That was all that mattered. Dominic sat on his divan with Woolly, watching her sleep, curled in a ball in the deep circular chair.

*

Two days later, Dominic was surprised when he answered his phone to find the New Zealand pedigree analyst Freddie Vine on the other end.

'Hello, Dominic, remember me?'

'I certainly do. What can I do for you?' asked Dominic, wondering why the horse expert was getting in touch.

'Actually, I was thinking I could help *you*!' Freddie replied. 'I'm in Sydney and I'm heading out to visit a studmaster I work with every so often. I thought you might like to come along, learn more about the breeding business.'

As Dominic hesitated, Freddie added, 'Plus, I think he could be interested in those books that Joe Gordon compiled. The progeny studies and such.'

'Really?' Dominic paused, thinking. 'Well, okay, where and who and when?'

*

A day later, in bright full sun, the roads now cleared after the heavy rain, Dominic was driving to the other side of Sydney, to where the last private estates of the expansive and expensive horse studs were located in what had once been serene and isolated bushland.

The estates were oases of manicured lawns, with monied mansions set behind elaborate gates and walled entrances, all surrounded by immaculate white-painted fences and where, in the distance, mega sums of money frisked about on fine thoroughbred legs.

But the once forested area was now surrounded by felled trees, cleared land scraped to bare earth as far as Dominic could see. Parked heavy equipment and signs announced that this was to be a super highway linking yet another new world of urban housing and sterile suburbia.

Once inside the grounds of Carthaggi Stud, Dominic realised he was breathing the refined air of the high-end racing fraternity. It seemed a contrast to the down-to-earth plain speaker Freddie Vine.

A friendly, pretty young woman, dressed in casual jeans, riding boots and a T-shirt with a Carthaggi logo on it, directed Dominic to the office building which was close to a cluster of stables and neat sheds.

There were several people in the office. The walls were cluttered with photos, framed certificates and press cuttings. A bookcase was filled with trophies, awards and various memorabilia.

Dominic picked out Freddie straight away as he looked the most out of place among the horsey set – short, tufted grey hair, neat moustache, a pressed shirt with a knitted Fair Isle vest and corduroy pants with polished shoes.

Freddie shook his hand warmly. 'Thanks for coming all this way. Do you want to look around? Meet Mr Hollander, the owner?'

'Of course, thanks,' said Dominic.

'Okay, I'll give you a bit of a tour round the place first.'

An hour later Freddie and Dominic leaned on the railings of a paddock, watching two thoroughbreds.

'Beautiful animals,' said Dominic.

'I can watch them all day,' said Freddie. 'Fascinating seeing the results from the paperwork play out in the living, breathing animal. I know their pedigree, family history, genetics, little traits and habits that they've inherited as well as the potential result if I match them with certain mares,' he added.

'It sounds very . . . absorbing,' said Dominic.

'Not even close. It's an obsession,' admitted Freddie.

*

Back in the office, Dominic was grateful to sit down with a cup of coffee as Stephen Hollander joined them.

'You got the tour from Freddie here, eh?' He smiled. 'So you're not in the racing business yourself, Freddie tells me. How'd you get interested?'

Briefly Dominic explained about learning of Joe Gordon's hobby.

'From what Freddie has told me, this Joe was pretty darn knowledgeable for an amateur,' said Hollander. 'Where is he?'

'It's an odd story,' put in Freddie. 'The fellow went missing years ago. No one knows what happened to him.'

Hollander raised an eyebrow. 'Did he dabble in the gambling business? I've never heard of him.'

'He was one of us,' said Freddie.

'He was actually a schoolteacher. It seems to have been a hobby . . .' said Dominic.

Hollander nodded. 'Freddie's caught it.' He grinned. 'Anybody who studies pedigrees has rocks in their head and would be advised to take up chess instead, as that would be easier. The breeding industry is a very small one. Frankly, most commercial breeders give no thought at all to their matings, but simply breed for financial outcome. Evidently people like this Joe Gordon and myself find it incredibly challenging and rewarding – in every sense.' He shook his head. 'Pity Mr Gordon couldn't continue with this. You say he left behind lots of records? They would be highly sought after by a small circle of people.'

'But they'd be kept, right?' interjected Freddie.

'Of course, if they are as good as you say. Some of them should go on display in the Racing Museum at Flemington. I'd like to have a good look through them myself,' Hollander said with a smile.

'There you go,' said Freddie, turning to Dominic. 'I thought Mr Hollander might be keen.'

'I'll speak to Mrs Gordon and have her contact you if she's interested. There's quite a few books of notes and files. A suitcase full,' said Dominic.

'Then that'll keep me quiet of an evening for a bit,' chuckled Hollander, getting to his feet. 'Nice to meet you, Dominic. Stay in touch.'

'See, I told you,' said Freddie as they walked back to Dominic's car. 'Pedigree analysis is not a hobby; it's a passion. It would have been too shocking if your friend's papers had been tossed out. Might be old papers to some, but a potential goldmine and great reading for the likes of Hollander and myself.'

As he drove back to WestWater, Dominic mulled over everything he'd learned about Joe's connections to the racing world. He certainly hoped that Maggie would be open to Hollander's idea of sharing the fruits of Joe's passion with the Racing Museum – it would be another way for him to leave a meaningful legacy. But as much as Dominic had hoped that this new information could lead to a breakthrough in the mystery of Joe's disappearance, he just couldn't see anything nefarious in it. The more he considered it, the more he was sure the answer lay elsewhere.

*

Dominic parked next to the buzzy little Burmese restaurant in the inner city.

'Looks a bit crowded and noisy for a meeting,' said Holly.

'Oh, Rob will have made some arrangement. Apparently the food is brilliant.'

The smiling hostess in her traditional colourful *longyi*

led them to a private room at one side which was quieter and decorated with traditional Buddhist artefacts and candles.

'Oh, nice,' said Holly appreciatively.

Rob and Alicia were already there and Rob rose to greet them.

'Thanks for coming at last. Shame we had to postpone because of the rain,' Rob said, smiling.

'Can't help rain,' said Dominic.

Holly and Alicia nodded to one another, Holly rather guardedly, each noting the other's dress. Holly was in pale lemon linen. Fresh, smart, businesslike. Alicia's outfit was flaming red, low-cut, clinging. Sexy. Then Alicia surprised Dominic by stepping forward and saying to Holly, 'No hard feelings, hey? I was only teasing the other day. It's a bad habit of mine. Let's start over.'

Holly looked slightly taken aback but she nodded and said, 'Sure.'

There was a general settling as drinks and starters were ordered and a light repartee was exchanged with the owner. Then a solemn waiter arrived to take their order for the mains, but Rob cut in with, 'Bring us whatever you think we'll like.'

Once he'd left, Rob raised his glass in a toast and the others followed suit. 'Here's to La Hacienda!' he said.

Alicia was instantly businesslike and took control of the meeting.

'So now is La Hacienda's time,' said Alicia.

'Has the property been bought already by Mr Marchant? What's his plan for it?' asked Holly. Dominic had filled her in on the broad brushstrokes of his idea before the meeting, but he was pleased that she had got off on the front foot.

'No, he hasn't. And it is *our* plan,' answered Alicia with a slight smile.

'Actually, it was Dominic's plan first,' said Rob. 'Harold Marchant hasn't seen the place yet. But after Dom's suggestion Alicia floated the idea to him,' added Rob. 'It's up to us to sell it to him. With your help, Holly, we hope to get the project over the line and have Harold put his hand in his pocket.'

'Oh, I see. A makeover to sway him, a plan and sales pitch to convince him,' said Holly, and Alicia nodded, glancing at Dominic with a small approving nod.

'How long have we got, and how much will it take?' asked Holly.

Alicia named a figure. 'And we have two weeks.'

'Sounds tight but doable,' said Holly. She turned to Rob. 'How many and what sort of clientele or entourage do we invite to convince Mr Marchant?'

'His hangers-on, the social set, a few bean counters, but in the end, Harold will make up his own mind.'

'With our help,' said Alicia.

'So where do I fit in?' asked Holly forthrightly. 'If Harold bites the bullet, is this a launch-only assignment or an ongoing management role for me? I have launched and managed some high-end properties all over the place for a number of years. Happy to give you references.'

Dominic looked at Holly who was poised, calm, businesslike. And impressive.

Rob looked at Alicia.

'One step at a time. Let's see if Harold takes the bait first, shall we?' said Alicia.

'Expensive fishing exercise.' Holly shrugged. 'But if it's the best way, fine.'

'Okay, let's talk strategy,' said Rob. 'And who's doing what.'

Alicia needed no further prompting. She was all business, beginning with her list of plans and ideas for the venture and how to get them under way.

Holly pressed the *Record* button on her phone as Alicia spoke, and pulled a small notebook and pen from her handbag and made notes.

Rob leaned back, listening, interjecting with a small comment here and there as Alicia spoke, and Holly asked the occasional question or made a clarification.

Dominic sipped his drink, marvelling at the interplay between the two women which continued until they were satisfied they'd covered every contingency.

'Is that it then?' asked Rob as they finished dessert and Holly tucked her phone and notebook back into her handbag.

'Have we missed anything?' Alicia smiled at Dominic.

'Short of having Harold sign on the dotted line, I wouldn't think so. I don't know how anyone who could afford to buy the hacienda would knock it back. Sounds like a winner to me. A big job, though.'

'The pitch to Harold or the whole deal?' asked Alicia, looking at him with her head cocked quizzically to one side.

'Both.' Dominic was about to comment on the state of the interior of the old mansion, but quickly closed his mouth.

*

In the car on the way back to WestWater, Dominic shook his head in admiration. 'You were sensational, Holly. I was so impressed. I could tell Alicia was, too.'

'It's the guests at this event we need to impress,' said Holly. She paused then said, 'I don't know Harold Marchant. But I now know Alicia better, and I'd say he doesn't stand a chance.'

'You reckon he'll buy it?'

'Yep.'

Dominic grinned. 'Between the three of you, I think you might be right.'

*

It was barely past first light. Yet there were vans, trucks, a pantechnicon and people unloading furniture as Dominic pulled up and spotted Rob. Dominic chuckled.

'Hey, big boss, got your clipboard, eh? What's happening?'

Rob grinned. 'Happy chaos. We'll get there.' He turned as Holly stepped out of Dominic's car. 'Righto, over to you, Holly.' He handed her the clipboard.

'It's fine, Rob. I have my own system.'

'Whatever it takes. Man, I hope the weather holds,' said Rob, looking at the sky.

'It will,' said Holly. 'Okay. Is everything unlocked, open, cleaned and ready to go?' she asked.

'Yep. Getting those front doors open was like trying to get into Fort Knox,' said Rob, pointing to the old wooden front doors which now stood open. 'Impressive when you go through that entrance, though,' he added.

'Make sure guests only do that, no using the side entrances,' said Holly. 'We want the *wham bam thank you ma'am* right up front from the start.'

'Pity you couldn't whitewash the stucco exterior, but at least it looks clean,' said Dominic.

'Yep. Didn't want it to look like a quick new paint

job. We want to keep the old lustre and mystery. But they've done the windows and walls inside; there was a bit of mould here and there. Now it's all fresh and smells clean,' said Holly.

'But old,' added Rob. 'In a good way. Hey, Foxy, come over here, would you?' he called.

A wiry man with sharp features, pointed nose and chin and darting brown eyes joined them. Holly and Dominic exchanged a quick glance, amused at his appropriate nickname. Rob did some quick introductions and then said, 'Come on, bring your notes, let's walk through this so we're all on the same page and sure we haven't missed anything.'

'I'll leave you to it,' said Dominic. 'I have a few things to do.' Turning to Holly he said, 'I'll be back here this afternoon to pick you up so you can whip home and get changed before the big reveal tonight.'

'Where are you off to?' Rob asked him. 'Must be important. Why're you wearing a tie?' he added, as if only noticing just now.

Dominic shrugged. 'Taking my parents to lunch. Would you like me to postpone and give you all a hand?'

'No way, mate. Alicia has hired an army.'

*

Later that afternoon, Holly texted him: *It's going well, the expected hiccups. Won't be done till this evening. Still lots to do. Would you mind bringing my outfit in here when you come? No time to go back home. Mum has it all ready. I'll see you soon!*

After a very pleasant lunch, Dominic drove back to WestWater and changed into shorts to while away the few hours until the soiree started at 5 pm.

Sam wandered down and joined him at the jetty.

'How's this "makeover" going that Holly's doing?' he asked.

'Tonight's the night. Unbelievable job to pull it off. But the three of them are quite a team,' Dominic replied.

'Good luck. Let us know all about it. Getting Marchant out of our hair here would be damn good. I'm on my way to the store; better keep moving.'

Dominic swung past Maggie's and picked up Holly's things, and then headed to the hacienda, arriving early. Most of the trucks and tradies had gone, although a van with *Atmos Lighting* on the side was still parked out the front.

Dominic was tempted to go in the side gate and texted Holly who texted back – *FRONT DOOR!*

Dominic pushed the heavy carved door ajar and suddenly felt as if he were stepping into . . . what? A movie set, another world, or had he slipped on virtual reality goggles?

There were candles everywhere casting a mellow glow, and a drifting aroma of some sort of tantalising flower. Haunting guitar music came from somewhere. Two men were working to hang a massive dramatic photo, the size of a single bed, against the back wall of the atrium. It was a stunning portrait of a flamenco dancer, one arm to the sky, her hand clasping a castanet, the other grasping her red dress and revealing layers of frills and a shapely leg with an arched foot in black tap shoes.

Holly walked into the marble atrium foyer. 'So? What do you think?'

'*Olé!* Holly, this is incredible.'

'Not too OTT, is it? The Spanish feel is softened else-where. Come and see. Still doing the finishing touches as quickly as we can.'

Dominic could tell Holly was pleased, excited even, at the stunning transformation she had wrought, though obviously there was more to be done. Men came in with massive urns filled with exotic plants to stand in the black and white atrium.

She took Dominic's hand and led him outside. 'I'm concentrating on this area. The rooms will be done later. We've just made up one suite for now. Keeping them simple but stylish.'

Dominic could only follow Holly in silent amazement as she chatted and described the plants, props, mood makers and stylish simple furniture that married with the fixtures to give an impression of Art Deco meets Tiffany. But he stopped dead as they came out to the loggia and the sheltered garden. The old pool had been cleaned and was floodlit, a statue fountain splashing in its centre.

'Did you buy out a garden centre?' Dominic managed to say as he looked at the new lawn, the tiers of plants and flowers in large pots. A long table and chairs, benches and cast-iron love seats were scattered around a portable bar beneath the vines, which he saw had been draped cleverly over the loggia roof, providing shade and shelter.

Holly chuckled delightedly. 'Doesn't it look great? We'll start out here with hand-picked staff circulating with trays of food and drinks. It's a drinks evening, after all, although we have several baristas who will do the nightcaps and coffee.'

'What's "hand-picked staff" mean?' asked Dominic.

Holly smiled at him. 'Attractive, handsome, sexy and really good at their job.'

'Of course,' said Dominic. 'Rob's idea?'

'Naturally,' said Holly. 'Though I think Alicia gave him a few hints.'

He followed Holly past a small raised stage under an arbour facing the lawns by the pool to a glassed conservatoire which had been temporarily transformed into a food and serving area, where staff in crisp white were preparing hors d'oeuvres.

Giant mock-up pictures and plans of the finished hacienda were hung along a wall, presenting a stunning visual of the anticipated final layout. Photos that caught Dominic's eye showed discreetly separated suites which had garden balconies with private open-air showers and quaint bathtubs under luscious grapevines.

Dominic walked around the huge images of the formal function room, the dining room, the outdoor settings, the golf course, the spa and the private beach where cabanas faced the ocean a short distance away.

'There's a mock-up brochure as well. We didn't have the budget to leap in too far, but we want Mr Marchant to be able to visualise the possibilities. I've kept a particular clientele in mind,' said Holly.

'All this for one night?' said Dominic.

'Hopefully it will be a sales pitch that does the job. It's a fine line between classy and kitsch,' said Holly.

Dominic stared at her. 'You're amazing. You seem to be able to adapt to any situation and be wonderful at them all,' he said.

'I'm also good at handling pain-in-the-butt millionaires,' said Holly, taking his hand.

'I can believe it,' said Dominic. He remembered the bag he was carrying and handed it over. 'Here's the things your mum sent.'

'Thanks. We invited her, but she said she didn't want to run into Harold Marchant,' said Holly. 'By the way, you look very schmick.'

'Thanks. I picked up my jacket from Mum's place this afternoon.'

'Nice lunch? I'm looking forward to meeting your family.'

'Oh, you will,' said Dominic firmly. 'So who's coming this evening?'

'Alicia is rounding up the money. People, that is. She's inviting some of Harold's rich mates tonight before he goes public for investors.'

'It's another world,' said Dominic, shaking his head.

'I'd better get dressed. Rob and Alicia are around somewhere. I have the staff on the job, but I'll need to do the last-minute checks. Are you okay to hang around?' asked Holly.

Dominic nodded. He was more than happy to watch Holly be the smart and confident general manager she so clearly was.

*

Guests were beginning to arrive. They were ushered from the entrance through to the dramatic romantic loggia gardens overlooking the pool. Waiters began to drift from the conservatoire with drinks in crystal flutes and goblets along with tantalising finger food.

Four charming hostesses greeted people and circulated, wearing figure-hugging silver dresses with a flower pinned to their shoulder and a badge that read *Welcome to La Hacienda*. Fit young male hosts in red silk shirts, black pants and matador jackets also moved among the guests.

Unobtrusively, guests were taken by staff on tours through the hacienda to the prepared suite, dining and private function rooms, where again large mocked-up photographs showed how the rooms would eventually look.

'*C'est magnifique! Étonnante!*' commented one man, and the tour host replied in flawless French, explaining some further plans.

Dominic was impressed, and as the group moved on he asked the young male tour host where he was from. The man explained he was Australian but had studied abroad, and that all the hosts and hostesses for this evening were required to be multilingual.

Dominic nodded. Another tick to Alicia and Holly.

As he returned to the gardens by the pool, there was a flurry of activity and it was obvious Harold Marchant had arrived.

Dominic spotted Holly, who looked stunning in a long clinging dress of pale pink, her hair piled up with a spray of flowers giving an exotic touch. Alicia was channelling a flamenco look in black ruffles, her sleek hair in a bun, with dramatic eye make-up and a vermillion smile. They were standing beside Harold as a photographer recorded the occasion.

Harold looked around, taking in the astonishing scene, but revealing no particular reaction. He was obviously playing his cards close to his chest.

Dominic stood in the back of the crowd as Alicia and Rob made the presentation they'd rehearsed, explaining the future plans for La Hacienda. While they were speaking, Holly made her way over to him through the assembled guests.

'You look fabulous,' Dominic whispered to her.

'Alicia booked hair and make-up for us all.'

'If Harold doesn't sign on the dotted line by 10 pm, I'd be surprised.'

'Alicia says he's hard-nosed, but we'll see. It's been a bit of fun, if crazy,' replied Holly.

'There's no getting away from the fact this is a magical place,' said Dominic.

'Like WestWater is, right?' said Holly.

'You bet,' said Dominic. 'The same, but different.'

'I know which I prefer,' said Holly, leaning against him.

Dominic gave her a quick kiss on the cheek. 'Me too.'

*

It took Harold forty-eight hours.

Holly rang Dominic. 'It's a go!' she said jubilantly.

'Really?! Harold is going to do it?'

'Yes. Alicia and Rob are going over to see him now with the contracts and so on.'

'Alicia had them all ready, yes?'

'Of course she did.' Holly laughed. 'I'm so pleased. Plus, Alicia told me that *unusually* – she made a point of stressing that – Harold has asked that I be offered the GM's job.'

Dominic suddenly couldn't stop smiling. 'So you're not going anywhere, then.'

'Nope. I can't thank you enough for bringing me into this, making the introductions. I'm so happy.'

'Me too. I knew they'd be impressed when they met you,' said Dominic. 'We need to celebrate. Come for sunset?'

*

Dominic changed his shirt, got out Nigel's best glasses and a cold bottle of champagne he'd been saving . . . just in case.

He was setting out candles on the deck in the last golden rays of the day when his phone rang. 'Bet it's Rob,' he said to Woolly.

'Hey, Dom. It's me, Nigel. I'm back.'

Dominic's heart sank. 'Oh, hi, Nigel. Did you have a good trip?' he asked, trying to keep his voice light.

'Yes, very productive, thanks. I'm staying in town for a bit to sort a few things out – not sure about my future plans at this stage. Just wanted to let you know I'll be moving back down there after that. I need some time to chill. Will that be okay?'

'Of course,' Dominic managed. 'For sure.'

'Two weeks okay with you? I'll confirm the date in the next few days. See you then.' He hung up.

Dominic stared at his phone. Two weeks until he had to leave WestWater. Just as Holly was settling in.

14

DOMINIC WATCHED SAM'S FERRY chug across the bay from The Point, where it had been moored during the rain event. It headed towards the creek then reappeared half an hour later returning to Sam's own wharf. Gloria got off with a small bag while Sam threw his bag onto the wharf and began to moor the ferry.

Dominic jogged around to the wharf and stopped Gloria. 'Need a hand, Gloria? Let me carry that up for you,' he said.

'Oh, that's kind of you, Dom. Thanks.'

'How was the break with your son?' Dominic asked.

'It was nice seeing them. But now that it's stopped raining Sam was anxious to get back to work. In fact, he had a passenger to drop off on the way home just now, and you know what Sam's like – they got chatting and the trip took even longer!' Gloria shook her head good-naturedly. 'Sam's sorting out the ferry but he said he'll pop down and see you later. Is that okay?'

*

An hour later Sam gave a 'yoo-hoo' as he rounded the deck where Dominic was waiting with two cold beers.

'Well, that's what I call a welcome home,' Sam said with a grin.

'Pull up a chair,' said Dominic. 'You were away longer than I expected.'

'Tell ya what, if we're not frying, we're drying. Step out the door to a drought or else you can't see for rain. Then I asked my mechanic mate to check the ferry and he found the engine was playing up. Took days to find the parts.'

He clinked his beer bottle against Dominic's. 'I hear you pulled off a major rescue. Holly was damned lucky you got to her in time. Good on you. Well done, lad.'

'Sheer luck, thank God.'

Sam raised his eyebrows and broke into a grin. 'I bet Holly is thanking her lucky stars.'

Dominic smiled, and Sam lifted his beer. 'Well, that news deserves a toast. Congratulations. We're jolly lucky you moved to WestWater.'

'Actually, I've just had a bit of a spanner thrown in the works. Nigel's coming back in a couple of weeks so I need to move out.'

'Oh. Hell's bells, eh? Well, I'm sure he won't stay too long. He never does. You can stay with us in the meantime if you want?'

'Thanks, that's kind of you, Sam. But I'm kind of

thinking it's a sign. Get my act together, make some decisions, that sort of thing,' said Dominic.

'What's Holly say?'

'I haven't told her yet. I'm thinking, but I don't have any answers.' He sighed.

Sam sipped his beer, looking thoughtful. 'What do you want to do, Dom?'

'I have a few irons in the fire with my former boss. I'm doing a project for her now, which I'm finding interesting –'

'No, I meant, where do you really want to live?'

Dominic gave him a frank look. 'I'd like to stay here. In WestWater.'

Sam leaned back. 'I might have an idea for you. Leave it with me,' he said.

*

'Dom . . . it's Josie. Any chance you can come and get Snowy? He's ready to be discharged and he's like a bull at a gate. My shift doesn't end for a few hours and I'm worried he's going to walk out of here on his own steam if someone doesn't collect him.'

'No problem. I'll be right over.'

The road to The Glades was open but still banked with debris from the rainstorms.

Dominic nodded to the old fellow who sat on a chair by the entrance reading a newspaper and acting as the unofficial doorman.

As Dominic hurried down the hallway he could hear raised voices. The door to the tearoom was shut, but looking through the glass panel he could see as well as hear Snowy and Dean Banks arguing.

Dominic pushed the door open and saw Josie pleading with Dean Banks who was in his wheelchair beside the tea-making bench. He was shaking his fist at Snowy while Josie was trying to placate him.

'Get him away from me . . .' Dean Banks's voice was contorted, his words hard to understand.

'Shut up, you silly old bugger. You're talking crap!' shouted Snowy. 'I'm leaving today anyway, and not a moment too soon.'

'What's the problem?' Dominic said, looking at Josie.

She threw up her hands in frustration. 'These two! They've been at each other's throats ever since Snowy arrived. There was never any love lost between them but it's got really bad lately.' In an undertone she added, 'Mr Banks is quite lucid today. But that's not necessarily a good thing; he ends up provoking people and aggravating a lot of old arguments. It's quite exhausting, to be honest.'

Dominic turned to the two old men. 'Snowy? What's going on?'

'Banks's just a mongrel. Always has been. Mean bastard, mean to his wife – no wonder she left – mean to his kid, mean to his neighbours. And, Jesus wept, when Joe went missing, everyone was out looking for him except this bugger,' shouted Snowy, looking furious.

Josie, who'd been relatively calm until this point, suddenly looked upset. Turning to Dean she said, 'Why wouldn't you go and help search, Mr Banks? Everyone liked my father.'

'Not everyone!' snarled Banks. 'I didn't like that Pommy bastard. Always interfering. Always spying on me, whingeing about stuff.'

'What's he talking about?' asked Dominic.

'Joe looked out for Leo,' said Snowy. ''Cause Banks was a mean sod, even to his kid.'

'What did my father ever do to you?' demanded Josie, trying to hold back tears as she glared at the old man.

'Your father stuck his nose in where it wasn't wanted!' Banks shouted.

Snowy stabbed his finger at the furious old man in the wheelchair. 'You're a lousy father. Always been a bloody bully. That poor kid was scared to death of you. And you couldn't stand that he used to run to Joe's place and hang out with his family, could you?'

The two men glared at each other.

'No one's going to tell me how to run my life! Not then, not now,' said Banks coldly. 'Anyway, lucky for me, that problem went away . . .' The corners of the old man's mouth twitched in what was almost amusement, Dominic thought.

A strange silence descended, and Dominic blinked. An idea drifted into his consciousness, fully formed.

'Mr Banks,' he said slowly, 'you saw Joe Gordon on the day he disappeared, didn't you?' Dominic had no idea if this was true, but he thought it worth a try.

'No.' Dean Banks glanced at Dominic, then away.

'He came to your place to speak to you, didn't he? You've mentioned that before.' Dominic felt bad using the old man's confusion against him, but this was too important.

'Oh –' Mr Banks looked wary. 'Y-yes. The nosey so-and-so. Telling me how to raise my own son. I sent him packing!'

'But he didn't just go home, did he, Mr Banks?' said Dominic quietly. 'He intended to do something about it. That must have been very irritating. Had he got the wrong end of the stick?'

Mr Banks was turning red. 'Yes he had! He wouldn't

stop. On and on. Going to call the cops, he said! For what? The odd smack? He needed to mind his own goddamn business, that's what. I told him if he didn't, I'd mind it for him! That shut him up. Shoved him out the door in the end.' Mr Banks was breathing hard. Josie was frozen to the spot, looking horrified.

Dominic paused, picturing the Banks house, the house the young couple now owned, up a flight of steep stone steps next door to the Gordons'. Suddenly an image took form in his mind.

'That's right,' he said slowly. 'You shoved Joe out the door, didn't you, and then he fell, down those steps . . .' Dominic knew he was taking a big risk, but he paused, letting this idea sit between them.

Mr Banks had turned purple. 'Well, I had to shut him up!' he screamed, and then stopped short.

The words hung in the room as they all stared at him. Josie was the first to speak.

'What are you saying . . .? What happened to my father?' she asked in a shaking voice. 'Mr Banks?'

'What did you do, you bastard?' growled Snowy.

Josie knelt down next to the wheelchair. *Are you saying you know what happened to my father?*

Banks looked furtively left and right, then began to shout. 'He came at me, was going to call the cops . . . and I pushed . . . and down he went . . . down them steps . . .' The old man's eyes were bright in his scarlet face. He started to laugh. 'I showed him! I stopped him!'

There was a frozen silence for a moment. Banks opened his mouth again then suddenly clamped it shut, glancing at the shocked faces around him. His bravado seemed to falter and he turned away. 'Bastard deserved it,' he muttered. 'Wasn't my fault.'

'Mr Banks . . . Dean . . . where is my father?' cried Josie.

'Wouldn't you lot like to know!'

Seeing Josie's anguished expression, Dominic stepped over and leaned close to Banks's face. He said loudly and clearly, 'Mr Banks. Did you kill Joe Gordon?'

Josie's hand was at her mouth, a look of horror and disbelief on her face as she shook her head.

Banks gave a kind of manic laugh. 'No. No. He fell. He fell down. Wasn't my fault –'

'You need to tell us now, Mr Banks. What happened to Joe Gordon?' Dominic asked.

Something seemed to dislodge in Dean Banks. It was almost as if he was relieved to finally be able to tell his story. Gripping the arms of his wheelchair he said, 'That devil came to my place, wanting to interfere with me and my boy. It was none of his business . . . I shoved him out and he fell down the back steps. Hit his head and didn't get up. Not my fault.'

'You killed Joe, you bastard . . .!' Snowy said in a strangled voice.

'Wasn't my fault!' shouted Banks over and over.

'Mr Banks,' Dominic cut in loudly, 'where is he? Where is Joe?'

Josie was white-faced, too stunned to speak.

Banks gave a nasty smirk. 'Shark bait. Had to get rid of him . . .'

As Josie stepped back in shock, Dominic continued to speak, quietly and as calmly as he could.

'You threw his body into the sea? Where?' he demanded.

Banks was struggling to breathe now, but managed to spit the words, 'Outside . . . took him past the island in me boat that night . . .' He started to choke.

Josie stepped forward. She grabbed the old man, pulling him onto the floor as Banks began gasping, the colour draining from his face as his eyes rolled back in his head.

'Dominic, hit that emergency button.'

Josie started CPR, rhythmically pummelling Banks's chest, as another nurse rushed in.

'Ambulance on its way. Here, let me, Josie . . .' said the nurse gently, laying her hands on Josie's and continuing the pumping.

Dominic helped Josie to her feet as Snowy linked his arm through hers. 'Let's sit down.'

The two men sat on either side of Josie on a small couch by the windows.

Josie sat still, tears streaming down her pale face.

'My poor dad . . . after all this time . . . how awful for him.' She dropped her face in her hands. 'Do you think it was really an accident or not?'

Snowy patted her shoulder. 'I don't think we'll ever know for sure, love. He said he pushed your dad. And we all know Banks's old place has dangerous bloody steps.'

Dominic was speechless, numb with shock as he sat beside Josie. After all everyone had told him, he had never expected this outcome.

Two paramedics rushed in with a stretcher and medical equipment and began to move Banks.

'I'll have to call Leo. Tell him to go to the hospital,' said Josie, pulling out her mobile.

Dominic and Snowy sat on either side of her as she made the call.

'What now?' asked Dominic. 'You'll have to notify the police.'

'Must I?' Josie looked suddenly fragile, not her strong

and organised self but a hurt and sad young woman. She shook her head. 'Of course. I'm finding it so hard to take this in.'

Dominic looked across at Snowy. 'Do you think Leo knew what happened to Joe?'

Snowy shrugged. 'Hard to say, he was only about nine or ten. His old man always gave him a hard time. What a bastard Banks is, keeping this to himself all these bloody years.'

'Scared he'd be implicated in a death, no doubt,' said Dominic. 'And with good reason.'

'Indeed,' exclaimed Snowy. 'He killed poor Joe whether he meant to or not. But he got rid of him rather than face up to an accident. Everyone knew he had a temper.'

'If only he'd come forward. Told us . . . it's been the not knowing . . . the hoping . . . oh, my poor mother.' Josie dropped her face in her hands again.

Awkwardly Snowy put his arm across her shoulders.

Dominic was thoughtful. 'I have to ask . . . do you think it's true? I mean, he's not making it up for some weird reason? You said he's been out of it a fair bit lately.'

Josie stared at Dominic. She shook her head. 'I believe him. I could tell he meant every word.' And she burst into tears.

'Josie, let me take you home,' said Dominic gently.

She straightened up, taking a deep breath. 'I'll just call Riley. I have to get to Mum and tell her and we'll call the police. Poor Mum, this will be so hard for her.'

'What hospital did they take Banks to?' asked Snowy.

'I assume The Vale.' Josie stood up, suddenly businesslike. 'Thanks, Dom, Snowy. I'll call you both later. Oh, Snowy, you were leaving . . . there's paperwork . . .'

'Josie, I'll deal with it. I'll get Snowy home,' said Dominic quickly. He touched Snowy's arm. 'Snowy, rather than tackle getting you to your place – there's no food or anything – come and stay with me for a day or two. There's a divan that makes up into a bed . . . nice and comfy, great view. We can barbecue a couple of chops, have a beer, just till we've got your place fixed up, okay?'

'Good plan. Thanks, mate.' Snowy cracked a big smile, causing Josie to raise her eyebrows.

'I'll let you know what's happening. Thanks again, Dom,' said Josie in a faltering voice. 'I'm not sure that would ever have come to light without you.'

They watched her leave.

'Snow, what Banks said – what's "outside" mean? Where he took Joe's body?' asked Dominic.

'It's what the fishing blokes call the ocean – outside. Once you pass Crouching Island you're out in the wide Pacific Ocean.'

'How awful,' said Dominic with a sigh. 'Look, I guess we'll have to tell Leo what his father just said and ask him what he remembers, but first, let's get you out of here.'

'Bloody oath, yes,' said Snowy, standing up. 'I'll get my stuff.'

While he waited, Dominic wondered when Josie would break the news to Maggie and the rest of the family, and how they would take it.

Snowy appeared in his socks, carrying his boots and a haversack. He dropped his boots and bag and bent down, pulling his boots on unaided and lacing them with a great show of strength. Then he lifted his fists above his shoulders like a triumphant boxer, making Dominic smile.

'That's pretty impressive, Snowy.'

'The day I can't put my boots on myself, you'd better shoot me!'

*

As they drove to the boatshed, Dominic was still trying to absorb all that had happened. 'It's unbelievable,' he said to Snowy. 'An argument, a single moment of anger, and everyone's life changed.'

Snowy shrugged. 'Banks was regarded as a cranky old fart by everyone. People kept away from him. His poor kid.' Snowy shook his head. 'I might be a bit rough around the edges but when I grew up you didn't bash women or kids.'

'Nor anyone else,' added Dominic.

Snowy looked out the window. 'Unless it's a war and it's you or him.'

Dominic glanced at Snowy and decided not to pursue this remark.

By sunset Snowy was ensconced in the boathouse, befriended by Woolly – 'That's a big tick of approval,' Dominic told him – and they were both relaxing on the deck with a beer in one hand and a fishing line in the other.

'This is the life,' Snowy declared.

'Like being on a holiday, eh?' Dominic smiled.

Snowy shrugged. 'Dunno. Never been on one of those.'

'Living in WestWater *is* a holiday,' said Dominic.

'Yeah. Joe used to say that. Missed his family back in Pommy land, but had no desire to go back permanently.' He shook his head. 'Poor bastard. He was a good man, it was far too soon for him to go.'

'I hope this brings some resolution for the family,' said Dominic. 'All of them told me that it's been the not

387

knowing that's been hardest to deal with.' Dominic glanced up the hill towards the Gordon property. 'I reckon they're all up there together, by the sound of cars arriving,' he added. 'I won't go up unless they need me.'

'No. This is a family thing. We'll talk to them tomorrow,' advised Snowy. 'Fewer people involved now the better.' He yanked his line. 'Ah! Good bite.'

Dominic wound in his line. 'I'm just going to check my emails,' he said, 'then I'll start the barbie.'

'Okay,' said Snowy easily. 'I want to land this fella for dinner.'

*

Snowy was relaxing in a chair by the barbecue while Dominic turned the chops and sausages when a figure came along the track.

'That smells damn good,' called Sam.

'Pull up a chair, Sam. Want a chop? Sausage? Or a bit of the bream Snowy just caught?' Dominic asked.

'Wouldn't say no to a sausage sandwich. All getting a bit intense up there at the house.' He turned to Snowy. 'So what do you reckon, Snow? Did mad old man Banks kill poor Joe?'

'Says it was an accident.' Snowy shrugged. 'Either way, though, yep, it was him.'

'I can't believe he took Joe's body out to sea,' said Sam, shaking his head. 'It's too horrible to think about. Where's Leo?'

'He had to go to hospital with his dad. He doesn't know what Banks said yet. It looked like the old bloke had some sort of episode,' said Dominic.

'Yeah, Josie once said old Dean had a dicky heart,' said Sam. He glanced up at the Gordon house. 'Maggie's still in shock. All the kids are there,' he went on. 'Riley and Josie seem to be running the show. Gloria is in the background making pots of tea and doing a meal. I wanted a bit of fresh air. Hard to take it in after all these years.' He sighed. 'Why did Banks suddenly come out with this now, d'you know?'

Dominic looked at Snowy.

'He kept having a go at me the whole time I was in the respite place . . . screaming and shouting rubbish,' said Snowy. 'I never liked the bloke. We all hated how he treated Leo as a kid. And he knew it. I guess he just snapped.'

'Sounded to me like he was trying to prove something,' said Dominic.

'He was pretty wild; told us more than he meant to, I think, and then it was too late to take it back.'

'So that caused a heart attack or something . . .?' asked Sam.

'Must've. He was like a boiler fit to burst,' said Snowy.

'Grab a plate, guys,' said Dominic as he served up the food. 'There's garlic bread, a bit of salad.'

The three men sat quietly eating, talking little as darkness softly enveloped them.

'I s'pose I'd better head back up and see how things are,' said Sam. 'You need anything, Snowy?'

'Right as rain. Never felt better.'

Sam and Dominic smiled at him.

'I'll go get your bed ready, Snowy. Then I might stay up and throw another line in, seeing as we've eaten your bream,' said Dominic.

Surreptitiously Dominic and Sam watched Snowy carefully walk straight-backed into the boatshed.

'Y'know what I reckon?' said Sam. And as Dominic raised his eyebrows, Sam added, 'He's lonely. Managed on his own so long and didn't need anyone. That fall has made him feel fragile. He's wanting company – maybe even enjoying it – for the first time in his life.'

Dominic nodded. 'You might be right. Just for now, at any rate. Snowy is a loner. But this Banks thing has come as a big shock to him.'

'That's putting it mildly,' said Sam. 'But we take Snowy as he is. He's always there if anyone's in trouble. I imagine that's why he's kept an eye on Maggie and the kids. Banks had better keep out of Snowy's way now.'

'Won't Banks be charged?' asked Dominic.

'Don't know. It'll be up to the authorities, I guess,' said Sam. 'At least it's some sort of closure for Maggie and the kids.' He stood up, resting a hand on Dominic's shoulder. 'Can't help thinking it might never have come to an end without you, son.'

*

Later, Dominic sat quietly sipping a coffee while he fished, then decided to call it a night and wound in his line.

His mobile rang. His heart smiled when he saw the glow of Holly's name and number.

'Hi,' he said quietly. 'You okay?'

'Sort of. Sorry, you still up?'

'Just. Everything all right up there?'

'We're just all bunking down for the night. Riley went back to their kids. We just got a call from Leo . . . Dean Banks died.'

'Oh no! Have you told your mother?'

'Josie gave her something to help her sleep. We're going to wait and tell her in the morning.'

'Good idea.' Dominic paused. 'Settles things a bit.'

'It does. Is Snowy okay?'

'I'll tell him about Banks in the morning. I think he's out like a light.'

'Okay. Sleep well.'

'You too. Sending you a kiss and a hug.'

'You're sweet. Thanks, Dom.'

Dominic drew a deep breath, realising again how much Holly meant to him.

He walked into the front room and saw Snowy sleeping in his singlet, one arm flung out, and curled against it was Woolly.

'Fickle cat,' said Dominic, smiling.

*

Early next morning Holly texted to ask if Dominic would meet the family at Maggie's around ten.

Dominic walked into the house to find everyone doing something. Holly was drying some glasses which Jason was handwashing. She came over and Dominic hugged her.

'Where's your mum?' he asked.

'On the deck with a coffee. How's Snowy?'

'Fine . . . he's fishing. He didn't want to interfere; said he'll catch up with you all later.'

Simon shook Dominic's hand. 'Glad you're here. While it's a relief to have some closure, it's all very shocking. Thanks for your part in it. Josie told us what happened.'

Dominic murmured an acknowledgement then walked out to the deck, nodding to the rest of the family as he gave Maggie a quick hug.

'You okay?' he asked her quietly.

Maggie nodded. 'I guess so. Still a bit shocked. Sad. We've called the police. They're sending someone over this afternoon. I presume they'll want to speak to you and

Snowy at some point about what Dean said yesterday. Leo is coming over here this morning too. It's not going to be easy, but we need to tell him what happened yesterday. He doesn't know yet.'

Dominic nodded, thinking Leo might be a bit fragile at being confronted by the entire family of the man who had been killed by his own father, who had just died.

'I can't believe that bastard is taking his crime to the grave,' said Paul grimly. 'Doesn't seem fair.'

'No, it doesn't,' said Maggie softly. 'But listen, Leo is going to be here in a minute,' she added firmly. 'None of it is his fault, and his father has just died. And for what it's worth, Banks did raise Leo on his own.'

'With your help,' interjected Josie.

'Leo was just a kid at the time. Only a bit older than me,' added Holly as she and Jason joined them.

'Not even ten, I think,' said Maggie.

Everyone suddenly stopped talking as Leo called from the front door.

Maggie got up and went to greet him, giving him a quick embrace.

Leo looked tired and a little taken aback as he saw the entire family gathered together. But Josie stepped forward and gave Leo a brief hug as Jason and Paul shook his hand.

Simon gave a curt nod and looked away.

'Sorry about your old man,' said Paul somewhat stiffly.

'Heart attack. Bit of a shock. Though he's had a few heart issues,' said Leo.

They poured Leo a coffee and he sat down. There was a rather awkward silence.

Maggie wrung her hands and then began. 'Leo, you

know you've been like part of our family, in a way, since you were all kids. We know you had a bit of a tough time of it.' Maggie glanced at him.

Leo nodded, swallowing hard. The slick, assured salesman Dominic had seen was absent. Leo was a man whose father had just died unexpectedly.

Josie broke in gently. 'There's something we need to tell you. We know this will be hard for you, but it is also hard for us. You've just lost your dad, but we want you to know what happened to our father.'

Leo looked at her in surprise and some shock.

Carefully, slowly, she recounted what had happened at the nursing home, and what Dean Banks had said.

Everyone was silent, watching Leo struggle. He had gone very pale. Then he burst out, 'But – no – that can't be right. Are you sure? I can't believe it. Why would Dad say that?' There were tears in his eyes as he looked around at them all.

Dominic spoke up. 'I was there too, Leo. It's what he told us: that he and Joe were arguing. He shoved Joe out the door and Joe fell down the steps, hitting his head. Your dad just exploded and came out with it. Like a dam bursting.'

'I know this must be very difficult for you –' started Josie.

'It's horrible!' For a moment Leo looked enraged, but then he broke down, putting his hands to his face, his shoulders heaving. 'You know,' he said after a long moment, his voice shaky, 'Much as I wish this weren't true, I really think it might be. I was always so scared of Dad. I didn't ever really feel free of him until he went into the home.'

Josie spoke quietly. 'I think in a way he was glad to

confess. To tell someone what had happened after all this time.'

Leo nodded miserably.

'Do you remember anything of that night?' asked Dominic gently.

Leo lifted a stricken face. 'No. That time is a blur now. Dad was always angry; he could lash out over nothing. I used to come here, or run into the bush and hide, or sneak round to a friend's place. Sometimes they'd be asleep and I just slept on their verandah or under their house so I didn't have to go home . . .' He took a ragged breath and looked straight at Maggie. 'I'm so, so sorry, Maggie. You and Uncle Joe were so good to me, and it sounds like Uncle Joe was trying to protect me.' Leo's face crumpled again.

Maggie reached over and took his hand. 'None of it is your fault, Leo. Never was. My Joe was only doing what he did best – looking out for kids. Nothing is going to bring him back . . . but I'm glad that he was trying to do something to help you when he died.' Then Maggie seemed to crumple too, just for a moment. 'Oh, my poor Joe,' she said brokenly.

Suddenly there was a release of emotion in the room, years of pent-up pain and hurt, the doubts and fears and wondering, washed away in a sad and bitter knowing.

Dominic moved quietly beside Holly, who reached for his hand. Simon put his arm around Maggie and she straightened up, dabbing her eyes with a tissue.

Josie spoke up. 'Leo, it's all too late now and your father has gone. At least we know . . . what happened. We will have to inform the police – they're coming over later. We'll deal with it. I'm sure you understand.'

Leo nodded.

Shaking, Josie reached for the coffee pot, but Riley picked it up to pour her coffee.

Maggie rose, turning to look from the deck out to Joe's favourite view.

There was a quiet murmur between Paul and Jason, and then the three brothers joined their mother, arms around each other, and no words were needed.

Dominic turned and put his arm around Holly's shoulders as she leaned against him.

Quietly, Leo walked from the house.

*

While Dominic was making breakfast for himself and Snowy, Rob rang.

'Hey, I only just heard about you having to move on from the boatshed. Listen, I know a great place you could get, or if you're broke, Alicia suggested we set you up on site at La Hacienda for a bit . . .'

'It's okay, Rob . . . really. It's probably time – things happen for a reason, as they say. I've got some irons in the fire, don't worry.'

'Do your plans include Holly?'

'I hope so.'

'Okay then. I await them with bated breath. So what's happening with the Joe story? I was thinking you could do a podcast that could become a novel . . .'

'No. No, Rob. I'm leaving it up to Maggie and Josie and the family whether they want me to do something with it or not,' said Dominic. 'It's their story, not mine.'

'Really?' Rob paused. 'That's a waste, you could sell it for sure.'

'Money isn't everything, Rob. Let's just leave it for now, okay?'

'Your call,' said Rob good-naturedly. 'So what are your plans workwise, then?'

'Julie wants me to come back into the fold. For the moment I'm doing some research and writing for her, which I'm enjoying. And since I've been living in WestWater, I've heard so many fascinating stories about this place, that I'm also thinking of writing a book about them.'

'So long as you're happy, mate.'

'I am. And you?'

'I'm good. Really good. Life's never dull with Alicia around!'

*

Dominic could hear Snowy outside the boatshed yarning with Marcia. He walked out to the deck.

'Oh, Dom, I was just popping in to see you on my way up to Maggie's. I wanted to say thank you for heading out to rescue me! What a time it's been!'

'It has.' Dominic smiled.

'Such a nice surprise to see Snow here.'

'Just a pit stop,' said Snowy. 'I'm heading back home today.'

'You've been away a while, do you need a hand to settle in?' Marcia asked him.

'No thanks, love,' said Snowy. 'Sam and Holly took my chooks back yesterday and cleaned up a bit, they said.'

'Sam is going to miss those chickens. I bet he'll get some of his own now,' said Dominic.

'I'll catch you all later then. There's a community picnic coming up. They're a lot of fun. I'll let you know the details,' enthused Marcia.

'Sounds great, Marcia. See you.' They waved Marcia

off, then, turning to the older man, Dominic said, 'Okay, Snowy, let's get you home.'

'Let's take the boat,' said Snowy.

'Okay, fine. I'll let Holly know we're ready.'

*

Holly and Dominic helped Snowy into the little boat, both watching him like hawks, but they were pleased to see he was moving confidently.

It was a bit of a hike up to his house along the track from the old landing, but they were surprised to find the pathway had been cleared of loose rocks and sticks, the bracken hacked back.

'Good on Sam and his mates,' exclaimed Holly.

As they came in sight of the house they could hear Snowy's chickens. Snowy stopped and took a deep breath. 'It ain't much, but it's heaven to me. Plus an egg for supper, eh?'

'Snowy, if you did ever want to sell, this place could be worth a lot of money. You'd have no end of offers from people wanting to build a fancy house,' said Holly.

'Nah. I'll leave it all to some worthy cause.' He winked. 'Let's get inside and have a cuppa.'

As they drank their tea and watched Snowy move around the tidy house and yard, settling back in, Dominic and Holly felt reassured he could manage. Finally, Dominic said, 'If you're sure you'll be right, Snowy, we'll head off.'

Holly gave the old man a hug.

'Sorry about your dad, Holly. It's sad but at least we all know what happened to him now. Your father was a remarkable man. You should be proud of him,' said Snowy gruffly. 'And thanks for the bit of a holiday, Dom,' he added.

'No worries, Snow. Now that Nigel's coming back, I'll have to move, but I'll be sure to pop in and hang out with you sometimes,' said Dominic cheerfully.

'You do that! We can have a fish.'

'Sounds good, Snowy.'

*

As he and Holly headed back towards the old landing, Dominic paused.

'Let's go and check out the poet's house while we're here,' he suggested. 'Snowy keeps an eye on it for the owner, but as he hasn't been around, we could cast an eye about instead.'

'Good idea. Haven't been there for years. I went once with Josie and her friends for some reason, I don't really remember why,' said Holly.

But as they headed along the path, Holly, who was in front, suddenly stopped. 'There's someone there. The doors and windows are open!'

'Ah. Well let's go and say hello,' said Dominic. 'We're here now.' As they approached the gracious old home, he called, 'Hello! Anyone home?'

An older man appeared on the verandah and waved.

Dominic went up the steps, followed by Holly.

'Ah, Mr Cochrane? Hello. Nice to meet you,' said the man, shaking Dominic's hand.

'And you. This is Holly Gordon. Holly, this is Mr Ambrose. Sam put us in touch.'

Holly gave Dominic a querying look, noting this unexpected familiarity, but smiled and shook Mr Ambrose's hand.

'Do you want to look around? Please, help yourselves. I'll perch out here. Such a glorious view,' said the older man.

Dominic walked straight through the house to the outside patio as Holly followed, whispering, 'Why does he want us to look around? Does he think we're tourists, or fans of the old lady?'

Dominic looked at her, then took a breath. 'Time to come clean. Mr Ambrose is the owner. Sam brought him over here on the ferry the other day and they got talking. It turns out Mr Ambrose wants to sell this house; wants it off his hands. And the price isn't unreasonable . . .' As Holly's eyes widened, he added, 'There's a catch. He doesn't want to be bothered with clearing and selling a lot of the furniture. So it's a walk-in, walk-out deal.'

'*Whaaat*?'

'I wanted to see what you think of it. I looked through this place with Snowy and CeeCee a few weeks ago and I fell in love with it. It needs some work, but –' Dominic took her hand. '– I was thinking if I sold my flat, I could just about manage it.'

Holly stared at him. 'Buy this place?' She looked a little dazed. 'Let me have a look around,' she said slowly.

Dominic trailed behind Holly as she walked through each room, taking everything in, then paused in the study.

'Wow, this is pretty amazing. Are those the poet's things?' She pointed to the desk.

Dominic nodded. 'And her books.'

'Oh goodness. Make a great study for you. Even a small fireplace. I love the big one in the living room. The kitchen needs updating but it looks like it's all functional,' said Holly. She looked at Dominic, her eyes bright. 'It's magic. Can you really afford this? There's a lot of land too.'

'I'll get a silly price for my trendy city flat,' said Dominic, 'which will cover a good deposit. It will still be tight . . . unless, that is, you'd like to throw some of your savings into a romantic old home that comes with history and a view . . . and me?'

Holly's hand flew to her mouth. 'Buy it together and move in with you? Here?'

'Just a thought,' said Dominic. He stepped towards her and took her hands. 'These months at WestWater have made me realise it's time I took life by the horns. Your dad should have had decades more of life to enjoy, and he didn't. I have that opportunity – *we* have that opportunity – and I would love to do this with you more than anything.'

Holly flung her arms around him. 'Then my answer is yes,' she said, smiling wide. 'This is crazy, but it feels absolutely right. We could move in almost straight away!'

'Really? You're up for this?' asked Dominic, aware his voice was shaky.

Holly leaned in and kissed him.

'I am. Let's do it. We've got a lot to discuss, though. So what's the deal –'

Dominic threw his head back and laughed. 'Hang on, we'd better look around some more and see the place properly. Then . . . yes, let's make it ours!'

*

'What do you think?' asked Mr Ambrose after they'd looked in every room and the outside area.

'Before we start peering into cupboards, can we ask a few more questions?' said Holly.

'Of course. There's one condition that I must make you aware of, though. I know I told Sam I don't want to be fussed with furniture and possessions and such, but I do want to take my grandmother's few items from her study. I promised them to the Mitchell Library.'

'Of course. There are paintings as well,' said Dominic. 'They're quite valuable, surely.'

'They are valuable to those who appreciate them,' said Mr Ambrose. 'All I ask is that if there are any you don't treasure and enjoy, please donate them to those who will.'

'Of course,' said Holly and Dominic together.

'Could you tell us some of the family history of this house?' asked Holly.

'Indeed. Perhaps a coffee or tea might be in order?'

*

Two hours later they farewelled Mr Ambrose and went down to the boat, both talking at once and all the way back to the boatshed. They had learned a lot – including confirmation of the fact that he was the great-nephew of the poet. Dominic vaguely remembered Snowy saying as such, but now he'd heard it from the man himself.

'Shall we just pop up to Mum's and tell her Snowy is settled in – and that, by the way, we just bought a house together?' said Holly.

'Why not?' Dominic chuckled, taking her hand.

*

It was sunset a few days later when Maggie appeared at the boatshed, and as Dominic greeted her she handed him a bottle of expensive wine.

'What's this for, Maggie?'

'To drink. For your last night here. In the boatshed, anyway. It was Joe's favourite. I happened to find it in the back of a cupboard yesterday. I'd like to share it with you. Everybody has gone home and Holly is with Josie tonight.'

'It just so happens I have something that will go with the wine – truffle cheese and quince paste. With some toast squares,' said Dominic.

'Good grief, do you eat like this every day? You'd better get a fulltime job,' she smiled.

'I stocked up to impress Holly,' said Dominic as he pulled the cork from the wine. 'I'll let this breathe; don't see many corks in wine any more.'

'Aha, you discovered that Holly's susceptible to good food!' Maggie tilted her head and gave him a quizzical look. 'Moving in together is one thing. Buying a house together is quite another. So you're serious?'

He looked her in the eye. 'Very.'

'Strange how things can evolve. A loss and a gain.' Maggie sighed.

'Is that how you feel? A loss of Joe . . . or Holly?' Dominic asked gently.

'Well, I've gained you in my family. And finally I feel I can close the door on what happened to Joe. I'll have some little ceremony, out on the water, when I'm ready,' she added.

'Let me get the food. Could you light the candle? Let's sit on the deck.'

They settled at the little table as Dominic poured the wine slowly into Nigel's best glasses.

'I'm going to miss this,' he said.

'Me too,' said Maggie.

'We'll be just around the bay, Maggie. Still pretty close! Let's savour Joe's wine,' said Dominic, breathing in the aroma of the mature claret. He lifted his glass and leaned towards Maggie.

They touched glasses gently, saying together, 'To Joe.'

Maggie inhaled the wine and closed her eyes, then said, 'This brings back a lot of memories. All good.'

They sat quietly.

Maggie looked at the dark stretch of shining mudflats, musing, 'The tide is on the turn. Joe loved to be there as the tide came in at night. It meant all was right with the world; the day had been swept away and in the morning everything would be fresh and full, busy and new.'

Dominic nodded. Words were not necessary.

In the deepening darkness the wavering candle was a small speck of light in the wide surrounds. The two figures were silhouetted in silence as the familiar night sounds began.

As they always had.